MANHUNTER

Chris Ryan was born in Newcastle. In 1984 he joined 22 SAS. After completing the year-long Alpine Guides Course, he was the troop guide for B Squadron Mountain Troop. He completed three tours with the anti-terrorist team, serving as an assaulter, sniper and finally Sniper Team Commander.

Chris was part of the SAS eight-man team chosen for the famous Bravo Two Zero mission during the 1991 Gulf War. He was the only member of the unit to escape from Iraq, where three of his colleagues were killed and four captured, for which he was awarded the Military Medal. Chris wrote about his experiences in his book *The One That Got Away*, which became an immediate bestseller. Since then he has written over fifty books and presented a number of very successful TV programmes.

To hear more about Chris Ryan's books, sign up to his Readers' Club at bit.ly/ChrisRyanClub

You can also follow him on social media:
Twitter: @exSASChrisRyan
Instagram: @exsaschrisryan
Facebook: ChrisRyanBooks

CHRIS
RYAN

MANHUNTER

ZAFFRE

First published in the UK in 2021 by
ZAFFRE
An imprint of Bonnier Books UK
80–81 Wimpole St, London W1G 9RE
Owned by Bonnier Books
Sveavägen 56, Stockholm, Sweden

A CIP catalogue record for this book is
available from the British Library.

Hardback ISBN: 978–1–83877–520–9
Trade paperback ISBN: 978–1–83877–521–6

Also available as an ebook and an audiobook

1 3 5 7 9 10 8 6 4 2

Typeset by IDSUK (Data Connection) Ltd
Printed and bound in Great Britain by Clays Ltd, Elcograf S.p.A.

One

At eight o'clock in the morning, on a damp grey Saturday in late March, Josh Bowman felt the pain flooding through his system.

It came on suddenly, without warning, as he waited in the lobby of the Broxbury Hall Hotel, a swanky five-star establishment located just across the road from Hyde Park. The pain started as a sharp scraping inside his head, clawing along the surface of his brain and quickly migrating through his bones, pricking his skin. It would only get worse, Bowman knew. Twelve hours since his last pill, and he could already feel the first pangs of nausea in his guts. Soon the stomach cramps and the sweats would kick in. Then the hallucinations. Like the flu, but a million times worse. A few hours from now, he would be a pale, shivering wreck.

You know what you need to do, the voice at the back of his head told him. The one that had hijacked his brain, rewiring his pathways. The voice was always there nowadays, invading his every waking moment.

You need another hit.

Just one pill, that's all.

Something to get you back on the level. Make the pain go away.

Bowman shoved the voice aside, forced himself to concentrate on the sleek TV mounted on the wall opposite. On the news, vast crowds lined the streets around Westminster Abbey, ahead of the day's wedding between Princess Amelia and her investment banker fiancé, Lucas Wentworth. Bowman saw a huge cheering mass of people dressed in red-and-blue hats or jackets, many of them waving Union Jack flags. There was a definite buzz in the air, despite the crap weather. The biggest live audience for a royal wedding ever, the commentator said. A clock in the bottom corner counted down the time until the ceremony began. Three hours twenty-nine minutes.

Christ, Bowman thought. *I'm supposed to be preparing for a mission.*

Instead, I'm getting the bloody shakes.

The pain briefly faded. Dave Kember glanced at his watch and cursed.

'What's taking these idiots so long?' the SAS sergeant snapped. 'They were supposed to be here by now, for Chrissakes.'

Bowman glanced at his colleague. With his pitted skin and slab-like forehead, Dave Kember was one of the ugliest guys in the Regiment. The lads had nicknamed him 'Toxic' on account of his bad breath. A teetotal clean-eating fanatic, he also had a reputation as a world-class moaner. The kind of bloke who could have a Virginia ham tucked under his arm and still complain that there wasn't any food to be had. Bowman couldn't decide which was worse. The withdrawal pains, or the prospect of spending the next sixteen hours working with Kember.

They had arrived in London the previous afternoon, as part of a four-man team sent up from 'The Wing', a covert unit within the SAS working alongside MI5 and MI6. According to the briefing they had been given, Six had uncovered intelligence of a plot by dissident rebels to assassinate Ken 'The Viper' Seguma, the president of the tiny but mineral-rich Central African state of Karatandu, and a close friend of the royal family. Bowman and his colleagues had been tasked with boosting the president's security during the royal wedding.

While the other two guys on the team carried out security checks at the Abbey, Bowman and Kember had been ordered to rendez-vous at the Broxbury with the president's personal entourage. They had driven over from their hotel, stowed their armoured Land Rover Discovery in the underground car park and sent a message to the president's flunkey to let her know they had arrived. Then they had settled down to wait.

Thirty minutes later, they were still waiting.

Kember checked his watch for the hundredth time since they'd arrived. 'Bloody typical. Bodyguard duty. Always a pain in the arse, waiting for some fucker to show up.'

'I thought you'd be well up for this job, Geordie,' Bowman said. 'Rubbing shoulders with royalty and all that.'

It was one of the worst-kept secrets at Hereford that Kember was planning to leave the Regiment in the next few months. At forty-one, he was four years older than Bowman, a veteran soldier with more than fifteen years of service under his belt. The contacts gleaned from close-protection duty for a foreign head of state could be priceless for an ex-SAS man looking for work on the private circuit.

Kember said, 'Aye, it'll look good on our CVs, I guess. But that's the only good thing about this op.'

Bowman looked away, gritting his teeth. *Jesus*, he thought. *This bloke really is a serial whinger. It's only eight in the morning and he's already getting on my nerves.*

'It's not that bad, mate,' he said, trying to lighten his mucker's foul mood.

Kember snorted. 'Ain't it? We're staying in a crap hotel, living on shite food and sitting around waiting to take orders from some jumped-up flunkey.' He nodded at the TV. 'And the bloke we're safeguarding is a murderer.'

Bowman looked up. The cameras had cut away from the streets of Westminster to a grey-haired presenter in a news studio, rounding up the rest of the morning's headlines. There was a report on the protests in Karatandu. Some sort of violent government crackdown against pro-democracy activists. People were fleeing through the streets, pursued by security forces decked out in black riot gear. Several officers opened up with tear gas canisters while their colleagues battered the helpless civilians with sticks and batons. The background was a tableau of burning cars and bloodied corpses and screaming children.

The camera cut to a short, stout figure dressed in army fatigues, aviator sunglasses and a purple beret. A chinstrap beard accented the officer's strong jawline. He sat on a mountainside, flanked by a couple of tough-looking soldiers, their massive arms crossed in front of them. The caption at the bottom of the screen identified the guy in the middle as General Moses Kakuba, leader of the main rebel opposition. He smiled at a question asked by a journalist off-camera, revealing a pair of golden front teeth.

'We will not be cowed into surrender,' Kakuba was saying. 'If Seguma thinks we are afraid, he is badly mistaken. We are ready to fight . . . even if it means death. Our lands have been ransacked. Our people have been tortured and murdered in the thousands. We have nothing to lose. We will not stop fighting until we have achieved a new dawn for Karatandu, for our people. A new socialist dawn.'

The camera cut again to a shot of President Seguma waving at his supporters as he boarded a plane. Kember shook his head in disgust. 'I still can't believe we're having to protect this twat.'

Bowman said, 'We've protected worse, mate.'

'The guy is nicknamed the Viper, for fuck's sake. He tied up one of his political opponents and tossed them into a pit of poisonous snakes.'

'Come off it, mate. That story isn't true.'

'How would you know?'

Bowman shrugged. He was on the verge of an opioid withdrawal. He didn't want to get dragged into a debate on ethics with Kember.

'What about all those other stories about him personally torturing victims?' said Kember. 'Cutting off fingers and ears and toes, burying people alive, crucifying protestors and putting their heads on stakes? Are you saying it's all bullshit?'

'It doesn't make any difference. We're here now.'

'You're telling me you're OK with this?'

'We've got a job to do,' Bowman replied tersely. 'That's it. Whatever you personally feel about the bloke, it doesn't matter.'

4

Kember shook his head. 'He's a world-class psychopath. He's slaughtering his own people. We shouldn't be protecting him.'

'It's not that simple,' Bowman said quietly.

'Yeah, it bloody is.' Kember nodded at the news report. 'We're putting our balls on the line for some tinpot dictator committing atrocities.'

'This isn't about Seguma. His country's sitting on a load of gas and oil. It's in our interests to keep him onside. If he gets plugged, the next bloke might not be so friendly.'

Kember sneered. 'I don't care if the country's paved with gold. Doesn't mean we should let the prick get away with murder.'

'Your feelings about Seguma are the least of our problems.' Bowman nodded at the screen. 'Those protests are getting hot.'

'What's that got to do with our op?'

'Think about it, Geordie. Seguma's enemies will be even more motivated to get rid of him now.'

'You ask me, they'd be doing the world a favour,' Kember muttered. 'But it ain't gonna happen.'

Bowman turned to him. 'You don't think the threat is real?'

'We're talking about a few protestors in some African backwater,' Kember argued. 'They're not exactly Delta Force. There's no way they've got the organisation to plan a hit.'

Bowman shook his head, slowly. 'I wouldn't be so sure.'

'Bollocks,' Kember said. 'There's no threat. You heard what they said at the briefing yesterday. Five thousand officers on the ground, plus sniper teams on the rooftops, the guys from Five and Six and the private security teams. No way anyone could get close enough to slot the principal.'

Bowman didn't reply. The grating flared up between his temples once more. There was a strange tingling sensation in his muscles, like a million invisible ants crawling under his skin. Every cell in his body screamed at him to make the sickness go away, before it became unbearable.

With the pain came the first terrible murmurs of memory, the resurfacing of the nightmarish images he had tried desperately to forget. Like the echo of a bad trip, creeping up on him when he least expected it. Except these visions never faded away. They grew stronger, stalking Bowman. He remembered stepping through the front door. The stillborn quiet in the air, where there should have been laughter, noise. He remembered, too, the knife discarded on the carpet. The blood splashed across the kitchen floor. The bodies . . .

Bowman closed his eyes, as if he could somehow factory-reset his brain. As if it was that simple. Then the pain stabbed at him again, and he knew he couldn't last much longer without a pill.

Kember was watching him closely, a quizzical look on his mug.

'Fella? You all right?'

'Fine,' Bowman said. He could feel the sweat running freely down his back, seeping through his shirt. 'I'm fine.'

'Don't look it,' the Geordie said. 'You ask me, you look like a bag of shite.'

'It's nothing.'

Kember shook his head. 'I know what your problem is.'

Bowman tensed. Did Kember know he was using drugs? Or was that just the paranoia talking?

If he knows about my addiction, I'm done for.

'It's all that processed meat you've been eating,' Kember went on. 'No good for your body. Plant-based, that's the way you want to go. Clean all that crap out of your system.'

'Yeah,' Bowman said non-committally. 'Maybe.'

The pain intensified. Like holes being drilled into the sides of his skull. Nausea clogged the back of his throat. His hands were trembling. Bowman realised he was perspiring heavily.

He stood up. 'Wait here,' he said.

'Where the fuck are you going?' Kember asked.

'Gotta take a piss.'

He hurried across the foyer towards the toilets, brushing past a group of Chinese tourists. The decor inside the toilets matched the rest of the lobby. Polished marble floor, granite countertop, brass taps. Luxury handwash, a posh brand Bowman didn't recognise.

His hands were shaking as he fished out the plastic pill crusher he always carried. There was a storage compartment above the crusher but the pills inside weren't the kind of thing you bought over the counter at your local Boots. Four tablets left in the container. Bowman knew he'd have to score a fresh supply soon, but he didn't have time to worry about that now.

He flipped the cap open, plucked out one of the oval-shaped tablets and placed it in the crusher on the underside of the bottle. He secured the base and twisted the cap several times, grinding the tablet down to a fine white powder. Tipped the contents onto the countertop, dug out a ten-pound note from his wallet, rolled it up and inhaled the lines. The powder burned in his nostrils. Then he clamped his eyes shut.

After a couple of minutes, he felt a buzz as several milligrams of opioid flowed into his blood. Slowly, the pain in his body faded. The sickness ebbed away. He stopped sweating.

Bowman put the note back in his wallet. He looked up, caught sight of his reflection in the mirror. He saw a face he barely recognised. The body was still lean and hard, his hands were rock-like, his shoulders broad. But the hair was streaked with grey now. His skin was pale. His pupils were the size of pinpricks.

You're supposed to be a staff sergeant in 22 SAS, Bowman told himself. *A decorated soldier with more than a decade of experience in the world's most elite SF unit. You can't be a bloody addict.*

But in that moment, Bowman didn't really care. He didn't care about much, not now. He had long ago stopped looking to the future, to a time when things could be better. His dreams, such as they were, had been shattered in an act of horrific violence fifteen years ago. Now he had no plans, no hopes. He kept his distance from others. He had no real friends. He looked no further ahead than his next pill. Nothing mattered except shutting out the pain. Getting from one day to the next.

He took a deep breath and headed out the door.

* * *

The tourists were still hanging around the reception area as Bowman emerged from the washroom. He strode past them, a warm feeling from the pill washing over him. Kember sat alone, staring at his phone screen. Bowman glanced round but there was still no sign of the president's lackeys.

He planted himself in the armchair next to Kember. The news had switched back to the royal wedding. People were getting into the spirit of the occasion, smiling and waving at the cameras.

Twelve minutes later, two figures stepped out of the nearest lift. A burly guy in a black suit and a tall slender woman in a mustard yellow dress, matching jacket and heels. The woman paused while she scanned the lobby. She spied Kember and Bowman and walked over, nodding at the two SAS men as they rose to their feet.

'You're the soldiers, yes?' she asked.

'That's us,' Kember said, extending a hand. 'I'm Dave, but you can call me Geordie. This is Josh. We're from the Regiment.'

The woman stared at his outstretched hand as if it belonged to a leper.

'Martha Lungu,' she said. 'Personal assistant to President Seguma.'

She sized the men up with a look of disapproval. She was in her late twenties or early thirties, Bowman guessed, with the high-cheekboned, pouting look of an ex-model. She was wearing enough jewellery to fill a Hatton Garden vault. Diamonds the size of fists sparkled in her earrings. The pearls on her necklace were as big as golf balls.

Lungu waved a bejewelled hand at the guy in the suit.

'Samuel Jallow. Mr Seguma's chief bodyguard. He's in charge of Mr Seguma's security arrangements.'

Bowman turned to the bodyguard. He was enormous. The biggest guy Bowman had ever seen. In the top three, certainly. His tightly corded neck muscles were as thick as anchor chains. His arm muscles bulged inside his suit. Pinkish scars ran down both of the bodyguard's cheeks. His head was mostly clean shaven, except for a belt of short curly hair running down the middle.

'Where's the principal?' asked Kember.

'Mr Seguma is upstairs in the presidential suite,' Lungu replied. 'He's a very busy man, as you might expect. You'll meet with him shortly. In the meantime, you will liaise with us.'

Bowman nodded.

'I'm guessing you know why we're here?' he asked.

Lungu said, 'Our friends at the Foreign Office called last night. They mentioned something about a potential incident today.'

'It's possible that there's going to be some trouble with a few protestors,' Bowman replied, repeating the line that they'd been told to use at their earlier mission briefing.

The powers-that-be had decided not to share the details of the assassination attempt with Seguma or his staff. Too risky. There was a serious danger of leakage. The president or one of his advisers might post a message online about the threat or share the news with a journalist. With an audience of two billion people, the last thing the government wanted was widespread panic overshadowing the wedding itself.

'As you know,' he went on, 'a small group of activists planned to stage a protest in Hyde Park this morning.'

Lungu said, 'I thought they were denied permission?'

'They were.'

'So what is the problem?'

'We don't have specifics, but we think that a few of their mates are planning to go proactive. Disrupt the ceremony somehow.'

'How so?'

'As I said, we don't know the details. The protestors might try to infiltrate the crowd. Or they could be planning something later on, at the reception party.'

'Is Mr Seguma in any danger?'

'We don't think so, no.'

'The protestors want to embarrass your boss on national TV,' Kember put in. 'Throw paint on his car, toss eggs at him. Shit like that. There's no real threat.'

'That's why they've sent you here? Because you're worried about a handful of troublemakers?'

'We're here as a precaution, ma'am. To make sure nothing untoward happens to your boss today. His safety is a top priority.'

A tiny groove formed on Jallow's brow. He stared at them with his dead, emotionless eyes.

'Mr Seguma's security is already taken care of,' he said. 'We are perfectly capable of keeping him safe.'

Bowman held up a hand. 'We're not looking to tread on anyone's toes here. We'll be in the background, at your disposal if you need us.'

'Shouldn't this be a job for the police?' said Lungu.

'Ordinarily, aye,' Kember said. 'But the royal protection officers have got their hands full today as it is, as you can imagine.'

'Mr Seguma is a high-profile target,' Bowman stressed. 'The police are very good at what they do, but this kind of job calls for certain skills. That's why they've asked us to be here.'

Lungu silently regarded them both. The look on her face suggested that, in a contest between a pile of dirt and the two soldiers, she would marginally favour the dirt.

Jallow stood there, eyeballing the soldiers.

'Have you done any courses?' Lungu asked.

'We've both completed close-protection training at Hereford. We've got plenty of experience guarding VIPs around the world.'

'Are you armed?'

'Aye.' Kember nodded. 'Pistols and longs.'

Bowman and Kember had been authorised to carry service-issue pistols for the mission. Both men had Glock 17 semi-automatics concealed beneath their grey jackets, secured in leather pancake holsters fastened to their belts. For the heavier stuff they had a pair of Heckler & Koch HK416 assault rifles stored in a lock box bolted into the boot of their Land Rover. The compact variant, with shorter barrels and suppressors attached to the muzzles. They also had plated body armour, spare ammo, and covert radio harnesses strapped to their left shoulders. The radios were connected to earpieces to allow rapid secure comms between the different members of the team.

Jallow said, 'Where are the others? We were informed that there would be four of you.'

'They're at Westminster Abbey right now,' Bowman said. 'Liaising with the police, securing the venue. They'll be inside throughout the ceremony. If there's any trouble, they'll step in.'

Alarm flashed across Lungu's face. 'You're not expecting problems at the Abbey itself, surely?'

'It's highly unlikely. The police have thrown up a ring of steel around the area. But we don't want to take any chances.'

Kember said, 'We'll also be taking an alternative route to the venue.'

'Why can't we take the normal route?' asked Lungu.

'It passes through Pall Mall and Trafalgar Square. Lots of people, obviously. We should avoid those hotspots.'

'You could arrest the protestors instead.'

'That's up to the police, ma'am. But even if they did round them up, some of their friends might slip through the net. For all we know, they might already be in the crowd somewhere, waiting to cause trouble.'

Jallow snorted with contempt. 'This would never be allowed to happen in Karatandu. We have ways of dealing with such scum.'

'I bet you do,' Kember murmured.

Lungu glared at him before she turned to Bowman. 'This new route . . . you're sure it's safe?'

'We've recced it. The police have sent in a clearance party to check the drains, lamp posts, choke points, all of that.'

Lungu looked at him sceptically.

'Trust us,' Bowman said. 'This is for the best.'

Lungu looked from the SAS men to Jallow. 'Samuel, you're happy with this arrangement?'

The bodyguard shrugged. 'I guess.'

Lungu said, 'You'll have to notify Mr Seguma's driver, of course. Go through the changes to the route with him.'

'Yes, ma'am.'

'Fine.' She nodded, brushed a rogue strand of hair back into place. 'Now, there are a few things we must cover before you meet Mr Seguma. First, remember that you are working for a great man. You will behave appropriately at all times in his presence. That means no smoking or drinking while you are on the job.'

Bowman said, 'We're trained professionals, ma'am. We won't be doing any of that shit.'

'No swearing, either,' Lungu replied. 'Don't talk to Mr Seguma unless spoken to. When you speak, you will address him as "sir" or "Mr President". If you have any questions or concerns, you should raise them with myself or Samuel,' she added.

'Anything else we should know?' asked Bowman.

'Mr Seguma doesn't like being touched by strangers. Anyone from outside his own tribe. He thinks it transmits bad juju. You are to keep a respectful distance from him at all times.'

'Yes, ma'am.'

'You have your own transport, I presume?'

'We've got wheels,' said Kember. 'But it's better if one of us travels with the principal in his own vehicle. We can respond much faster if something goes wrong.'

'Out of the question,' Lungu said. 'Mr Seguma doesn't allow strangers to travel with him. He'll never stand for it.'

'That's going to make our job tricky.'

'Too bad. Even Mr Seguma's personal bodyguards are forbidden from travelling in the same car. You will have to follow us, and that's the end of it.'

Kember started to protest but Bowman cut him off. 'We understand, ma'am. We'll ride in our own wagon.'

'Good.' A thin smile flickered across her lips. The gatekeeper to the big man celebrating another small victory. Putting the two foreigners in their place.

'We'll be leaving here at ten thirty.' She glanced at her Cartier watch. 'Two hours from now. Mr Seguma is due to arrive at Westminster Abbey at ten forty-five. There's a holding area a few streets away, I believe. For the bodyguards. I assume you'll wait with Mr Seguma's security detail?'

Bowman shook his head. 'We've got clearance to enter the Abbey. Me and Dave will have eyes on the principal during the wedding.'

'But you just said there's no danger at the Abbey.'

'There isn't, in all likelihood. But it's better to be on the safe side.'

'What's your boss's schedule for the afternoon?' asked Kember.

Lungu said, 'Once the wedding is over, Mr Seguma will return here. Around two o'clock. Then we'll head over to the Greybourn Hotel for the party. You'll be joining us for that, I assume?'

'Yes, ma'am,' Bowman said.

'The party begins at six. Mr Seguma's driver will pick us up fifteen minutes beforehand. You can follow us to the venue.'

'We'll need somewhere to station ourselves close by. Keep an eye on the principal.'

'Shouldn't be a problem. Mr Seguma's security team will have a table near one of the exits. I'm sure they can accommodate you.'

'When is this big bash supposed to end?' Kember asked.

'Who knows? Could be midnight. Could be later. The president is a man of great energy, you know. He likes to party.'

'Great,' Kember muttered.

Lungu's phone vibrated. She reached into her jacket, took out an oversized handset sheathed inside a crocodile leather case and moved away as she swiped to answer. She spoke to the person on the other end of the line in a language Bowman didn't recognise. After half a minute she killed the call.

'Follow me,' she said, pacing back over to the soldiers. 'Let's go and meet the president.'

Two

They followed Lungu and Jallow across the lobby and crowded into the next available lift. Lungu retrieved a card from her jacket pocket, touched it against a reader below the control panel and thumbed the button for the fourteenth floor. The lift whispered upwards, the doors sucked open and then Lungu led them towards the suite at the far end of the corridor.

Two figures sat on a pair of chairs outside the presidential suite. One of the guys was slender with close-cropped hair, a pencil moustache and a pair of dark tinted sunglasses. His mate was thickset and lighter-skinned, with a wide nose and a round head shaped like a bowling ball. They were both dressed in the same plain suits as Jallow. Both of them had the same peculiar scars on their cheeks. The other members of the president's BG team, Bowman assumed. At the sight of their colleagues they rose slowly to their feet and nodded greetings at Jallow. The latter exchanged a few words in his mother tongue with the bodyguards. Then he turned to the soldiers.

'This is Isaac Deka,' he said, gesturing the guy with the pencil moustache. Then he pointed to the guy with the bowling-ball face. 'And this is Patrick Okello. My colleagues.'

Jallow addressed the bodyguards and gestured towards Bowman and Kember, making the introductions. Okello, the guy with the bowling-ball face, slanted his eyes towards the soldiers, slowly. Stared at them with naked hostility.

Kember said, 'What's the craic with them scars?'

'Tribal marks,' Jallow explained. 'Every man in our tribe is scarred on his twelfth birthday.'

'Lots of tribes, are there?'

'Hundreds. But ours is the most warlike in Karatandu. Only men from our tribe are trusted to guard the life of the president.'

There was a clear note of pride in his voice. Which was understandable, Bowman thought. Personal bodyguard to the president was a position of great trust. Their appointments would have had less to do with their capabilities than their absolute loyalty to the boss. Now they were reaping the rewards. Foreign travel, the chance to line their own pockets. The perks of the job. Probably an honorary leadership role in their tribe as well.

Lungu said, 'Wait here. We have some business to discuss with Mr Seguma first.'

'How long is that gonna take?' Kember asked.

'Not long. We'll call you when Mr Seguma is ready.'

She tapped her smart card against a reader above the lock, waited for the light to blink green, then wrenched the handle and disappeared inside. Jallow and Deka and Okello shuffled in after her. The door clicked shut.

Bowman took the chair Deka had just vacated. Kember sank into the chair next to him and scowled.

'Can you believe this shit? Here we are doing them a favour, and they're treating us as if we're a pair of turds they've trodden in.'

'Leave it, Geordie,' Bowman replied.

Kember shook his head. 'We're Regiment. We shouldn't have to put up with this crap.'

'We don't have a choice.'

'Yeah, we do. We could tell Mr T and his mate to go fuck themselves.'

Bowman glanced sidelong at his colleague. 'That's not a good idea,' he said. 'It's not worth the hassle, mate.'

'You think we should let this lot talk to us like we're scum?'

Bowman drew in a breath. 'Look, we both know that we're in charge of this op. But we can't piss these guys off. They've got the ear of the president. It'll make our lives easier if we get along with them.'

16

Kember shook his head. 'This mission is a joke.'

'That's a bit extreme.'

'Come on, Josh. We both know that this is a job for the plod, not us. The threat is low level. Some amateur nutcase with a butcher's knife trying to hack his way into the principal's car. Nothing that the royal protection squad couldn't deal with.'

'What's your point?'

'It's obvious. This op is a PR exercise. We've been drafted in to make this guy feel appreciated.'

'Six wouldn't send us up here just for that.'

'Wouldn't they?' Kember cracked his knuckle joints before he went on. 'Everyone knows Seguma is a big fan of the British army. He was a cadet at Sandhurst and everything. Sending us in to guard him is bound to put a big smile on his mug.'

'Even if that's true,' Bowman said, 'it doesn't change our mission.'

'It ain't right. We're being used.'

'Could be worse.'

'Aye? How's that?'

'If we weren't doing this, we'd be doing some other crap. We could be out in the desert right now, sleeping in tents and shitting in a hole in the ground. At least here we've got a warm bed, clean dry clothes, a good wash. There are worse jobs.'

That drew a scornful look from Kember. 'Frankly I'd rather sleep in the desert than put up with any more shite from that PA.'

Bowman glanced at his colleague, fighting a strong urge to punch him in the face. Kember was beginning to really piss him off.

I'm trying to concentrate on the mission, he thought, *and this guy is dragging me down with his constant negativity. If he keeps this up, I'll give him a slap.*

They waited several minutes. Kember tapped out messages on his phone, checking in with the two guys at Westminster Abbey. The advance party. A pair of experienced SAS sergeants, Lomas and Studley. Kember's phone buzzed with incoming texts from the guys on the team, confirming that the location had been cleared and they were in position at the Abbey.

Bowman checked the time on his G-Shock Gravitymaster.

08.39.

A little over an hour since they had arrived at the Broxbury. Less than two hours until they were scheduled to leave for Westminster Abbey.

Six minutes later, the suite door swung open. Then Lungu stepped outside.

'OK,' she said. 'Mr Seguma is ready to meet you now.'

She guided them into a high-ceilinged room adorned with oriental rugs and gold-framed mirrors. In the middle of the room stood a pair of gilt-trimmed armchairs and a sofa arranged in a semicircle around a marble-topped coffee table. Gift boxes from luxury department stores littered the floor. None of them had been opened. Suit bags and dresses spilled out of a Louis Vuitton suitcase to one side of the room. A pair of Rolex watches, still in their leather boxes, had been carelessly discarded on an antique side table. On the left, a set of double doors led through to the bedroom. There was a door on the right side of the room connecting to an adjoining room. The PA's quarters, Bowman guessed.

Jallow, Okello and Deka had spread themselves on the nearest armchairs, watching an episode of *Rick and Morty* on a flat-screen TV as big as the national debt. In his peripheral vision, Bowman glimpsed two young women lying on the unmade bed in the bedroom. A blonde and a brunette. They were tanned, long-legged, dressed in complimentary dressing gowns. Neither of them paid any attention to Bowman or Kember as they tapped away on their phones.

Lungu ushered them towards the far end of the room. A broad-shouldered figure stood in front of the French windows, smoking a cigar as he gazed out across Hyde Park. Lungu cleared her throat.

'Sir, the soldiers are here. The ones I told you about.'

The man in front of the balcony slowly turned to greet the new arrivals. Bowman recognised his face instantly from the various reports he'd seen on the news.

Ken 'The Viper' Seguma.

The president looked somewhat shorter than he'd appeared on TV. Two or three inches under six feet. He had been living well, apparently. Better than his famished people. His face was plump; his prominent belly threatened to burst out of his tartan waistcoat. His small, round eyes were pressed deep into his skull. A rack of military medals hung from the left lapel of his morning suit. The designer's label was still attached to the sleeve of his jacket, Bowman noticed.

Seguma took a puff on his stubby cigar. Smoke veiled his face as he studied the men closely.

'You are from the Special Air Service, correct?'

'Yes, sir, that's us,' Bowman said.

'Wonderful. Splendid!' he exclaimed. 'It is always an honour to meet the men of the famous SAS.'

His voice was strangely stilted. An African tyrant, trying to imitate the accent of an English aristocrat.

'Yes, I am a big fan,' he continued. 'You men are the real deal. Real killers!'

'Thank you, sir,' said Bowman.

Seguma tapped cigar ash into an empty coffee cup. He said, 'Martha tells me that some worthless dogs are looking to cause trouble today.'

'It's just a possibility, sir. We've been sent here to make sure everything runs smoothly.'

The tyrant swatted away his concerns. 'A few miserable exiles and dissidents. They don't scare me.'

Bowman didn't reply.

'They are nothing but rats, you understand. A great man such as myself does not fear rats. There are rats back home, too, in my country. You've seen the news?'

'Yes, sir.'

'There will be outrage, of course. The media will turn me into a hate figure. But they don't understand what I'm up against.'

'No, sir?'

'These people, you cannot negotiate with them. General Kakuba and his mob talk of a new dawn, but they are only interested in themselves. That is why I call them rats, do you see? You do not take a rat, sit down and discuss policy details with it over a bottle of Beaujolais. You exterminate it. Crush it.'

The president made a clenched fist, strangling imaginary foes.

'And that is what must be done in my country,' he went on. 'I must wipe out the rats, before they spread their disease.'

He spoke matter-of-factly, as if he was talking about the weather, or the cricket score. There was something weird about this cartoonish figure with the voice of an English toff, blandly discussing the slaughter of his own people. Something comical, almost. Bowman found it hard to take him seriously. He was less intimidating in real life than the tyrannical despot he'd seen on the news reports, working himself up into an apoplectic rage.

Lungu's phone vibrated, breaking the awkward silence. She wandered off to take the call. Seguma watched her, a hungry look in his eyes.

'Miss Karatandu, two years in a row.' He grinned at Bowman, revealing a set of pearly white teeth.

'Yes, sir,' Bowman said. Because he didn't really know what else to say.

'Beautiful women are attracted to me,' Seguma said. 'They cannot help it. They are attracted to greatness, I suppose. It is a kind of spell.'

Bowman nodded politely.

Seguma said, 'Are your brother soldiers guarding anyone else today?'

'Not as far as we know, sir.'

His grin widened. 'That is good news. Very good news indeed. It means that my British friends must know that I am very important, do you see? That is why they have sent their best men to protect me, and no one else. I am their top priority.'

'Yes, sir,' Bowman said.

'You agree, then? That I'm an important man?'

'Of course, sir.'

The president searched their faces. 'And you would sacrifice yourselves to save me?'

'If it comes down to it, sir. That's why we're here.'

'Good, very good.' Seguma took a hit on his cigar and said, 'It is a great day for our two countries. Our burgeoning friendship, and the marriage of a princess. We should celebrate.'

He barked an order at the bodyguard with the pencil moustache. Deka sighed and brought over a bottle of Macallan 25-year-old single malt and three glasses. He set them down on the desk, sank back into his armchair. Seguma cracked open the whisky, filling his glass to the brim. He offered the bottle to the soldiers.

'You will join me?'

Bowman said, 'No thank you, sir. We're fine.'

'I insist.'

'We can't, sir.'

'This is good whisky, you know. The best. Very expensive.'

'That's very kind of you, sir, but we're on the job. Me and Dave won't be drinking.'

Seguma clapped his hands. 'Excellent! The right answer. Well done.'

Bowman said nothing.

'I was just testing you both, you see,' Seguma added.

'Yes, sir.'

He reached for his tumbler and sipped his whisky. He smacked his lips, wiped his mouth with the back of his hand.

'You're very professional, I see. Only a good soldier would refuse such an offer.'

'Thank you, sir.'

'I know such things, because I am a great warrior too. First in my class at Sandhurst, you know.'

Bowman made no reply. In the background he could hear the two women giggling in the bedroom. Lungu chatted on the phone, shouting over the sounds blasting out of the TV. Seguma took another sip of whisky, pointed to the medals pinned to his jacket.

'Do you like these?'

'Very impressive, sir,' Bowman replied, trying to mask his growing irritation.

There's nothing we can do, he told himself. *We're on the job. We've just got to indulge this guy.*

He listened as the president pointed out each medal.

'This one is for bravery,' Seguma said. 'This one, for valour. And this one, this is very special.' He tapped a fat finger against a silver cross-shaped decoration with an engraved medallion in the centre. 'Do you know it?'

'No, sir.'

'The Karatandu George Cross,' Seguma explained proudly. 'It is the highest honour our country can bestow. I earned it for an act of outstanding heroism, fighting against my enemies. I believe you have a similar award in your country.'

'Aye,' Bowman replied. 'We do.'

'Mine is better, naturally,' Seguma said.

'Yes, sir.'

The tyrant set down his whisky glass, reached for the bottle and poured himself a refill. Some of the liquid splashed across the desk. He tipped more booze down his throat and burped.

'Enough talk of medals. Tell me about the guns,' he said. 'I like to know the make of the guns my men carry,' he added.

Bowman swallowed his irritation and talked the president through their hardware. The pistols, the longs. Seguma listened attentively.

'And you're absolutely sure there is no threat to me?' he asked.

Bowman caught a flash of something in his eyes. Something like fear.

He said, 'We're simply here as a precautionary measure. If anyone does try it on, it will be to embarrass you, sir. Nothing more than that.'

Seguma nodded slowly. Bowman was thinking about that momentary look he'd seen in the president's eyes. Then Lungu hurried over, interrupting his train of thought. She glanced contemptuously at the soldiers before addressing her boss.

'Excuse me, sir. We need to go through those papers now. The ones I was telling you about?'

'Yes. Of course.' Seguma gestured to Bowman and Kember. 'I was just speaking to these brave warriors.'

The anxious look in his eyes had vanished. He was back to his old self. Like an actor on stage, changing impressions mid-performance. Seguma puffed out his chest and nodded at the soldiers.

'We will speak again later,' he said. 'We can exchange war stories. I'll tell you the story of how I won the George Cross.'

'Yes, sir.'

* * *

They left the suite thirty seconds later. They had offered to run through the details of the new route to Westminster Abbey with the bodyguards, but they had merely shrugged and told Bowman and Kember to discuss it with the driver. They seemed oddly disinterested in the safety of their leader, Bowman thought.

He made his way down to the lobby with Kember. They showed their SIS-issued ID cards to the concierge and asked to speak with Seguma's chauffeur. The concierge made a call. Two minutes later, a thin stern-faced man with silvery hair trotted into the lobby and introduced himself. A diplomatic driver employed by the local

Karatandu Embassy. He had spent the past forty minutes sitting behind the wheel of a stretch limo in the underground car park and seemed grateful for the opportunity to stretch his legs. Kember showed him the maps he'd been carrying, pointing out the directions to the venue, the various escape routes if the principal came under attack. Once they had gone through the details, Bowman and Kember hustled back up to the fourteenth floor and took up their stations outside the suite.

At ten o'clock, Kember checked in with Lomas and Studley, the two guys in position at the Abbey. Bowman watched his partner wander down the corridor, phone clamped to his ear as he searched for a decent signal. He waited until Kember's back was turned, hastily grabbed a tablet from his pill crusher and popped it into his mouth. He stashed the crusher back in his jacket pocket moments before Kember marched back over.

'What's the craic?' asked Bowman.

'All clear. The lads are in position. They're ready.'

Kember stared at his partner, his brow heavily furrowed.

'What the fuck is wrong with you?' he said. 'You're sweating like a Russian athlete at a dope test.'

Bowman shrugged and said, 'Just a bit of a chill. Think I'm coming down with a cold or something.'

Kember stared closely at him. 'You sure that's all it is?'

'It's nothing, Geordie.'

'We've got a long day ahead of us. The last thing we need is you coming down with the fucking flu.'

'I'll be fine.'

'You'd bloody better be. I really don't want to have to bodyguard this twat by myself.'

Twenty-nine minutes later, the suite door clicked open.

Lungu swept into the corridor first, clutching a small leopard-print handbag. President Seguma followed a couple of paces behind, wearing his trademark trilby hat. In his right hand he gripped a stout rattan cane topped with a gleaming gold crown. The bodyguards brought up the rear, all three of them decked out in dark sunglasses in spite of the grey English weather.

Lungu took out her crocodile-leather-cased phone and called down to their driver. Letting him know they were on the way down. Then Okello, Bowman and Kember rode the lift down to the underground car park. Okello hopped into a black Mercedes S-Class sedan, while Bowman and Kember made for their Land Rover Discovery. They were driving the petrol model, with bullet-proof glass, armour-plated sides and enhanced brakes and suspension. The Discovery also came fitted with a covert radio, allowing them to stay in touch with the other guys on the Counter-Attack Team.

They got into the wagon, Kember took the wheel and steered out of the parking space. He followed Okello in the S-Class as the latter drove up the ramp and parked in front of the hotel, two metres behind the president's car. Which turned out to be another S-Class, but the stretch limo version, with blacked-out windows and a Karatandu national flag mounted on the front fender.

Kember pulled up directly behind Okello's S-Class, with the presidential limo ahead. A few moments later, Jallow and Deka strolled out of the lobby. Jallow shoved aside a businessman blocking the entrance, needlessly drawing attention to the team. An amateur move. Seguma walked a few steps behind his bodyguards, swinging his gold-crowned cane. Jallow yanked open the rear passenger door and said something to the president. Bowman didn't catch the words. But the tone wasn't friendly. Not a polite request. More like an order. *Hurry up.*

Seguma and Lungu ducked into the rear of the stretch limo. Jallow slammed the door shut, then swung round to the S-Class sedan parked to the rear. Jallow crammed his enormous frame into the back seat while Deka took the front passenger seat.

Then the convoy set off. The limo departed first, steering into the mid-morning traffic. Then the bodyguards in the sedan, followed by the SAS men in the Discovery. Thirty seconds later, they were motoring south on Park Lane, leaving the hotel in the rear-view.

Heading for Westminster Abbey.

Three

The column tooled south for half a mile, dominating the road in a loose line formation. The stretch limo in the lead scout position, the three bodyguards in the sedan four metres behind, Bowman and Kember bringing up the rear in their Discovery. Riding almost bumper to bumper with the S-Class in front. The roads around Buckingham Palace, Pall Mall and Victoria Street had been closed off to traffic, but the police had been notified of the alternative route being taken by President Seguma and the small convoy was swiftly waved through.

As they carried on, Bowman felt a vague anxiety creeping through his bones. He wondered when he'd be able to take his next pill, how long he'd have to wait. The anxiety gnawed at him as they motored south-east on Vauxhall Bridge Road. Kember was driving on the right side of the road, ready to overtake the two vehicles in front in case of an immediate threat to the president. Making sure they owned the road. Like a fat guy in the street, dominating the pavement, not allowing anyone to get past on either side.

'Look at that shit,' Kember said, pointing with his eyes at the sedan. 'Those tossers are too far back from the principal.'

Up ahead, the limo eased to a halt at a set of traffic lights. The sedan carrying the bodyguards stopped two whole car lengths from the lead vehicle.

'Bloody amateurs,' Kember said as he stopped behind the sedan. 'They should be riding bumper to bumper with the principal. If it kicks off, they'll be too far away to do anything.'

Both soldiers automatically lowered their hands to the chrome door handles. Standard operating procedure when the target went static. If the principal came under attack, you could spring the handle and instantly debus from the wagon, rather than having to fumble with the lock. A tiny detail but in the heat of an ambush it could save a second or two. The difference between saving the principal's life or failing to stop an assassin.

The lights stayed red. Bowman checked the side mirror, the pavement. He was looking for anyone approaching the limo, on foot or from another vehicle. He figured the most likely method of attack would be a gunman riding pillion on a motorbike. Easy enough to execute. Pull up alongside the limo while it was static. Empty a clip through the window, speed off again. By the time either bodyguard team had debussed, the killers would be long gone.

The lights changed.

Six metres ahead of the Discovery, the stretch limo set off again. Four metres further back, the sedan was slower off the mark. The limo started pulling ahead, increasing the distance between the principal and the three bodyguards in the second vehicle. Six metres, then eight. Then the sedan set off, moving slowly past the lights as it made no attempt to catch up with the limo.

'Fuck this,' Kember said.

He stamped his foot to the floor, mashing the accelerator. The engine roared as the Discovery surged forward, racing ahead of the sedan. As soon as they had overtaken it, Kember wrenched the wheel hard to the left, nudging the Discovery into the limo's slipstream. Taking up the position in the middle of the column. They were directly behind President Seguma in the lead vehicle now, the rear of the limo no more than a bumper's width ahead of them, with the bodyguards in the sedan trailing six or seven metres behind the Discovery.

Kember eased off the pedal, dropping the speed to twenty miles per hour, sticking close to the limo as they continued south on the near-empty road.

'The BGs won't appreciate that, Geordie,' Bowman said.

'I don't give a crap. They're pissing me off with their schoolboy tactics.'

'Thought you said the threat to the president ain't real.'

'It isn't,' Kember said. 'But I'm not having these twats make us look useless.'

The puzzling thought nicked at the base of Bowman's skull again. 'I don't get it,' he said.

'What's that?' said Kember.

'These guys are supposed to be the president's top bodyguards. But they don't seem bothered about keeping him safe.'

'Hardly surprising, is it? They're poor quality.'

'It's not just their training, mate.'

'What is it, then?'

'It's their behaviour. The way they act around Seguma. They're not timid. It's almost as if they don't respect him.'

'Maybe they've got some leverage over him. They might know about the skeletons in his cupboard. Or maybe they just hate working for the prick.'

'They're working for a violent dictator, mate. You'd think they'd be treading on eggshells around him all the time.'

'What else could it be?'

'I don't know,' said Bowman. 'But there's something off about him. He seems small.'

'He's hardly gonna be a bloody giant, is he?'

'I mean, he looks ordinary. I can't see anyone being afraid of this guy.'

Up ahead, the limo turned off to the left. Kember took the same turn, following the limo and the sedan as they trundled down a side street flanked by white stucco terraces. They hung a left at Millbank and shuttled north towards the Houses of Parliament.

They were getting close now. Bowman could hear the whump-whump of helicopters circling overhead. The area was swarming with police. Armed officers in dark uniforms, tactical vests and baseball caps patrolled the streets, clutching their Heckler & Koch MP5 carbines. Yellow-and-blue liveried cars and motorbikes lined the sides of the road.

Bowman kept his eyes pinned to the limo, searching for any potential threats. But apart from the heavy police presence the area was deserted.

'Look at this,' said Kember. 'You can't swing a cat without hitting a police officer or a bodyguard. There's no way anyone could get close to the president.'

'Seguma has got plenty of enemies,' Bowman reminded him. 'Someone might slip through the net, even with all these guys about.'

Kember looked at him. 'Weren't you a cop once?'

'Three years,' said Bowman. 'In the Met. Before I enlisted.'

'You weren't one of them tossers with a speed gun, were you?'

Bowman laughed. 'Nah, mate. I never did traffic duty.'

'What were you, then? Plod?'

'I did two years as a constable. Then I went into specialist work.'

'Doing what? Arresting climate change activists?'

Bowman shook his head. 'Undercover operations. Infiltrating gangs. Drug traffickers, arms dealers, that sort of thing.'

Kember gave him a long look. 'Where? London?'

'Sometimes. But I worked all over the country. Liverpool, Birmingham, Manchester. Wherever they needed me. Sometimes I'd be undercover for months at a time.'

'You make it almost sound dangerous.'

Bowman heaved his shoulders in a shrug. 'There were less stressful ways to make a living. You had to have your wits about you all the time. One wrong move and your cover would be blown.'

'You miss it?'

'Not really,' said Bowman. 'I was a different person back then.'

'Meaning?'

'The police have a different priority to the army. They're interested in putting the bad guys in handcuffs.'

'And you ain't?'

'I want to kill bad guys,' Bowman said. 'That's why I joined the Regiment, mate.'

The first weak shafts of sunlight were breaking through the clouds as they passed the Houses of Parliament. They took another left, turning on to Broad Sanctuary, and then Bowman saw the crowd.

A sprawling mass had gathered on Parliament Square, hemmed in by steel barriers, cheering and hollering. Dozens of police lined the side of the road, some dressed in black-hatted, white-gloved ceremonial uniform. Others wore less formal hi-vis jackets. Further to the west, a hundred metres away, a temporary stand had been erected for the world's media. Camera crews jostled with reporters for space on the tiered benches, preparing for the arrival of the bride. No one was filming at the moment: the government had imposed a media blackout during the arrival of the VIPs.

Kember stayed bumper-close to the limo as it continued west on Broad Sanctuary. Bowman looked behind him and was surprised to see that the bodyguards in the sedan were still lagging several metres to the rear, making no attempt to close the gap to the rest of the column.

Up ahead, more spectators had been crammed into the space in front of the media centre. Many of them waved flags or clutched balloons, shouting ecstatically. After a hundred metres the limo veered off to the left, abruptly pulling up at the drop-off point on the west side of the Abbey. Twenty metres to the south, a tongue of red carpet ran from the kerb to the grand West Door.

Kember steered towards the drop-off point. Bowman mentally rehearsed the next few minutes. The president, his PA, Jallow, Deka and Bowman would debus and head towards the western entrance. Okello and the limo driver would ferry their vehicles to the holding area located a couple of hundred metres further along. Kember would join them, ditch the Land Rover and hurry back to the Abbey. With the principal safely inside, Bowman and Kember would then take up their positions in the Abbey. The other bodyguards had orders to wait in their cars until Seguma was ready to leave.

A row of police officers faced out towards the crowd in front of the media centre. At his three o'clock, fifteen metres away, Bowman noticed four more police officers. Three of them were dressed in hi-vis jackets. They were standing together near a line of trees at the roadside. A fourth officer loitered a few paces further back from his colleagues, beside a shuttered kiosk, arms folded across his chest.

They pulled up behind the limo. The sedan stopped a few metres further back. Kember turned to Bowman and said, 'I'll dump the wagon. See you in five minutes.'

'Roger that, Geordie.'

Bowman stepped out into the damp chill of early spring. He slammed the door shut, and then Kember took off in the Discovery, following the signs to the VIP holding area. Bowman hastened over to the limo and stopped beside the rear passenger door, giving Seguma room as the latter climbed out. Lungu got out after her boss, clumsily navigating the opening one-handed while she held her pillbox hat in place.

Six metres to the north, Jallow and Deka debussed from the sedan. They trotted over to the president as the sedan pulled away again. Seguma shot the two bodyguards a mean look as they approached. The look suggested they might spend the rest of their lives breaking rocks in a labour camp. If they were lucky.

'We will talk about this later,' Seguma hissed.

Jallow shrugged. As if he wasn't scared of the tyrant. Or possibly he just didn't care.

The limo edged from the kerb.

Seguma set off at a brisk pace towards the western entrance, the cleated foot of his walking cane rapping against the pavement.

Lungu fell into step two paces behind him, with Bowman third in line. The two other bodyguards, Jallow and Deka, casually brought up the rear as the tail-end Charlies.

To the west, the police officers stood with their backs to the Abbey, watching the sea of excited faces in front of the media centre. To the east, the three officers next to the trees and the guy beside the kiosk were also keeping a close eye on the crowd opposite.

They were twenty metres from the red carpet when Bowman saw a sudden blur moving towards them.

He snapped his eyes to his left and caught sight of the lone police officer near the kiosk. The man had spun away from his three colleagues. Now he was moving across the pavement.

Heading directly towards Seguma.

For a split second Bowman wondered whether the officer was trying to get their attention. Warning them about a possible threat, perhaps. Some random guy with a knife in the crowd. Then Bowman saw the man's shoes. They were brown, he noticed. Not the standard-issue black shoes of a ceremonial police uniform. He wasn't wearing gloves, either.

The two bottom silver buttons on his tunic had been undone. Something bulged beneath his tunic.

The officer was ten metres from Seguma.

Now nine. Eight.

Bowman processed everything in a fraction of a second. Directly ahead, Seguma carried on towards the red carpet, Lungu walking alongside him. Neither of them had seen the threat coming from the left flank. Nor had the bodyguards. The three cops at the trees were still looking across the road at the spectators. Oblivious to the drama happening behind them.

The officer slowly moved an ungloved hand towards his navel.

Bowman sprinted towards the assassin.

The man didn't see him coming. Not until it was too late. His eyes were laser-focused on the target. There was a look of wild excitement on his face. As if he couldn't believe his luck. Like a contestant on a game show who suddenly found himself on the verge of winning the grand prize. He hadn't expected to get this far. Now his plan was going to work. He was going to be the big hero. The saviour of a nation.

The man slid his right hand under his tunic.

Bowman snatched his Glock from his holster as he charged towards his target. The assassin had just enough time to look surprised before Bowman clamped a paw on his shoulder and brought his right knee up between the guy's legs in a rapid jerking motion, crushing his balls. The officer gasped in pain and sank to his knees, momentarily paralysed.

'Are you all right, mate?' Bowman said, loud enough for the officers nearby to hear him. Playing the role of concerned citizen. 'What's wrong? You feeling OK?'

The hitman croaked. Bowman shoved the Glock against his ribs and lowered his voice to a menacing hiss.

'Make a move and I'll fucking slot you.'

Bowman kept the muzzle pressed against the assassin as he glanced round. Seguma, Lungu and the two Karatandan bodyguards had stopped in their tracks several paces from the Abbey and turned back towards the kiosk, their faces stencilled with confusion.

'Get him inside the Abbey!' Bowman barked at the two bodyguards. 'Now! I'll meet you at the door.'

Jallow and Deka snapped out of their stupor. The latter grabbed hold of the president by his bicep, hustled him towards the West Door. Lungu hurried after her boss, struggling to keep up in her high heels. Bowman watched them pass through the wrought-iron gate and disappear into the Abbey. Then he looked over at the police officers near the trees.

'Give us a hand here!' Bowman yelled.

The officers rushed over. One of them knelt down beside Bowman and the assassin with the bruised balls. A thickset guy with pale skin and a beard the colour of rust. The two female officers took a knee either side of him, forming a tight protective semicircle. The older woman was fortyish, with short blonde hair and dark circles under her eyes. Her colleague was fifteen or twenty years younger, Asian, with a heart-shaped face and narrow pointed chin.

'What's going on?' the guy with the ginger beard said. 'Is someone hurt?'

Bowman reached with his free hand into his jacket pocket and waved his SIS identity card at them.

'I'm with the security services. Listen carefully. Do not react to what I'm about to tell you. Plasticuff this fucker, then get him out of here.'

Ginger Beard's eyebrows knitted together.

'Why? What—'

'This guy isn't a cop. He just tried to assassinate our principal.'

'Is anyone hurt?'

'Everyone's fine,' said Bowman. 'I spotted him before he could fire. The principal is inside the Abbey, but I need your help suppressing this bastard.'

'What do you need us to do?' the older woman asked.

'Get him cuffed. Put him on his back, so no one else can see them. Do it quietly. We don't want to cause a panic. Is there an ambulance nearby?'

'I can call one,' the woman with the heart-shaped face said.

'Do it. Get this guy on it. Don't make a big fuss. Pretend he's fainted. Load him onto a stretcher and take him away to the nearest police station. Get him in a cell and put him on suicide watch.'

'What about our bosses? Someone will need to tell them what's happened.'

'We'll take care of that. The guys I'm working with will notify the security services. They'll send someone down to the station to receive him. Just make sure he gets taken away without making a scene.'

The younger woman moved away, relaying orders over her police radio. Bowman turned his attention back to the shooter. He was still badly winded, groaning and retching. He jabbed the gun against his side, drawing another sharp hiss of pain.

'Lie down. On your fucking chest.'

The man dropped down, hugging the ground.

'This is a mistake,' he said.

'Face down,' Bowman said. 'Hands at your sides.'

The man did as he was told.

'Please. I didn't do anything.'

'Shut up. Move and I'll put a hole in your guts. Got it?'

The man didn't react. Bowman shoved the pistol harder into his side.

'OK, OK.' The man winced.

Bowman kept his finger on the trigger while Ginger Beard pulled the man's arms together behind his back. The officer grabbed a pair of plasticuffs from his utility belt, slipped the looped cables over the guy's knuckles and cinched them around his wrists, pulling them tight. Then Ginger Beard and the older woman rolled him on to his back, hiding the ties from view. Bowman re-holstered his pistol and snatched the weapon concealed beneath the man's tunic. A Glock 19 semi-automatic. The same basic specs as the Glock 17, but smaller. More compact. Bowman thumbed the release catch on the side of the Glock, ejecting the clip. He dropped the mag in his left jacket pocket and stuffed the gun down the front of his trousers.

'Ambulance is on the way,' the woman with the heart-shaped face said as she jogged back over. 'Be here any minute.'

Bowman nodded at the shooter.

'Wait here with this prick. When the ambo shows up, bundle him on to the stretcher. Keep it quiet.'

'What if he struggles?'

'Give him another dig in the bollocks. That should shut him up.'

Bowman sprang to his feet.

'Where are you going?' Ginger Beard asked.

'I need to liaise with my team. Tell them what's happened.'

He turned away, leaving the three officers to form a protective cordon around the assassin, shielding him from the view of the crowd across the street. Already some of the spectators near the media centre had switched their attention to the curious incident unfolding near to the kiosk. Several of the uniformed police officers were also glancing over at their comrades, straining to see what was going on.

As he neared the western entrance, Bowman spoke into his covert radio.

'Principal on site,' he said. 'There's been an incident. Repeat, there's been an incident.'

There was a pause, and then a Scouse voice fizzled over the secure comms.

'We're coming out now. Meet us at the entrance.'

Bowman forced himself to walk calmly towards the Abbey, in spite of the tension throbbing in his chest. Jallow and Deka stood beside the West Door. Kember was there too, having raced over from the holding area. He was deep in conversation with Lomas and Studley. The two other guys on the Counter-Attack Team.

Bowman nodded at the bodyguards.

'Where's the principal?'

'Inside,' Jallow replied. 'They're showing him to his seat. What's going on?'

'I'll explain later. Right now, I need you two to get over to the holding area. Secure the vehicles.'

'What for? There's no danger there.'

Bowman drew in a deep breath. He wanted the bodyguards elsewhere, away from the situation. The Regiment was taking control now. These guys would only get in the way.

He said, 'Our team has got the Abbey covered. You're needed elsewhere.'

'To watch over some cars? What's the point?'

'There's a risk someone might try and deface the limo while this thing is going on.'

The bodyguard shrugged his massive shoulders. 'So?'

'You think it'll look good if your boss has to drive back to the hotel in a car covered in paint?'

Jallow muttered something to his partner. The pair of them turned and traipsed down the street towards the holding area. Bowman watched them for a beat. Then he hurried over to Kember and the two other grey-suited guys from the Counter-Attack Team. Lomas and Studley.

The shorter of the two guys glared at Bowman, face twitching with anger.

'What the fuck just happened?'

Bill Studley, the team leader, was a squat Scouser with dark curly hair, and a temper that snapped more easily than a biscuit. What he lacked in height he made up for in fighting skills and sheer aggressiveness. The bloke at his side, Stan Lomas, was physically at the opposite end of the scale from Studley. He was built like a rugby prop, with hands the size of ham hocks and bulging arm muscles.

Bowman briefed them on the attack. The assassin disguised as a cop, the situation with the police. The plan to make it look like a fellow officer had fainted.

Studley cleared his throat and said, 'Everyone get into your designated positions. We'll cover the main entrance. You two head for the muniment room, just as we discussed. We'll have to be as vigilant as fuck from now on.'

'You think there might be another attempt?' asked Kember.

'These guys tried once. They might try again.'

'Or it might be a decoy,' Bowman pointed out. 'A false attack. Get us to relax our guard before the real hit goes ahead.'

'Stick with the principal closely,' Studley said. 'Eyes in the back of heads, yeah?'

Bowman said, 'Shouldn't we be getting more bodies down here now?'

Studley said, 'There's no time.'

'But we need more pairs of eyes on this guy, Bill. These guys know what they're doing.'

'You fucking deaf, pal? I just told you, the plan stays the same. We'll stick with what we've got.'

Kember said, 'The incident will need reporting. Someone has to tell Scotland Yard what's gone down.'

'I'll phone it in. Give the liaison officer the heads-up.'

'Someone should double-check the backgrounds of the catering staff,' Bowman said.

'Why?' Studley demanded.

'They might try to repeat the trick. Sneak in another assassin dressed as a waitress.'

'We'll mention it to Five. For now, we stick to the plan as agreed.'

Studley looked round, daring the other guys on the team to defy him.

'Get into your positions,' he added. 'I'll see you again when the principal leaves. You see or hear anything suspicious, tell us immediately.'

Studley turned and swept back through the Abbey door, Lomas hard on his heels. They moved off to the right just inside the nave, taking up their positions in the small chapel to the side of the entrance. From their vantage point they would have a clear view of anyone coming in or out through the main entrance. Bowman and Kember would set themselves up at an elevated position in the muniment room, overlooking the guests seated around the quire and the transepts.

As Bowman moved to follow the others inside, his eyes were drawn back to the kiosk. An ambulance had pulled up at the side of the road, lights pulsing. Two paramedics jumped down from the cabin and wheeled a gurney across the concrete towards the three police officers huddled around the suspect. To anyone watching nearby, it would look like an officer had fainted and was being escorted to hospital for treatment. A trivial event. The story would merit a line or two in tomorrow's newspapers, buried beneath an avalanche of stories about the wedding itself.

Kember watched the paramedics and let out a breath. 'Shit, this thing is really happening.'

'It was always real,' Bowman said. 'I've been saying that all along.'

'Yeah, well. Who knew these rebels were capable of staging an attack like this? Disguising one of their own as a cop, for Christ's sake.'

The paramedics slid a plastic stretcher under the suspect. On a count of three they hoisted him on to the gurney. Once he was secure the medics manoeuvred him towards the rear of the ambulance, flanked by the three police officers.

'One thing's for sure,' Bowman said.

'What's that, fella?'

Bowman looked back at his colleague.

'We're dealing with professionals. We got lucky this time. But if the next attack is as well planned as this one, we're in serious trouble.'

Four

Most of the guests were already seated by the time Bowman and Kember swept through the doors of the Abbey. They presented their SIS identity cards to a solemn-faced official at the entrance, waited a few beats while he checked in with his boss, then made their way down the long belt of red carpet. Guests sat along rows of chairs either side of the central nave, clutching their orders of service and gossiping amongst themselves in hushed tones. Bowman recognised some of their faces from TV: geriatric musicians, ex-footballers, a handful of respectable actors. The usual faces, wheeled out by the establishment to sprinkle some stardust on the big day.

They passed the quire stalls and reached the crossing. Directly ahead of them was the high altar, dripping in gold. Guests moved around the transepts, mingling with one another. Some chatted in small groups. Others pointed out famous faces across the floor or gazed up at the vaulted ceiling. Royal officials patrolled the aisles, directing guests to their seats.

'You get into position,' Bowman said. 'I'll check on the principal.'

'Roger that.'

Kember set off towards Poets' Corner at the far end of the south transept, making for the entrance to the muniment room. Bowman turned his gaze towards the crowd of guests near the area of seating reserved for foreign heads of state, worthies and senior MPs. He spotted Seguma sitting on the front row, hands planted on his knees, glancing nervously at the entrance. As if he expected a gunman to storm inside the building at any moment. Lungu sat to his right, her long-nailed fingers clasped around her handbag. She looked round, watching the crowd. Seemingly more interested in the other guests than her boss's welfare.

The president stood up as Bowman approached. He was sweating profusely, Bowman noticed. The tip of his shirt collar was soaked through. There was an unmistakable look of fear in his eyes.

'Everything OK, sir?' Bowman asked.

'Yes, I think so.' Seguma hastily recovered his composure. 'What happened out there?'

'False alarm, sir. One of the police officers on duty fainted.'

'In this weather?'

'Must have been dehydrated, sir. Can happen to anyone.'

'Yes, I suppose so.' He peered at Bowman. 'Can I ask a favour?'

'Sir?'

'Don't take your eyes off me from now on.'

'Yes, sir.'

'Where are my men, by the way?'

'In the holding area. They're watching the cars. The situation is under control.'

'Perhaps they should be here as well? It would be safer.'

'We've got two guys covering the main entrance you just came through. Me and Dave will be up there.' Bowman pointed up towards the loggia on the western side of the transept. 'No one is getting in or out of here without us knowing about it, sir.'

'You could take these seats, next to me, perhaps?'

Bowman said calmly, 'Those seats are reserved, sir. We'll be able to keep an eye on you from where we are.'

'And when this is over? What then?'

'As soon as it's time to leave, the other lads will bring the cars round. Me and Dave will escort you out of the Abbey.'

'You did very well back there. I'm grateful.'

'Just doing my job, sir.'

He left the president and threaded his way across to Poets' Corner, sidestepping a woman with a hat so wide you could land a helicopter on it. A small door had been built into the south-east corner of the transept. The door led to an unseen part of the

Abbey: a secret network of staircases and passages leading to the upper levels of the Abbey. Bowman ducked through the opening and climbed a dusty spiral staircase to a narrow walkway on the south side of the transept. He walked carefully along the passage and ascended the steps to the mezzanine gallery. Then he found Kember sitting in the far corner, watching the guests. From their position the two soldiers had a commanding view of the action below. If anyone tried to breach the Abbey via the north or south entrances they would be instantly spotted, giving the team time to act before the principal came under threat.

'How is he?' Kember asked as Bowman drew up alongside him.

'Shaken,' Bowman said. 'But otherwise okay.'

'Does he suspect anything?'

Bowman considered for a beat, recalling the look of raw fear in his eyes. 'I don't think so. He just looks shit scared.'

'That's hardly surprising, is it?' Kember said. 'His people are out to get him. I'd be worried too, if I was in his boots.'

'He's a tyrant, mate. He's spent twenty-four years in power. You'd think he would be used to people having a pop at him.'

Kember grunted. 'Maybe he's losing his nerve.'

Amid the crowd, Bowman caught sight of a guest approaching Seguma. A broad-shouldered man dressed in a striped morning suit and a pink tie, a pocket square jutting like a shark's fin out of his breast pocket. The man wore a pair of thick-rimmed glasses; his large round eyes were as black as his slicked-back hair. He had the build of a retired boxer, with hands the size of shovels and a prominent scar running like a tear down his left cheek.

The man pumped Seguma's hand, slapping him on the back and whispering into his ear. The president nodded along, occasionally glancing at Bowman and Kember in the gallery above.

Kember nudged his partner, inclining his head towards the man chatting with the president.

'That's one of the Lang twins, isn't it? Those Cockney mobsters.'

'Freddie,' Bowman said. 'That's Freddie Lang.'

'How can you tell?'

'He's the one with the scar on his cheek.'

'You ever run into them when you were working undercover?'

Bowman laughed drily. 'Not a chance. The Langs are too smart to get involved in street-level trouble. They keep their hands clean.'

'What's Freddie doing here, anyway?'

'He's a friend of the groom. Freddie Lang is mates with all those City boys,' Bowman said. 'Makes himself out to be a property tycoon.'

'I wonder what he's doing talking to the principal.'

'The Lang brothers are a big deal in Karatandu,' Bowman explained. 'Have been for years. They own loads of real estate down there. Hotels, holiday resorts, diamond mines, shopping malls. They own half the country.'

'They must be worth a fucking fortune.'

'They are. But they're still a pair of evil fuckers. Freddie and his twin brother have been involved in crime since they were out of nappies.'

Kember stared at him. 'How d'you know so much about them?'

'I grew up in the same area as the Langs,' said Bowman. 'Romford. In Essex. They lived a few streets over from us.'

Kember looked at him with widened eyes. 'You knew the Lang brothers?'

'Not personally. But everyone knew about them. The Langs were practically royalty around those parts when I was growing up. Everyone knew about them. Everyone feared them, too.'

'You ever get mixed up in all of that?'

'A few of my mates did, but I managed to stay out of it. I was one of the lucky ones.' He shrugged. 'Maybe things would have turned out differently, if I hadn't escaped.'

'You must have some stories.'

'I've heard one or two,' Bowman admitted.

'Are the Langs as bad as people say?'

'Worse. They were animals. They ruled through fear. David, the older one, he was the brains behind their operations. But everyone knew Freddie was a psychopath. If he came into the pub, you finished your pint and got the fuck out of there. One time, he didn't like the way the barman looked at him. Freddie dragged the guy outside, broke his legs and beat him within an inch of his life. Poor bastard ended up in a wheelchair, pissing and shitting into a bag.'

'Christ. I thought growing up in Sunderland was rough.'

'The Langs are nasty fuckers,' said Bowman. 'They might be rich, and they like to pretend they're legit businessmen these days. But don't be fooled. Those two are as cruel as they come.'

As they looked on, Seguma said something and pointed up at Bowman and Kember. *Look*, his body language appeared to suggest. *Those are my two SAS bodyguards.* Freddie Lang slowly lifted his gaze to the gallery. He caught Bowman's eye and frowned. Then he turned back to Seguma, pointed at Bowman and uttered a few words. As if asking a question. Seguma nodded. Lang looked up again and stared at Bowman for several long beats, his frown deepening.

Bowman stood frozen to the spot. Kember glanced at him with a puzzled expression. 'I thought you said you didn't know Lang?'

'I don't.'

'Then why is he staring at you?'

'Maybe he thinks he's seen me somewhere before,' Bowman answered quickly. 'That fucker never forgets a face.'

Groups of royal officials paced the transepts, gently steering the guests back to their seats. In his earpiece, Bowman heard Studley reporting that the groom's party had just left their hotel. Lang slapped Seguma heartily on the back and then strutted back to his seat, his arms swinging at his sides like a couple of punchbags.

Up in the gallery, Kember and Bowman took their seats.

'Do you think Studley was right?' Kember asked in a low voice. 'About the president's enemies trying to have another crack at him today?'

Bowman sucked in air through his teeth. 'After what just happened, we can't rule anything out.'

But even as he sat down he heard the voice at the back of his head again. Telling him that he had nearly messed up. If he had been suffering with the cravings, Bowman knew, there was no way that he would have spotted the assassin. A fraction of a second later, and the president might have been killed.

The next time, I might not be so lucky.

* * *

The ceremony started at exactly twelve o'clock. The groom arrived first, a City poser with fashionably mussed hair, a swaggering gait and the kind of impermeable confidence you can only acquire after you've made your hundredth million. The organ music built to a booming crescendo, the guests hushed and then the bride appeared. Princess Amelia, sixth in line to the throne, plain and gangly, stuffed into a dress as white as uncut cocaine.

The service proceeded in a rigid, orderly fashion. Later, Bowman would remember it as a blur of Bible readings and hymns and vows. He wasn't really paying attention. He was too busy thinking about his next pill and watching the guests below. At exactly one o'clock the newlyweds glided back down the red carpet, into a great wall of noise from the spectators. They rode off in their landau, and then the VIPs rose to depart.

As soon as the first guests got to their feet, Lomas and Studley hurried out of the Abbey to retrieve their wagon from the parking area. Kember left to fetch the other Discovery, while Bowman slipped out of the muniment room and jogged down to the ground floor. He moved alongside Seguma and Lungu, then they joined the bottleneck forming at the nave. There was a delay as the guests at the front waited for their coaches and private cars to collect them. Then the bottleneck cleared, and Bowman spoke into his mic, notifying the other guys that the principal was on the move. Thirty seconds later, they walked out of the Abbey into the weak grey light of the early afternoon.

They ferried Seguma back across town to his hotel, sticking to the back roads. Then the team split up again. Lomas and Studley continued on towards the reception venue while Bowman and Kember stuck with the principal. They took up their positions outside the presidential suite and settled into a tedious routine of sitting around and checking their phones.

At four o'clock, Bowman snuck into the lobby toilets and popped another pill. Which left him with one tablet in the container. To last him another forty-eight hours.

Not enough.

Nowhere near.

The thought of running out filled him with dread. One way or another, he was going to need to source some more opioids. Tonight, he knew. Before the withdrawal pains started again.

Eighty minutes later, they left for the reception party.

Five

They arrived at the Greybourn Hotel at six o'clock. The team went through the exact same procedure as the journey to the Abbey. The same three cars with the same occupants moving in the same column formation. Except this time, they hung a left off Park Lane, zigzagging east and then south. Passing the neat Georgian squares and the trendy Russian restaurants. Plunging deeper into the heart of Mayfair. Three minutes later, they drew up at the side entrance to an imposing redbrick building shaped like a medieval castle, with cone-roofed turrets and tall arched windows and stone columns.

Bowman, Jallow and Deka left their vehicles. They formed up in front of the limo and accompanied Seguma and his PA towards the side entrance. Bowman stuck close to the principal, eyes shifting from side to side, alert to the slightest danger. The roads surrounding the Greybourn had been sealed off to the public; every room had been booked out for the occasion by the wedding party. The chances of an attack at the reception were low. But Bowman didn't want to take any chances. Not after what had happened at the Abbey.

An elderly doorman greeted them with a polite nod as they entered the foyer. Seguma's personal bodyguards split off from the rest of the group and headed through a pair of doors on the right, towards the main lobby area. The heightened threat to the principal had resulted in a change of plan. Jallow and Deka would now guard the front of the hotel. Lomas and Studley would base themselves on a side street, watching the rear staff entrance and fire exits. Bowman and Kember, meanwhile, would remain inside the ballroom during the party. Okello, the president's other bodyguard, would watch the vehicles parked in a secure area near the hotel. Bowman had expected some resistance to the plan from the bodyguards. But to his surprise they had agreed without a word of protest.

Seguma snatched a champagne glass from a silver tray and swept through a wood-panelled door on the left. Bowman walked alongside the principal down a short corridor and through another set of doors into the ballroom. Which was huge. The size of two basketball courts. The walls were lined with mirrors; the domed ceiling decorated with gold leaf. There was a dance floor to the north, in front of the head table. To the west, on the far side of the room, a band on a stage went through a warm-up routine.

Most of the guests were already seated. At least three hundred of them, Bowman guesstimated. They chatted with one another, chortling and guzzling flutes of Bollinger. Waiters circled the room, topping up half-empty glasses.

Seguma grinned.

'Now *this* is more like it! Food, wine, women. A real party, eh?'

'Yes, sir,' Bowman said.

'And you'll be here all evening? You and your friend won't leave me?'

'Don't worry, sir. We've got the hotel covered.'

A member of staff came over to escort them to their seats near the main stage. Bowman left them and cut across to the southern end of the room. An area of seating had been reserved for the security details close to the fire exits. He took one of the free tables, realised he hadn't eaten since breakfast and beckoned over the nearest waiter.

'Yes?' The waiter looked him up and down, as if deciding whether he was required to address Bowman as 'sir'. He evidently decided against it.

'Bang us a couple of sarnies, mate,' Bowman said. 'Before the rest of the scoff comes out.'

50

The waiter stared dumbly at him, as if Bowman was talking in tongues.

'Pardon?'

'Sandwiches,' Bowman said. 'For me and my partner. We're with the principal.' He pointed out Seguma across the room. 'We don't need anything fancy, just some basic grub.'

The waiter made a supreme effort to mask his distaste, failed, and smiled thinly. 'I'll speak to the kitchen. See what the chef can rustle up.'

'There's two guys in a black Land Rover Discovery parked on Townsend Street. Any chance you can take out a few sarnies to them?'

The smile thinned even more. 'I'll see what I can do.'

He turned and disappeared through one of the service doors. Bowman swept his eyes across the ballroom, looking for anything out of the ordinary. It might be someone with an unnatural body posture or gait, perhaps indicating that they had a weapon concealed on their body. Or it could be something as simple as a member of staff taking a peculiarly keen interest in Seguma. Any one of those signs might reveal an assassin in their midst.

As he looked round, he caught sight of Freddie Lang.

The mobster was sitting at a table to the right of the dance floor. He was talking with another guest. The other guy did most of the talking. Lang looked bored, twisting the stem of his champagne flute. He spotted Bowman across the dance floor and stared curiously at him. Bowman quickly dropped his gaze. When he glanced up again, Lang had turned back to his fellow guest.

Two minutes later, Kember slipped into the ballroom and dropped into the chair next to Bowman. After a few more minutes, the same waiter returned to their table carrying two platefuls of sandwiches. Ham and cheese, egg and watercress, corned beef. Bowman wasn't hungry but he dug in anyway. The first rule of bodyguard work: eat when you can, as fast as you can, because there's no telling when your client might suddenly decide to get up and leave.

Kember regarded his plate as if it carried the plague.

'What's wrong with you?' Bowman asked between mouthfuls of bread and cold meat. 'Not hungry?'

'I ain't touching that shite. Full of carbs and fats.'

'You should eat something. Better than sitting here on an empty stomach.'

'And put that crap in my system?' Kember screwed up his face. 'No chance, fella. I'm sticking to water.'

'Suit yourself,' Bowman said, helping himself to another sandwich.

The reception was more relaxed than the stuffy formality of the ceremony. The VIPs were letting their hair down, now that they were no longer on public display. More champagne was poured. Speeches were made. Then dinner was served. The waiters brought out plates of smoked salmon, followed by lobster for the main course. Seguma hunched over his plate, hacking messily at his food. He talked as he chewed, pausing only to slurp champagne. Some of it dribbled down his chin, staining his tuxedo.

As the waiters brought out dessert, Seguma reached for the finger bowl. He popped the flower into his mouth and chased it down with the warm water. Clearly mistaking the bowl for some sort of soup. He drained the water and let out a loud belch, patting his stomach in satisfaction. The other guests watched him with a mixture of fascination and horror.

'Can you believe this bloke?' Kember muttered.

'Maybe they do things differently in Karatandu,' said Bowman. 'Different culture. Different customs and all that.'

'Even so, you'd think he would have been invited to enough state functions to know the score by now.'

Bowman sighed. 'We've got more important things to worry about, Geordie.'

'You're still worried about someone else having a crack at him?'

'Aren't you?'

Kember swept an arm across the room. 'There must be fifty bodyguards here. No one's going to have a crack at him tonight. Not here.'

'You said that earlier. Look what happened.'

He grunted. 'Let's just hope he doesn't decide to party too hard. If he starts breaking moves on the dance floor, we'll be here until the sun comes up.'

The meal finished, and the staff rolled out a wedding cake with more tiers than a pandemic. The guests cheered the traditional cake cutting before they gathered around the dance floor. A freckled red-headed singer in a silk gown took to the stage and sang a slow folksy ballad for the couple's first dance.

Bowman paid her no attention. He was observing the guests, the staff, the security details. Watching them closely. The next attack on the principal could come from anywhere. At first he had been convinced that the biggest risk came from the agency: the caterers, the cleaners, the extra help brought in for the party. Someone attempting to penetrate the inner security cordon. But they had been thoroughly vetted weeks before, and after the near-miss at the Abbey the security services had gone through their records again to see if they had missed anything. They had come back clean.

The guests began migrating to the dance floor. The booze was flowing freely now, the band blasting out seventies and eighties covers. Whitney Houston, Stevie Wonder, George Michael. Seguma remained in his seat beside Lungu, eyeing up some of the talent. Bowman tried to focus on his mission but the cravings were getting worse.

At nine thirty, he slid out from behind the table.

'Where are you off to?' Kember asked.

'Toilets.'

Kember arched an eyebrow. 'Fuck me, mate. You should see a doctor. That must be your twentieth piss of the day.'

Bowman moved away without replying. He circled around the tables, pushed through the doors on the eastern side of the room and paced down the corridor leading to the foyer. Three women staggered past him, giggling and rubbing their noses. He slipped into the men's toilets, locked himself in an empty cubicle, crushed his last pill. Snorted it. Then almost immediately started obsessing about where he was going to get his next supply from.

He knew he couldn't wait until they were back in Hereford. They had at least another day on the job, guarding Seguma until his return to Karatandu. Which meant he would have to text his regular dealer later on. Arrange to meet. Tonight, preferably. He'd have to think of an excuse to get away from Kember after the party, too.

He left the Gents, started down the corridor.

Then stopped dead in his tracks.

Freddie Lang came bounding towards him from the direction of the ballroom. With a sudden panic, Bowman realised there was no way of avoiding the gangster. Before he could make a decision, Lang fronted up to him, jabbing a finger in his face.

'Don't I know you from somewhere?' he joked. His fat lips spread into a grin. 'All right, Bowman. How's it going, son?'

There was nothing friendly in his voice, or the look in his eyes.

'Hello, Mr Lang,' Bowman muttered.

Lang stared closely at him from behind his thick-rimmed glasses.

'Bit of a surprise, seeing you here. The brother-in-law of one of my top lieutenants, bodyguarding my old mate Ken Seguma. Then again, maybe not.' He pushed up his glasses and sniffed. 'This place is crawling with fucking filth.'

He spat out the last word. Bowman said nothing. He glanced past the huge rock of the mobster's shoulder, praying that Kember or one of the other guys from the team didn't catch sight of them.

'A little birdie told me you're in the army these days,' said Lang. 'Is that right?'

'Yes, Mr Lang.'

His throat constricted. Sweat beaded his forehead. He had to get away from Lang, but he couldn't risk pissing the guy off.

Lang tutted and wagged a finger at Bowman, like a schoolteacher lecturing a misbehaving student.

'You see, you've made two bad choices in your life. Joining the pigs, that was number one. Then this business of enlisting in the army. Bunch of bleeding mugs. You should have taken a leaf out of your brother-in-law's book and worked for me.'

Bowman didn't reply. He stole another glance past Lang's enormous shoulder. *If I'm spotted with Lang, it'll kill my career.*

'Don't say much, do you, Bowman?'

'Sorry, Mr Lang,' Bowman said. He shifted on his feet. 'I can't really talk. I'm working tonight.'

'So I heard.' Lang's eyes narrowed to slits. 'What are you doing here?'

'I can't discuss it.'

'Top secret, is it?'

'I really can't say, Mr Lang,' Bowman replied firmly.

Lang grinned. 'I guess you know all about secrets, don't you?'

Bowman stood still but said nothing. Lang stepped into his face.

'You've been a naughty boy, Bowman. Very naughty. You've got a bit of a habit, so I've heard.'

He tapped a finger against his nose conspiratorially. Bowman felt a cold shiver run down his spine.

'You've been using your brother-in-law to score pills,' Lang said. 'Carter is a good boy, he'd always help out his family. But I was surprised when I found out he was selling stuff to you. I didn't know they allowed junkies in the army.'

Bowman didn't reply. Lang took a step towards him and lowered his voice.

'Some free advice, son. In business, it always pays to under-stand your enemies. Know their weak points. Now I know yours, don't I?'

He patted Bowman on the shoulder with a grizzled paw. A hand that had crushed windpipes and beaten faces to a bloody pulp.

'It's a good job Carter works for me,' he went on. 'Otherwise, who knows what I might do with that information? An ex-copper snorting opioids?' He smiled cruelly. 'You could end up in trouble.'

Just then Bowman spied two guys lingering close to the ball-room door. They were dressed in plain dark suits and rigged up with covert earpieces. Bodyguards, perhaps. The shorter guy was medium height and build, with the kind of clean-shaven corporate face you forgot ten seconds after seeing it. The second man was a few inches taller than his partner and maybe fifty pounds heavier. His head was shaped like a bucket with a pair of holes drilled into the side. Both men glanced up and down the corridor, as if waiting for someone.

Lang glared and poked a finger at his chest. 'I want to know what's going on here, Bowman. What are you and your mates up to?'

Bowman sighed. 'I'm sorry, but I can't talk. I need to get back to work.'

Lang stared at him with dark slitted eyes. Then his face relaxed into a crafty smile.

'You secret squirrels.' He formed his right paw into an imagi-nary pistol and pretended to shoot Bowman in the head. Then he winked and said, 'See you around, son.'

He turned and headed into the bathroom. Bowman watched him leave, Lang's threat replaying in his head.

Most guys in the Regiment knew about his background, grow-ing up in an area infested with gangsters. How he'd escaped a life of crime and violence to join the police, and later on the army. But if Kember or anyone else discovered the true nature of his relationship with Lang – his reliance on his brother-in-law's contacts to supply him with powerful opioids – then his career was over.

He started back down the corridor, towards the ballroom.

The two men in suits were moving briskly towards him. The bland-faced man and the guy with the bucket for a head. They swept past Bowman, glancing at him before they continued down the corridor. As Bowman passed them he noticed a grey-blue strap dangling from Bucket Head's pocket. The guy had something bulky hidden under his jacket, Bowman realised. Not a gun. Something bigger.

He carried on towards the ballroom and spoke into his integrated mic.

'Two guys in suits,' Bowman said. 'Jacked up with comms. Just spotted them. From one of the other BG teams, I think. Something's wrong with them.'

Studley said, 'Can you be more specific?'

'I don't remember seeing them around any of the VIPs. They weren't at the Abbey, either. They just don't look right.'

He gave a brief description.

'Any idea who they're working for?' Bowman asked.

'We'll check. Leave it with us.'

The party was in full swing as Bowman made his way back to the table. Kember glared at him. 'You were gone ages. What took you so bloody long?'

'Sorry, Geordie,' Bowman said.

'Fuck it. Wait here.' Kember scraped back his chair, stood up. 'Going for a piss myself.'

He stormed off towards the washrooms. Bowman signalled to one of the waiters to fetch him a Diet Coke. He took a long sip, keeping one eye on the president while he scanned the room for any sign of the guys he'd passed in the corridor. But they were nowhere to be seen.

57

He got back on the radio. 'Any word on those two BGs, Bill?'

Studley's voice hissed in his earpiece. 'They check out. Both of them. There's no threat to the principal. Repeat, no threat.'

Bowman said: 'Are you sure? Could they have been looking at the wrong blokes?'

'There's no mistake. Everyone in that room has been cleared. Ignore them. That's an order.'

Studley clicked off. Bowman sat at the table, listening to the music, eyes locked on the principal. Kember returned to the ballroom four minutes later, wearing a look that could gut a rat.

'Bloody useless,' he growled. 'Toilets are out of order. Had to go all the way over to the other side of the hotel.'

'That's strange. They were fine a few minutes ago,' Bowman said.

'Someone must have had an accident,' Kember said, his features stitched with anger. 'Can't say I'm surprised. Considering all the shite this mob are stuffing up their noses.'

Bowman stayed quiet, drinking his Coke while he watched the guests. Twenty metres away, to the left of the dance floor, Seguma roared with laughter at something one of the guests said. He sank another slug of whisky, liquid splashing down his front. To the north, Princess Amelia sat at the head table with the older members of the royal family. Her new husband stood to the right of the dance floor, boozing with his City chums and ogling the arse of a young waitress. He saw Lang across the room and waved him over.

Lang stumbled towards him, unsteady on his feet. He brushed past the dance floor, almost fell and steadied himself against a chair. Someone handed him a glass of water. Lang held it and swayed on the spot. Too much drink, thought Bowman. Or he'd overdone the cocaine.

He kept surveying the area but there appeared to be no imminent danger to the principal. Just people dancing, gossiping and joking with one another. A normal, noisy, drunken wedding party.

Seguma barked at a waiter and held up his empty glass, making the universal gesture for a refill. To the west, at the edge of the ballroom, Lungu sat tapping out messages on her phone.

Then a scream pierced the air.

Six

The scream came from across the ballroom. From the direction of the dance floor. Bowman swung his gaze back to the president. Seguma sat rigid, still holding his whisky tumbler. Staring at the body seven or eight metres away.

Freddie Lang.

The mobster lay sprawled on his back to the right of the dance floor. Arms locked at his sides, his body writhing spasmodically. Broken glass scattered around him. Some of the guests hurriedly backed away from Lang. Putting a safe distance between themselves and whatever was happening to him. Others stood transfixed. On the stage, the band was still playing a Bonnie Tyler cover.

Bowman leaped up and dashed across the room, shouting at the top of his voice. 'Out of my way!' he yelled. 'Security services! Stand back!'

He cleared a path through the crowd. Kember hurried after him, shoving people aside. They knelt down either side of Lang while Bowman made a quick assessment. The guy was in a bad way. His skin was pallid. His glasses had slipped off; his eyes were like egg whites, his pupils the size of pinpricks. His jaw was so tight it looked as if it had been wired shut. His clothes were soaked through with sweat.

'Mr Lang?' Bowman peered into his eyes. They were drowsy, vacant, dull. 'Can you hear me? Are you OK?'

Lang made a choking sound. Bowman fixed his gaze on one of Wentworth's mates. A chubby, round-faced guy with curly dark hair. He stared at Lang, as if in a trance.

'You. Call an ambulance,' Bowman said. 'Everyone else, get back! Back, now!'

The chubby guy fumbled for his phone in his jacket pocket. Lang started convulsing.

'What's wrong with him?' Kember asked. 'Drug overdose?'

'I don't understand,' Wentworth cut in. 'He was fine a few minutes ago. Then he came out of the washroom and started going on about how someone had mugged him.'

Bowman looked up at him. 'Who?'

'He didn't say. I just thought he'd had too much to drink. Or someone might have been playing a joke on him.'

Bowman glanced over at the door leading to the foyer and the toilets. He thought about the two BGs he'd seen. The strap, hanging out of Bucket Head's jacket pocket. He remembered what Kember had said about the washroom being closed off.

Kember bent down to administer mouth-to-mouth resuscitation to Lang. Which was an understandable reaction to a potential drug overdose. Clear the airway. That was rule number one for overdose victims, when you didn't have any naloxone to hand. Get oxygen into the lungs. Revive the patient.

Kember reached out to tilt Lang's head back. Bowman grabbed him by the shoulder, yanking him away from Lang.

'No!' he said. 'Don't!'

Kember rounded on his partner. 'Are you mad? He's struggling to breathe. We need to get air into his lungs.'

'Don't do it,' Bowman said. 'It's too dangerous.'

'He's OD'ing, for fuck's sake. There's no time.'

Bowman shook his head, slowly.

'No, he's not,' he said.

Lang's chest heaved and then he vomited, spewing milky fluid down his tuxedo. The bystanders edged away from the stricken mobster, some gasping in revulsion. A few other guests stood further away from the action, recording the drama on their phones.

Lang was foaming at the mouth, convulsing in agony.

'This isn't an overdose, mate,' Bowman said in a soft whisper. 'He's been poisoned.'

Kember frowned. 'How can you tell?'

'He's got the same symptoms as that Russian ex-spy they poisoned a few years ago. This is exactly the same.'

'I don't know, mate . . .'

'Look at his eyes, Geordie,' Bowman said. 'This is textbook.'

Kember looked. Lang's pupils were dilated. One of the telltale signs of nerve agent poisoning.

'Jesus,' he whispered. 'What have they given him?'

'Novichok, maybe. Could be anything.'

The colour drained from Wentworth's face. He backed away a step. 'What did you just say?'

'Nothing,' Bowman growled.

Wentworth stabbed a finger at them. 'You just said something about Novichok.'

'No one said anything, sir.' Bowman forced himself to reply as calmly as possible.

'Rubbish. I heard you. Novichok, that's the chemical they used to kill that Russian spy,' Wentworth said, raising his voice. 'This man has been poisoned, hasn't he?'

Wentworth saw the hesitation on Bowman's face and back-pedalled away from Lang. A boxer stepping out of range of an uppercut. His eyes widened with terror.

'My god,' he exclaimed. 'This is a chemical weapons attack!'

'Stay calm,' Bowman ordered.

Panic quickly spread through the ballroom. The guests closest to Lang gasped in shock and terror. Those further away heard the rumours of an attack and panicked. The bodyguard teams were the first to respond. They rushed over to their principals and began shepherding them towards the fire exits on the southern side of the ballroom, barging waiters out of the way. Those less fortunate souls, the ones without security details, quickly realised what was happening and fled the scene. Others stood paralysed. After a few moments the music stopped as the band abandoned the stage and joined the mad scramble at the exits. At the head table, Princess Amelia suddenly burst into tears. Three well-built bodyguards ran over and dragged her away.

Kember stared at Lang, dumbfounded. 'Fucking hell.'

'Secure the principal,' Bowman said. 'Get him out of here.'

Kember tore his gaze away from Lang and hurried across the empty dance floor. He seized hold of Seguma, bellowed an order at Lungu and led them south, towards the phalanx of bodyguards and VIPs converging on the rear emergency exits. The president stumbled along, Kember moving ahead as he pushed his way through the guests.

Amid the commotion, Studley's voice crackled through Bowman's earpiece. 'What the fuck is going on in there? Where's the principal?'

'Suspected poisoning,' he reported. 'Principal is unharmed. Repeat, principal is unharmed and en route to your position.'

There was a long, cold pause. 'Who's the victim, Josh? Anyone we know?'

Lang made a guttural sound of pain. A trembling grey hand reached out towards Bowman.

'Bowman . . . ' he rasped. 'Help me.'

He coughed, groaning in pain. The security guard on the phone saw Lang spit out the dregs of vomit and took a few steps further back.

'Josh?' Studley asked.

'I'll update you as soon as possible,' Bowman said into the mic. 'Notify Scotland Yard and the security services. Get a specialist team down here immediately.'

He snatched a napkin from the nearest table and wiped foamy saliva and chunks of vomit from Lang's mouth, careful not to get too close in case the gangster spluttered on him. Lang tried to say something, but Bowman only heard a faint croaking sound escape from his cracked lips. He reached for another napkin to shield his nose and mouth and inched closer.

'What is it, Mr Lang?'

'They got me, son,' Lang said hoarsely. 'Stabbed me in the back. Should have . . . known. So stupid.'

'Who?' Bowman drew closer. 'Who did this to you?'

'Russians. They've killed me . . . '

Bowman felt acid dripping into his guts. 'The Russians did this?'

Lang nodded weakly. He clenched his eyes shut, suddenly gripped by a wave of pain. When he opened them again, there was a look in his eyes Bowman had never seen before.

The look of terror.

'You have to stop them,' Lang said.

'Stop them from what?'

'They're meeting my brother. In Monte Carlo. With . . . Seguma.'

'That can't be. The president is right here.'

The guy's delusional, Bowman thought. His brain was playing tricks on him. One of the side effects of the poison infecting his bloodstream.

Lang shook his head and groaned.

'He's a body double,' he barely whispered.

The words hit Bowman like a fist.

He thought about Seguma. His odd behaviour. The fear he'd seen on the man's face at Westminster Abbey. His lack of aura. Drinking the water from the finger bowl. Not the sort of amateur mistake a foreign head of state was likely to make.

Suddenly, he understood.

'It's too late for me,' Lang said, his voice fading to a low murmur. 'But you can still save my brother.'

Lang swallowed painfully, struggling with the effort to go on. Saliva pooled at the corners of his mouth.

'We had a deal,' he said. 'But they lied to us. I see that now.'

He closed his eyes, summoning one last ounce of strength.

'It's a trap. They're going to kill David,' he said. 'Just like they killed . . . me. You must . . . stop them.'

'What's happening in Monte Carlo? Where are they meeting?'

But Lang didn't appear to have heard him. He shivered. 'So cold . . . Jesus, fuck.'

'Mr Lang.' Bowman's voice was urgent. 'Stay with me.'

Lang had a faraway look in his eyes. His breathing shallowed to a faint rasping noise. His jaw slackened. He was slipping in and out of consciousness.

Bowman gently eased him into the recovery position. He grabbed a bottle of still water from the nearest table, unscrewed the cap and doused his hands and face, removing any spores he might have unwittingly picked up.

The ballroom had almost emptied. A handful of guests hung back near the fire exits, rubbernecking the scene. One or two had gone into shock and sat down on chairs, or in the street outside. Some of the waiters watched from the service doors; others hurried back into the kitchen, shouting at their co-workers. On the other side of the room, two police officers burst through the doors connecting to the main lobby. A heavyset man and a petite blonde-haired woman with an upturned nose. They scurried over to Lang.

'Step away, please, sir,' the big guy said. 'Stand clear.'

'Don't touch him,' Bowman said as he moved away from Lang.

'Why?' the button-nosed woman said. 'What's wrong with him?'

'He's been poisoned,' Bowman said. 'If you come into contact with him, you might get some of the same stuff on your skin.'

'Who are you?' the man asked.

'Security services.' Bowman showed them his ID. 'We're protecting one of the VIPs. Where are your mates?'

'On their way.'

Bowman pointed to the stragglers and the people filming on their phones. 'Get this lot out of here. Secure the exits. No one in or out except emergency services personnel. The last thing we want is some idiot blundering in here and getting infected.'

The officer saw the urgency written on his face and relayed a string of urgent instructions into his police radio. Bowman watched them both from a safe distance.

Lang had stopped moving.

He heard Studley's voice in his earpiece: 'Principal is secure. He's on the move. What's going on in there?'

'Victim is unconscious,' Bowman said. 'It's Freddie Lang. He's been deliberately poisoned. Ambulance is on the way.'

'Stay where you are,' Studley said. 'I'm coming in.'

Bowman retreated to a table in the corner of the ballroom, twenty metres from Lang. A safe distance, probably. But who really knew? More police officers swarmed inside, dashing over from their positions at the front of the hotel and the surrounding streets. They quickly began securing the area, sealing off doors and ushering the remaining stragglers and hotel staff towards the exits.

Two minutes later, Bill Studley charged into the ballroom. He breezed past two police officers guarding the fire exit and marched straight over to Bowman. He saw Lang's chalk-white face and abruptly halted.

'Jesus,' he said.

'Where are the others?' asked Bowman.

'Lomas and Kember are taking the principal back to his hotel,' he said. 'He'll be staying in his suite. Him and his BG team. He won't be setting foot outside his room. Not until we've figured out what the fuck is going on.'

'He's a body double,' Bowman said, barely concealing his rage. 'Seguma. We've been protecting a nobody.'

Studley pulled a face. 'Bollocks. Says who?'

'Lang.'

A deep frown creased Studley's face. 'Half a mo. You spoke with him?'

Bowman nodded. 'Right after it happened. He wanted to talk.'

'Why would Seguma send a body double here?' Studley asked.

'Lang reckoned the real Seguma is in Monte Carlo,' Bowman said. 'With Lang's twin brother, David. He said they're out there to meet with some Russians.'

'Doing what?'

'I don't know. He didn't go into specifics. Lang mentioned something about a deal. But they're walking into a trap. He says the Russians are going to betray them.'

'You think he was telling the truth?'

'Lang knew he was dying,' Bowman said. 'He knew the Russians had got to him. He wanted to confess.'

'Fuck me.' Studley ran a hand through his hair. 'Who else knows about this?'

'No one.' Kember had gone outside to raise the alarm. 'Why?'

'No reason.'

'We need to talk to those two BGs,' said Bowman. 'The ones I told you about.'

'What for?' Studley snarled. 'I told you already, them lads checked out.'

'They were involved, Bill.'

'You don't know that.'

Bowman said, 'One of them had something hanging out of his jacket pocket. I didn't know what it was at the time. Or at least, I couldn't remember where I'd seen it before. It's a respirator strap.'

'Why would a couple of BGs be carrying respirators?'

'To protect them from the nerve agent,' Bowman explained. 'They would have needed gloves too, probably. They must have followed Lang into the toilets, put an out-of-order sign outside and then jumped him. That's how I would have done it.'

Studley puckered his brow. 'Let me see if I've got this right. You're suspicious, because of some fucking strap you glimpsed for half a second?'

'Why else would they be carrying masks around?' He pointed to the corridor. 'We've got a witness who says Lang told him he was mugged in the toilets. We need to get hold of the CCTV footage. That'll show us what those BGs were up to.'

'But we can't be sure he was attacked here,' said Studley. 'How do you know he didn't drink it in his morning tea?'

Bowman shook his head. 'The BGs had something to do with this. I'm sure of it. We need to find them.'

Studley said, 'I'll ask the suits at Five and Six to look into it. But if they are involved, they'll be long gone by now.'

'We should notify the other guys,' Bowman said. 'Tell them they're not needed at the hotel anymore. Now that we know that this guy isn't the principal.'

'I'll take care of it.'

Studley's phone hummed. He moved away to take the call, barked a few words down the line before he hung up again.

'Officers from Counter Terrorism Command are on their way,' he said to Bowman. 'They'll want a word with you, I imagine. Someone from the Cell is heading over as well.'

'The Cell?' Bowman frowned. 'What's their involvement?'

'How would I know?' Studley replied moodily. 'No one ever tells us anything about them.'

Bowman looked away, his mind racing ahead of him. Every SAS man had heard of the Cell. It was a covert unit within the Wing, a small inner circle of veteran SAS men tasked with carrying out clandestine operations at home and abroad. The guys in the Cell kept a low profile: no one outside the unit knew anything about their activities, except that they worked closely with the security services and the police. In a world of shadow warfare, fought between non-state actors, the Cell was the ultimate deniable force.

And now they wanted to speak with Bowman.

What was their interest in this op? Why would they care about a hit on Freddie Lang?

And what do they want with me?

'Wait here,' Studley said. 'Don't say anything or speak to anyone until the others show up. Then you can tell them exactly what Lang said.'

Seven

The first paramedics arrived on the scene six minutes later. Half a dozen of them, jogging along either side of a gurney. Like soldiers at a siege, lugging a battering ram towards the enemy's gate. They huddled around Lang, checking his vitals. One of the medics shone a pen torch into his eyes. Another swabbed the inside of his mouth. A third asked Lang if he could hear them. Lang didn't respond. There was a big discussion amongst the medics interspersed with radio chatter, messages bouncing back and forth. Decisions being made. Then a complicated operation to lift Lang onto the gurney. Bowman looked on as they wheeled him away to the waiting ambulance. He felt no remorse for Lang. The guy was a sadistic psychopath. He'd inflicted untold misery in his life. He didn't deserve a happy ending.

And if he dies, thought Bowman, *my secret is safe.*

After fifteen minutes the last of the VIPs had been driven away from the hotel. By that point the police had managed to evacuate the remaining civilians from the building. A steady stream of staff, security officials and caterers traipsed through the emergency exits to a cordoned-off area across the road. Another team of paramedics treated guests for minor injuries. Some were in shock. Others had fallen or hurt themselves in the crush to escape the ballroom.

A short while later, a smartly dressed figure stepped in from the cold.

He was in his mid-fifties, though his weathered face suggested someone at least a decade older. His greying hair was swept back in a silver wave. His eyes gleamed with menace, like knife tips catching the sun. He had the lean greyhound physique of a Regiment veteran, a body built for endurance and hardship and killing, rather than grunt work. But he was dressed more like a partner at a City law firm on casual Friday: dark blazer, light blue shirt, black trousers and tobacco-brown suede shoes, a stainless-steel Breitling watch clamped around his wrist. Bowman recognised him at once.

John Mallet. A former legend of 22 SAS.

The leader of the Cell.

Studley tucked away his phone and greeted the ex-Regiment man as he marched over. He seemed small next to Mallet, thought Bowman. It wasn't a physical thing: Studley was only two or three inches shorter than the other man. It was something in the way Mallet carried himself. Composed, still, a quiet but robust confidence. Studley seemed deferential towards the older man. Subservient, almost. As if he was in the presence of a superior being.

The two men approached Bowman. Studley gestured to the silver-haired ex-officer at his side.

He said: 'You've met John before, haven't you? He runs the Cell these days. He's got a few questions.'

Bowman nodded keenly. Almost every lad at Hereford had met Mallet at one time or another. Or at least heard of him. The guy was something of a mystery. A Glaswegian, born and bred in Govan, he had joined the Regiment in the early 1990s, eventually attaining the rank of colonel. He was rarely seen around the camp, always going on obscure postings overseas, working on shady special projects and team jobs. No one knew where he went, or why. There were rumours that he had deep connections to both Five and Six. The older guys in the Regiment claimed that Mallet had been one of the founders of the Cell. He had done the business in Iraq, Bosnia and Sierra Leone, they said. Along with a bunch of other places. A true hero of 22 SAS.

Another thought crossed Bowman's mind. *If Mallet is personally involved, the situation must be serious.*

Mallet smiled at him and said, 'Hello, Josh.'

Christ, Bowman thought. *He remembers me.* Bowman had only met him once before. Eight years ago. Bowman had collected his first gallantry award, and Mallet had come over to congratulate him. *Eight years, and the guy still hasn't forgotten my name.*

'Hello, boss.'

'I'll have to keep this brief,' Mallet went on in his strong Scottish burr. 'Our friends from Counter Terrorism will be here in a few minutes. I understand Lang spoke to you, before he fell unconscious.'

'Yes, boss,' said Bowman.

'Perhaps you can tell me what Freddie said. Word for word, if possible.'

It wasn't a direct order, but Mallet's charm and the attentive look on his face made Bowman want to please him anyway. He had the manners of a career politician. That ability to make you feel as if you were the most important person in the room.

Bowman told him everything. Lang's dying confession. The president's body double, the secret meeting in Monte Carlo. His desperate plea to save his brother before the Russians got to him.

'Did Freddie say anything else about this meeting?' Mallet asked. 'What his brother is discussing with the Russians, perhaps?'

'Nothing like that, no.'

'You're sure he said nothing else?'

'I've told you everything. Which is a lot more than anyone has told us.'

Mallet frowned. 'I'm not sure I follow.'

'We risked our necks for that body double,' Bowman growled. Anger flared in his chest. 'Any one of us could have been shot trying to save him. Someone dropped a bollock on the intelligence for this op, and I want to know who.'

'That's none of your business,' Mallet replied sternly.

73

'Sorry, boss, but that's not good enough.' Bowman felt the rage simmering in his veins. 'One of our lads could have died tonight. I want to know what the fuck is going on.'

Mallet showed no sign of irritation. He remained perfectly composed. A teacher patiently dealing with an irate student.

'I can't go into specifics,' he said. 'All I can tell you is that this business about a body double was nothing to do with us. If we had known anything about it, we would have told your team. You have my word on that.'

Bowman watched him closely, looking for a tell. But Mallet's expression was utterly unreadable. He might as well try to read a brick wall. Something else occurred to him then.

He said, 'The Russians must have planned that attack at Westminster Abbey as well. The assassination attempt.'

'What makes you think that?'

'Something that bothered me at the time. That assassination plot was well planned. A few anti-government protestors wouldn't have the discipline or the resources to mount an attack like that. It's got to be the Russians.'

Studley scratched his head. 'Why would the Russians sanction a dummy attack on the president?'

'To create a distraction. The killers knew we'd be focused on Seguma after the attempt on his life. No one would be looking at Lang. They staged the hit to throw us off the scent.'

Studley puffed out his cheeks and exhaled. 'The Kremlin must have really wanted this guy dead.'

'Them, or the Russian mob,' said Bowman.

'Isn't that the same thing these days?' A knowing smile crept across Mallet's face.

'What about David Lang?' asked Bowman.

'What about him?'

'If what Freddie Lang said is true, he's in trouble.'

Studley contorted his face into a contemptuous sneer. 'I wouldn't shed any tears over him, Josh. That fucker is probably out in France fixing a drug deal. If the Russians do get to him, it'll be one less thick mobster to worry about.'

Bowman shook his head forcefully. 'David Lang isn't stupid. He might be a bastard, but he's clever.'

'He's a gangster,' Studley said. 'They're all idiots.'

'David Lang is different. He's not like other crime bosses. The bloke has got an IQ of 182. That makes him a genius. He reads philosophy books for fun, studies economics in his spare time. He's evil, but first and foremost he considers himself a businessman.'

Studley grunted. 'You sound like you admire the prick.'

'I'm just telling you how it is. And I'll tell you something else. Whatever he's doing in Monte Carlo, it must be big. David isn't the kind of bloke who spends his time arranging petty drug deals. He's always been more interested in the big picture, even when he was a kid.'

Mallet narrowed his eyes to razors. 'How do you know all this?'

'I grew up around the Langs.'

'A Cockney boy, eh?'

'Romford born and bred,' Bowman said. 'Toughest people in the country, boss.'

Mallet grinned. 'Except for us Scots, of course.'

'Maybe. But we're craftier.'

Mallet laughed. 'I expect you're right,' he said. Then he looked intently at Bowman. 'So you knew the Lang twins, eh?'

'Everyone did, boss. We were a tight-knit community.'

'Any criminals in the family, Josh?'

Bowman knew better than to lie. 'My uncle had friends in the underworld,' he said. 'My granddad too. Every family knew someone linked to the Langs or one of their gang associates. It was just a way of life for us back then.'

He left out the part about his brother-in-law and oldest friend, Carter Grant, working as a lieutenant for the Lang twins. His drug dependency. The opioids he bought from Lang's dealer.

Mallet stared at him thoughtfully. 'I understand you used to be a police officer.'

'That's right, boss. Three years in the Met.'

'Undercover work, I hear. Gang stuff.'

Bowman nodded.

'Rather unusual, isn't it? Someone from your background, joining the force. Like siding with the enemy.'

'Not really,' said Bowman. 'I spent years growing up around gangsters. I saw how they really operated. How they bullied people and ruined lives. I figured I should do something about it. And I knew how to behave around them. How to talk like them, how they thought. That gave me an edge, working undercover. Helped me to blend in.'

'You're something of an expert on mobsters, then.'

'I know a fair bit. More than most, I guess.'

Mallet was silent as he sized the younger man up. He looked at Bowman the way a butcher assesses cattle at a market. Bowman couldn't tell what he was thinking. Reading Mallet's face was like picking up a book and finding it was written in a foreign language. You knew there were words on the page, but that didn't make it any easier to read.

Then Mallet's phone buzzed. He glanced at the screen without answering, nodded at Bowman.

'Forget about Davey Boy,' he said. 'He's not your concern. But there is one thing I must ask you to do.'

'Yes, boss?'

'Do not repeat anything Lang told you to the police.'

If anyone else had told him to withhold information from the cops, Bowman would have questioned it. Or at least demanded to know why. But for reasons he couldn't quite understand, he didn't want to disappoint Mallet.

'No worries, boss,' he said.

Mallet looked him in the eye and said, 'If they press you for information, just say Freddie was out of it and babbling like an idiot. You couldn't understand a word he was saying.'

'I was a copper once,' Bowman replied coolly. 'I know the procedure, what questions they'll ask. I know what to do.'

Mallet placed a hand on his shoulder. 'Good man.'

'What about the two BGs? Any word on them?'

Mallet exchanged a quick look with Studley. 'The security services are looking into it,' he said. 'But I wouldn't get your hopes up. Whoever did this will be out of the country before we can identify them.'

'Someone needs to get hold of that CCTV footage. Find that, and you'll find the blokes responsible.'

'We're looking into it,' Mallet repeated coolly.

His phone rang again. He took the phone call and beelined towards the emergency exits. Studley watched him walk away and made a grunting noise deep in his throat. 'Looks like you made a good impression,' he said.

Bowman rubbed his jaw. 'It didn't seem that way to me.'

'John only takes an interest in people he likes,' Studley replied. 'People who interest him. Everyone else is invisible. Take it from me, pal. You caught his eye.'

'He's got a funny way of showing it.'

He watched Mallet disappear through the exit and thought: *The guy is a crafty operator. I've spent the last few minutes telling him my life story, and he didn't reveal a thing about himself.*

Studley said, 'Those officers from the Met will be here shortly. They'll give you a quick interview. Stick to the plan and you'll be fine.'

'What then?'

'Get yourself checked out by one of the medics. Make sure you're not at risk from whatever crap they gave Freddie Lang. The last thing we want is your scruffy arse wandering around town, smearing deadly chemicals all over the place.'

'What about the other guys?'

'They're staying with the bodyguards and Seguma's assistant. Officers from Five are on the way over there to question them.'

'They won't know anything,' Bowman said. 'They're just flunkies.'

'You're probably right. But it's worth a shot. They might have seen or heard something about this top-secret meeting.' Studley sighed as he looked round the ballroom. 'What a fucking mess.'

The floor was littered with broken glass, hastily abandoned stilettos, jackets and jewellery. Amid the clutter Bowman saw Freddie Lang's trampled thick-rimmed glasses.

'I'll be in touch later,' Studley added. 'Once I've finished briefing the head shed on this clusterfuck.'

* * *

Studley left to make some calls. Bowman sat and waited. At around ten thirty, a pair of plain-clothed figures swept through the fire doors. A man and a woman. The man looked like the deputy manager of a suburban bank branch. He wore a jacket the size of a circus tent, a pair of badly scuffed shoes. His face was soft and doughy, his body a shapeless mass of flesh. The woman was perhaps ten years younger, thirty-five or thereabouts, dressed in a dark pencil skirt, white blouse and a black jacket. Her hair was pulled back in a tight ponytail. She looked unfussy, businesslike, and a lot healthier than her partner.

They showed Bowman their identification and introduced themselves. The guy with the doughy face was DI Rob Hardcastle. The woman was the more senior officer. Detective Chief Inspector Joanna Tatum. Which put her in the senior ranks of Counter Terrorism Command. She looked like she had earned it the hard way, through graft and commitment, rather than anyone doing her favours. She had an honest face, a refreshing lack of front. Bowman liked her immediately.

Tatum asked most of the questions. Hardcastle stood there, sweating and looking uncomfortable. Bowman told them he was ex-job, that he knew the score in terms of the debriefing and what was required of him. Establishing a rapport with the officers. Letting them know that he had once been part of their gang, that they could trust him. Tatum didn't grill him too hard. She could see that he'd had a rough day. Bowman handed his ID card to Tatum and promised to swing by the following day to provide a full statement. Tatum gave him a pleasant smile and thanked him for his assistance. It was all very civilised. Which was just the way Bowman wanted it. He wished them good luck and headed for the exit.

He ignored Studley's advice and bypassed the medical teams. If anyone started shining pen torches in his eyes or testing his blood, they'd quickly realise he was on opioids. Besides, if he had been infected by Lang, he would soon know about it.

At the door, he gave his details to an officer with a clipboard. The officer handed him a card and told him to get in touch if he developed any symptoms. Sweating, fever, stomach cramps, nausea, dilated pupils, muscle aches.

Congratulations, he thought. *You've just described a textbook opioid withdrawal.*

He left the ballroom soon after eleven o'clock. Bowman paced down a maze of backstreets, turned left past Bond Street Tube station and continued west along Oxford Street towards Marble Arch. After maybe five hundred metres he turned right again and cut north until he hit the hotel.

The Gold Star Lodge was no one's idea of luxury. The brickwork was crumbling, the windows were filthy. Bird shit and chewing gum spackled the pavement outside. It had been chosen purely on the basis of its availability, budget and proximity to the principal's hotel. Bowman assumed the second of these was the deciding factor. But, at that moment, he didn't care. He just needed to get out of his clothes, clean up and source some more pills. Fast.

He took the lift to the sixth floor, slipped into his room and hung the 'Do Not Disturb' sign on the door handle. He found his washbag next to the sink in the grotty bathroom and fished out a tobacco tin hidden in a secret compartment at the bottom of the bag. He took out a spare SIM card and paperclip from the tin, teased out his phone's SIM card holder with the bent clip, replaced it with the spare SIM. Then he powered up, tapped in his passcode and opened the secure messaging app. The most secure app on the market. Military-grade encryption. The Regiment used the same one, for covert comms on ops.

He dialled the only number stored in the contacts list. The person on the other end picked up on the third ring.

'I was wondering when you'd call,' the throaty voice said.

Lenny Scavell, his dealer.

Bowman preferred to buy the opioids through Carter Grant, his brother-in-law, and one of Freddie Lang's most trusted lieutenants. Which was a pain in the arse, involving frequent trips up to Roomers, a club in east London owned by the Langs, to meet with Lenny Scavell. Lenny was a long-time associate of the Lang twins. A risky set-up. But safer than buying stuff on the streets in Hereford, he figured.

Bowman said, 'I need a score. The usual.'

Scavell hack-coughed. 'When?'

'Tonight, mate. Soon as.' He added, 'I'm in town.'

There was a long pause. Bowman could hear dance music thumping in the background, voices. Several of them. Scavell said, 'Tonight ain't good. You seen all this stuff on the news? Some terror attack at the royal wedding or something. Fucking madness.'

Bowman said, 'I can't wait until tomorrow, Lenny.'

'Tough shit. I ain't going anywhere tonight. Not with all that chaos. Come down the club.'

'I can't.'

He didn't want to be seen anywhere near the Langs' club right now. Not for a long time, not after what had happened to Freddie.

A long sigh whispered down the line.

'Where are you?' Scavell asked.

Bowman gave the address of the hotel.

Scavell paused again. 'Wait there. I'll call you back in a minute.'

He hung up. Two minutes later, Bowman's phone trilled again.

Scavell said, 'One of my boys will sort you out. But it'll cost double. Consider it a delivery charge.'

'Fine.' Bowman wasn't in the mood to argue. 'When can your man get here?'

'Two o'clock. Earliest he can do.'

Bowman glanced at his G-Shock. Half eleven. Two-and-a-half hours until Lenny's man would arrive with the goods. A long time to wait. But no choice.

'There's a car park around the corner from the hotel,' he said. 'Opposite a Vietnamese takeaway. Tell your man I'll meet him there.'

Scavell gave him a description of his associate's car. Then Bowman killed the call, ejected the spare SIM card from his phone and replaced it with his regular SIM. He stashed the other SIM in the secret compartment in his washbag, threw off his suit, showered and changed into his off-duty gear. Dark jeans, plain T-shirt, Timberland boots. He dropped into the frayed armchair, scooped up the remote and flicked through the channels on the TV.

A small army of reporters had camped out in front of a police cordon outside the Greybourn Hotel. No one knew about the poisoning yet, it seemed. There were unconfirmed reports of a terrorist attack, the reporter said. She seemed very keen to reassure viewers that the royal family was believed to be safe. Police lights pulsed in the background.

Bowman's mind drifted back to the night his world collapsed. It always did, in the end. He could never escape that gruesome memory. Christ knows, he had tried. Fifteen years had passed since that evening, but the images were so vivid it sometimes felt as if it had happened yesterday. He would be sitting in the pub, or walking down the street in Hereford, and suddenly he would see his young family dead on the kitchen floor. A momentary snapshot. Like a subliminal message spliced into a film reel. He would see his wife, Amy, her beautiful face ruined by the smile the gangsters had drawn on it with the tip of a kitchen knife. His little girl, Sophie, wearing her favourite princess dress. A sleepy look in her eyes, as if she had nodded off beside her mother.

And the blood. Always he would see the blood.

In the years since their horrific murders, Bowman had tried to move on. He had sought to escape in booze, sleeping pills, other drugs. Nothing had worked. Only the opioids gave him some semblance of peace. They didn't block the memories – no drug in the world could do that – but they did numb the pain. They turned him into a kind of zombie. Helped him make it through the day.

But lately, the images had been getting stronger.

He had started popping a few extra pills each day, upping his dosage. Anything to dial down the grief. Put the lid on it. Bowman knew he was playing a dangerous game. The more pills he took, the more he needed to stay on the level. And the bigger the risk of getting caught. Bowman had gone to greater lengths to conceal his addiction, but if he kept this up, sooner or later someone in the Regiment was going to find out the truth . . .

He watched TV and waited, growing more restless with each passing minute. At ten minutes to two he grabbed his coat, wallet, phone and left his room.

The dealer was waiting for him in the car park at the end of the block, in a red Audi A4 saloon, the engine low-rumbling. Bowman halted in front of the takeaway and looked up and down to make sure he wasn't being watched. Then he stuffed his hands into his coat pockets, lowered his head and walked across the road. As he approached, the window on the driver's side of the Audi cracked open. Bowman took out the four twenties from his coat pocket. A hand poked out of the window and snatched the cash. It reappeared a moment later gripping a plastic baggie filled with pink-coloured pills. Bowman jammed the bag into his coat pocket and walked on.

He took a roundabout route back to the hotel. He looped round Marble Arch, doubling back on himself and occasionally pausing to glance in the reflection of shop windows. The usual anti-surveillance measures.

Bowman returned to his hotel room and flicked on the bathroom lights. He set the plastic baggie down, took out one pill and emptied the rest into the storage compartment in the pill crusher. He mashed the other tablet into a fine powder using the crusher, tipped it onto the counter. Prepared to inhale.

Then there was a knock at the door.

Bowman froze.

His first thought was: I've been followed. The police have seen me buying drugs. I'm about to get arrested. But no. He had been vigilant. The chances of someone tailing him back from the drop were vanishingly small.

So who the fuck is outside?

The knuckles rapped on the door again.

He left the opiate powder on the counter, slipped out of the bathroom and padded over to the door. Slid off the deadbolt and eased the door open.

Two figures stood in the corridor.

They had the attitude of security service heavies and the wardrobes to match. Off-the-rack suits, cheap haircuts. Next to each other, they were like the before and after photographs for a dietary supplement commercial. The guy on the left was grey-haired and running to fat, with a heavily lined brow and a wonky nose. His partner was leaner and square-jawed, with the glowing skin of someone in peak physical condition.

They showed him their security badges. Bowman glanced at them both. The guy with the wonky nose was called Henderson. The guy with the perfect skin was called Williams. They were UKNs. Bowman had seen their type before. Freelancers used by Five and Six to carry out surveillance work and other duties. They did the jobs out of some deep loyalty to Queen and country, Bowman presumed. It certainly wasn't because of the piss-poor pay.

'Josh Bowman?' the latter asked.

'Yeah?'

'You need to come with us,' Williams said. His voice was as nondescript as his clothes, his face. 'Now, if you don't mind.'

'We've been told to tell you to bring your ghost ID from the Wing,' Henderson added.

'Why?' Bowman demanded. 'What's going on?'

'John Mallet says hello. He wants a word.'

Eight

They gave him three minutes to pack his bags and insisted on waiting inside. Which meant there was no time to snort the crushed-up pill. Bowman left them watching TV while he hurriedly scraped the dust-like powder off the countertop and emptied it into the toilet bowl. He flushed, disposing of the evidence, then shoved his washbag into his black leather holdall, along with his spare kit and Glock. He grabbed the passport issued to him by the Wing under his cover story name. Checked the room one last time, then followed Henderson and Williams down the corridor. They took the lift down to the lobby and led Bowman outside towards a meteor-grey BMW 7 Series. He dumped his bag in the boot, then slid into the back seat. Henderson and Williams squeezed in either side of him, man-spreading their legs, their huge hands planted on their knees. A third guy with a buzzcut sat behind the wheel. He glanced at Bowman in the rear-view, nodded at his partners and pulled out into traffic.

Bowman sat quietly in the back as they took a circuitous route north and then east away from Marble Arch. There was no point asking where they were going, or why. Bowman had served with the Wing long enough to know how they operated. Henderson, Williams and Buzzcut were foot soldiers. Guys who could be trusted to do a job and keep their mouths shut. They wouldn't have been told anything except the bare minimum.

But that didn't stop him from fearing the worst. Questions pinballed inside his head. Why does Mallet want to see me at this hour? Why had the UKNs told me to bring my ghost ID? He decided it couldn't be good news. Most likely Six had found out about his drug habit. Now they were shutting him down. They had called him out so Mallet could confront him with the evidence of his addiction, take away his ghost ID and tell him his time in the Wing was over.

They hit Middle Temple and scudded east along the Embankment. The city blurred past them. Bowman saw grandiose Victorian buildings and brutalist concrete offices, gleaming glass-and-steel towers and cranes slanted against the skyline, like the masts of sailing ships in a crowded port. All of it illuminated by the glow from a million street lamps and apartment windows. Buzzcut took the Blackfriars underpass and carried on east, through Cannon Street and Monument. At two in the morning, the roads were quiet apart from the trickle of black cabs and night buses.

Buzzcut kept the BMW purring along, sticking to a steady thirty miles per hour as they headed towards Whitechapel. Ripper country. He wondered, again, where the heavies were taking him. He thought about the pills, too. If Henderson and his mates had knocked on his door sixty seconds later, he would have had time to snort the pill. Instead, he'd have to wait until after his meeting with Mallet. However long that took . . .

They passed the Tower of London, hit a junction the size of a great lake and then Buzzcut steered into an empty taxi bay in front of the old Royal Mint. He slit the throat of the engine.

'What's going on?' Bowman demanded. 'Where's Mallet?'

'Patience, sunshine,' Williams said, blandly.

Henderson's eyes shot forward. Bowman looked in the same direction and descried a figure standing in front of the southern gatehouse, smoking a cigarette.

Mallet.

He took a final drag on his cancer stick, dashed the butt and circled round to the rear of the vehicle, then knocked twice on the passenger window. Henderson buzzed down the glass. Mallet leaned through the opening and glanced briefly at Bowman before he nodded at the heavies.

'Right, you lot,' he said. 'Get out. Stretch your legs. Give us a few minutes.'

The heavies obeyed without question. Partly because they were lower down the food chain than Mallet. But also because the guy talking to them wasn't the kind of person you wanted to piss off. Mallet stood back while Henderson and his mates removed themselves to a spot two metres from the BMW. Then he dropped into the back seat, slamming the door shut behind him. The hubbub of London reduced to a faint hum. Bowman waited anxiously.

Here it comes, he thought.

The end of my career.

Mallet stared out of the window at the old Royal Mint.

'Shame about this place,' he said in a low mutter, as if talking to himself. 'This building is a big part of our history. They moved the Mint here from the Tower, two hundred years ago. Back when our ancestors were busy slogging it out with Napoleon. Two years ago, we sold it off to the Chinese. Beijing will use it for their new embassy.' He shook his head sadly. 'We used to keep the enemy at the gates. Now we welcome them with open arms. All we care about is whether they've got deep pockets.'

Bowman looked at the ex-SAS man in puzzled silence. *Is this why Mallet dragged me out of my hotel room? To give me a history lesson at two thirty in the morning?*

'Why am I here?' he demanded. 'What do you want with me?'

Mallet stared levelly at him.

'I'll cut right to it,' he said. 'I'm here to give you an opportunity, Josh. The kind that doesn't come around very often.'

'Opportunity for what?'

'To fight mobsters.' A crafty grin played out on Mallet's face. 'I'm offering you the chance to come and work for the Cell.'

The words hung in the air between them, like apples from a tree. Bowman felt a surge of relief sweep through him. *Mallet didn't call me here to give me the boot.*

87

This is a job interview.

'Why me?' he asked.

'I'll explain everything in a moment. But first, let me remind you that what I'm about to say is strictly confidential. You are not to repeat this conversation to anyone. Not your mates, your OC, not even your own mother. What I'm about to tell you stays between us. Clear?'

Bowman nodded. 'Crystal, boss.'

A hot feeling of excitement swelled up inside him. *A few minutes ago, I thought I was about to get booted out of the Wing. Now I'm being offered the chance to join the inner sanctum of the Regiment.*

'Tell me,' Mallet said. 'How much do you know about what we do?'

'Not much. The same as the other guys at Hereford, I suppose. You're part of the Wing. You work closely with the police, Five and Six. Something to do with organised crime.'

'That's true. But we do a lot more than that.'

He gestured past his window at the Tower of London. The Shard rose above it on the far side of the Thames, the spire illuminated like some ancient beacon warning of an imminent invasion.

'Our real job is to protect all of this. The state. Which, in this day and age, means defending British business interests.'

'From what?' asked Bowman.

'From whatever hostile forces threaten it,' Mallet explained. 'Mostly, it's organised crime groups working within or alongside foreign governments. These groups aren't seeking to engage us militarily, do you see? Their main point of attack is on British businesses, at home or abroad. We're talking about some of the world's biggest companies. Huge deals. Billions of pounds at stake.

'The spooks don't like to admit it, but British business is what keeps our place at the top table in world affairs. Not nuclear subs or foreign aid, but cold, hard cash. Our task is to protect these interests at all costs, at home and abroad.'

'Isn't that Six's job?'

Mallet's smile played out across his face. 'It used to be. But Vauxhall can't handle the new threats we're facing. Not alone, anyway. They don't have the skills for the task. They're smart people, with their Oxbridge degrees and City contacts, but they're not good at the rough stuff. They need guys like you and me. That's why we created the Cell.'

'To protect some greedy bankers and tax dodgers?'

'That's not what we do. We're the only specialist team dedicated to fighting the gravest threat to our country: foreign criminal elites.'

His Scottish accent grew more pronounced as he warmed to his subject. Bowman listened as he went on.

'The world has changed, Josh. The desk jockeys in Whitehall like to say that we're no longer living in a unipolar world. What they really mean is that the rules of the game have been thrown out of the window and we're in a free-for-all. Traditional state spies are no longer the main threat. It's not from terrorist groups, either. Some nutter mowing down a few civvies in a truck is a tragedy, but it's not a serious threat to national security. No,' Mallet added, 'these days, it's all about mobs and big business, working together.'

'Like Russia, you mean?'

'Exactly. We all know that Russia isn't a country, not anymore. It's a mafia state run by organised crime groups, oligarchs and the security services. Those guys aren't interested in ideology or state spycraft, and they're not looking to go toe-to-toe with the West in some direct military confrontation. Bad for business. They're only interested in lining their own pockets. Their motivation is pure greed.'

'They don't sound much different from the gangs in Romford, mate.'

'Amateur thugs. Small-time crooks,' Mallet said with a sneer. 'These guys are different. They're a cut above your average criminal. And it's not just the Russians, either. This is a global problem.

Everywhere you look, organised mob networks have infiltrated governments. Central America. Eastern Europe. Africa, Asia. In some places they've taken complete control. We're dealing with a whole new criminal elite. These guys pose a serious threat to our interests, at home and abroad. *That* is why the Cell was created. To fight the criminal groups threatening our security.'

Bowman noticed a hard gleam in Mallet's eyes. He thought: *This man hates mobsters. He hates them almost as much as I do.*

'What has all of this got to do with me?' he asked.

Mallet thrust a hand into his jacket pocket and plucked a cigarette out of a crumpled packet, lowered the window. He looked at Bowman. 'Do you mind?'

'My mother smoked forty a day. She died of lung cancer.'

'I agree. It's a terrible habit.'

Mallet sparked up. He sucked in a deep lungful of air, blew it out through the open window.

Bowman waited for him to continue.

'We're being given the green light for a hard arrest,' Mallet said at last. 'It's a fastball operation, and it's going to happen soon. I can't go into any details at the moment. There's a briefing later – if you accept our offer. But if you agree to join us, there's no going back. Once you're in, you're in.'

'Who's the target?' asked Bowman.

'I can't say right now. That will be explained later. All I can tell you is that if you agree to do this job with us, you'll be doing your country a great service. This is a highly sensitive mission, lad, and you're made to measure for it.'

Bowman looked at him doubtfully. 'What do you mean?'

Mallet tapped the side of his head with a thick finger. 'You know mobsters. Better than most people. You grew up around them, you went to school with them. You worked undercover in gangs with the Met. That means you know what makes them tick.'

'That's why you're interested in me? Because I've hung out with a few gangsters?'

'It's one of the reasons, aye. There are others.'

'Like what?'

Mallet sucked on his cigarette one last time and tossed the butt out of the window. The burning tip somersaulted through the frigid night air. He closed the window.

'I've seen your file,' he carried on. 'The Cell keeps a close eye on the rest of the SF community, naturally. We're always on the lookout for people with particular skills. People such as yourself.'

Bowman shook his head. 'I'm no different to the other blokes at Hereford.'

'I disagree,' Mallet said. He rested his hands in his lap and stared out of the windscreen. 'You did your undercover work in the Met. Then you left the force and did three years in Special Forces Support Group. Then the Regiment. Multiple tours in Afghanistan, Iraq, followed by a two-year secondment in the Special Reconnaissance Regiment, so that's your surveillance skills sorted. You've done a posting with E Squadron, so you've got experience of working with Vauxhall and Thames House. That makes you unusual, you see.' Mallet hesitated. 'I know what happened to your family, too,' he added in a low voice.

Bowman felt something cold and wet slither down the base of his spine. Everyone at Hereford knew the story, the tragedy that had wrecked his life fifteen years ago, but they never mentioned it in his presence. They knew better.

'What those Albanian thugs did to your wife and daughter was despicable,' Mallet continued quietly. 'No husband or father should ever have to deal with that.'

Bowman closed his eyes for a moment. The violent images flashed across his mind again, tormenting him. He saw the blood splatter, the mutilated bodies. His wife and daughter. Murdered.

'There's no need to . . . to bring that up,' he stuttered. 'There's not a day that goes by without me thinking about . . . what happened. You can't imagine . . .'

His voice trailed, he looked away.

Mallet said, 'This is your chance for revenge. You can't bring your loved ones back, but I'm offering you the next best thing. The opportunity to avenge their deaths.'

'It's too late for that,' Bowman said. 'Those Albanian bastards got away with it. *That's* in your bloody file, isn't it?'

'Aye, lad, I know. But if you agree to work with us, you'll be waging war against the criminal elite. The David Langs of the world. The same type of scum responsible for murdering your family. This is a chance to make them pay.'

Bowman stayed silent as he weighed up Mallet's offer. But he already knew his answer. He'd tried repeatedly to push past the grief, the raw anguish. But somehow, he had never been able to move past it. The one thing he craved – vengeance – was always out of his reach. The pills had dampened the pain, but they had never given him closure. Now he had the opportunity he'd always been looking for.

A tiny voice at the back of his mind told him that he shouldn't trust Mallet. *This guy might be a Regiment legend, but he's also a world-class manipulator.* But at that moment he didn't really care.

'And if I say yes?' he asked. 'What then?'

Mallet stared at him. 'Let me be very clear. This is a temporary posting. There are no guarantees that you'll be kept on once the mission is over. If you screw up, you'll be straight back to the Wing.'

'I'll take the chance. What about Hereford?'

'Everything's been cleared with the CO,' Mallet said. 'I've spoken with Studley as well. It's all sorted. You're with the Wing, so you've already been positively vetted. In terms of processing – fake passports and ID, cover story – all of that stuff will be sorted later.'

'I'll need accommodation,' Bowman said. 'Somewhere to kip, while I'm based up here with you lot.'

'We'll sort out something for you,' Mallet assured him. 'But it won't be glamorous. A bedsit in Acton, that's the best we can offer.'

'I grew up in worse,' Bowman said, recalling the dilapidated terrace from his childhood. 'Where's your base of operations?'

'I'll explain that in a bit,' Mallet replied. 'But before we go any further, we need to establish a few ground rules.'

Bowman listened as Mallet counted them off on his fingers.

'One. Our work in the Cell is top secret and absolutely deniable. That means you don't ever speak about anything you do, see or hear to anyone on the outside. Working for us is like going on a bender in Vegas. What goes on in the Cell, stays in the Cell.'

'Fine,' said Bowman. 'What else?'

'There's no need to call me "boss". You can call me John from now on. The nature of our work means that we'll sometimes find ourselves in the company of people outside the Regiment. People who won't know who we are, or what we do. I don't want you dropping a bollock in that type of situation.'

'I can manage that . . . John.'

Mallet paused and gave him a long hard look. 'One more thing. Your brother-in-law. Carter Grant.'

'What about him?'

'He's a criminal. No point denying it. It was flagged up when you joined the Wing. The head shed decided to overlook it at the time, but you'll need to stay away from him now. You can't be seen in the presence of organised crime figures . . . however hard that may be for you personally.'

Bowman felt a stab of anxiety. He recalled the vetting process he'd undergone when joining the Wing. They had listened to his phone calls, read his text messages, emails and social media posts. They had even dived into his bank accounts to search for dodgy transactions. At the time, he had assumed he was in the clear. But now he started to wonder what else they might have uncovered. He mentally reviewed the trips he'd made to Freddie Lang's club in Romford over the past few months, the pills he'd scored from Lenny Scavell.

Does Mallet know about my addiction? If so, why is he offering me a job with the Cell?

'I understand it will be difficult not seeing your sister and your niece,' Mallet went on. 'But that's the sacrifice you'll have to make if you want to join the Cell.'

Bowman sighed inwardly with relief. *He doesn't know.*

'Well?' Mallet spread his hands. 'Are you interested?'

'Fuck it,' he said. 'I'm in.'

'Good.'

Mallet turned and rapped his knuckles on the glass twice. Through the tinted glass, Bowman saw the heavies turn round and yank open the car doors before they folded themselves back inside the BMW. Henderson rode shotgun. Buzzcut took the wheel. Williams squashed in the back, next to Bowman and Mallet. The latter signalled to the driver in the rear-view mirror.

'OK, guys. Let's go.'

Buzzcut met his eyes in the rear-view and fired up the engine. He steered smoothly away from the taxi bay, glanced over his shoulder and pulled out into the main road. They cantered on past the old Royal Mint and headed east, beyond Tower Bridge.

'Where are we going?' asked Bowman.

'Headquarters,' Mallet said. 'There's a team briefing in half an hour. Then we'll tell you all about the mission.'

Nine

They drove east and then north, away from the river. Bowman sat in the back, fighting off a wave of exhaustion. Things were moving fast. Faster than he'd expected. Bowman had assumed that the UKNs would ferry him back to his hotel after the meeting with Mallet. He could pop a couple of pills, get his head down and grab a few hours of kip, before getting a full briefing the next morning.

Instead, they were going straight to work.

Push through it. There'll be plenty of time to rest later.

Buzzcut kept the BMW ticking along as they motored through Aldgate. They passed a chaotic mishmash of ancient churches, new-build apartment blocks and fried chicken shops. Fragments of the old city poked through the clutter: an old-school boozer named after a long-dead admiral, a greasy spoon, a curry house that looked as if it had been doing business since the Gordon Riots. Buzzcut made several quick turns, and then they rolled down a wide street flanked by steel-and-glass apartment blocks and trendy co-working spaces. At two forty in the morning, the streets were empty. After three hundred metres Mallet motioned for him to pull over.

'OK,' Mallet said. 'This is fine.'

Buzzcut parked the BMW at the side of the road but kept the motor running. Bowman looked enquiringly at Mallet. They had been driving for about six minutes since setting off from the old Royal Mint.

'The Cell is *here*?'

'Get out,' Mallet said. 'Follow me.'

They slid out of the back seat, breath misting in the night air. Henderson swerved round to the boot, popped it open and handed the leather holdall to Bowman. He dived back into the front passenger seat, and a few moments later, the BMW sped away.

Bowman followed Mallet as he started across the road, towards a drab grey building sandwiched between a gastropub and an accountancy firm. Blinds covered the windows on every floor of the building. There was a canopied entrance, but no company sign. Nothing to indicate what sort of business went on inside.

'What is this place?' asked Bowman.

'Used to be a police station,' Mallet said. 'Back in the seventies. Before your time. It closed down a few decades ago. Been empty ever since. There's a range in the basement. The lads in SO19 use it for shooting practice, but no other fucker knows about it.'

'This is where you lot are based?'

'For now. Some day, it'll be sold off to a property developer for big bucks,' he grumbled. 'But for now, this is our HQ.'

Bowman gazed up at the six-storey building. In his head, he'd imagined the Cell would be based somewhere remote, far from the public eye. A disused industrial estate in Hertfordshire or Essex, maybe. Not a few minutes' walk from the bustle of the City.

'Isn't this a bit conspicuous?' he asked.

'The Regiment hid in plain sight in Ulster,' Mallet reminded him. 'We're simply doing the same thing. And it gives us the chance to keep an eye on those pricks in the City.'

Bowman followed him up the steps. They stopped in front of the intercom panel fixed to the wall. Signs either side of the door warned that security cameras were in operation. Mallet pressed a large button and glanced up at the camera above the door, identifying himself to whoever was watching. Several moments passed. Then the door buzzed, and Mallet ushered Bowman into a sparsely furnished enquiry office. The decor was horribly dated: worn carpet, nicotine-stained walls, panel lighting. Every surface was thickly covered in dust. A fat, bored-looking security guard sat behind the glass partition, staring at a bank of computer screens.

Mallet held up his security pass. The podgy guard glanced briefly at it then waved the two men through and went back to screen-watching. Mallet led Bowman down a bland corridor until they reached a bank of lifts. He punched the call button, the scuffed metal doors scraped open, and they stepped inside. Mallet swiped his card against the reader, pushed another button on the panel and the doors thunked shut again.

The lift creaked and clanked as they descended into the bowels of the building.

'We're on the lower basement,' Mallet explained. 'The range is on the floor above. The lads from SO19 know not to bother us. If we ever want to use the range, we make a call and it's booked out.'

'Who else knows we're here?'

'Just the top brass at Vauxhall and Thames House. One or two figures in the Foreign Office. The police chiefs. Nobody else. We're the best kept secret in London.'

Bowman suddenly understood why the Cell had chosen this place as their headquarters. It was fully secure, anonymous and within easy distance of Whitehall, Scotland Yard, the City. No one would ever bother to find out what was going on inside the build-ing, and if they did, the guards would take care of them. The Cell could go about its business in complete secrecy.

The doors scraped open, and then Mallet guided him down another short corridor. They came to a halt in front of a thick steel door secured with a biometric lock.

'Access is via fingerprint recognition,' Mallet said. 'We'll get your prints into the system as soon as the briefing is over. You'll be given a security pass, too.'

He pressed his index finger against the sensor panel. The door unlocked with a cheerful beep. Mallet levered the door handle, took a step inside, then paused in the doorway.

'This is it. Once you step inside this room, there's no turning back.'

Bowman eased out a breath. 'I'm ready,' he said.

'Good lad.'

He crossed the threshold and entered a cavernous, brightly lit space with ductwork on the ceiling and exposed brick walls. The room was huge. The size of half a football pitch. There was an armoury at one end of the space, secured behind a separate steel door. Nearby was a row of computer terminals, a stack of handheld radios and mobile phones on charge. In another corner he saw an open wardrobe. Suits and athleisure gear and dresses hung from a clothes rack, along with four sets of courier overalls: bright-blue shirts with orange trim, matching baseball caps and dark trousers. Next to the wardrobe was a make-up station with a vanity mirror surrounded by LED lights, a wig stand, a make-up case with powders and liners and brushes. Bowman saw shoe racks filled with high heels, trainers, walking boots, leather brogues. There was a kitchen countertop to one side of the entrance, with a microwave, kettle, drip coffee maker, toaster, sink. Further along, there was a breakout area with a flat-screen TV, two sofas, a few armchairs. Bowman saw a snooker table, a dartboard. Lockers. A row of bunk beds with bags scattered across the floor.

Across the room, two figures in plain civvies stood hunched over a map. One of the guys was very short. Five-four or maybe five. The man next to him was at least six inches taller and dark-skinned, with close-cropped hair, like a black leather skullcap. They paid no attention to Bowman. As he looked on, a slightly built woman hurried over to her two colleagues. She was dressed in a pair of tight black jeans, blouse and dark blazer. She had a plain face, short dark hair and lips the colour of strawberries.

'The rest of the team,' Mallet said. 'You'll be introduced to them in a few minutes. In there.'

He pointed to a large structure in the middle of the floor space. At first glance it looked like a steel container. Six metres long and three wide, with corrugated metal sides. The kind of thing you saw stacked up on transport ships or freight trains. A metal door had been fitted to one of the longer panels, Bowman noted.

'We call it the Shed,' Mallet added. 'It's fully soundproofed and screened for bugs. That's where we have our briefings.'

Bowman looked round in amazement. 'How long has all this stuff been down here?'

'Nine years. Since we first created the Cell.'

'How many guys on the team?'

'Six, including myself,' said Mallet. 'You're the seventh. Two of the lads are on another job right now. Overseas posting.'

Bowman barely heard him. He was buzzing with adrenaline. The tiredness he'd felt earlier that evening was a distant memory now. An hour ago, he had been sitting in his crappy hotel room, watching TV. Now he was being drafted in for an urgent mission with the Cell. Something big was about to go down, Bowman sensed. And he was going to be right in the thick of the action.

That's exactly where I want to be.

Mallet said, 'Drop your stuff off at the bunks. Then meet me in the Shed. I want to show you something.'

He started towards the Shed. Bowman beat a path across the room, dumped his holdall on one of the empty beds. Then he hurried over to the soundproofed room and stepped inside.

There was a boardroom table in the middle of the Shed, with eight chairs arranged around it and a conference speakerphone in the centre. Wires snaked through the square cut-out, leading to unseen plug sockets and modems beneath the table. The walls were covered in eggcrate-patterned foam tiles. Soundproofing. Bowman had seen it before, in MI6 safe houses elsewhere in the city.

Mallet was standing in front of a large display board against the back wall. The board was covered in postcard-sized photographs, linked to one another with lengths of red string. Bowman saw a picture of a palatial mansion overlooking a bay, an exterior shot of a gleaming apartment block. A photo of Ken Seguma, along with some other faces he vaguely recognised. Members of the president's family.

In the middle of the board was a snap of David Lang.

Bowman drew up alongside Mallet and took a closer look at the photo. It appeared to have been taken at some sort of party. A private gathering. Lang sat at a table, between a couple of burly guys in dark suits, a bottle of wine in front of them. The two stocky guys were smiling as they posed for the camera. But not David Lang.

He looked almost identical to his twin brother. He was slimmer than Freddie, lean-hipped and slender, and his hair was sprinkled with grey. But he had the same arched eyebrows as Freddie. The same thin lips and cruel, cold eyes. He was smartly dressed in a linen jacket; the top two buttons on his shirt were popped, revealing a tuft of chest hair and a gold chain as thick as a hanging rope. On his left wrist he wore a chunky watch with a spider on the dial. Bowman had seen that model before. The Russian president owned the same one. He remembered reading about it somewhere. A limited-edition model, costing almost half a million quid.

He turned to Mallet and jabbed a finger at the pinboard. 'Is that who we're arresting? David Lang?'

There was a menacing glint in Mallet's eyes. A smile cut like a machete across his lips. 'I told you we'd be fighting mobsters, laddie. Lang's the target, all right. We've had eyes on him for a while.'

'What's the plan?'

'We're going to head to Monte Carlo,' Mallet said. 'This morning. A few hours from now. Then we're going to snatch Lang and make him an offer he can't refuse.'

Ten

Silence hung heavy in the air for a beat. Bowman scrutinised the faces on the pinboard, his head spinning. His exhausted mind was struggling to process what was going on. He looked round at Mallet.

'You knew about the meeting in Monaco? With the Russians?'

Mallet dipped a hand into his jacket pocket, took out a packet of nicotine gum. 'No smoking in the basement,' he said. 'Health and safety.'

He pushed out a piece of gum from the foil pack, popped it into his mouth.

'We knew some of the details,' he continued. 'The basic facts of the meeting. But we didn't know about President Seguma's involvement, or the trap the Russians have been planning. Now we do. Thanks to you.'

'What's Lang doing out there?'

Mallet chewed loudly as he indicated two other photos pinned to the fabric board. The guy on the left was puffy-faced and balding, with heavily lidded eyes and wispy beard. The pale face on the right had a pointed nose, eyes like bullet holes in a paper target.

'Lang is due to meet two Russian nationals,' Mallet explained. 'Today. Eight hours from now. One of the attendees is Alexei Bezuglov, the Russian ambassador to Monaco.'

He tapped a finger against the picture of the bald guy with the wispy beard.

'The other is this man,' he added. 'Sergei Galkin.'

'Never heard of him.'

'You wouldn't. Galkin is one of the original oligarchs. Late nineties moneyman. Part of the president's inner circle, back when he was mayor of St Petersburg. Keeps a low profile. He's the Kremlin's Mr Fix-It. When they need to make something happen, Galkin is the guy they bring in.'

'Any idea what this meeting is about?'

'Six has got a few ideas. They reckon Lang is fixing to make some sort of deal with the Kremlin behind our backs.'

'What kind of deal?' asked Bowman.

'Pressuring him into changing allegiance, maybe. But we don't know for sure. That's why we're going in. To find out what the bastard is up to.'

'Lang is playing in the big boys' league now, isn't he?'

Mallet laughed. 'He's come a long way from breaking legs in dodgy East End boozers. That's for sure.'

'Where's the meeting?'

'At Galkin's mansion, down the coast in Antibes. Lang is due to meet the Russians at midday local time. We've been planning the operation to arrest him for the past week. Now we're being green-lit.'

Bowman nodded. He'd worked on plenty of similar ops in the past. He could imagine how the planning would have taken shape. First the Cell would have devised an immediate response. A crude plan, simple but effective. Like a guy walking into a bar and punching someone in the face. The plan would have been adapted and honed each day as new information came to light, allowing the team to put together a planned response. Which would be more sophisticated than the emergency plan. They would keep on working on it each day, fine-tuning the details until the team got the go-ahead.

His eyes focused on another photo on the board, next to Seguma's family members and advisers. A sun-bleached face, long and lean, with long dark hair and a bushy beard. He wore a short-sleeved khaki shirt and stood next to a couple of soldiers in combat fatigues.

'I know that face,' Bowman said. 'That's Mike Gregory. He was my old OC in B Squadron. I served under him in Iraq.'

'He had less facial hair back then,' Mallet said with a grin. 'He's hairier than Bigfoot these days.'

'What's he doing mixed up in all of this?'

'Mike is the chief security adviser to the president. He's been in the job for the past three years. I assumed you knew.'

Bowman shook his head. 'I'd heard he was operational in Karatandu, doing jobs on the Circuit. But I didn't know he was working directly for the president.'

'Mike had a contract to protect one of the big mines. When the job ended, Seguma kept him on. He's one of a handful of confidantes the president trusts. Maybe the only one, outside his immediate family. Seguma doesn't take a dump without consulting him first.'

'He's done well for himself. Good for him.'

'You're a fan of his?'

'Mike's one of the good guys. Best officer I ever had. Saved my arse on Selection.'

Mallet knitted his brow. 'How's that?'

'He was with Training Wing at the time. I got into a fight one night in a pub in Hereford. It wasn't my fault, I was minding my own business, but some drunken idiot wanted to have a go. One thing led to another and the police showed up and arrested me. I could have been RTU'd for that, but Mike stepped in and defended me.' Bowman frowned. 'He's not in any trouble, is he?'

'We don't think so. Mike is on the fringes of this thing. He's holding the fort while his boss is in Monte Carlo.'

'How did you find out about the meeting in Antibes?'

'We've had Davey Boy under surveillance for months. The guys at Six have infiltrated every corner of his business empire. They've hacked his computer, his phones. His properties have been rigged up with mics. They've flipped his accountant, his PA, even his cleaner.'

Bowman kept his face composed but felt a twitch of anxiety. For a moment he wondered if Six had discovered the truth about his addiction when they'd ripped Lang's life apart. But he immediately dismissed the fear. No. There was no way Mallet would have invited him to join the Cell if he knew about his opioid dependency.

At least there was no chance of David Lang recognising his face, Bowman reassured himself. Unlike his twin brother, David had always maintained his distance from street-level crime and violence. He didn't associate with thugs or drug dealers, he ran legitimate businesses. He didn't hang out at the club in Romford.

My secret is safe. For now.

He said, 'Where's Lang now?'

'His apartment,' Mallet replied. 'Overlooking the beach in Monte Carlo. That's where we'll make the arrest. Then we'll give him a choice. He can come back with us and go into protective custody, or he can come back to something a lot less pleasant. But either way, that scumbag is coming back to the UK.'

'What if he refuses?'

'He won't. Trust me.'

Bowman returned his gaze to the pinboard and sucked air between his teeth. 'It's not gonna be easy to isolate him. The principality will be crawling with police and cameras.'

'We've got a way inside,' Mallet said.

'How?'

Mallet frowned at his Breitling. 'There's no time to go into the details right now. The other guys will bring you up to speed later. Fill in any blanks.'

'But why bring me on now? You've been planning this thing for days.'

'We had two other guys due to take part in the operation. An advance party from the Special Reconnaissance Regiment. They were brought in specifically for this mission. We've had them on the ground in Monte Carlo for the past forty-eight hours, keeping an eye on Lang. They're out of the picture.'

'What happened?'

'They were arrested late this evening in Monte Carlo. A car accident. That leaves us two short, and we can't do the mission with three guys. It's not enough. We need someone to make up the numbers. That's you.'

Bowman nodded guardedly. It wasn't unheard of for a Regiment man to be recruited for a mission at the eleventh hour. A guy on a team might suffer a freak injury during training, and someone else would be brought in as a last-minute replacement. Accidents happened. But it wasn't ideal. There wouldn't be much time to go through everything: the plan, his job, the SOPs.

'When do we leave?' he asked.

'Straight after the briefing. Our contact at Six will explain more.'

Mallet straightened his back and marched over to the door.

'Everyone inside the Shed!' he ordered. 'Team briefing in five.'

From outside, Bowman heard the scraping of metal against concrete, the shuffling of papers, the clicking shut of laptop screens. Mallet circled round the table, took a place close to the speaker-phone and waved a hand at the empty chair next to him.

'Sit down, Josh. You've got questions. That's understandable. Everything will be clear soon.'

Bowman sat and stared at the board, questions cycling through his head. He thought about the meeting in Monaco. He thought about David Lang's involvement with Galkin and Bezuglov and President Seguma. He wondered what the fuck was going on in Monte Carlo.

Then there was no time to think, because the three other members of the Cell filed into the Shed. First came the woman with the strawberry lips, then the black guy with the cropped hair. The short guy entered the room last. As he shut the door a red light glowed above, signalling that the Shed was fully secure. He took a seat next to his colleagues.

'Everyone, this is Josh Bowman,' Mallet said. 'He'll be joining us for this operation. He's coming on board as a replacement for those two other idiots. One or two of you might have worked with him before. For those of you who haven't, Josh is a Regiment lad. From B Squadron. My old crew.'

Mallet gestured towards the short guy. Keith 'Tiny' Loader was the smallest man in 22 SAS, but also one of the toughest. A widow's peak sat atop his craggy face; his hands were criss-crossed with scars. But the smile was warm, and there was a kindness to his large round eyes.

'I'm sure you know Tiny from your time at Hereford,' said Mallet.

Bowman nodded. 'We did Selection together. He beat me on the Long Drag.'

Loader grinned, revealing a graveyard of stained brown teeth. 'You were a cocky bugger back then, boyo.' He spoke in a sing-song Welsh accent, redolent of the valleys.

'Typical bloody Para. Always wanting to kick the front door in and kill everyone in sight.'

'Engineers,' Bowman quipped. 'Always think you know best.'

'That's because we do, mate. We sneak through the back door while you idiots are going through the front.'

Bowman laughed.

'How's the madhouse these days?'

'Fine,' Bowman said. 'The lads are all fine.'

'Is Sally Stevens working the bar at the Green Dragon?'

'I wouldn't know.'

'She's a good woman, that one. Gorgeous. If I was still down there, I would have been giving her the old Loader vaccine by now.' He winked. 'A seven-inch injection, if you know what I mean.'

'If you did,' said Mallet, 'it would be the first time you'd pulled anything in a pub other than a pint, Tiny.'

Bowman and Mallet shared an easy laugh. Although the other guys in the Regiment often teased Loader, everyone respected his abilities as a soldier. He had a smart, thoughtful attitude, like many of the recruits from the Corps of Engineers. He was also loyal to a fault. In public he fancied himself as a ladies' man, but everyone knew that he secretly adored his childhood sweetheart Mary and their eight kids. One of the bullying sergeants had nicknamed him Tiny after he'd passed Selection, but Loader wore the name like a badge of honour. The piss-taking had only motivated him to work harder, to prove himself the equal of every other guy in the Regiment. Bowman was genuinely glad to see him on the team.

Mallet said, 'Tiny's the team medic. He also deals with anything related to entry, breaking security systems. As you know, he used to run the lock-picking wing at Hereford. If there's a safe that needs cracking, he's your man. Or if you need a terrible chat-up line.'

He pointed to the man to the right of Loader. The figure with the cropped hair. Under the glare of the overhead lights in the Shed, Bowman saw that his chin was a knot of pinkish scar tissue. He was lean and tough, with muscles like cement and a fierce look in his eyes. There was a quiet intensity to the guy, Bowman noted. As if he might explode into violence at the slightest provocation.

'This is Sergeant Patrick Webb,' Mallet said. 'He's from the Special Reconnaissance Regiment.'

'All right, mate,' Bowman said. 'How's it going?'

Webb nodded a curt greeting.

Mallet said, 'Patrick is our lead surveillance operator and team linguist. Fluent in seven languages. He did three years with SRR before he was picked up by Thames House. Now he works for us.'

Bowman nodded. The Special Reconnaissance Regiment was the modern successor to The Det, the shadowy surveillance unit that worked alongside the Regiment in Northern Ireland. SRR candidates were trained in many of the same skillsets as their predecessors in the Det. They were the ultimate grey men and women, able to operate in areas others couldn't, recceing targets and observing enemy positions. Their skills were highly prized by the security services, who often recruited SRR operators to carry out surveillance work.

'Josh did two years in SRR himself,' Mallet said to Webb.

'When did you join SRR, mate?' Bowman said. 'I don't remember seeing you around the ops room when I was there.'

'Four years ago,' Webb replied in a heavy Birmingham accent. 'We don't know each other.'

'You're a Brummie, eh? Villa fan?'

'City.'

He said nothing more and stared blankly at Bowman, his lips pressed into a hard line. A long moment passed between them. Bowman figured he was the kind of guy who preferred silence to small talk.

Mallet turned to the third member of the team. The dark-haired woman with the strawberry lips.

'Captain Alex Casey,' he said. 'She's also from SRR.'

Casey smiled at him. She had a small mousy face, with a button nose and a slender neck, but the big green eyes were constantly alert, observing everything, missing nothing. Her side-parted hair was the colour of coffee grounds.

'Alex is our electronics specialist,' Mallet said. 'She's in charge of our surveillance equipment, comms, nano-drones. Anything technical, Alex can take care of it.'

'You can take care of my handset any day of the week, love,' Loader said.

Casey stared at him with flat eyes. 'That's not funny, Tiny. It doesn't even make sense.'

She spoke in a clipped Home Counties accent. She sounded more like a Pimlico book editor than a member of Britain's covert reconnaissance unit.

'Alex was in 18 Signals before she joined SRR,' Mallet added. 'Which means she's good at all the cyber stuff too. If you've ever looked at porn, she'll know about it.'

Bowman nodded thoughtfully. The men and women of 18 Signals handled secure comms for UKSF. It was the largest regiment in the British Army, with a dedicated selection course lasting for six months. The signallers were a talented bunch, highly educated, tech-savvy.

Mallet said, 'I'm sure you lot would love to sit around bumping your gums, but we're on the clock. We've got a team briefing with Six in two minutes.'

'Who are they sending down from Vauxhall?' asked Bowman.

'No one,' said Loader. 'It's all done remotely, boyo. She just speaks to us through that.'

He tipped his head at the speakerphone in the centre of the desk.

'Don't you see her face?' said Bowman.

Casey shook her head quickly. 'We don't even know her name. Assuming it's a woman, that is. It could just as easily be a man's voice disguised through a modulator.'

'What do you call her?'

'The Voice,' said Loader. 'What else?'

Bowman pursed his lips. He'd worked with the security services on numerous ops in the past, during his time with E Squadron, and later with the Wing. He'd met with MI6 officers for mission briefings in safe houses, sometimes in hotel suites, sometimes elsewhere. But whatever the situation, he had always known the identity of the officer in charge. He wondered: *Why would Six go to such extreme lengths to hide their identities?*

I don't know. But we're about to go on a mission, and we don't have a clue who we're really working for.

Mallet checked his watch again. 'Mic is going live in one minute,' he said.

The team members waited in tense silence. Casey drummed her fingers on the polished walnut surface. Loader folded his arms and unfolded them again, fidgeting nervously. Webb sat immobile, looking at the wall, as if he was locked in a staring competition with it and the prize was a million quid.

'Thirty seconds,' said Mallet.

Casey stopped drumming her fingers. Loader sat up straight. Webb continued his staring contest with the soundproofed wall. Mallet watched the sweep hand tick round on his watch. Seconds ticking by. Twenty-five seconds later, he reached over and pressed a button on the speakerphone. A sibilant noise bled out of the speaker, filling the room.

Then the Voice spoke.

'John? Are you there?'

'I'm here,' Mallet responded.

'And your colleagues?'

'Everyone is present,' Mallet said. 'Josh Bowman is here as well. He's been brought in, as we discussed earlier.'

'Has he been briefed?'

'He knows the basics. We'll update him fully later.'

'Good.'

The Voice had an echoing, synthetic ring to it. The sort of automated tone you heard at airport terminals and train stations, making important announcements. A speech synthesiser, perhaps, as Casey had suggested. Or a piece of software that did the same thing. Probably encrypted at both ends.

Another layer of deniability.

'I'll get straight down to brass tacks,' the Voice continued. 'There's been a critical development in the situation with the Lang brothers. Earlier this evening, there was an attack at the royal wedding reception in Mayfair. I'm sure you've seen the reports on the news.'

'What's that got to do with our mission?' asked Casey.

'The victim was Freddie Lang.'

Loader stiffened. Webb and Casey looked at one another.

'Freddie's dead?' Casey asked.

'Not yet,' the Voice replied. 'He's currently in the ICU at University College Hospital. But I'm told the outlook is grim. Frankly, it'll be a miracle if he survives the night. He ingested a significant dose of poison. Enough to kill several people.'

'Do we know who's responsible?'

'Could be anyone,' said Loader. 'Let's face it, Freddie's got more enemies than I've had women.'

'More than one, Tiny?' Bowman joked.

Mallet chuckled. Casey rolled her eyes in disdain.

The Voice said, 'Actually, we know, with reasonable certainty, who carried out the attack.'

'Who?' asked Loader.

'It's early days. The guys at Porton Down are still running tests. We won't have official confirmation for some time yet. But we have reason to believe that Lang was poisoned with a nerve agent. Something from the Novichok family. We're working on the assumption that the Russians are responsible.'

'But the Russians have used Novichok before,' said Casey.

'Correct. Your point being . . . ?'

'Why would they risk carrying out another attack with the same type of poison? Everyone would know they were behind it.'

'This is the Russians we're talking about,' Bowman cut in. 'They don't give two shits about plausible deniability. They just wanted to make a statement.'

'Josh is right. Poisoning is the Kremlin's MO,' Mallet added quickly. 'They know they can get away with it, and the worst that happens is we expel a few diplomats. Frankly, I'm surprised they haven't carried out another attack sooner.'

111

The Voice said, 'We're not here to discuss the details of a criminal investigation. That is not the purpose of this meeting.'

Even through the artificial modulator, Bowman detected a certain hostility in the MI6 officer's voice. *The snooty Vauxhall attitude rearing its ugly head*, he reflected. Bowman had encountered it before. Oxbridge-educated spooks, looking down their noses at the military, regarding them as little more than a bunch of musclebound idiots.

'There's more,' the Voice added. 'John. Perhaps you'd care to explain.'

All eyes in the room turned to the Cell team leader. Mallet laced his hands in front of him and cleared his throat.

'Shortly before he slipped into a coma, our old pal Freddie spilled his guts about the meeting between David Lang, Galkin and Bezuglov in Monte Carlo. Which, of course, we already know about. But Freddie provided us with some new information.'

'What information, exactly?' Casey asked.

'Lang isn't going to the meeting alone. He's got Ken Seguma with him.'

'Seguma?' Loader repeated. 'Wasn't he at the wedding today?'

'That's not the real president. He sent a body double in his place.'

'What's he doing in Monte Carlo?'

'I think we can be reasonably certain that it involves the meeting Lang has arranged with the Russians.'

Casey said, 'How do we know all this?'

'Josh spoke to Freddie, moments before he slipped into a coma,' Mallet replied. 'Freddie told him everything.'

Loader looked at Bowman with renewed interest. 'You were at the wedding?'

'We had orders to bodyguard Seguma. Me and three other guys from the Wing,' Bowman replied. 'Putting our lives on the line for a nobody, as it turns out.'

Loader edged backwards in horror. 'Bloody hell, are you infected?'

'Piss off,' Bowman said. 'I should be worried about catching something from you, mate. All the groupies you claim to have had.'

Casey said, 'How can we be sure that Freddie is telling the truth?'

'Thames House has questioned the man purporting to be President Seguma,' the Voice responded in its train-station-announcement tone. 'He's confessed to the scam. It appears the president's personal assistant and bodyguards were in on it as well. But they don't appear to have been involved in the wider plot.'

'Freddie also claimed that his brother is blundering into a trap,' Mallet chipped in. 'Reckons the Russians are planning to ambush the meeting. Stab David Lang in the back.'

Bowman heard the rustling of papers. The Voice said, 'It's imperative that we intercept David Lang at once, before he walks into a trap. You'll set off immediately, as soon as this briefing has finished.'

Mallet said, 'As you all know, Lang is meeting Galkin and Bezuglov in Antibes at noon local time. Eleven o'clock our time. Galkin's mansion is a one-hour drive from Monte Carlo. Which means we'll need to isolate Lang before eleven o'clock, local time. Less than seven hours from now.'

'What's the deal with transport?' asked Bowman.

The Voice said, 'There's a private jet waiting for you at RAF Northolt. It's been booked through a private firm in St Albans. You've been granted priority clearance onto the airfield. Everything has been arranged in advance. Wheels up at five o'clock this morning. A Caravelle will take you there. Should be with you in the next thirty minutes.'

'Do we need a blue-light convoy?'

'That won't be necessary. We've checked the route. Traffic is light. Shouldn't be any problems getting to Northolt.'

Bowman made a rough mental calculation. Northolt was approximately an hour's drive from their location. The Caravelle would pick them up at 03.50. Which meant they would be arriving at the airfield with a few minutes to spare before they took off. There would be no time to go through the mission before they departed. He wondered when he was going to be told the full picture.

'The jet has been booked under the name of PLQ Trading Limited,' the Voice went on. 'As far as the staff and crew are concerned, you're a group of wealthy businesspeople flying out for a jolly in the south of France. It's a two-hour flight to Nice. It'll have to be Nice as there's no airport in Monaco. In case anyone asks questions, we've made reservations at the Orleans Hotel in the city centre.'

'How do we get to Monaco?' said Webb.

'Helicopter transfer. Which has also been booked. You'll arrive in the principality at around eight o'clock, local time.'

Bowman said, 'What happens once we land?'

'You'll head to your prearranged RV to collect vehicles and weapons. John has the details. That should leave you with around two hours to get to the apartment complex and make your move before Lang departs for the meeting in Antibes.'

Bowman sucked the air between his teeth. 'We're gonna be cutting it fine. What if Lang leaves his flat early? He might decide to take the scenic route to the meeting. Check out some sights on the Riviera.'

'Our analysts consider it unlikely. Lang doesn't move around much when he's in town, by all accounts. He's a reclusive fellow. Stays indoors most of the time, entertaining his friends or watching the boxing.'

'Don't forget, he's got Seguma with him as well,' Mallet added. 'Which makes him even less likely to set foot outside unnecessarily. That prick will want to keep a low profile.'

The Voice said, 'As an extra precaution, we've asked the guys at GCHQ to ping his mobile every sixty seconds. If Lang makes an unexpected move, we'll know about it.'

Mallet said, 'You all know the plan to arrest Davey Boy at his apartment. There's no need to run through the details again right now. I've told Josh he'll receive a full update after this briefing. As soon as we've got Lang where we want him, we'll turn the screw.'

'What makes you think Lang will spill his guts?' asked Bowman.

'He won't have a choice,' the Voice said simply. 'Once you present him with the facts of his brother's poisoning, Lang will realise that he's being set up. That ought to get him talking.'

'Lang will suspect it's a trap. Even if he doesn't, he won't tell us the truth. He'll spin some bollocks story.'

'We're well aware of that.' The Scot looked meaningfully at Bowman. 'That's where you come in.'

'Me?'

'You've got the inside knowledge on mobsters. You grew up around the Lang twins. You know their world. Their mindset. You can help us to anticipate how Lang might react, identify any weak points. Chinks in his armour.'

'I don't know the bloke from Adam.'

'But you know how gangsters think. How their minds work.' Mallet spread his hands across the table. 'Then there's all that undercover work you did with the Met. You must have learned a thing or two about what makes criminals tick.'

'That was donkey's years ago.'

Mallet swatted away the words with his hand. 'You never forget that kind of stuff. And another thing. You're the one who heard Freddie's confession. You can tell David how his brother suffered, how the life slipped out of him right in front of you. It'll feel authentic.'

Bowman shook his head determinedly. 'Lang won't talk to you. Or me. Or anyone. It would make him a snitch.'

'Then we'll torture him,' Mallet suggested. 'Slap him around a bit. Waterboard him.'

Loader looked horrified. 'You can't do that, John.'

'Why not?'

'Torture won't work.' Webb hadn't said a word during the briefing, but now he addressed the others in his thick Brummie accent. 'I've seen blokes tortured before. Only works on a certain type. It ain't the likes of Lang. He's a tough bastard.'

'He's right,' Bowman said. 'You can't make Lang talk, not through pain.'

'What do you suggest, then?'

Bowman considered. 'There is one thing that might work.'

'Go on.'

'Lang is rumoured to run a paedophile ring. Him and his brother supply underage boys and girls to a bunch of rich bastards. Politicians, lords and businessmen. They smuggle kids in from group homes and host secret parties at David's mansion in Essex. The guests are secretly filmed, to entrap them.'

'Unsubstantiated rumours,' the Voice said. 'Street gossip.'

'There's more to it than that. I've heard that Lang has a taste for young girls as well.'

Mallet tilted his head at Bowman. 'How do you know that?'

'I heard it while I was doing an undercover job. Up in Liverpool. No one talks about it publicly, because they're all shit-scared of the Langs, but it's well known in the underworld. It's his dirty secret.'

'Even if that's true,' the Voice said, 'we can't threaten to prosecute Lang. It would never stand up in court.'

'You don't need to charge him,' Bowman countered. 'Just smear his reputation. You lot are experts in destroying lives. You must have a few tricks up your sleeves.'

Casey steepled her delicate fingers on the table. 'That could work. Lang likes to think of himself as a legitimate businessman, after all. He'll want to protect that.'

'I'll speak to our team,' the Voice said. 'See what they can do.'

'What's the plan once we've questioned Lang?' asked Bowman.

'That depends on his level of cooperation.'

'What about the attack on Freddie?'

'What about it?'

'It's all over the news. Lang is bound to find out that his brother has been poisoned. If he hasn't found out already. What if he works out what's afoot and calls off the meeting?'

'We've anticipated that. Scotland Yard has been briefed. They've been instructed to withhold details of the investigation for a few days. News outlets have been told that the victim's identity won't be made public until his family has been notified. That should buy you enough time to complete your mission.'

Mallet leaned forward and looked round the room. 'Any questions?'

Loader said, 'What do you want us to do with Seguma?'

'He's a great friend of the British government,' the Voice responded. 'Make sure he doesn't come to harm. That's priority number one.'

'Do you want us to bring him back with us?'

'We can hardly leave him high and dry in Monaco, can we?' The Voice was undeniably sarky despite its flat neutral tone.

Webb said, 'Seguma won't be pleased to see us, if he's planning to strike a deal with the Kremlin behind our backs. He might cause us problems.'

'Leave the president to us,' said the Voice. 'Just focus on getting Lang to tell us what he knows.'

'There's one thing I don't get,' Bowman said after a pause. 'Why would the Russians kill the Lang twins, if they're supposedly brokering some big deal with them?'

Mallet stared silently at the speakerphone, as if deferring to a higher authority.

'We don't know,' the Voice said. 'Perhaps there's a financial incentive. The Russians might have decided it's in their interest to cut the middlemen out of the deal. Increase their profit margin.'

Casey said, 'But the Russians must have known that if word leaked about Freddie's death, his brother would call off the meeting. Why would they take the risk?'

'We don't have time for this sort of idle speculation,' the Voice replied tonelessly. 'Now, unless you have any more questions, I suggest you prepare to leave for Northolt. The next time we speak, I expect to hear David Lang on the other end.'

'We'll get the bastard,' Mallet said. 'Don't worry about that.'

'Make sure that you do,' the Voice warned. 'Whatever David Lang is planning with the Russians, we need to put a stop it. I don't care what you do, or how you do it,' she added. 'Just get to Lang and make him talk. Before it's too late.'

Eleven

The line cut out. Mallet reached across the table and tapped a backlit button on the speakerphone, shutting the unit down. He checked his watch, then glanced round the room with his hard Glaswegian stare.

'The Caravelle will be here in twenty minutes,' he said. 'Remember, this is a fastball operation. We'll load up the wagon and then head straight to the airfield. The plane will be waiting for us on the pan, fuelled and ready to go. Any questions?'

Loader did a double-take. 'You're coming with us?'

'Change of plan,' Mallet replied.

'It's a bit late for that, isn't it?'

'We need boots on the ground. The original plan was for a five-man team. You've lost two guys. Josh will fill one slot. I'll fill the other. If the other lads were here, I'd send them along. But they're both tied up on a posting, so you've got me instead. Besides, I'm already up to speed. Unless you've got a problem with that?'

Loader held up his hands. 'You won't get any arguments from me, John. The more the merrier, as far as I'm concerned.'

'Good.' Mallet turned to the others. 'The seventh dwarf approves, so we can all breathe a sigh of relief. How about the rest of you? Anyone have anything to add?'

Casey and Webb both shook their heads. Mallet looked round at Bowman and said, 'There's no time to go through the plan right now. We'll update you fully en route to France. As soon as we're in the air. Rat runs, equipment, procedures on capture.'

'Capture?'

Mallet laughed. 'When I say "capture", I mean arrest. We might be driving to the target and get involved in a pile-up. Or a kid might run out in front of us and get hit.'

Bowman was starting to see the picture more clearly now. They were going in on a deniable operation to arrest a suspect during the day, in the middle of a packed urban environment. Which meant the team would need to make contingency plans for any number of situations and emergencies. Murphy's Law. *Anything that can go wrong, will go wrong.* Bowman would have to commit every procedure to memory before they touched down in the south of France.

'Will we have enough time?' he asked. 'On the plane?'

'It's a two-hour flight to Nice. Should give us plenty of time to go through everything. Unless you're planning to spend the flight like Tiny, using crap chat-up lines on the stewardess.'

He boosted up from his chair, signalled the end of the meeting.

'Hurry up and get your kit sorted,' he barked. 'We're out of the door in eighteen.' Everyone stood to leave.

'A word, Josh,' Mallet added.

Bowman stayed put while the others trooped out of the room. Mallet rooted around in his pockets and chucked another stick of nicotine gum into his mouth. 'You've got your ghost ID on you?'

'In my pocket,' Bowman said, recalling the two UKNs banging on his hotel door in the dead hours, ordering him to bring his Wing-issued passport with him to the meeting at Tower Bridge.

'Why?' he asked. 'What's the deal?'

'We'll give you a new cover story in the next few days,' Mallet said. 'In the meantime, you'll have to go with the cover you used in the Wing. It's not ideal, but it'll have to do.'

'What about my phone?'

'You'll be using your existing encrypted handset for the mission. You can stick the battery on charge during the flight.' He paused. 'We'll need to sort you out with a uniform as well.'

Bowman frowned. 'What's my role in all of this, John?'

'You're going in as part of a two-man team disguised as couriers,' Mallet said. 'That's how we'll gain entry to Lang's apartment. You're one of the couriers.'

'Who's the other?'

'Patrick. You'll pretend to have legal documents that need to be countersigned by Lang. It's the only way we can sneak in and out of the block without anyone spotting us.'

'I'm playing catch-up, John. I need to know what the plan is.'

Mallet glared at him. 'There's no time to discuss this right now. It'll have to wait until we're en route to France.'

Bowman hesitated. 'Are you sure this is a good idea?'

'Dressing up as couriers?'

'Bringing me on the op.' He pointed to the pinboard. 'I'm coming on to this thing late in the day. I still don't know the ins and outs of the op, any of the SOPs, none of it.'

'What's the problem? I thought you wanted to fight mobsters.'

'I do. But I didn't expect to be going in half-cocked.'

'You won't be. We'll go over every inch of the plan on the jet. By the time we land, you'll be fully in the loop.'

'That's all I needed to know.'

Mallet straightened up.

'You can leave your Wing-issued weapon here,' he said. 'Along with any spare clips, radio, your SIS ID. Someone will be along later to collect it all. Did you leave anything in your room?'

Bowman thought of the crushed pill he'd flushed down the toilet. 'No, boss—I mean, John.'

'Someone from Six will give it the once-over anyway. Leave the card with the rest of your Wing kit.' He hesitated. 'One more thing. This business with the nerve agent. Since you're not foaming at the mouth, I reckon you're in the clear. But Six wants a bit more reassurance. Risk of transmission and so on. You'll have to get tested once we're back home.'

'Fine,' Bowman said. Then he remembered something else. 'Any news on that CCTV footage from the ballroom?'

'Five has looked into it,' Mallet said flatly. 'It's a dead end. The cameras weren't working.'

121

'All of them?'

'That's what they said.'

'Can't they trace the suspects through their mobile phone signals?'

'The Russians only carry burners with them on these ops. They're professionals. They're probably on their way to Moscow by now.' He glanced at his Breitling. 'We've wasted enough time. Go and find Casey. She'll get a uniform for you.'

They left the Shed. Mallet marched over to his makeshift office near to the computer terminals. There was a flurry of activity around the basement as the rest of the team hastily snatched up maps, documents, laptops. All the items they would be taking with them on the op. Bowman found Casey at the vanity table, packing a blonde wig into her rucksack.

'I need a uniform,' he said.

Casey tilted her head to one side as she cast an eye over the hard figure standing in front of him. She took in his impressive shoulders and honed biceps, his eyes as grey as stones.

'What size are you?' she asked. Bowman started to reply but Casey quickly shook her head and said, 'Forget that. Stupid question. You're definitely a large.'

She hurried over to the wardrobe, fetched one of the courier outfits. The logo of a well-known international delivery firm was stitched onto the breast pocket of the shirt and the front of the baseball cap. She held the uniform up alongside Bowman, judging cut and length and shape. Nodded.

'There. That ought to fit. Pack that in your bag.'

Bowman draped the uniform over his forearm. Casey bit her lower lip, deep in thought. 'Are you sterile?' she asked.

'I bloody hope not.' Bowman grinned. 'Not at my age.'

Casey gave him a disapproving look. 'Let's pretend to be adults and dispense with the sexual innuendo for a minute. I mean, do you have anything identifiable on you? Jewellery, engraved rings, bracelets, anything like that?'

'I've come straight from a job with the Wing. I'm clean.'

She smiled sympathetically. 'Sounds like you've had a rough day.'

'I've had better.' He pointed his head at Webb. He was standing over his bunk bed, methodically checking the kit in his holdall, packing a load of paperback books. 'What's his deal? He doesn't say much.'

'That's just Patrick for you.'

'Has he got a problem with me?'

'Don't take it personally. I've spent three years in the same unit and I hardly know a thing about him.'

'Is he good?'

'The best I've worked with,' said Casey. 'He once spent three weeks outside an apartment in Jordan, dressed as a beggar, observing a target, and no one rumbled him.'

Bowman grunted. 'As long as there's no problem between us.'

'There isn't. Believe me. He's the same with everyone. But he knows his stuff.' She paused. 'They say he used to roll with a gang, you know. In Birmingham. Before he joined the army.'

'Jesus. How did he get out?'

'I'm not familiar with the details. Another SRR guy told me. Something about Patrick's dad getting killed, he said. That's all I know. Patrick won't talk about it.' She shrugged. 'I guess we've all got our secrets, haven't we?'

Bowman ignored the question.

'How long have you been with the Cell?' he asked.

'Six months. Why?'

'Does Six always brief us over the mic?'

'As far as I can remember.'

'You don't think that's strange?'

'I think lots of things are strange. Right-wing conspiracy theories. People who have never shopped online. Male banter.'

'You know what I mean, Alex.'

Casey gave a slight shrug. 'Who knows what they think over at Vauxhall? They're an entirely different species from the rest of us.

123

Perhaps they don't fancy slumming it in a basement in Aldgate. Not their scene, I imagine.'

'Maybe,' Bowman said, uncertainly.

'You think there's another reason?'

'I don't know,' Bowman muttered.

Something doesn't feel right, he thought. *The suits at Vauxhall were going to a lot of trouble to insulate themselves from this unit. Cleary, they didn't want anything to connect them to the Cell or its operations. But why?* Bowman wondered.

Casey took a band of euros from the vanity table and handed it to Bowman. 'Here. You'll need this as well.'

'What for?'

'In case we get separated. Keep receipts, won't you. Six hates it when we don't keep receipts.'

Bowman hastened over to the bunk beds. He unzipped his holdall and stuffed his uniform, cap and the bundle of notes inside. Bowman had packed his go-bag before leaving Hereford two days ago. The bag contained all the essential items: his washbag, a spare T-shirt, jeans, underwear and socks, a pair of trainers, a basic medical pack, a pen and notebook, a small HD camera. Everything an operator needed to function for forty-eight hours.

He zipped up the bag and joined Loader and Webb at the breakout area. Casey hurried over to them a short time later. Mallet hovered next to the landline, waiting for the call from Six to let them know the Caravelle had arrived.

The others watched the news. The rolling coverage of the poisoning in Mayfair. A red-headed reporter summarised what they knew so far. Which wasn't much. Three people had been hospitalised, she said. One of them was in a critical condition. The others were seriously ill but stable. The police were in the process of notifying the families of the victims. The police were appealing to any witnesses to come forward. A Cobra meeting had been called.

Buckingham Palace had issued a tersely worded statement condemning the attack.

There was nothing in the report about Lang, or Moscow, or nerve agents.

Loader shook his head. 'You've got to hand it to the Russians. They've got some brass balls on them, staging an attack at a royal wedding. Bloody cheek of it.'

Casey said, 'I didn't know you were a fan of the royal family, Keith.'

'I'm not. I couldn't give two hoots about them. But my Mary, bless her, she loves them. She'll be upset, watching this with the kids.'

'What do you think they're discussing at this meeting?' Webb said.

'It's obvious, ain't it, Brummie?' Loader replied. 'They're gonna apply the pressure to the president. Get him to change teams. Make him see the light and pledge his allegiance to Moscow.'

Bowman scratched his grizzled jaw. 'Whatever they're planning, Lang doesn't want anyone to know about it.'

'Why do you think that?'

'They sent a body double to London. That was a risky move. Could have easily backfired. If the royals had found out the truth, it would have created a big stink. Why bother doing that unless they wanted to keep this meeting secret?'

'But if this is about changing sides,' said Casey, 'why would Seguma turn his back on London? We've kept him in power for twenty-four years. He owes us everything.'

'Money,' said Loader. 'It's always about the readies, love.'

Casey shook her head slowly. 'There must be more to it than that. Seguma wouldn't risk everything for the sake of a few million.'

'I would, if I was in his boots.'

'You have eight mouths to feed on Special Forces pay.'

'Meaning?'

'Seguma is already very rich. He's pilfered millions from the oil profits. He doesn't need the cash.'

'Perhaps Lang has changed his mind,' Bowman offered. 'Maybe he stands to gain from the arrangement somehow.'

'Greedy, is he?' asked Loader.

Bowman laughed cynically. 'That bastard would crawl over his crippled sister and shag his own mother for the sake of a few quid.'

Four minutes later, a phone rang across the floor space. Mallet grabbed the receiver, listened for several beats, then hung up again without replying. He snatched up his luggage and marched over to the breakout area.

'Everyone ready?'

They nodded.

'Let's go, then. The wagon's waiting.'

* * *

They left through the service yard, at the rear of the building. The same entrance once used to securely transfer prisoners to and from the adjacent cell block, back when the building had been a public-facing station. It was still fully dark as they swept outside. Four o'clock in the morning in late March. Technically spring, but the experience on the ground was somewhat different. The night was cold and dank. The air was so crisp you could almost snap it. Bowman followed the rest of the team across a litter-strewn yard towards a sliding metal gate flanked by a high fence topped with anti-climb spikes. There was a pedestrian door built into the panel to the left of the gate. An external keypad was fixed to the brickwork. A security light affixed to the metal lintel flickered intermittently.

Mallet halted in front of the door. He kicked aside the mountain of takeaway cartons, energy drink cans and cigarette packets at the foot of the door and pressed the release button on the keypad. The entrance unlocked with a whirring buzz. Mallet yanked it open and led the team down a sloping ramp towards a narrow side street. They walked past a line of cars and approached a jet-black Volkswagen Caravelle, headlamps burning in the semi-darkness of the street.

Mallet knocked twice on the passenger window. The side door sucked open, and then Loader got in. He took one of the middle seats and dumped his bag at his feet. Casey jumped in after him, then Webb squeezed into one of the bench seats in the rear of the van.

As Bowman shaped to follow him, Mallet reached out and grabbed his arm.

'Are you fully focused, lad?' he asked.

'Yeah. Sure. Why?'

'I need you razor sharp on this one,' Mallet said quietly. 'I can't have any of my guys getting sloppy on the job.' Before Bowman could protest, he added, 'I know you've had a long day and no kip. That's why I'm asking, you understand.'

His expression was kindly, but there was a knowing look in his eyes. Bowman started to suspect that Mallet knew more about him than he was letting on.

'It's all good,' he replied flatly. 'I'm ready.'

'OK then.'

He released his grip on Bowman's bicep. Bowman ducked into the van and took the bench seat beside Webb, the holdall resting between his feet. Mallet boarded last, dropping into the empty seat next to Bowman.

The side door whirred shut, and the driver glanced round to check on his five passengers. Bowman was surprised to see a familiar face looking back at him. Buzzcut. One of the three UKNs who had collected him from his dingy hotel room earlier that night. A little over two hours ago, but it felt more like two days.

'We're ready,' Mallet said. 'Let's move.'

Twelve

The guys kept to themselves as the Caravelle cruised west out of the city. They spent the time rechecking bits of kit or gazing out of the window. Casey swiped and tapped at her phone screen, getting live updates from Six on Lang's current position. Mallet chewed his nicotine gum. Loader showed Webb pictures of one of his kids in a Swansea City kit. Webb pretended to look interested. As they skated west, Bowman tried to ignore the cravings. They had been getting worse since they'd left the police station, nibbling away at him. It wouldn't be long before the shakes started again. A few hours at most. Maybe sooner.

I'll need a few pills to get through the op, he told himself. He remembered what Mallet had told him when he'd offered him the job with the Cell.

This is a temporary posting. There are no guarantees that you'll be kept on once the mission is over.

If I'm struggling with opioid withdrawal, Bowman thought, *there's no way I'll be able to perform today. My career in the Cell will be over before it's begun.*

The first hint of dawn tinged the horizon as they neared the airfield. A guard in a high-vis jacket stepped out of the guardroom as Buzzcut drove up to the front gate. Buzzcut lowered his window and flashed his security pass. The guard studied it closely, cross-checking the details against the flight manifest on his clipboard. He handed the pass back to the driver and gave him a set of directions, thrusting his arm towards a row of buildings on the south side of the airfield.

The Caravelle coasted past the guardroom and down the access road for a quarter of a mile, passing maintenance buildings and a fuel dump and a half-empty car park. They raced past the terminal, turned left and hit another checkpoint. There was a short pause, then the boom barrier lifted and the Caravelle drove on, and suddenly they hit the pan: a lake of smooth asphalt two hundred metres due south of the runway. Further to the north, on the other side of the aerodrome, Bowman could just about see the lights coming from the RAF base.

They sheared off to the left and approached a Gulfstream business jet resting on the pan. The airstairs were in the lowered position. A long-legged woman in a bright pink flight attendant's uniform and black pumps stood at the bottom of the steps, a pink scarf wrapped like a collar around her neck.

'Remember the story,' said Mallet. 'Six rented this jet through a private company. The one we're supposed to be working for. As far as this lot is concerned, we're five high-powered execs going on a luxury trip to the French Riviera to enjoy some fine dining.'

Bowman nodded his understanding. He'd flown on deniable ops before with the Wing. The security services didn't own private planes. They were too expensive to operate and spent too much time idle on the ground to justify the taxpayer expense. Far cheaper, and more convenient, to lease them privately through one of the dozens of front businesses MI6 operated. The companies themselves were untraceable, their ownership structures hidden behind a web of offshore shell companies.

The Caravelle pulled up alongside the Gulfstream, the side door flew open and the team snatched their bags and scrambled out. The attendant stepped forward from the stairs and flashed a pearly white smile at the team as she greeted them. She had the enthusiasm of a make-up counter assistant and the perfumed scent to match.

'My name is Calypso,' she said. 'I'll be looking after you today.'

Loader winked at her. 'You can look after me any time you want, sweetheart.'

She smiled politely. 'Do you have any special requests for your flight?'

'Not today,' Mallet said brusquely.

'This way, sir.'

They ascended the steps, passed the galley and entered a main cabin divided into three salons. There was a lot of soft leather on display, a lot of polished wood and luxury furnishings. Enough seating to accommodate a dozen passengers. A flat-screen TV mounted on a credenza in the middle section of the cabin. A conference table, a minibar stocked with bottled water and soft drinks. There was a separate office at the front of the cabin equipped with a printer, fax machine, shredder and ultra-fast Wi-Fi, the attendant said. Everything a business executive needed.

If this op does go pear-shaped, thought Bowman, *at least Six is sending us off in style.*

They stowed their bags and buckled up. Nine minutes later, the Gulfstream was climbing through the low clouds. As soon as the jet levelled out, the team relocated to the conference area in the middle salon. Bowman, Mallet, Casey and Loader dropped into the four seats either side of the table. Then Webb hauled over one of the holdalls stowed in the aft luggage compartment. He retrieved a lap-top and a thick manilla folder from inside, set them down on the table and dumped the holdall on the floor and perched himself on it, using it as a makeshift beanbag. The attendant sauntered over from the galley, wearing her pearly smile.

'Can I get you anything?' she asked. 'Breakfast? Coffee? Champagne?'

'No thanks,' Mallet replied in an amiable but firm tone. 'We'll be fine, lass. Me and the guys here are having a business meeting. We don't want to be disturbed.'

'Well, if you need anything, just let me know.'

'We will, sweetheart,' Loader said with a wide grin. 'We will.'

His eyes followed the attendant as she wandered back down the aisle to the galley, hips swaying gently. Mallet said, 'Forget it.'

'I didn't say anything.'

'You didn't have to. It's all over your face. You wouldn't stand a chance. She's not interested in your Welsh arse.'

Loader looked hurt. 'You don't know that.'

'Aye, I do. Do you want to know why?'

Loader shook his head.

'Because she's got taste.'

'Sometimes you can be a real bastard, John.'

'Life is harsh. Get used to it.' He nodded at Casey. 'Get the map out. We've got a lot to run through.'

Casey reached into the folder and unfolded a detailed street map of Monte Carlo. Mallet tapped a gnarled finger at an apartment block circled with black marker pen. Bowman leaned in for a closer look. The building was situated on Avenue Princesse Grace. One of the most expensive streets in Monaco. The most expensive address in the world, twenty years ago. Before the moneyed elites took up residence in Kensington and Fifth Avenue and St Moritz. Now it was probably lucky to make the top twenty. There was a promenade to the east of the apartment, straddling a narrow crescent of artificial beach. To the north, a short distance away, stood a rocky promontory with a sprawling casino and hotel resort extending across it. Casino Square was maybe half a mile to the south.

'This is Lang's residence,' Mallet began. 'The Du Veil apartment block. Lang owns a three-bedroom apartment on the eighteenth floor. There's a twenty-four-hour concierge, security cameras covering all the entry and exit points, remote alarms, the works.'

He pointed to a spot on the map a hundred metres due south of the building on Avenue Princesse Grace.

'This is the drop-off point,' he said. 'You'll make your way on foot from here to the building. Patrick will handle the concierge.'

'You speak French?' asked Bowman.

Webb laughed and said, 'My mother's side of the family is from Martinique. It's all I spoke around my grandparents.'

'What's our story?'

Mallet said, 'You'll claim to have urgent legal documents that need to be countersigned by David Lang,' Mallet said. 'Six have drawn up a couple of ID cards, in case you get arrested. That should get you past the front desk.'

'Won't Lang get suspicious?'

'Six doesn't think so.'

'I don't care what they think,' Bowman said. 'It's my neck on the line, not theirs.'

'And mine,' Webb added.

Mallet sighed irritably. 'It won't be a problem. Lang likes to think of himself as a reputable businessman. That's why he's pumped his money into hotels, casinos, mining companies. All that legit money comes with paperwork. This won't strike him as unusual.'

'What's the plan once we're inside?'

'You'll subdue Lang and Seguma and clear the apartment. Patrick will watch over them. Meanwhile, you'll change into Lang's clothes and head down to the underground car park. There's a private lift, so no one will see you entering or leaving. Lang keeps a Range Rover down there. We'll give you the licence plate, so you'll know which one to look for. You'll take his wagon out for a spin,' he added, tracing a finger south along the main road, 'drive down as far as this roundabout, swing round and head north again to pick me and Alex up. That way, no one will see us entering the building.'

'Why me?' asked Bowman.

'You're roughly the same build as Lang. You could almost pass as his third twin. There are cameras in the underground parking facility. When the security staff see you getting behind the wheel, they'll naturally assume it's Lang popping out for a pack of ciggies.

'Once we're inside,' Mallet added, 'we'll take the lift back up to Lang's apartment and question him. I'll be leading the interrogation.'

'What about Tiny?' Bowman asked.

'He'll wait in the car. Keep an eye on the entrance to the block. That's the plan. But knowing Tiny, he'll probably pass the time eyeing up the local talent and wishing he was taller than an elf.'

'Size ain't everything, John.'

'Fuck me, is that the line you use on women? No wonder you can't get laid.'

Casey gave them both an eye-roll and said, 'If someone shows up – one of Lang's associates, or the police – Keith will let you know. That'll give you a few minutes' warning to get out.'

Bowman said, 'What's the exfiltration plan?'

'We'll escort President Seguma down to the car park and drive out in Lang's wagon. A UKN will RV with us on the way to the airport. We'll dump the kit, get on a private jet and fly home. By the time anyone has figured out what's happened, we'll be long gone.'

'And Lang?'

'He'll come with us too,' Mallet said, icily. 'But we're not asking him nicely.'

Bowman stared at the map as he mentally reviewed the plan. 'It's risky,' he said.

'So is getting in a car. Or going on a date with Tiny.'

'This thing could easily go south.'

'The plan isn't up for debate.'

'What if there are BGs in the building, though? Seguma might have some of his bodyguards with him.'

'We think that's unlikely.'

'He's the president. He'll want some sort of protection.'

'Not at this meeting, he won't.'

'The president doesn't trust his BG team,' Casey explained. 'He's getting paranoid in his old age. Believes some of them are spies. He sacked a bunch of guys on his team six months ago.'

Mallet said, 'As you know, Seguma has gone to great lengths to keep this meeting secret. That means keeping his BG team out of the loop as well. The smart money is on him going to this thing alone.'

'They won't want to meet with the Russians alone, John.'

'I agree. It's possible that Lang might have one or two of his heavies with him,' Mallet conceded. 'Minders. Dumb muscle he can trust. But we're talking about one or two guys. He won't have any more than that.'

'And if he does?'

'You'll have to stay fluid. React to any unexpected threats. Staying flexible comes with the territory, especially when you're fighting gangsters.'

'I'm beginning to realise that.'

They talked through the courier plan for a solid thirty minutes. Webb broke out the laptop and brought up the exterior of the apartment complex on Google Street View, pointing out the various entry and exit points, the position of the team in the vehicle. Bowman studied the original architectural drawings for Lang's apartment, making sure he'd committed it to memory. Then they switched their focus to the situation around the building: roadworks, tourist hot spots, likely traffic jams, rush-hour times, parking zones. From time to time, Mallet asked Bowman if he had any questions. There was no negativity, no judgement. The rest of the team had spent the past seven days pulling the op together. They knew the whole thing backwards. As the newcomer, Bowman was having to absorb every aspect of it at lightning speed.

'What about our kit?' he asked.

Mallet leaned back, giving the floor to Loader. 'Tiny will explain. That's his area of expertise. Along with lessons in how to repulse women, of course.'

Loader gave him a look and stabbed a finger at the southern edge of the principality.

'A local UKN will RV with us at the heliport here,' he said. 'He'll drive us to the car park beneath the football stadium. We'll collect our kit, then drive straight to the target location.'

'Are we packing heat?' asked Bowman.

'Pistols. One for you, one for Patrick. But you shouldn't need them.'

Mallet said, 'We need to discuss rules of engagement.'

He leaned forward and looked Bowman hard in the eye.

'Let me be very clear. Your weapons are to be used as a last resort only,' he said. 'If you're danger close, if rounds are coming in, you may engage. But don't go plugging anyone if you can help it. The clean-up would be a nightmare, it's the last thing we need. And do not engage the cops under any circumstances.'

'I know the drill,' Bowman said. 'I've gone through all this stuff before in the Wing.'

'It'll stand a repeat,' Mallet growled. 'We're not in the business of making trouble with the cops. If you're arrested, don't kick up a fuss. Keep your mouth buttoned and sit tight. Don't make up some cock-and-bull story. It'll only encourage the police to get curious, and we don't want that. Six won't like it, either. As soon as you're captured, the balloon will go up and someone from the Embassy in Paris will come down. You'll receive full legal representation. The Whitehall folk will do their usual string-pulling behind the scenes. You'll be back on a flight to London before you know it.'

'Let's hope it doesn't come to that.'

'It's a routine hard arrest,' Loader said. 'We do this kind of stuff all the time in the Cell.'

'There's no such thing as routine, Tiny. Not in the Regiment.'

'It's hardly Rorke's Drift, is it? We'll be back home and on the beers a few hours from now.' He gave Bowman a cheeky nudge and a wink. 'Me and you can hit the town together. Check out the talent.'

'You won't see much,' Mallet said. 'Tiny clears out the bars faster than a bomb threat.'

'That's not true,' Loader protested. 'I ain't the tallest, but I've got a way with the ladies.'

'Aye, I suppose you have. It's called scaring them shitless.'

Bowman shared a laugh with Mallet. Even Webb permitted his lips to form a smile. Casey stared at them with a look of dismay.

'Let's crack on,' Mallet said. 'There's still plenty of ground to cover.'

Casey took over the briefing. She handed Bowman a piece of paper with a list of phone numbers and a map detailing various pick-up locations. The numbers belonged to individuals the team could contact in the event of an emergency. There was a guy with a small boat in the Fontvieille district, she said. A doctor across the border in Nice. A pair of retired spooks living in a town forty miles to the west, in Trigolins.

They discussed escape plans and rat runs. Emergency pick-up procedures. Locations in the area, safe places where they could hide out for a day or two. Worst-case scenario stuff. Bowman tried to memorise every detail, but he struggled to focus. The lack of sleep was catching up with him. His tired body craved another hit of opiates. Something to keep him wired. He was sweating badly under his shirt. He took a pull of bottled water, tried to refocus.

There was time for one last general run-through around the conference table. Everyone talked through their specific roles, making sure that there were no grey areas, no loose ends. Then the pilot announced they would shortly be making their final approach to Côte d'Azur, and Webb and Loader quickly gathered up their belongings and carried the bags back to the aft compartment. Casey cleared the papers from the table and hurried over to the office to feed them into the shredder.

While they were busy, Bowman levered himself up from his seat and quietly slinked off to the toilet.

The cabin shuddered as he moved down the aisle. Bowman almost lost his balance, recovered as the jet began pitching and plunging through the air. On the speaker, the pilot explained they were going through a patch of turbulence. Bowman ignored the request to stay seated and staggered into the toilet, his palms greased with sweat. He felt like shit. The cravings had been getting worse for the past hour, but he'd soon be feeling normal again. He dipped a hand into his jacket pocket, removed the cap on the base of the pill crusher and tipped one of the tablets into his shaking hand.

The cabin jolted.

The plane banked hard to the right, throwing Bowman off-balance. He lurched backwards, crashed against the door, steadied himself against the countertop, then looked up in despair as he saw the pills clattering around the basin. Like balls on a roulette wheel. He stumbled over to the sink, panicking. The plane pitched heavily again as he clawed at the pills, but they disappeared down the plughole before he could scoop them up.

A few moments later, the plane stopped shuddering.

Bowman stared unblinking at the plughole, feeling the cold hand of dread clench around his throat. His stash of pills – gone. All of them.

For a moment he didn't know what to do. He contemplated unscrewing the pipe but figured the pills would have dissolved by now. Then he began to think more clearly. The situation wasn't good. He had no spare tablets in his luggage. No emergency stash of meds. Somehow, he was going to have to wing it for the next few hours without any pills. And pray that the shakes didn't get too bad.

He walked back down the aisle, sat down opposite Casey. She half smiled, a questioning look on her face.

'Everything all right? You look like you've had a fright.'

'Just a lack of sleep. I'll get over it.'

He looked away, panic rising in his chest. He tried telling himself to stay calm. But it was no use.

We're about to go in and arrest a violent mobster, and I'm staring down the barrel of an opioid withdrawal.

And there's nothing I can do about it.

A few minutes later, the Gulfstream began its descent.

Thirteen

They landed at eight o'clock in the morning, on a grey wind-swept day on the French Riviera. The Gulfstream taxied off the runway to the tarmac stand, the engines dialled down to a whine, the airstairs unfolded. Loader gave the attendant a parting smile, and then the team deboarded. It took them only a few minutes to clear through security and transfer to the heliport. Mallet had explained that they were on the fast-track programme. Something called the Elite Service package. Which brought with it certain privileges, such as a streamlined check-in procedure. A short, squat official gave their passports a cursory glance, and then a pair of waiting airport buggies whizzed them round to the heliport.

The chopper was an AgustaWestland AW109. The civilian variant. Helicopter of choice for the executive community. The team ascended the retractable steps and made themselves comfortable in the six-seater cabin while another official loaded their holdalls and rucksacks into the luggage compartment. The twin engines screamed, the rotor blades swathed through the air. The pilot performed a series of final checks, testing bits of equipment, gauging dials and meters.

The Agusta soared into the air above Nice. The pilot rounded the beaches of Cap-Ferrat, roughly following the coastline running north-east towards Monaco. Cruise ships and yachts were strung out like stepping stones on the deep blue water. As they neared the principality, Bowman's hands began to tremble. His palms were clammy with sweat; veins of it slicked down his back, gluing his shirt to his skin. With the tremors came the deep throbbing pain. The involuntary twitching of his muscles, the drip-drip of anxiety into his guts. Bowman balled his hands into tight fists and hoped the others hadn't noticed.

They might realise I'm getting withdrawals, he thought.

Or worse . . . they'll think I'm afraid.

He tried to stay calm. Which wasn't easy. The cravings were getting intense. He clung to the hope that he might find a stash of drugs at Lang's apartment. Lang himself didn't smoke or drink, but he was known to host parties for his friends. Celebrities, financiers, models. The kind of people who dabbled in narcotics. Bowman didn't know for sure, but there was a slim chance he might find something there. Maybe pills. Maybe something else. Right now, he'd take anything.

The Agusta approached Monaco from seaward. Below them, Bowman spied a harbour crammed with small fast boats and flashy yachts. Apartment blocks hugged the edge of the marina. From this height they seemed as small and white as sugar cubes. Further inland he glimpsed the football stadium, partially obscured behind a cluster of offices and hotels.

Seven minutes after they had taken off, the chopper descended towards the marina. They landed at the heliport at the water's edge, the engine whined and then the team piled out and made for the terminal. Casey consulted her phone, verifying Lang's last known location, pinching and swiping. Bowman avoided the border official's gaze as he gave his passport a quick scan. The tremors were much worse now. His left hand began shaking as he strolled out of the terminal building. An hour from now, he would be a shivering wreck.

You need to get something in your body, the voice in his head warned. Any opioid will do. It doesn't matter. Just get to Lang's apartment and find something.

An enormously overweight man in a Hawaiian shirt and shorts waited for them outside. His face was glossed with sweat. A great hammock of flesh sagged beneath his chin. He had no neck; it had been submerged beneath the fleshy folds of his jowls and shoulders. His arms and legs protruded from his torso like sticks out of a snowman. The man wiped perspiration from his brow with a pocket handkerchief, a seemingly futile exercise, and offered a moist hand to Mallet.

'You must be Peter,' he said, using the name of Mallet's ghost ID. UKNs were never told the real names of the people they worked with.

Mallet shook the man's hand with great reluctance.

'I'm Barry Vokes,' the man went on. He spoke with a strong Mancunian accent. 'I was told to expect you guys.'

Bowman had been given a few details about Vokes, the UKN, during the briefing. Vokes was ex-Special Branch, a retired detective who had worked with Five and Six on several occasions in the past, carrying out basic surveillance duties, setting up weapons caches and scouting escape routes. He had sold up his place in leafy Hertfordshire and now lived in the south of France, although Bowman couldn't understand why. The climate clearly didn't agree with him.

Mallet surveyed the car park and said, 'Where's your ride?'

'This way, guys.'

Vokes started towards a Peugeot Traveller parked thirty metres away. His thighs chafed as he waddled along. Vokes periodically daubed his sweat-glazed brow.

'Hot today,' he said as they reached the Traveller. 'I'll crank the air con up, don't worry.'

'It's sixteen degrees, if that,' Loader remarked, squinting at the overcast sky.

'Is it? Feels a lot warmer, if you ask me.' Vokes turned and nodded at Bowman. 'I'm not the only one struggling in this heat, by the looks of it.'

Loader gave his colleague a long searching look. 'What's wrong with you, pal? You've been sweating like an activist in Hong Kong since we landed.'

'Got a cold,' Bowman snapped. 'That's all. It's no big deal, mate.'

They piled inside the Traveller. The door thudded shut, and then Vokes backed out of the parking bay.

'First time in Monaco, is it?' he asked.

'Something like that,' Loader muttered.

'It's all right here, I suppose,' Vokes said, answering a question no one had asked. 'But me, I prefer somewhere a bit quieter. Too much noise here, too many people. The bars are too busy. Takes forever to get served, and the drinks cost a fortune.'

Vokes was a talker.

'Is that right,' Mallet said, feigning interest.

'That's why I moved to the Languedoc, see. Cheaper than here. And you can always get a drink. Tell you what, though. I don't miss England. Not one bit. All that rain.' He shuddered in horror at the memory. 'Not for me.'

'How long to the car park?' Mallet said.

'Four minutes,' Vokes replied.

Mallet met Bowman's eyes in the rear-view mirror. 'Get changed. Both of you. Hurry.'

As soon as they had pulled clear of the heliport, Bowman and Webb ripped open their bags and started changing into their courier uniforms, their movements obscured from view through the tinted windows. Casey retrieved a male wig from her rucksack and handed it to Bowman. He pulled the wig down tight over his head, covering his dark hair with a mop of wavy blond locks. He planted the baseball cap on top, slipped his phone and company ID badge into his trouser pockets and shoved his civvies into his bag, along with his passport and wallet.

'Any word from Six?' Mallet asked.

Casey swiped and scrolled on her phone. 'They just pinged Lang's phone again. Target is still in place.'

'Let's hope he doesn't move in the next twenty minutes,' Loader said.

They skirted around the football stadium, sheered off the road and rolled down the entry ramp to the underground car park built directly under the pitch. Vokes descended the levels until he found the vehicle he was looking for: a silver Mercedes-Benz E-Class estate parked in the far corner. A big roomy vehicle, with space enough to accommodate five adults and a whole stack of luggage.

Vokes nosed the Traveller into the space next to the E-Class. A scruffy-looking guy in a polo shirt and chinos climbed out of the Merc. One of the other UKNs, Bowman presumed. Another member of the ex-pat community in the south of France. He looked a decade older than Vokes. Early sixties. His face had more lines in it than a Shakespeare play. His hair had been styled into a comb-over in a poor attempt to conceal his balding pate.

The Cell team disgorged themselves from the Traveller, grabbed their luggage and met the guy with the comb-over at the back of the E-Class. He chucked a set of keys at Loader and jerked a thumb at the E-Class's boot compartment.

'Hardware's inside,' he said.

'It's all there?'

'Everything you asked for. She's got a full tank.'

'Paperwork?'

'In the glovebox.'

Comb-over swung round to the passenger side of the Traveller and hopped into the cabin alongside Vokes. A few moments later, the Traveller skulked off in the direction of the exit. Mallet popped the boot on the E-Class. Grabbed the black sports bag from the otherwise empty compartment, beat a path round to the front passenger side.

'Get in,' he ordered. 'Let's move.'

The rest of the team dumped their holdalls in the boot and bundled inside the E-Class: Loader behind the wheel, Mallet in the shotgun seat, Casey, Bowman and Webb in the back. Thirty seconds later, daylight flooded the vehicle as they glided out of the car

145

park. As they motored away from the stadium, Mallet passed the sports bag to the guys in the back. Bowman ripped it open with sweat-slicked hands. A pair of Ruger American Compacts lay in the bottom of the bag. Lightweight pistols, easy to carry and conceal, chambered for the 9 mm Luger round. Each one had a two-inch snub silencer attached to the barrel. Bowman handed one of the weapons to Webb and checked the other himself. His hands were shaking as he released the magazine from the underside of the grip. The clip was full. Seventeen rounds of nine-milli brass.

He eased the clip back into the mag well, tucked the Ruger into the pancake holster threaded through his waist belt. The holster sat flush against his skin, close to his side. Beneath his thick outer layer, the pistol wouldn't be visible to anyone. He fished out four pairs of plasticuffs from the bag, handed two pairs to Webb, shoved the others into his trouser pocket.

'Here,' Mallet said. 'You'll need this.'

He gave Bowman a document wallet with Lang's address printed on the front.

'Four minutes out,' said Loader, as they emerged from a tunnel. 'Get ready.'

Bowman gazed out of the window, hiding his dilated pupils from his colleagues as they rounded Port Hercules. They carried on east down Avenue J. F. Kennedy, past rows of super yachts, ugly high-rise blocks and tacky restaurants. Casey checked her phone again. Loader stuck to a moderate speed, staying well under the limit.

We're almost there, Bowman told himself. *Just keep your shit together for a few more minutes. Then you can get into Lang's apartment, find his drugs stash. Sort yourself out.*

And if he doesn't have anything? What then?

I don't know.

They cleared a wide roundabout, passed an underground parking garage and shuttled north along Avenue Princesse Grace. One of the world's most expensive streets, twenty years ago. But it didn't look like it. Not anymore. Bowman saw dated 1970s apartment blocks the colour of orange peel, roof awnings hanging over the tiny balconies, a handful of drab cafés and garish nightclubs. They tooled on for another hundred metres, past a glass and steel conference centre and a monument to Grace Kelly.

Getting close now.

They rolled on for another hundred metres, and then Mallet pointed to a parking area at the side of the road next to the promenade.

'Pull over here,' he said.

Loader nudged the E-Class into a free space, parallel with an ice-cream parlour and opposite a luxury car dealership. The engine died. Then they waited. Casey tapped open an encrypted messaging app on her phone and quickly read the text.

'Got another ping on Lang's phone,' she said. 'He's still in his apartment.'

'This is it,' Loader said. 'We're in business.'

Mallet and Loader checked their side mirrors, watching for pedestrians. They had talked through this part of the plan in detail on the jet. Bowman and Webb wouldn't step out of the vehicle until they had confirmed that the coast was clear. If someone happened to see two guys in courier gear getting out of a civilian car, they might get suspicious. Safer to wait until they had a clear run to the apartment.

Seconds ticked by. Bowman waited impatiently for the signal. He started seeing things. Vivid waking hallucinations. Memories of the night his family had been butchered, seeping into the real world. He saw blood puddled on the pavement. A girl was lying dead on the street, her throat slashed open. Bowman was about to alert his colleagues when he realised she was wearing the same princess outfit as his dead daughter. His Sophie. His wife was there too, a neat bullet hole in the middle of her forehead. Both of them stared at him with accusing eyes.

He blinked. The images vanished.

Christ, I need a pill.

A handful of people passed the E-Class: an elderly man out for a stroll, a young female jogger in leggings, a grey-haired woman in a fur-trimmed coat, walking her toy poodle. None of them gave the estate a second glance. They weren't driving a supercar, they didn't have a VIP escort. Therefore, they were unimportant.

As soon as the dog-walker had moved on, Mallet half turned in his seat and nodded at the guys in the back seats.

'We're clear. Go.'

A mild breeze thrust in from the sea, mussing Bowman's blond wig as he got out and set off north with Webb. Ahead of them, a hundred metres away, the Du Veil apartment building towered over its neighbours. A glassy structure shaped like a tower fan, twenty-three storeys high. To the left of the building was a chic restaurant with a rooftop garden. To the right, an older pastel-coloured block. Monegasque flags fluttered above the entrance.

They hit the zebra crossing and approached the entrance in short, brisk strides. Just another pair of couriers in a powerful hurry. They swept through the sliding glass doors and entered a wide lobby decorated with abstract sculptures, chandeliers and designer furniture. The floor looked as polished as a green army recruit's boots on parade day. A slim, tanned concierge stood behind a dark wooden desk, dressed in a suit so sharp you could hack through bamboo with it. There was a framed picture behind him. Prince Albert II and his wife, beaming for the camera.

The concierge stared at the two men as they drew near, as if deciding how to deal with them. His eyes dropped to their logo-branded jackets and caps, and when he looked up again, he flashed a polite but firm smile at them. As if signifying that he was prepared to tolerate their presence, as basic human courtesy, but no more than that. The tag above his breast pocket gave his name as Raymond.

'*Oui, messieurs*?' he asked sharply. 'Yes, may I help you?'

'We're from HLO Global,' Bowman said. 'Got some legal documents for Mr David Lang to sign.'

'HLO?' The concierge's eyebrows came together. 'But your caps, *monsieur*, they say you are from HLX, *non*?'

Bowman opened his mouth, but no words came out. He couldn't focus. Started to panic. 'Yeah. No, I mean—'

Webb hastily stepped forward and said a few quick words in French to the concierge. He made an exaggerated gesture, waving a hand at Bowman and shrugging as if to say, *What can you do? I've got to work with this idiot for a living.* The concierge smiled. His expression visibly relaxed. Webb gestured to the document and tapped his watch. A clear signal. Emphasising that the job was urgent. His body language said: *We've got to get these papers signed. Can you help us out?* Bowman watched his colleague with surprise. The quiet, shy soldier had completely transformed himself into a chatty, cheerful French delivery driver.

The concierge picked up the phone and dialled a number.

Lang answered on the fourth ring. The concierge addressed him in a grovelling tone of voice, telling him about the couriers, the important papers. There was a pause before Lang barked something inaudible. Then the line clicked dead. Raymond replaced the receiver. Looked up.

'You may go up,' he said in English, for the benefit of Webb's colleague. 'Monsieur Lang, he will see you.'

'We will have to wait upstairs,' Webb pointed out. 'For the other parties to arrive. We must have all the signatures before returning the papers to the office.'

'*Bien*. Not a problem. This way, please, *messieurs*.'

They followed him across the foyer, towards a bank of private lifts reserved for the building's wealthiest residents. The concierge touched a master key card against a magnetic reader below the control panel and selected the eighteenth floor from the touchscreen display. The leftmost lift doors pinged open, and then Bowman and Webb stepped inside the gold-decorated car. The concierge trotted back to his station. The doors slid gently shut.

The soldiers kept their heads low as they rode upwards, shielding their faces from the security cameras.

'What the fuck was that about?' Webb said icily.

'I forgot the name of the company,' Bowman muttered. 'It's no big deal, mate.'

'You almost blew the op.'

'It was a mistake,' Bowman said in a low voice. 'Won't happen again.'

'You'd better hope not.'

'What did you say to that guy?' asked Bowman.

Webb glanced at him, a flinty look in his eyes. 'I told him it was your first day on the job,' he said. 'And probably your last, too.'

The lift announced their arrival on the eighteenth floor with a strident ring. Bowman and Webb stepped out into a private landing. Bowman had studied the floor plan during the flight to Nice and the layout was instantly familiar to him. Two doors on the right led through to the emergency stairwell and a maintenance room. There was a service lift on the left side of the landing, next to a storage compartment.

At the far end was the front door to David Lang's apartment.

Bowman gripped the document wallet tightly as he walked up to the door with Webb. He felt the Ruger grip beneath his thick jacket, pressing against his torso as they halted in front of the door. Webb rapped the brass knocker twice and took half a step back. He slid his right hand down to his side. Ready to draw his weapon. Bowman did the same.

The door snicked open. A figure stood in the doorway, hard-edged and thin-lipped, with a massive gold chain draped like a garland around his neck and eyes so cold they could freeze a lake.

David Lang stared impatiently at the two men in the corridor. He was dressed in a fine shirt the colour of champagne and a pair of slim-fit jeans. The spider-faced watch on his wrist gleamed under the soft glow of the ceiling lights. He had no scars on his face, but in every other way he was identical to his twin brother Freddie.

'What the fuck do you want?' Lang said, looking from Bowman to Webb with narrowed eyes.

Webb reverted to his Brummie accent.

'Papers for you to sign, sir. We were told it's urgent.'

He indicated the plastic wallet Bowman was holding. Lang's eyebrows came together in suspicion. 'First I've heard about it. Who are they from?'

'That's none of our business, sir. We were just asked to make the delivery.'

Lang sighed. 'Well, don't just fucking stand there. What have I got to sign?'

'The documents are just here, sir,' Bowman said.

He fumbled with the tamperproof zip, distracting Lang. As Bowman reached inside for the documents, Webb tore his Ruger free from his holster and brought it up to shoulder height, shoving the barrel close to the mobster's face.

'What the f—'

'Step away from the door,' Webb said coolly. 'Now.'

Lang glowered at the soldiers but didn't argue. Sound logic. He couldn't hold a debate with a nine-milli pistol two inches from his face. He held up his hands and retreated two slow steps from the doorway, his nostrils flared with rage. Bowman deholstered his pistol and crept into the hallway behind Webb, the semi-automatic unsteady in his clammy grip. He closed the door, dumped the wallet on the side table, next to a leather bifold wallet and a Range Rover key fob, and took up a position at Webb's right shoulder.

'You're making a big fucking mistake,' Lang said. 'You don't know who you're dealing with.'

'Shut up,' Webb snapped. 'Make a move and I'll blow your brains out.'

In the same breath Bowman glimpsed a sudden movement to the right of the hallway. He whirled round to his three o'clock, his index finger tense around the safety built into the Ruger's trigger mechanism. A pot-bellied man in a tweed suit stood five metres away in the middle of the living room, his mouth hanging open in dumb surprise. A trilby hat and a gold-crowned rattan cane rested on the coffee table in front of him, along with a half-full bottle of Lagavulin single malt and a couple of tumblers.

The real Ken Seguma.

'Stay where you are,' Bowman said. 'Sit and don't move.'

Seguma stood his ground. His wide eyes darted between the soldiers and Lang. 'Who are you? What the hell is going on, David?'

'Sit down,' Bowman ordered. 'Last chance.'

'Do as he says, Ken,' Lang said.

Seguma lowered himself onto the leather sofa. He looked numb with shock and confusion. Bowman kept his weapon trained on the tyrant while Webb dug out a pair of plasticuffs from his back pocket. He brought Lang's hands behind his back, cinched the plastic ties around his wrists. Then Webb grabbed him by the upper arm and manhandled him into the living room, shoving him towards the sofa.

'Sit the fuck down,' Webb barked.

Lang set himself down beside Seguma. He stared up at Webb with a sadistic look in his eyes, his lips set in a hard line.

'You'll regret this,' he said. 'I'll make sure of it.'

'Shut up,' Webb snapped. He nodded at Bowman. 'Clear the other rooms.'

Bowman backed out of the living room and set off across the hallway. He was sweating freely now, his body ached, as if a million needles were pricking his skin. He charged into the kitchen and visually swept the area for threats. He hooked round an island the size of a sarcophagus, peeked into the laundry room, then backed out again and hurried past the study and the dining room and the staff quarters. He knew from studying the floor plan that the sleeping quarters were located at the far end of the apartment.

If Lang did keep any drugs in his place, he'd want to keep them hidden away. Lang was a naturally cautious guy. He wouldn't leave illegal substances lying around the place for an unsuspecting cleaner to find. Which ruled out the living room and kitchen, the other communal spaces. Lang would keep them somewhere safe, Bowman figured. The master bedroom, perhaps, or the bathroom.

There, if anywhere, he might find something useful.

He pushed through another door and found himself in a bright, airy corridor shaped like a T junction, with bedroom doors to the left and right. Bowman swerved to the right and crashed through the door to the master bedroom. The withdrawal pains were severe now, his hands shaking uncontrollably. The room was tastelessly furnished. There was a diamond pendant chandelier, nude bronze statues of winged cherubs on the desk and bedside table. Bowman staggered over to the king-sized bed. He yanked the table drawer open and rooted through the contents. He saw no pill bottles, no plastic baggies. Nothing containing opioids. Just cigarette packets and condom wrappers, a load of other junk.

He must have something here. Surely.

So where the fuck is it?

He stood up and stumbled through the door to the master bathroom. Floor-to-ceiling windows looked out over the waterfront, cars and people as small as ants. He set his Ruger down on the marble countertop and rifled through Lang's black leather washbag. Nothing. He flipped open the mirror cabinet, scanned the rows of luxury grooming products. On the top shelf, he found half a dozen medicine bottles. Bowman reached in for them, scattering designer shaving products and anti-ageing creams across the vanity unit. He glanced at the printed label on one of the plastic bottles, unscrewed the cap. Aspirin.

This is just a bunch of regular meds. He hasn't got anything.

Bowman kept searching. He checked three more pill containers. He hit the jackpot with the fourth bottle. It was unmarked, but he recognised the yellow tablets inside. The letters and numbers stamped on the face of each pill identified them as a moderate-strength opioid. The kind of thing prescribed for severe pain relief. Not as powerful as the stuff he bought from his dealer. But better than nothing.

Bowman thought: *Lang must be in a lot of pain to take this stuff. Or maybe he's like me. Maybe he has a secret habit no one else knows about.*

Then the sickness came back, cramping in his stomach. Bowman hastily ground down one of the tablets and inhaled it off his fist. A faster delivery system than swallowing the pills. He ran the chrome tap, wiped his face with an Egyptian cotton towel. Turned off the tap.

Looked up.

Saw the figure in the doorway.

Fourteen

Bowman stood still for a beat. The fog behind his eyes instantly cleared as two billion years of survival instincts kicked in. The guy in front of him was huge, broad in the arms and shoulders. His legs were as wide as temple columns. His fingers were the approximate size of beer cans. About the only small thing about the guy was his head. It was small and round, like a medicine ball, the pale fleshy face crowned with a trim Mohawk. He had the bloated, acned look of a steroid addict. *Not one of Seguma's bodyguards*, Bowman decided. *He didn't have the facial scars. Which meant he must be one of Lang's heavies.*

Minders. Dumb muscle he can trust.

Bowman reached for the Ruger.

In the next fraction of a second, the heavy lunged forward.

Roidhead wasn't fast. Bowman had seen oil tankers move with more speed. But he had time on his side. Lots of it. The Ruger was on the countertop beside the sink. It would take Bowman two or three seconds to snatch up the pistol, aim at Roidhead's centre mass and squeeze the trigger. No way he could reach it in time. Not with two hundred and fifty pounds of muscle bearing down on him.

Roidhead jacked his right arm back, winding up for a clean strike to Bowman's jaw. He was going for broke. Aiming to land a killer blow before his opponent could react. Not a sophisticated plan. But then again, it didn't need to be. Sometimes the crudest strategies were the best. Like the equivalent of a long ball in a game of football, pumping it forward to the striker. Route-one stuff. One punch and he could win the cup.

Bowman parried the punch, palming it away. He shaped to throw one of his own, but the shakes had badly slowed him down.

His arms and legs felt as if they had lead weights tied around them. Roidhead saw the balled fist driving at him and jerked his head to the side, sidestepping the blow. Then he pushed forward, slamming his forehead into Bowman's skull. Bowman saw white briefly. Something jarred inside his skull. He tasted blood and stumbled backwards. His vision cleared just in time to see Roidhead swinging at him again. He gasped as the heavy's hard knuckles collided with his stomach, driving the air out of his lungs.

He glanced up, saw Roidhead stomping forward, his right shoulder dropped as he shaped to throw another punch. Bowman deflected the blow with a ragged swipe of his forearm, then stamped down on Roidhead's toes with his right heel, as if he was crushing a cockroach underfoot. He followed up with another quick attack, then snatched a glass tumbler from the countertop and smashed it against the side of his opponent's temple. Roidhead groaned and staggered backwards, claret dripping down his face.

'Bastard!' he rasped.

Bowman whirled away from him and lunged for the Ruger. Roidhead recovered with astonishing speed and launched himself at Bowman with a maddened roar. He smashed into the SAS man shoulder first, as if he was barging through a locked door. The blow winded Bowman and sent him flying backwards. Pain shot up his spine as he fell back and crashed against the tiled floor. Bowman blinked, looked up and saw Roidhead grabbing the semi-automatic from the countertop. The heavy whirled round to face his floored opponent, his thick finger curled around the trigger. Blood streamed down his waxen face.

Roidhead began squeezing the trigger.

A sudden blur appeared behind the man.

There was a dense metallic thunk, and then Roidhead spasmed and his eyes rolled into the back of his head. The Ruger tumbled from his grip as he pitched forward and dropped to the floor. Like a puppet with the strings cut. Bowman looked up from the slumped figure. He saw Webb standing in the bathroom doorway, gripping a nude statue of a cherub. Fresh blood glistened on the cherub's bronze face.

Webb nodded at him.

'You all right?'

Bowman shook his groggy head clear. 'Thanks, mate.'

'I heard shouts. Figured you were in trouble.'

'Bloke had the jump on me. Came out of nowhere. Must have been hiding in one of the guest rooms up the corridor.'

'Why didn't you check them rooms first?'

Bowman didn't answer. Webb looked from the pill bottle to the floored heavy and back at Bowman. A question formed on his lips.

'Get back to Lang,' Bowman said as he picked himself off the floor. 'I'll plasticuff this fucker.'

'What's with the pills?'

'How the fuck should I know? Lang must have left them out.'

Webb gave him a curious look. Then he turned and left the bedroom, tossing the statue aside on his way out. Bowman dropped to a knee beside Roidhead. The guy was barely conscious. Blood oozed out of a shallow wound on the back of his head, matting his hair. Bowman pinned the heavy's arms behind his back, slipped the plastic restraints around his wrists and pulled them tight. He patted the guy down, found a creased leather wallet in his back pocket. There was a thin sheath of twenty-pound notes, credit cards, receipts. A driver's licence gave his name as Tony Hutton.

Bowman picked up the Ruger and pushed the tip against the guy's cheek.

'Christ, don't shoot!' Hutton begged. 'I'm just the driver!'

'Any more of your mates in the apartment?' Bowman growled.

'No. It's just me, the boss and his guest.'

Bowman's finger tensed around the trigger. He shoved the barrel harder against the heavy's cheek. 'You sure about that?'

'It's the truth, I swear! There ain't no one else.'

Bowman stood up and stuffed the bottle of pills into his pocket. He left Roidhead on the floor moaning in pain, skulked out of the master bedroom and quickly cleared the three guest bedrooms down the other side of the corridor. Once he was sure no one else was lurking inside the apartment, he moved back into the master bathroom and heaved Roidhead to his feet. He pressed the cold tip of the Ruger barrel against the nape of the heavy's neck.

'Get moving,' Bowman snarled, 'or I'll paint your boss's bathroom red.'

Roidhead staggered out of the master bathroom, cursing and moaning as Bowman forced him down the hallway and into the living room. Webb stood guard over Seguma and Lang, the Ruger at his side. Lang stared at the two soldiers, a look of sheer hatred etched across his face. Bowman frogmarched Roidhead across the room, and dumped him in one of the empty armchairs.

'Rooms are clear,' he said.

'You bastards,' Lang hissed as he caught sight of Roidhead's bruised and bloodied face. 'What have you done to Tony?'

'We had an argument,' Bowman said. 'Your man lost.'

'Sorry, boss,' Roidhead, aka Tony Hutton, mumbled. 'One of 'em clobbered me from behind. Couldn't do nothing.'

'Keep your mouth shut, son. Not a fucking word.'

Bowman nodded at the tyrant. 'Where are your bodyguards?'

'At the hotel,' Seguma said, his voice shaking. 'I left them there.' He glanced at Lang. 'David advised me not to bring them.'

'They're not downstairs? Outside? In the car park?'

'I came here alone.'

'Who drove you?'

'The chauffeur. From the hotel.'

'No one else knows you're here?'

'No one.' Seguma stared anxiously at Bowman. 'What's going on here? Who are you people working for?'

Bowman didn't reply. Instead, he turned to Webb and said, 'I'll get the wagon. You keep an eye on this lot.'

'I'd watch your mate, if I were you, son,' Lang said to Webb. 'He doesn't look too good from where I'm sitting.'

Webb's gaze skimmed across the room, looking from the mobster to his colleague. 'What's he talking about?'

'Nothing,' Bowman said. 'Just a touch of the flu, like I said.'

An ugly laugh escaped from Lang's throat. 'Yeah, that must be it.'

'Shut up,' Bowman said.

He bolted out of the living room, detoured into Lang's master bedroom and paced over to the walk-in wardrobe. Bowman ditched his courier-branded jacket, polo shirt and cap, grabbed a designer shirt and striped blazer from the rack. He found a pair of Gucci shades in a mirrored cabinet, completed the look with a baseball cap emblazoned with the crest of the yacht club. Then checked himself out in the mirror. The disguise wouldn't fool anyone up close. But from a distance, through a tinted car windscreen, he could pass for David Lang.

The pills were starting to kick in as Bowman returned to the hallway, the sweet warm buzz of the opiates spreading through his body. He extracted the magnetic key card from Lang's wallet, took the Range Rover fob from the side table, checked that his Ruger was concealed under his jacket. Then he left through the front door. He checked his phone signal on the landing, got two bars, and tapped open the encrypted messaging app on his phone. Dialled Mallet's number.

Mallet answered immediately.

'Well?' he asked.

'We're in,' Bowman said tersely.

'Any problems?'

Bowman told him about the heavy.

'Is he under control?' asked Mallet.

'He's tied up, with the others. Patrick's keeping an eye on them.'

'Where are you now?'

'Heading down to the car park. I'll be out in two minutes.'

'We're in the same spot,' said Mallet. 'We'll be waiting.'

The private lift plunged straight down to the underground car park. Bowman stepped out into what looked like the world's most expensive car showroom. Rows of Lamborghinis and Ferraris were parked side-by-side with Maybachs and Bentaygas. He located Lang's Range Rover and hit the unlock button. He got inside, dropped the fob into the cup holder. Then stamped on the brakes and pressed the start button. The instrument panels woke up. He released the parking brake, rotated the gear selector to Drive, followed the signs to the exit.

His hands had stopped shaking by the time he steered the Range Rover out of the garage. He hung a right on to Avenue Princesse Grace and drove south for half a mile, following the same route they had taken to the apartment block from the stadium, but in reverse. The relief he had felt at finding the pills quickly gave way to a gnawing unease. He had taken a big risk in searching for Lang's stash. And it had very nearly cost him his life.

He pushed the thought to the back of his mind as he hit the roundabout. He circled the roundabout counter-clockwise, sling-shot north again on Princesse Grace. Past the dull apartments and the cafés and the Grace Kelly monument. He motored on until he spotted the Mercedes-Benz E-Class parked at the side of the road, next to the ice-cream parlour. Then Bowman eased off the gas and drew to a halt parallel with the E-Class estate, blocking the line of cars behind him.

A car horn blared as Mallet and Casey jumped out of the E-Class and jogged into the road. Both of them wore baseball caps. Mallet was clutching a laptop in a neoprene sleeve. The driver immediately to the rear stuck his head out of the window of his Rolls-Royce Cullinan SUV and hurled abuse at Bowman, honking his horn as

Casey dived into the back seat. Mallet hopped into the front, pulled the door shut and said, 'Drive.'

They pulled away, leaving Loader behind the wheel of the E-Class. He would keep eyes on the front of the apartment block, watching for any sign of Lang's acquaintances or trouble from the police, while the rest of the Cell turned the screw on Lang.

Four minutes after leaving the parking garage, Bowman piloted the Range Rover back down the ramp. He berthed the wagon in the parking bay, and the three operators disembarked. The appearance of two strangers in the car park wouldn't strike the security staff as unusual. Webb had already told the concierge that more guests would be arriving later that morning to ink the contracts. Anyone watching the footage would conclude that Lang had picked up a pair of business associates and ferried them back to his apartment to get the paperwork signed.

Bowman touch-tapped Lang's key card against the control panel. The lift doors hissed open, the car rocketed them up to the eighteenth floor. They paced down the private hallway, and Bowman knocked three times on the front door to Lang's apartment, giving the correct signal to Webb. He cranked open the door, pushed inside the foyer a step ahead of Mallet and Casey. Led them across to the living room.

The temperature dropped as soon as Mallet swept inside. Like the devil had just entered the room. Or the moment the sheriff stepped into the saloon to arrest the villainous cowboy. Lang stared warily at the cruel-faced Scot with the ruthless blue eyes and the wave of silver hair. Mallet didn't say anything. He didn't need to. The mobster and the tyrant both seemed to understand they were in the presence of a terrible man. Like coming face to face with an eight-hundred-pound gorilla. A primitive reaction, stretching back millennia, to the days when their ancestors roamed the savannah.

Roidhead slumped heavily in the armchair, half dazed, his bovine face lacquered with blood. Mallet glanced briefly at him, then rested his gaze on Seguma.

'Step outside the room, sir.'

The president folded his arms defiantly. 'I'm going nowhere. Not until someone tells me what the hell is going on. Who are you? What are you doing here?'

'We work for the British security services,' Mallet said. 'These three are my associates. We know about your meeting with the Russians later today. We've got orders to arrest David Lang.'

Seguma's mouth went slack for a moment, before he swiftly recovered.

'This is an outrage. I have done nothing wrong.'

'You're not in any trouble,' Mallet said. 'We just need to ask your mate a few questions. Straighten a few things out. Now leave us, sir.' He motioned to Webb and Casey. 'These two will wait with you in the study until we're ready to talk.'

Seguma remained seated. He was the feared president of Kara-tandu. A man who commanded absolute loyalty and obedience from those around him. He wasn't used to being told what to do, especially by hard-faced Scots with harsh Glaswegian accents.

'Leave the room,' Mallet said coolly. 'If I have to ask again, it won't be nicely.'

Seguma caught the severe look on Mallet's face, evidently decided that the Cell team leader wasn't bullshitting, and stood up. He seized his cane and hat, and then Webb and Casey escorted him out of the living room. Mallet frowned at Roidhead, as if noticing him for the first time.

'Get that scumbag out of here,' he said to Bowman. 'Put him somewhere he won't bother us. Then you and me will have ourselves a little chat with Davey Boy.'

Fifteen

Bowman hauled Roidhead to his feet and shoved him out of the living room. The guy limped along, breathing heavily as they crossed the hallway and pushed through the doors to the staff quarters. Which was bigger than a broom cupboard, but only marginally. Bowman dumped him on the floor, closed the door and backtracked to the living room. Mallet had taken a seat at the dining table facing out across the balcony. He had the laptop set up in front of him, the screen flipped open.

'Close the door,' he said to Bowman. 'Bring Davey Boy over here. Let's have a friendly chat.'

Bowman grabbed Lang by his arm, marched him over to the table, set him down next to Mallet at the head of the table. Bowman sat in the chair to the Scot's right. Lang eyed Mallet suspiciously as the latter dragged his forefingers across the touchscreen pad, scrolling and clicking.

'What the fuck is this?' he sneered. 'You want to show me your private porn collection or something?'

Mallet said nothing. He typed, hit Enter.

Lang smirked. 'You're not a spook. I can tell. You ain't got the look. Not posh enough. You must be the muscle. Thicko soldiers, doing the heavy lifting. Am I right?'

Mallet didn't say a word.

'Fuck you, then. Miserable prick,' Lang said. He cocked his head at Bowman. 'How's that touch of the flu, son? Better?'

Bowman stayed silent. Mallet tapped another key on the laptop. Suddenly a long melodic ringtone filled the air. Mallet turned the laptop round, training the built-in camera on Lang. After six seconds, the caller on the other end answered, and an eerie, syn-thesised female voice filled the air.

'Hello, David,' the Voice said.

Lang stared at the blank screen, his eyes shrinking to dots. 'Who is this?'

'My name is not important,' the Voice said in its monotonous automated tone. 'All you need to know is that I'm from the security services.'

'Yeah? Then show us your fucking face.'

'That won't be necessary. Now, let me explain what's going to happen. The men in your apartment work for us. We're going to ask you some questions. And you're going to give us the answers.'

'I ain't saying shit to you poofs. Not to you,' he said, meeting Mallet's gaze, 'or to no fucking computer screen. For all I know, this is some wind-up.'

'We're not playing games,' Mallet said. 'You'll do as we say, Davey Boy.'

Lang eased back in his chair and chuckled. 'Or what? You and your mates will scare me to death? Is that it?'

Mallet glared at him with a look that could skin an animal.

The Voice said, 'It's in your interest to cooperate with us, David. We already know you're planning to meet with the Russian ambas-sador and Sergei Galkin in Antibes today, at midday.'

'It's a free country, last I heard. I can meet with mates. That's none of your business.'

'You've arranged a meeting with two well-known Kremlin associates behind our backs. We know you and Seguma both wanted to keep this meeting a closely guarded secret. That's why you conspired to send a body double to the royal wedding.'

Lang said nothing.

'You're trying to pressure Seguma into changing allegiance,' the Voice went on. 'That's the real reason for this meeting with the

Russians, isn't it? To persuade him to abandon his alliance with us and bend the knee to Moscow.'

Lang's shoulders heaved up and down as he let out a dirty laugh. 'You people don't know shit.'

Mallet gave him a menacing stare. 'The game's up, pal. You've been caught red-handed. Tell us what the plan is.'

'Fuck off.'

'We're doing you a favour, you idiot,' Bowman said.

'You stuck a gun in my face, son. I'd hardly call that good manners.'

The corner of Mallet's mouth teased upwards. A wicked glint flashed in his eyes. 'Tell me something. When was the last time you spoke to your twin brother?'

'A few days ago. Why?'

'You should treasure that conversation, Davey Boy. It'll be the last time you ever speak to him.'

Lang's expression darkened. 'The fuck are you talking about?'

'Freddie was poisoned,' the Voice said. 'Last night. At the royal wedding.'

They gave him an abbreviated version of events. Freddie's collapse and confession, the strong evidence linking Moscow to the attack. His brother's critical status in an intensive care bed, his dire prognosis. Lang listened in stony silence.

'You're lying,' he said after a long pause. 'Nah, you lot are playing mind games. This is some sick tale you lot have cooked up.'

'It's all true,' Mallet insisted.

'No. The Russians wouldn't do that. Not to Freddie. They ain't got no fucking reason.'

'We're not making it up.' Mallet gestured to Bowman. 'In fact, Josh was the one who ran to your brother's aid. He heard Freddie's confession. Ask him if you don't believe us.'

'Bollocks.'

'It's the truth,' Bowman insisted. 'The Russians got to your brother. Freddie said so himself. Those were his last words. He wanted me to warn you, before you walked into a trap.'

Lang shook his head angrily. 'It don't make sense.'

'We're just telling you how it is, Davey.'

'But if they poisoned Freddie, why haven't I heard nothing?' Lang jerked his head at the TV. 'That story is all over the news, but no one's talking about my brother.'

'We've withheld the victim's identity,' the Voice said. 'We thought you'd want to know from us first.'

'This isn't a game,' Bowman said sincerely. 'Your brother's seriously ill, David.'

Lang drew his gaze back to the solemn-faced figures at the table. He saw the sober look in Bowman's pale grey eyes, and something in him seemed to break. He looked away and fell silent. His lips began to tremble as he stared out of the balcony windows, beyond the terrace, at the forest of ugly high-rise apartments and skyscrapers. The white specks of cruise ships drifted lazily across the rim of the horizon.

'How is he?' he asked quietly.

'There's no point sugar-coating it,' Mallet replied bluntly. 'Freddie's going to die. It's going to be a fucking horrible death, he'll be in a great deal of pain, and you're next on the Russians' hit list.'

Lang searched the horizon, squinting, as if looking for answers. 'It can't be . . . Why would they do it?'

Mallet said, 'It's over, Davey. Your best bet is to come clean and tell us what's going on.'

Lang stared at the skyline for a few moments. When he slanted his gaze back to the table, the hard lines had returned to his face.

'Forget it. I ain't talking to the likes of you.'

'Don't be a fool,' the Voice said over the laptop speaker. 'The Russians are double-crossing you. They managed to get to your

166

brother at a royal wedding party. They'll kill you too, if they get the chance. Do you really think they'll let you walk away from this thing alive? If you tell us what you know, we can help you.'

'I don't need your help. I'm a big boy, I've made plenty of enemies in my time. I can take care of myself.'

'We're doing you a favour, you thick bastard,' Mallet hissed.

'You won't be safe in Monte Carlo,' said the Voice. 'The Russians have the run of the principality. They'll hunt you down and kill you. We can protect you, David.'

Lang gave a derisive snort. 'Don't make me laugh. How many Russians have been killed in London over the years? You couldn't stop them if you tried.'

'We can do better than your own men,' the Voice argued. 'We can offer you a private jet back to the UK, a safe house, round-the-clock protection for you and your family. If you cooperate.'

'I've earned some protection already, haven't I? All the work I've done for you in the past, I must have some credit left in the bank.'

A sharp jolt shot up Bowman's spine and tingled on the back of his neck. 'You've been working for Six?'

''Course I fucking have.' Lang's voice dripped with contempt. 'I've been supplying you people with information on the president for years. The people in Ken's inner circle, his business dealings, his meetings with foreign leaders. Ken hasn't taken a dump in the last decade without your mates knowing about it.'

Bowman glanced over at Mallet, but the older man showed no hint of surprise. *Did he already know about Lang's involvement with Vauxhall?* Bowman wondered. *What else isn't he telling me?*

The Voice said, 'We're not interested in the past. We're interested in the future. Start talking, and we'll get you and your family into a safe house.'

Lang's face hardened. 'Nah. I'm grateful for the warning and all. But you can untie me now.'

'You're making a serious mistake,' the Voice warned.

'Don't you people have anything better to do?' Lang jutted out his chin. 'Here I am, a respectable businessman, enjoying a nice weekend with an old friend, doing nothing wrong, and you come barging in here with your guns and your threats. It's fucking outrageous. I should sue.'

Mallet leaned back in his chair, rubbing his lightly stubbled jaw. 'Suit yourself,' he said. 'Play it that way if you want. But you can forget about getting that OBE you've been after.'

The Voice cut in: 'We know you've been paying a private lobbying firm to help you get on the Honours List. They've been pressing your claim hard, emphasising your charitable ventures in Karatandu. We have the power to make sure it doesn't happen.'

Lang snorted loudly. 'Is that supposed to be a threat?'

'We're serious.'

'You can't do nothing. I'm a good boy. I pay my taxes. If you had anything on me, you would have used it by now.'

'Are you sure about that?' Mallet asked.

He leaned across the dining table and smiled coldly. Lang shifted awkwardly in his seat.

'We know about the secret parties. The ones you've been hosting at your mansion in Essex.' He wagged a finger. 'The ones with the kids.'

Lang went pale. The arrogant look dropped from his face so hard and fast Bowman almost heard it thud against the parquet flooring.

'I don't know what you're talking about.' His voice was small and quiet.

'Yes, you do.' Mallet sat back with folded arms and said, 'What would your business partners and lieutenants think, if they found out you've been smuggling in underage kids for you and your Establishment mates? What would your wife say, come to think of it?'

168

Hatred flickered behind Lang's eyes. The look on his face suggested he wanted to reach across the table and strangle Mallet.

'You wouldn't . . . you wouldn't fucking dare,' he stammered.

'Want to bet on it?'

'You can't prove a thing.'

Bowman said, 'What about Beth McKee?'

'Never heard of her.'

'She was twelve years old when she went missing.' Bowman bristled with anger. 'I was in the Met at the time. We looked everywhere for that kid. Her mother was heartbroken.'

'Terrible. But what has that got to do with me?'

'You hid the body, didn't you, Mr Lang?'

'Fuck off.'

'I know for a fact that she was last seen at your mansion. Beth was the favourite of one of the lords, wasn't she? You lured that kid inside and let some rich old bastard abuse her. And when the lord went too far, when he throttled that poor girl to death, you buried her to cover it up. That's what happened.'

Lang's face gave nothing away. But the narrowed eyes were filled with the threat of violence, the veins on his neck bunched tight with rage.

Mallet said, 'Maybe we'll get the diggers round to your place in Billericay. Start tearing up the grounds. See what we find.'

'You can't . . . you don't have no proof.'

'We don't need any,' the Voice said. 'All we have to do is create a fuss, and the public will make up their own minds. We'll seed stories in the national newspapers. We'll populate chat rooms and social media with discussions about your sexual orientation. Our contacts will spread rumours among your friends and family. Our friends at Scotland Yard will begin an official investigation. Even if they can't find anything, it won't matter. By the time we're finished, your reputation will have been dragged through the mud. No one will want to go anywhere near you, not even with a barge pole. That'll have a ruinous effect on your businesses, of course.'

'Your own life might be at risk, too,' said Mallet. 'They don't tolerate kiddie fiddlers in your line of work. When your mob friends find out, they'll be arguing over who gets to cut your balls off.'

A pained expression formed on Lang's face. He swallowed hard and looked out of the window, as if searching for a sign from God. He took a deep breath.

'Before I talk, I want certain assurances,' he said.

'You're in no position to bargain,' Mallet replied.

Lang pretended to ignore him and continued to speak directly to the laptop. To the unseen voice in Vauxhall.

'If I tell you what I know, I want your word that you'll protect me and my family from the Russians. The gold-star package. Police protection, security details, new identities, the works.'

Silence.

'We can live with that,' said the Voice finally. 'But we can only help you if you answer our questions. If you cooperate fully, we'll do everything we can to keep you safe.'

Bowman felt his muscles tense with anger. He could barely believe what he was hearing. 'Why are we pushing the boat our for this guy?' he growled. 'He's a criminal, for Christ's sake.'

'Shut up,' Mallet snapped.

'Start talking, David,' said the Voice. 'Tell us what you're planning with the Russians.'

'There's a deal,' said Lang. 'Between President Seguma and the Kremlin. I've been working as a go-between for both sides. But you're wrong about one thing. It ain't about changing allegiance.'

'What, then?'

Lang hesitated.

'Talk,' Mallet hissed threateningly.

'The Russians are going to convince Seguma to stand down,' said Lang. 'He'll announce his resignation as president. Today.'

'That's why you're meeting the Russians later?' Bowman asked. 'To make this announcement?'

Lang nodded feebly.

'It's going to be broadcast on state radio and TV in Karatandu. Then the Russians are going to take over the country by force. Put their own man in charge. And there's nothing you can do to stop them.'

Sixteen

There was a beat of cold silence in the room. Bowman sat very still, the breath trapped in his throat. He saw Mallet's jawline visibly tense, the skin stretching across his weathered face. Lang hung his head low and stared at a spot between his feet. Then Mallet spoke up.

'You and your Russian mates must be living in la-la land. Why would Seguma agree to give up the throne?'

Lang slowly lifted his head. 'He doesn't have a choice. The Russians are going to launch a military coup, with the backing of the KUF.'

'Who the fuck are they?'

'The Karatandu United Front. The main rebel paramilitary force.'

Bowman said, 'I've heard of them. There was an interview on TV with their leader yesterday. Some bloke with golden teeth.'

'Kakuba,' Lang said. 'General Moses Kakuba. He's ex-army. Used to be one of Seguma's most loyal officers. He switched sides a few years ago. Reckons he was overlooked for a promotion because of his tribal heritage. Now he leads the armed wing of the KUF. Fancies himself as the next president of Karatandu.'

'He'll get it, if he's doing a deal with the Russians.'

Lang's lips twisted up at the corners in an ugly sneer. 'He's being played. The Russians are manipulating him. Kakuba thinks they're partners, but they're the ones calling the shots. He's just another lefty idealist taking whatever help he can get.'

'What if Seguma puts up a fight?' Mallet asked.

'He won't,' Lang replied. 'They've given Ken an ultimatum. Either he agrees to stand down peacefully, or there's gonna be a bloodbath.'

'It'll never work,' the Voice said. 'The army is loyal to Seguma. He's been very generous to the generals over the years.'

'That's why the Russians need the announcement from Ken. Once his men find out he's thrown in the towel, they won't stand by him. Not this time. Why fight for a leader who's given up?'

'What about the rest of his inner circle?'

'Some of them will come over. The ones we've paid off. The rest will get the old head-chopping treatment.'

Mallet glowered at him. 'That's why the Kremlin reached out to you. You're well connected in Karatandu, you know all the key figures to bribe. You and that dipshit brother of yours.'

'Don't talk about Freddie that way. I'm warning you.'

'See this?' Mallet pointed to his face. 'This is me shitting myself, Davey.'

Lang stared daggers at the Scot.

'The plan makes sense,' the Voice said. 'If Moscow can convince Seguma to step down, they can take over the country without a shot being fired.'

'They'd want to avoid getting sucked into a violent rebellion,' Bowman said. 'It could get ugly. People would be outraged.'

'Hasn't stopped the Russians before,' Mallet said.

'What's in this for Seguma?' asked Bowman.

'He gets to retire peacefully. Which is more than the bloke before him got to enjoy. Ken knows he's made plenty of enemies over the years. He also knows that you people take him for granted.'

'Britain is a loyal ally,' the Voice insisted. 'And we have been for many years.'

'That's not how Ken sees it. Far as he's concerned, the support he's had from Westminster is piss-poor. Yeah, you throw him the odd bone, but when it comes to hard investment, supplying arms and whatnot, you're not interested. All you care about is bleeding the country dry.'

'I still don't understand why Seguma would go along with the plan,' said Bowman. 'He's crushed uprisings before. He might think he stands a chance this time.'

'You fucking thick or something? Look at the news, son. Ken's losing his magic touch. He ain't as popular as he used to be with his people. Some of those ungrateful scrotes would like to see him hang. Ken knows that the moment he loses power, he's vulnerable. The Russians are offering him a way out. A chance to retire in peace.'

'And if he refuses?'

'He won't. Ken has already agreed to the deal.'

'That's why you set up this meeting today? To rubber-stamp this thing?'

Lang nodded. 'Once Ken has announced his resignation, the Russians will whisk his family over from Karatandu. He can enjoy a quiet existence in Monte Carlo or Malta or wherever, enjoying the company of his friends and family, his money.'

'The cash he's trousered from his country's oil and gas reserves, you mean.'

'Spare me your sermonising. Ken's a good man. He's made a few mistakes in his time, but who ain't? He brought stability to his country, peace. He put Karatandu on the map. If he was a white man, he would have been nominated for the Nobel Peace Prize by now.'

'Maybe,' said Bowman. 'If he hadn't butchered thousands of his own people.'

'Our government kills people every day.'

'That's different.'

'Is it?'

Mallet said, 'I can see what Seguma stands to gain from this arrangement. But what's your interest?'

'I get my cut,' Lang replied defensively. 'That's only reasonable. But I ain't doing this for the money. I'm doing what's right for Ken, and the good people of Karatandu.'

'That's what you tell yourself at night, is it?'

'Piss off.'

Bowman said, 'It's a good deal, but Seguma would never get away with it. He's a war criminal. The Hague would arrest him sooner or later. He'd end up in jail.'

Lang gave a lopsided smile. 'The Russians have thought of that. There's a back-up plan. If it looks like things might go that way, they'll whisk him off to Moscow. He'll see out his days in a luxury dacha.'

'When is the coup happening?' asked the Voice.

'I'm only the middleman, for fuck's sake. They didn't share the details of the operation with me.'

Mallet slapped a hand down on the table so hard the room seemed to shake. 'You'll have to do better than that, if you want our help.'

'You must have some idea of the timeline, surely,' the Voice said.

Lang sighed heavily. 'Look, all I know is that the Russians told me it would be happening sometime tomorrow. They didn't say exactly when. That's it. I don't know nothing else.'

'What about troops, tactics, key targets?'

'I don't know none of that.' He paused, wrinkled his brow. 'The Russian ambassador did mention something about a few guys they were sending in to Karatandu.'

'What guys?'

'Special Forces. Military advisers. We got pissed on vodka and the Russian started bragging about them. Said some blokes were going in to whip the KUF into shape. Turn 'em into professional soldiers. He reckoned Ken's army wouldn't stand a chance against them.'

'How many guys are we talking about?' asked Casey.

'I don't know.'

'They wouldn't need many,' Bowman commented. 'A handful of Russian Special Forces to coordinate the rebel forces, capture the main targets and infrastructure. One troop might do it. Ten or twelve guys.'

'Where are they now?' Mallet said.

'How the fuck should I know? Look, you're asking the wrong bloke. I'm just the broker.'

'You're a traitor. You've been playing both sides, double-dipping with the Russians. Betraying your country.'

'My loyalty is to Ken,' Lang replied curtly. 'No one else. I'm acting in his best interests.'

'Convincing him to hand his country to the Kremlin on a plate? That's hardly sound advice, Davey.'

'It's not as simple as that. Ken is backed into a corner. The new regime is taking over, whether he likes it or not. I'm trying to fix a deal that works for all parties.'

'Rubbish. Your man Seguma has had his nose in the trough for twenty-four years. Now he wants out, and you're going to make a percentage at both ends. Isn't that right?'

'I'm a businessman. I've got to have my taste.'

'You're a fucking crook,' said Mallet. 'And a crap one at that. An Essex boy with a shite haircut playing spy games. You thought you were being clever, but now you made one mistake, see.'

'Yeah? What's that?'

'You trusted the Russians. Big no-no, that. Now they're double-crossing you. That twat brother of yours is on life support, and you've got a big red target painted on your back.'

A spark of hatred flashed in Lang's eyes, his lips twitched. He turned to Bowman. 'Do you know something, son? I don't think I like your mate. He's got a terrible mouth on him.'

Bowman said, 'Why are the Russians so keen to get involved in Karatandu?'

'Cobalt.' Lang sniffed.

'Isn't that the stuff they use in batteries to power electric cars, laptops, phones and so on?'

Lang nodded and said, 'That shit is the new oil. There's a massive rush on it. Everyone wants a piece of the action: the Yanks, the Chinese. Karatandu is sitting on huge reserves of the stuff.'

'I thought most of that comes from the Congo.'

'It does,' the Voice cut in. 'That's where most of the high-grade cobalt is found. But the mining companies discovered large deposits in Karatandu last year.'

'Clean technology,' Lang said. 'It's the future. Oil and gas are history. Electric car batteries use several kilograms of cobalt. And the mineral is in short supply. Whoever gets their hands on the deposits in Karatandu will control the electric vehicle market. Which will be worth billions.'

'That's not the only reason the Russians are interested in Karatandu, though,' Mallet put in. 'Is it?'

Bowman looked towards the Scot as the latter went on.

'If the Russians take control of Karatandu, they're gaining a vital strategic foothold in Central Africa. Moscow would love that. Those bastards have been desperate for a slice of the action in the region. They could start making moves on the neighbouring countries. Like the old days, when the Soviet Union was a player in Africa.'

Lang shook his head vigorously. 'I don't know nothing about that. Look, I've told you everything I know, I swear.'

Mallet fixed his merciless gaze on him. The eyes of a born killer.

'You'd better not be lying to us,' he said. 'Because if we find out that you've withheld information, or sold us a pack of lies, we'll soon know about it.'

Bowman heard the clacking of fingers on a keyboard. Then the Voice said, 'This interview is terminated. John, we'll speak again later. Once we've consulted with our colleagues in the Foreign Office. In the meantime, sit tight.'

'What about my deal?' Lang demanded.

'Our team will have to put together a protection package. That will take some time. We'll be in touch.'

Bowman said, 'What are we going to do about the Russians?'

'Clearly, we cannot allow them to force President Seguma out of office. We'll have to discuss the situation, figure out how to respond.'

'How long will that take?'

'Half an hour, perhaps. The Foreign Secretary is on the other line, waiting to be briefed. We'll have something for you by ten o'clock.'

The call ended. Mallet closed the screen and turned to Bowman.

'Check in with Tiny,' he said. 'Let him know we might be here for a while.'

'We'll need to update the others, too,' Bowman said.

'Later. Once we've heard back from Six.'

'What about him?' Bowman pointed to Lang.

'Davey Boy can wait here with us.' Mallet grinned at the mobster. 'We don't want you in the same room as Seguma. You might put ideas in his head.'

Bowman typed out a short text message to Loader. He popped his head through the door to the staff quarters to check on Roidhead, then returned to the living room. They passed the minutes watching Sky News. The attack at the wedding was still the main story. The rest of the news barely warranted a look-in. There was a brief report on the trade war between the US and China. A thirty-second segment on the elections in Australia. An earthquake had struck in Italy. Another high-street fashion chain had gone into administration.

The fifth item focused on the growing unrest in Karatandu. The situation had deteriorated badly in the past twenty-four hours. The expected government crackdown had backfired. There was fighting in the streets. Protestors against the security forces. Molotov cocktails, bricks and clubs versus the AK-47. Some of the wealthier citizens were fleeing the capital, the reporter claimed. The US State Department had announced it was pulling its diplomatic staff from the country with immediate effect. General Kakuba gave another interview from his mountain hideout. The gold-toothed leader of the KUF angrily denounced Seguma's regime and called on his followers to take to the streets.

Bowman said, 'If they keep this up, the rebels won't need the Russians. They'll run Seguma out of town themselves.'

'Not likely,' Lang said. 'They don't have the resources to defeat the government. They'll loot some shops, burn a few buildings to the ground, maybe even kill some soldiers, but in the end, they'll lose.'

'Unless your Kremlin mates help them out,' Mallet quipped.

'Still won't be easy. Seguma's loyal supporters won't surrender, not without a fight. It would have been better if Ken had stepped aside gracefully. We could have spared the country a lot of grief.'

Mallet chuckled meanly. 'You don't give a crap about these people. The only thing you care about is your bank balance.'

'That's not fair. I've invested heavily in Karatandu over the years. I've poured money into hospitals, orphanages, roads. All sorts.'

'You must like the place.'

'Yeah,' Lang said, 'I do. The country gets a bad rap in the Western media, but it's a beautiful place. Once you get out of the cities, the landscape is like an English forest.'

'Pity.'

'What's that?'

'You won't ever see it again,' Mallet said. 'Not after today.'

Thirty-eight minutes passed. Mallet stepped out onto the balcony to take a call. Bowman snuck out to the kitchen, locked himself in the utility room and snorted up another one of Lang's pills. When he headed back into the living room, he noticed Lang giving him a funny look. Mallet was still out on the balcony, talking in a low voice on his phone.

Lang parted his lips into a sinister grin. 'How's that cold?'

'Fine,' Bowman muttered.

'I've seen that look before, you know. In your eyes.'

Bowman steered his gaze away from Lang. He felt a cold tingling on the nape of his neck.

'You must be in a lot of pain,' the mobster went on. 'People who have that look, they're usually trying to numb something horrible. Some shit they can't deal with in their lives. Know what I mean?'

'No,' Bowman said.

'Yeah, you do.'

He said nothing more. Another four minutes passed, and then the balcony doors swished open. Mallet stepped back inside, tucked his phone away. He nodded at Bowman.

'Six have liaised with their mates in the Foreign Office. They've reached a decision.'

'And?'

'We need to have a chat with Seguma. Bring him in. Patrick and Alex can sit in on this, too.' Mallet's eyes rested on Lang. 'You. Fuck-face. Wait on the balcony.'

'That's not very friendly, son.'

'We're from the Cell. We're not in the business of being nice.'

'What about my deal?'

'They're processing the paperwork now. Shouldn't take much longer.'

'Yeah, well, speed it up. I'm bored shitless sitting here with you mugs.'

Bowman left the room and hurried down the hallway. He levered open the study door, motioned for the others to follow him. Seguma glanced up at him, his face stricken with anxiety and fear. Webb and Casey pulled him up from the leather armchair and ushered him back down the hallway into the living room. He entered the living room behind Bowman and abruptly stopped as he caught sight of Lang. The latter was sitting on a chair on the balcony outside, looking miserable. The door had been locked, trapping him on the terrace. There was no other way off, other than the sheer drop to the streets below.

'Take a seat, sir,' Mallet said, stiffly.

His tone was friendly enough, but the look in his eyes carried a threat of violence.

Seguma dropped into the same chair Lang had occupied, took off his trilby hat, placed it on his lap. He watched the others in silence as they sat round the table.

'It's over,' Mallet said. 'Lang told us everything.'

Seguma glanced outside at Lang. 'David talked?'

'He spilled his guts. Gave us chapter and verse on your deal with the Russians.'

Mallet briefly explained the situation to Webb and Casey. The Russian conspiracy to force Seguma from power and put their own guy in office. The threat to violently overthrow Seguma's regime if he refused to agree to the terms on offer. Lang's role as an intermediary, taking a percentage from both sides. The cobalt rush.

Casey said, 'I'm surprised.'

Mallet said, 'About what?'

'How did Lang manage to keep this whole thing secret for so long? We've been watching him for months. Surely someone must have picked up on it at Vauxhall.'

'Not necessarily. A deal this big, Lang will have been cautious. More than usual.'

'But he must have left a trail. Electronic comms, messages.'

'The Russians could have advised him on all of that,' Mallet said. 'They'd have a system in place.'

'Lang meets with a lot of Russians in his business dealings,' Bowman added. 'He gets a lot of high-rollers at his casinos. It wouldn't have been hard to arrange a few clandestine meetings.'

Mallet turned to the president.

'You've been hoodwinked, sir. The Russians promised you a cosy retirement, but they're lying through their back teeth. They've poisoned your associate's brother. They even attempted to assassinate you in London.'

Seguma's eyes narrowed, pulling his eyebrows together. 'Someone tried to kill my double?'

'It was kept out of the news. The police arrested an assassin near the wedding venue. He's from Karatandu, but it looks like he was trained up and funded by the Russians.'

'But why would they kill me? We had a deal.'

'You're one of the longest-serving leaders in Africa,' Mallet said. 'The last thing the Russians want is you making noises in the background, stirring things up. It could cause problems for the new man.'

'But I promised them I would stay out of politics. I gave them my word.'

Mallet rooted through his pockets and pulled out a packet of smokes. 'That doesn't matter,' he replied as he jammed a cigarette between his teeth and searched for a lighter. 'The Russians will tell you whatever you want to hear, sir. But it's safer if they scrub you out of existence.'

He patted himself down, found a lighter in his jacket and sparked up. Then he said, 'We're about to go live on a call with a senior officer at MI6. The British are going to make you an offer.'

Seguma's expression tightened. 'What offer?'

'Something better than the one you had on the table from Russia.' Mallet blew out smoke, looked round and tapped ash into a glass ashtray. 'One that doesn't end with you getting a bullet in the back of the head.'

The cigarette dangled from Mallet's lips as he swiped a finger across the laptop touchpad. He pressed a key, the same musical ringtone filled the room, and a moment later the voice of the anonymous MI6 officer came over the speaker from six hundred miles away.

'John? Is everyone present?'

'We're all here, ma'am.'

'Have you explained the situation to Mr Seguma?'

'I've told him what's really going on, aye.'

The Voice said, 'Mr Seguma, I'm afraid I'm going to have to make this very quick, because we don't have a lot of time. In less than two hours, the Russians will realise that the meeting is off and initiate a military coup d'état. I'm sure you appreciate the urgency of the situation.'

'Who am I speaking to?' Seguma demanded. 'Give me your name.'

'That doesn't concern you, Mr President. All you need to know is that I am speaking to you on behalf of the British government. I've been authorised to make you an offer.'

Seguma laughed mirthlessly. 'Now you want to help me? Now, of all times? Surely this is a joke.'

'We're trying to help you out of this situation, Mr President.'

'Your foreign secretary, he never returns my calls,' Seguma said bitterly. 'I ask for aid from your country, military help to deal with my enemies. It never comes. I tell you I have big problems, drought, my people are starving, you don't care. But now, all of a sudden, the Russians take an interest in my country, and you pretend we are friends.'

'I'm deeply sorry you feel that way.'

'Lang was a fool for persuading me to do business with the Russians. But I had my reasons. You people never support me. It's all just words, words. Give us some cash and tell us to go away.'

'Britain considers you a dear friend,' the Voice said. 'We always have.'

'If that is true, you have a very strange way of showing it.'

'We've made mistakes. We're prepared to admit that. But that's all in the past, sir. Downing Street wants to start over. The government is keen to demonstrate its support . . . as long as you're willing to pledge your loyalty to us.'

'You are too late.' Seguma shook his head slowly. 'I cannot go back to Karatandu, not now.'

'Mr President, you cannot allow the Russians to coerce you into stepping aside. They can't be trusted. We both know that.'

Seguma spread his hands across the table, like a guy showing a weak hand in a high-stakes poker game.

'How can I go back now? If I refuse the deal from the Russians, they will infiltrate my country anyway. I will lose everything.'

Mallet took a final drag on his cigarette and stubbed it out in the ashtray. 'You'll lose a lot more than that, if you go to that meeting,' he said. 'In fact, I doubt you'd make it out of there alive.'

'They wouldn't kill me. Surely?'

Mallet answered with a shrug.

The Voice said, 'There is another way out of this situation, sir. One that doesn't involve surrendering to Moscow.'

Seguma turned his head to one side. 'How?'

'If you agree to remain in office, we can help you quell the rebellion.'

'With what? My army is poorly equipped, some of my generals cannot be trusted.'

'The British government is ready to back you with the full weight of our Special Forces teams. We're mobilising a squadron from the SAS, plus teams from the SBS and SFSG. They can be on the ground within the next twenty-four hours.'

Mallet said, 'We're talking about almost two hundred soldiers, plus weaponry and vehicles. Those lads will provide an immediate boost to your security forces. With their help, your troops will stand an excellent chance of defeating the enemy in detail.'

'But what happens after your men leave? I will be at the mercy of my own people. What if they take to the streets again?'

'We've discussed this with the Foreign Office. HMG is willing to increase its commitments to Karatandu,' the Voice said.

'It will need a big increase.'

'Which is why we're prepared to treble the current budget. We'll also send in training teams to bring your forces up to scratch, provide them with state-of-the-art weaponry. You'll be at the front of the queue from now on. Whatever you need, you'll get it.'

Seguma tapped his cane against his foot as he mulled the offer. 'It would have been better if you had made such a generous proposal before,' he said. 'None of this would have happened.'

'We're fully aware of that, sir.'

'And why should I believe you? After all these years of broken promises?'

'It's in our mutual interest to fully support you, Mr President. The foreign secretary wishes to make that point very clear. He sincerely hopes for a close relationship between our countries in the future.'

The president waved a hand at the laptop screen. 'If he considers me such a good friend, he can tell me himself.'

'I'm sure he will look forward to doing that, sir. Once this situation with the Russians has been resolved.'

Seguma stared at a spot on the wall. As if he was squinting at a rainbow in the distance and trying to figure out what was at the end of it: a pot of gold, or something a lot less promising.

'You won't lose any of your privileges,' the Voice continued. 'You'll get to keep your overseas properties, your Swiss bank accounts and the rest of it. But we can't let you retire in luxury, sir. Not with the Russians knocking on the door.'

'And if I agree to your proposal? What then?'

'We'll sign off on the deployment of the UKSF teams to Karatandu at once. They'll nip the rebellion in the bud, before the enemy can gain control of the infrastructure. In the meantime, we'll fly you via private jet to Libreville, Gabon. A team of diplomats will be sent over from London. They'll accompany you.'

'I should stay here,' Seguma protested. 'Where it is safer.'

'You can't, sir.'

'Why not?'

'Optics. It's not a good look if you're photographed sitting in a luxury apartment in Monaco, while your own soldiers are busy fighting a rebel army.'

'Yes. Yes, I suppose you're right,' he replied glumly.

'This is the right move, sir. Flying to Gabon will put pressure on the rebels. You'll be a hundred miles across the border from your capital, holding press conferences, issuing statements, projecting an image of strength. It'll boost morale on the ground.'

'I'll need protection.'

'We'll arrange that, sir.'

'General Kakuba will have to be dealt with as well. He has many devoted followers. My regime won't be secure as long as he is free.'

'Of course,' the Voice said.

'This is a good deal,' Mallet said. 'You won't get a better one.'

Seguma didn't reply. He stared at the gold crown on his cane, his face stricken with indecision.

'Mr President, we're running out of time,' the Voice said. 'We need an answer now.'

Seguma raised his eyes to the laptop. He took a deep breath, nodded.

'Very well. I'll go back. But on one condition.'

'What's that, sir?'

'You need to protect my family.'

'Are they in danger?' asked Casey.

'The Russians threatened to kill them if I did not cooperate.'

Webb said, 'Why would they target your family?'

The president stared at him as if he was mad. 'My relatives are some of the most important people in the country. My brother is the vice-president. His wife is the head of the Women's League in Karatandu. My wife is the party secretary. They are my closest allies. The rebels would do anything to get rid of them.'

The Voice said, 'Where are they now?'

'In Karatandu. At my palace in the capital, Marafeni.'

'Who else is there?'

'My children. My newborn son. My nieces. Some of my cabinet ministers. No one else.'

'What are they doing there?'

'It's the only safe place in the city. They've been holed up there for the past few days, making radio broadcasts denouncing the protestors, running the country in my absence.'

'Why didn't they leave with you, sir?' asked Bowman.

'I couldn't take the risk. I needed to keep them in place while I met with the Russians. Otherwise my enemies might have realised what was going on with my plans.' He rubbed his brow. 'You must protect them.'

'The Russians would want them out of the picture, that's for sure,' Mallet agreed. 'The army would throw in the towel double-quick.'

'There's another reason they would be interested in my family,' Seguma said quietly.

'Aye? What's that?'

Seguma looked down at the cane on his lap. 'Some of my relatives, they know my secrets. The Russians might put them on trial. They could use them to spread lies and discredit me.'

He spoke in a cold, impersonal tone. Bowman had the impression the president seemed more interested in his political credibility than the welfare of his loved ones.

'You must protect my family,' Seguma said. He lifted his eyes to the laptop. 'That is non-negotiable. I will not return to my country unless you can guarantee their safety.'

He leaned back, his arms folded across his ample chest. The Voice was silent for so long Bowman thought the connection had been lost. Then it spoke up in its train-station-announcement tone.

'Mr Seguma is correct. The security of his family is of paramount importance. Their capture, or worse, would represent a major victory for General Kakuba and his Russian backers. We cannot allow that to happen.' There was another pause. 'There's only one thing for it.'

'What's that?' asked Mallet.

'You're going to have to get over to Karatandu,' the Voice said. 'Locate the president's family and protect them at all costs. Before the Russians get to them first.'

Seventeen

The four members of the Cell looked round at one another. No one said anything for what felt like a long while but in reality was no more than five or six seconds.

Casey broke the silence. 'Why us?' she asked.

'Because there's no one else,' the Voice replied.

'What about those other SF teams? The ones going in to sort out the rebellion?'

'The SAS squadron is currently on an operation in Libya. That's D Squadron. Those fellows have got to get back to base, refit, get a full briefing and then fly down to Karatandu. That will take time. Twenty hours or so.'

'And the other units? SFSG, SBS?'

'They're scheduled to fly down from their respective bases in the UK and link up with D Squadron in Libya. We're expecting both teams to arrive in Tripoli shortly before midnight. They'll depart at one o'clock in the morning, local time. Libya is an hour ahead of Karatandu. Flight time is a little under six hours. Which means the combined SF force won't land in Karatandu until tomorrow morning. By that time, it might be too late. The coup might already have been triggered.'

'Besides,' Mallet added, 'when those lads do come in, they'll have their hands full stamping out the resistance. They won't have time to safeguard the family.'

'So it's down to us,' Webb said. 'Is that it?'

'More or less,' the Voice replied.

'And how are we supposed to get to Karatandu faster than D Squadron?'

'We're preparing a diplomatic jet for Mr Seguma for his flight to Libreville. Courtesy of our friends at the CIA. The jet is due to land at RAF Northolt shortly before heading down to Nice. You'll take the jet and accompany the president as far as Libreville. We'll arrange a connecting flight to take you from there to Karatandu. Once you're on the ground, it's a forty-minute drive to the palace. Should get you into the capital for around midnight. Six hours earlier than the other units.'

Bowman said, 'What's the plan once we get to the family?'

'You'll be the tip of the spear. The advance party. You'll locate Mr Seguma's loved ones, secure the perimeter and wait until the main strike force arrives to secure the country and snuff out the rebel forces.'

Bowman considered. 'It could go badly wrong. What if the coup kicks off before the other lads arrive?'

'It won't,' the Voice said. 'You'll have time.'

'Easy for you lot to say. You're not the ones putting your necks on the line.'

There was a long sigh before the Voice replied, 'Our analysts think the coup is unlikely to happen until first light. Which is around five thirty in the morning in Karatandu.'

'Sounds about right,' Mallet remarked. 'Standard military doctrine. First light and last light are the best times to mount an assault. If the Russians are launching the takeover tomorrow, it'll be at the crack of dawn. I'd bet my house on it. We won't be exposed for long before the strike force arrives.'

'If the timings are right,' said Bowman. 'If they're not, we'll be out on our arses.'

Mallet said, 'The KUF won't go for the palace first. General Kakuba and his men will want to establish a foothold in the country before they turn their sights on the family. By that time, the lads from D Squadron, SFSG and the SBS will be on the ground.'

'It's not just the KUF,' said Bowman. 'It might be some other group of rebels joining the fight. Or a gang of protestors looking to storm the palace.'

'Possibly,' the Voice interjected. 'But we're talking about a handful of poorly armed locals, at best. Surely you guys can handle that. You're elite soldiers.'

'We can take care of it, ma'am,' Mallet agreed. 'Should be a bread-and-butter job. Right, guys?' he added, his cold eyes glancing round the table.

Casey said, 'Why don't we escort the family across the border? That's got to be less risky than staying put in the capital while we wait for the cavalry to show up.'

'My family cannot leave.' Seguma tapped a finger against the table to emphasise his point. 'They must have a presence in the country. If they flee, it will look bad for me. My people will think I'm a coward.'

'They've got the radio transmitter at the palace too,' Mallet reminded them. 'They'll need to keep broadcasting messages to the army and the police. Boost morale.'

'There's no time to argue the merits of the mission,' the Voice said. 'You have your orders. The family must be protected, no matter what.'

'We're assuming they can hold out at the palace until we arrive,' Webb pointed out.

Bowman said, 'Patrick has got a point. Those protests in the streets are turning ugly. How do we know the mobs won't overrun the palace in the meantime?'

Mallet looked round at Seguma. 'Are there any guards with your family, sir? Anyone who's capable with a gun?'

'Some, yes,' Seguma replied. 'From the Presidential Guard. My best men.'

'How many guys are we talking about, sir?'

'Forty, perhaps more. I'm not sure. My chief security adviser is there. You could check with him. His name is Mr Gregory.'

Bowman stared at him in surprise. 'Mike is with your family?'

'Yes. You know him?'

'Mike was my old commanding officer in the Regiment. He's a top-class bloke. All the guys at Hereford respected him.'

A gleaming smile crawled like a colony of ants across the president's face. 'I couldn't agree more.'

Bowman recalled the photograph he'd seen pinned to the board in the Shed. The sun-blasted face, the wild hair and bushy beard. He remembered, too, how Gregory had stepped in to stop him from being RTU'd on Selection. The drunken fight outside the pub. The flashing lights from the police car. The night he'd spent in the cell. There had been no reason for Gregory to intervene. But he had argued Bowman's case anyway. Saved his career. Because it had been the right thing to do. Bowman had looked up to him during his time in B Squadron. Admired him. Gregory had almost been like a father figure, looking out for Bowman during those difficult early days in the Regiment.

'Does Mike know about this deal with the Russians?' asked Mallet.

Seguma shook his head. 'Lang told me not to mention it to anyone else. My mistake. If I had sought Mr Gregory's advice, I am sure he would have argued against it.'

'We can trust him, then?'

'Without question.' Something hard glinted behind the president's eyes. 'Mr Gregory would never betray me. Unlike some.'

He gazed through the floor-to-ceiling windows at Lang, scowling.

'Can we rely on him to hold the fort until we get there?' asked Casey.

'Mike is as tough as they come,' Bowman said. 'He used to come out on patrols with us in Iraq and Afghanistan. A lot of Ruperts would have hung back in the safety of the ops room, but not Mike.'

Casey stared at him. 'You really rate this guy, don't you?'

'I'm just telling you what he's like.' He nodded at Seguma. 'You don't have to worry, sir. Your family will be safe until we get there. Mike is a top soldier.'

'You don't need to remind me of his qualities.' The corners of his mouth curved upwards. 'Mr Gregory has been very loyal to me over the years. He has proved himself many times.'

'Those extra bodies from the Presidential Guard will even things up a bit,' Mallet said.

'Agreed,' said the Voice. 'Between yourselves, Mike Gregory and the Presidential Guard, you should have enough firepower to defend against anyone who might take a pop at you. More than enough.'

'We're going in half-cocked,' Bowman said. 'That's never a good idea.'

The Voice said, 'We're not asking you to go in and save the country. All you've got to do is secure the family and wait for the strike force to arrive. How hard can it be?'

Bowman clenched his jaws but said nothing.

'Someone should reach out to Gregory,' Casey said. 'Find out what's going on at the palace, how secure it is, how many men are there.'

Mallet nodded. 'First rule of reconnaissance. Get a report from the man on the ground.'

'Or a woman. We're not living in the eighteenth century anymore, John. In case you hadn't noticed.'

The Scot smiled condescendingly. 'Is that what passes for a sense of humour in Surrey these days?'

'Our team will contact Mike,' the Voice said in its artificial automated tone. 'Leave it with us.'

Bowman said, 'We'll need hardware as well. Longs, pistols, grenades, plate armour. The full package. If you want us to hold the palace, we're gonna need to be tooled up to the eyeballs.'

'Consider it done.'

'What are we going to do with Lang?' Webb said, glancing from the laptop to the balcony. 'You can't expect us to bring him with us to Karatandu.'

'Our team will make alternative arrangements for his return to London. I'll discuss that with John after this call. Then you need to get moving. Make your way across the border and head for the private terminal at Nice. We'll send you an update as soon as the diplomatic jet is on its way.'

'Any questions, guys?' asked Mallet.

No one spoke.

'As of this minute, rescuing Mr Seguma's family is our top priority,' the Voice said. 'I cannot stress that enough. If we lose the family, we lose the country. Do not fail.'

The line dropped. Bowman listened to dead air for a few moments. Then Mallet slid the laptop back into the sleeve, dug out his phone and pushed up from his chair.

'Wait here,' he said. 'I'll get on the blower with Six. Discuss Davey Boy's deal.'

'This isn't right,' Bowman said. 'We shouldn't be letting Lang off the hook. He's a traitor.'

Mallet shot him a savage glare. 'If I want your opinion on how to handle the interrogation, I'll let you know. Until then, keep your fucking thoughts to yourself. Got it?'

Bowman began to argue, then thought better of it. 'Fine,' he replied sourly.

'Good,' Mallet straightened. 'Right, you lot. We're on the road as soon as I get off the phone. You. Smart-arse. Send a message to Tiny,' he ordered Casey. 'Tell him to bring the car round and find somewhere to park near the entrance. We'll be out in a few minutes.'

Webb said, 'What about the heavy? We can't leave him here.'

'He's coming with us,' Mallet said. 'We'll deliver him to the UKN waiting for us en route to the airport.'

'Why don't we just clip the guy?'

'Can't. Five wants to question him in relation to several unsolved gangland murders.' A thought occurred to him. 'We'll get rid of the hardware and the kit at the RV, too.'

'It'll be a tight squeeze. Seven of us in the wagon.'

'The big bastard goes in the boot. No other way.'

Mallet stomped over to the balcony door and wrenched it open. Lang shot up from his chair. The faint drone of city noise drifted up from the streets far below.

'Inside,' Mallet ordered him.

Lang slid past him and stepped back into the living room. He glanced at Seguma, then slid his gaze across to Mallet. 'What's the news with my deal? It's taking fucking ages.'

'I'm discussing it with Six now. They're about to sign off on it.' He smiled thinly.

'Then what?'

'You'll travel with the rest of us to the airport. Some other poor sod will escort you back to London. Now wait here like a good boy.'

Mallet looked over at Webb, his face scrunched in thought. 'You'll have to change out of those clothes. Grab some of Lang's gear. Whatever you can find that broadly fits. Where's your courier kit?' he asked Bowman.

'Lang's closet.'

'Grab it. The document wallet too. Make sure we leave nothing behind. Not a trace, do you hear? I want everything removed, right down to the last skin cell.'

'Why? What's the big deal?'

Mallet didn't answer. His phone hummed. He stepped outside, pulled the balcony door shut and leaned against the railing as he took the call. Bowman and Webb left Casey on guard duty and darted out of the living room. They jogged over to the master bedroom, ducked into the walk-in closet. Webb changed out of his courier kit and threw on a striped shirt, cream jacket and a baseball cap with the crest of an East London football team on the front. Bowman stuffed their discarded gear into a Herschel holdall, trotted back down to the hall, snatched up the document wallet from the side table and shoved it into the same bag. He dumped the

Herschel by the door. Rushed over to the staff quarters, dragged Roidhead to his feet. Hustled the guy into the living room.

Moments later, Mallet stepped back through the balcony door. Lang stood up, straight-backed, like a defendant at a murder trial, waiting for the judge's verdict.

'Good news,' Mallet said. 'Your worries are over, Davey. All is forgiven. The deal has just been signed off. You're going into police protection.'

'About time. Now how about getting rid of these cuffs? They're killing me.'

Mallet nodded at Webb. 'Do the honours, Patrick.'

Webb left the room. He came back a few moments later clutching a pair of scissors and cut through Lang's cable ties. Lang rubbed his sore wrists and grinned at the soldier.

'Cheers, son.'

Webb glared at him.

'Don't say much, do you?'

Webb made no reply. He stared at Lang with barely concealed contempt. Lang stepped closer to him.

'You should watch yourself, sunshine. I might start to think you don't like me. I knew another feller once who didn't like me. Know what happened to him?'

Webb still said nothing. Lang took a forefinger and slowly traced a line across his neck, as if slashing it open with an imaginary knife. Then he took a step back and smiled. 'I'm just joking, you daft prick.'

Mallet said, 'Step outside with me for a moment, Davey.'

'Why?' Lang asked.

'Our friends at Six are sending a team to pick you up. They want to discuss your return to London. They've got a few questions.'

Lang swaggered confidently outside, a renewed spring to his step. Mallet beckoned him over and rested against the stainless-steel railing as he dialled a number. Lang waited while Mallet uttered a few words to the person on the other end of the line. Then Mallet said to the caller, 'OK.'

He hung up. Tucked his phone into his back jeans pocket. Lang frowned.

'What the—'

Then Mallet pushed him over the edge.

Lang screamed and fell backwards. He seemed frozen in mid-air for a split second, arms flailing, mouth open in horror, before he plummeted from view.

From below came the dull thump of a human body pancaking against metal.

A car alarm shrieked.

Bowman raced over to the balcony. He leaned over the edge and peered down at the side street below. Lang had crash-landed on top of a Porsche Cayenne parked at the roadside. His twisted body was slumped across the bonnet, arms and legs bent at unnatural angles.

'Jesus.' Bowman stared disbelievingly at Mallet. 'Jesus Christ.'

Mallet grinned wickedly. 'You didn't think Six would let that bastard get away with it, did you?'

A sudden chill ran through Bowman. *Did Six plan to kill Lang all along?*

Did Mallet lie to us?

He glanced briefly down at the street. Figures appeared on the balconies of the surrounding apartment blocks, rubbernecking the scene. A cyclist leaped off his bike and raced over to Lang, shouting at a middle-aged guy in a suit to call an ambulance. Several metres further away, an old man with a shopping bag stared up at the apartment block. And pointed.

'Move,' Mallet snapped. 'We're getting the fuck out of Dodge.'

Bowman pushed away from the railing and hurried inside. Casey and Webb both stared at the Cell leader with blank, neutral expressions. Neither of them seemed particularly surprised by the killing. Seguma stared out at the terrace, his face stamped with shock and fear.

'Sir, we're leaving,' Mallet said. 'Now.'

The president quickly cleared his expression. 'Yes, OK.' He spread his lips into a pitiless smile. 'I never really trusted that worthless dog anyway.'

'Grab the heavy,' Mallet said to Bowman. 'Let's go.'

Bowman took hold of Roidhead and shoved him roughly towards the front door. The team hastened down the hallway and squeezed into the private lift. Roidhead started bricking it as they rode the car down to the underground car park. Which was unsurprising. He had just seen his boss nosedive to his death. He was in the presence of stone-cold killers. People who spoke his own language, but with far more skill and ruthlessness. He pleaded in a small, panicked voice as Bowman marched the guy over to the Range Rover and sprang the boot. The rest of the team piled inside the vehicle as Bowman pressed the Ruger against the heavy's stomach.

'Get in,' he said in a low voice.

'Don't kill me. Please. I'll talk.'

'You're definitely gonna talk,' Bowman said. 'There's some people in London who are very interested in finding out what you know. Now get in.'

He rammed the gun harder against Roidhead, the metal tip digging into his ribs. Roidhead climbed awkwardly inside the void, rolling onto his side and bringing his legs up, his knees tucked against his chest. Bowman slammed the boot shut then jogged round to the driver's side door and scooched behind the wheel. Seguma sat hunch-shouldered in the back seat between Casey and Webb.

'Dump the guns in the bag,' Mallet said.

Bowman and Webb slid the clips out of their Rugers and then pulled back the sliders, checking the chambers. They dropped the pistols, holsters and magazines into the Herschel. Mallet stashed the bag in the footwell.

'Get us out of here,' he said.

They climbed the exit ramp and swung right. Loader had parked the Mercedes E-Class forty metres further along, in a loading bay in front of a post office. Bowman pulled up in front of the estate, kept the engine ticking over. Casey and Webb jumped out, ran over to the E-Class and hopped inside. Then both vehicles took off again. The Range Rover in the lead, Loader immediately to the rear, a two-vehicle convoy. A swift manoeuvre, taking no more than three or four seconds. And also necessary. Five guys crammed together in a single car would look suspicious. They might catch the eye of an overenthusiastic police officer. Too risky, especially with a thug in the boot and guns in a bag. Safer to spread the team out between the two motors.

Beyond the central reservation, on the other side of the road, an ambulance screamed past the late-morning traffic, sirens flashing. Two police cars raced after the ambo. Bowman caught sight of them in the rear-view as they hit the gap in the central reservation. They crossed over into the opposite lane, screeched to a halt in front of the apartment block. A small crowd had formed in the street outside.

'Stick to the limit,' Mallet said. 'And for fuck's sake don't run any lights.'

Bowman kept the speed below thirty miles per hour as he made for the border. For the entire journey he was the world's most diligent driver. He stopped at every set of lights, obeyed every line of the local highway code. Seguma sat silently in the back, his cane resting on his lap. Mallet punched a set of coordinates into the satnav. The RV point with the UKN. A lay-by, en route to the airport.

There was no border crossing. They simply followed the road signs pointing to Nice, steered into a one-way tunnel bored into a sheer rock wall, and when they came out the other side they were back on French soil. Sixteen miles from the airport, according to the satnav. A forty-minute drive through winding coastal roads and city traffic. Which meant they would arrive at the private terminal building shortly before noon.

Bowman stuck to the cliff road as it snaked around the mountainside, roughly parallel to the coastline. Loader, Casey and Webb tailed close behind in the E-Class. Several minutes later, Mallet's phone vibrated with an incoming message. He scrolled through a long message, hit Delete, put his phone away.

'Any word on that jet?' Bowman asked.

'It just landed at Northolt. There's going to be a short turnaround before it can take off again. They need to refuel the jet, procure our weaponry and kit, ferry the diplomats over.'

'How long before it gets here?'

'Three hours or so, Six reckons. We should be in the air by three o'clock at the latest.'

Bowman glanced at the digital clock: 11.26. The jet would land in Nice soon after two o'clock. There would be another brief turnaround before they took off again. Then a seven-hour flight to Libreville, followed by a sixty-minute connection to the only international airport in Karatandu. Both countries were in the same time zone as France, he knew. They would touch down in Karatandu at around 23.00.

'What's the word on the coup?' he asked.

'No news. It's all quiet at the moment.'

'Not for much longer.'

'No.'

Bowman gripped the wheel tightly. 'Let's hope this thing doesn't kick off before we land. I've had enough nasty surprises for one day.'

Mallet stared at him with narrowed eyes. 'Have you got a problem?'

'I thought we were going in to arrest Lang, not chuck him off a balcony.'

'The plan changed.'

'Is that really what happened?'

'Don't get shirty with me, lad. The decision was down to Six. We were following orders. There's nothing more to it than that.'

'I just want to know what's going on.'

'You're part of the Cell now. This is how we work. You've got to stay fluid. React to situations as they happen. Things can change very quickly in our line of work.'

Bowman glanced sidelong at him. 'The other guys didn't look too surprised to me.'

'They've been on the Cell for a while. They know the score. You don't fight criminals with kid gloves.'

'Still, you could have warned us before you threw Lang over the balcony.'

Mallet made a face. 'Christ, don't tell me you feel sorry for the bastard.'

'I couldn't give a crap about Lang,' Bowman said. 'I'm talking about the watch he was wearing. That was worth half a million quid, John.'

Mallet chuckled. 'I'll buy you a fake Rolex when we get back home. Call it even.'

They drove on. After a couple of miles, Mallet pointed to a rest stop at the roadside. Which was really just a patch of worn blacktop with an overflowing bin and a chicken-wire fence, bookended by tufts of dense vegetation. Beyond the fence, the ground sloped sharply away towards the glittering sea. A grey Volvo XC90 SUV was parked up on the far side of the lay-by. Bowman looked round but saw no other motors or people in the area.

'Pull over,' Mallet said.

Bowman pointed the Range Rover into the lay-by and skid-halted to the rear of the XC90. Loader pulled up a couple of metres behind, loose gravel crunching beneath the tyres. Bowman cut the engine.

Mallet said, 'Everyone out.'

Boots thudded on the worn blacktop as the three men got out. They waited while a familiar face debussed from the XC90. Bowman recognised him immediately. The guy with the terrible comb-over. The UKN they had met in the underground car park.

He lumbered over to the wagon, handed Mallet a set of keys.

'I was told to expect a live package,' he said.

'He's in the boot,' Mallet said back.

'Hardware?'

'Holdall in the front passenger footwell. Everything's inside.'

'Anything I need to worry about?'

'The guns haven't been fired. Nothing to link to any crime.'

'The wagon?'

'It's hot. You'll need to dispose of it.'

'Keys?'

'Inside.'

They swapped cars. Comb-over plodded over to the Range Rover and squeezed himself behind the wheel. Bowman, Mallet and Seguma took the Volvo. The president spread himself on the back seat, the soldiers sat upfront. Mallet tapped icons on the built-in satnav, entering the address for the airport. The Range Rover pulled away from the lay-by and motored west. Bowman waited until it was out of sight around the bend. Then he steered onto the mountain road, Loader and Webb and Casey shadowing them in the E-Class.

The satnav told him they were eleven miles from the airport. Twenty-three minutes away. Arrival time, 11.58. Bowman gripped the wheel tightly and clenched his jaw.

Eleven hours from now, we'll be landing in Karatandu, he thought. *And God knows what's waiting for us when we get there.*

Eighteen

Mallet spent the rest of the journey firing off messages and glancing at his phone screen, checking for further updates from Six. Bowman kept his gaze fixed on the road, barely able to keep his eyes open. He was knackered. He hadn't slept in more than twenty-four hours. The adrenaline he'd felt during the arrest had worn off. And now he was going to get on a plane and fly to a country on the brink of chaos, to protect the relatives of a despised tyrant. Every so often he glanced at Seguma in the back seat. The guy looked pensive. Three hours ago, he had been on the brink of losing his presidency. Now he was back in the game. The biggest gamble of his life. Like a guy at a roulette table, staking everything he owned on red. He could win big, or lose bigger, but the result was out of his control.

The convoy joined the slow crawl of traffic at the airport and hit the private terminal a few minutes before noon. Bowman swung round to the front of the terminal and stopped in front of the canopied entrance. Mallet and Seguma piled out and joined Casey and Webb at the side of the E-Class. The soldiers grabbed their luggage and escorted Seguma through the sliding doors to the reception. Then Bowman circled round to the complimentary parking bay and guided the Volvo into the nearest space. Loader went through the same manoeuvre with the E-Class, they gave the vehicles a once-over to make sure they had left nothing inside. Locked them. Then strolled into the terminal.

Bowman and Loader found the others waiting to one side of the reception area. Then Mallet led the group over to the main desk. A rose-cheeked blonde woman in a tight-fitting white blouse greeted them with a polite smile and immaculate English. Mallet handed over their passports, told her the tail number of the jet coming over to pick them up. Loader gave the receptionist a long admiring look as she glanced cursorily through the documents. She handed the passports back, wished them a safe trip and directed the team down a marble-floored corridor towards the private lounge.

'Really, Tiny?' Casey said as they walked away. 'Do you think about nothing else?'

'What's wrong? No harm in doing a bit of window shopping.'

'That's all you're doing,' Mallet said. 'There are monks who have had more action than you.'

'That's not true. I was a legend at Hereford. Ask any of the lads. The women couldn't get enough of me.'

'That's not how I remember it. I seem to remember the groupies running out of the pub to avoid your ugly mug.'

'Piss off, John.'

'Tiny, we all know you secretly love your wife,' said Casey, a trace of sympathy in her voice. 'You don't have to pretend to be God's gift to women.'

'No one's buying it, anyway,' Mallet said. 'They're more likely to believe in the fairy godmother than Tiny's powers of attraction.'

The team filed into the private lounge. Ten seconds later, Mallet's mobile rang. He wandered over to the kitchen area on the far side of the lounge and spoke to Six for several minutes. The voice on the other end appeared to have a lot to say. Mallet listened and said little except occasional one-word replies. *Yes. No. OK.* He hung up, marched back over and cleared his throat.

'The diplomats are heading to Northolt right now,' he said. 'The jet's due to leave in thirty minutes. Which means it'll get here for around two thirty. We'll take off at three o'clock.'

'What's the itinerary?' asked Casey.

'We'll fly direct to Libreville. Once we land, we'll transfer to another aircraft and head straight to Karatandu. An hour-long flight. We're scheduled to land at the main airport outside the capital at around eleven o'clock. From there it's a direct run to the palace.'

'What about me?' Seguma said, his mock-English aristocrat voice burning with indignation. 'I have been told nothing about my arrangements.'

Mallet said, 'A team from the Gabonese special forces will meet you on the ground in Libreville, sir. They'll escort you and the guys from the Foreign Office to a secure location. You'll wait there until it's safe to return.'

'And who gets to decide when it is safe, exactly? You cannot expect me to go back while there are still rebels running amok on the ground.'

'That's for you to discuss with the Foreign Office. Nothing to do with us.'

Bowman said, 'We need someone who can get us to the palace. Someone who knows all the army checkpoints and hotspots.'

'Six agrees,' Mallet replied. 'There's a military garrison at the airport. They'll accompany us to the palace.'

'What's the score with D Squadron?'

'They're returning to their camp now. Three Hercs are being prepared.'

'And the other SF units?'

'SFSG is due to fly out of their base in St Athan in a few hours. The SBS detachment will leave Poole at around the same time. They'll fly straight down to Libya and link up with D Squadron. Then the combined strike force will head on to the capital, Marafeni. Should get in at six o'clock tomorrow morning. Six hours after we land.'

Bowman pressed his lips together in a tight line. 'The timing is tight, John.'

'That's assuming the Russians are on schedule,' Mallet said. 'Right now, we've got those bastards on the back foot. They'll be wondering why the deal Lang brokered has collapsed at the last minute. They'll hear about his suicide and ask themselves what it means. It'll mess with their planning.'

'Or the opposite,' Bowman said. 'They might accelerate the coup.'

'I doubt it. They won't want to rush this thing. Too risky.'

'And if you're wrong?'

'I'm Scottish. We're always right. Part of our DNA,' said Mallet. 'Proving you English bastards wrong.' He chucked a stick of nicotine gum into his mouth. 'Worst-case scenario, we might have to hold out for a few hours before the cavalry shows up.'

'Has Six reached out to Mike yet?'

'They're liaising with him now.'

'And?'

'He's confirmed that the family is currently at the palace. We've given him orders. No one is to move until we get there.'

Seguma stared apprehensively at him. 'Is there trouble?'

'Nothing too serious, sir. Just a few protestors.'

'I see.' He stared anxiously out of the window at the tarmac. *He doesn't look thrilled to be returning home*, thought Bowman.

'Don't worry,' he said. 'As long as Mike is with your family, they'll be safe. He won't let you down, sir.'

'How many guards has Mike got with him?' asked Loader.

'About forty. Plus our gang, and Mike, that will give us forty-six bodies.'

Casey said, 'We should be checking all the social media accounts in Karatandu. Someone might post a picture or a message about gunfire they've heard, helicopters or aircraft coming in. Give us an early warning of trouble.'

'I'll get Six on it,' Mallet said.

'Tell them to check the local airline traffic, too. Look for any non-commercial planes coming in from Russia. Any planes circling over an area and turning back round again. That way we'll pick up any teams deploying via HALO.'

'Unless they're already on the ground,' said Bowman.

Mallet's phone trilled. He nodded at Casey. 'Get the laptop out. There's a packet of information coming through from Six. We'll go through everything in a few minutes.'

He moved away. Seguma flicked through a glossy magazine on wealth management. Webb sat and practised the art of silence. Casey worked on the laptop, her fingers moving across the keyboard at lightning speed. Bowman made coffee. Loader switched on the TV and flipped over to one of the 24-hour news networks. A French station, with English subtitles. There was nothing yet about a *coup d'état* in Karatandu, just two short segments about the continuing violence tacked on to the end of the main bulletins.

Mallet finished his call, the team gathered around the coffee table on the other side of the lounge from Seguma. They spent the next two hours running through the plan.

They studied satellite images of the palace and the surrounding neighbourhood, blueprints, the main routes to and from the building. Ideal firing positions, likely points of attack. Then they looked at the wider picture: the locations of the nearest embassies, crossing points to neighbouring countries if the shit hit the fan. Everything. They wouldn't have time to prepare later on. Once they landed in Karatandu, they were going to hit the ground running. Hard and fast. The Regiment way. Every so often Mallet got up and left to speak with their liaison officer at Six. He was getting a near-constant stream of updates on the status of the diplomatic jets and the UKSF teams, the military escort waiting for them in Marafeni.

'Jet's half an hour out,' Mallet said as he walked back over to the team.

Bowman frowned at the satellite pictures on the laptop. 'This is a tough ask,' he said.

'That's what Tiny's missus thinks, every time he's desperate for a shag,' Mallet joked.

Bowman didn't laugh. 'There's a lot of things that could go wrong.'

'It's a routine job. Get in, secure the stronghold, wait for the main force to show up and do the business, then get the fuck out again. Nothing we haven't done a hundred times before in the Regiment.'

'It's not that easy. If it goes right, great. We're heroes. But if we get caught out, it's going to go very bad.'

'Stop worrying, Josh,' Loader said. 'We're not expecting a scrap.'

'But we should be planning for one. If the rebels come at us in force, we'll get clobbered.'

'We've got those presidential guards to back us up. We'll have a small army to repel any attackers. Forty soldiers.'

'I've trained some of these teams before, Tiny.' He glanced across the lounge at Seguma and kept his voice low. 'They're honest troops, and brave, but they're nothing to write home about. We can't rely on them in a firefight.'

Loader gave him a look. 'Are you getting a bit twitchy?'

'I'm just trying to work out what the plan is if things go wrong.'

Mallet sighed deeply. 'The rebels won't hit us hard. Even if they launch the coup earlier than we think, General Kakuba and his men are going to be focused on securing the critical infrastructure first. The family won't be at the top of their list.'

'Karatandu is a small country,' Bowman pointed out. 'The size of Wales.'

'Aye. What's your point?'

'It won't take the KUF long to capture the key targets. Sooner or later, they're going to target the family.'

'But by then, the main strike force will have landed in-country. The worst that can happen is that we'll come under attack by a few opportunists who couldn't hit a barn door at fifty metres.'

'And if the rebels decide to come for the palace first?'

'That's a risk we'll have to take,' Mallet said.

'Maybe you'd prefer to sit this one out, Josh,' Loader said.

Bowman glared at him and set his jaw. 'I never said that, mate. I'm up for the job as much as anyone. I just want to make sure it's done right.'

Mallet's cold gaze centred on Casey. 'What about you, Alex?'

'What about me?'

'You've been as quiet as Patrick for the past hour. Usually we can't get you to shut up. Are you sure you're up for this?'

Casey folded her arms. 'Why wouldn't I be? Because I'm a woman?'

Mallet held up his hands in mock surrender. 'It's got nothing to do with that, and we both know it. I'm just asking.'

'What are you trying to get at, John?'

Mallet scratched the back of his neck and shifted. 'Look, everyone in the Cell rates you highly. You're smarter than the rest of us put together, you're skilled with the old cyber, brilliant at the tech and all that. But your books and gadgets won't come in much use where we're going.'

'You've never had a problem with me going on ops before.'

'This is different. There's a small chance this thing could turn very ugly, very fast.'

'I can take care of myself.'

'No one's suggesting otherwise. But if you've got doubts, you need to tell us. We can't be taking passengers, lass, not on this job. No one will think any less of you if you decide to stay behind.'

Casey took a breath and stared hard at Mallet.

'I've been trained in the same type of warfare as you,' she said. 'I might not have passed SAS Selection, but I've done the SRR course, which is the next best thing. I was the best shot in my training group, I've done surveillance work in war zones and I know how to fight. I'll be fine. And I'm not your bloody lass.'

Bowman glanced at the footage of the riots on the TV and gritted his teeth.

'Let's just hope the timing on this op goes like clockwork,' he said. 'Otherwise, we're all going to be in the shit.'

* * *

The Gulfstream landed at Nice at two thirty on the dot. Ten minutes later, a pair of diplomats strode briskly into the lounge. A man in his forties, six foot five, slightly stooped, with a bird's nest of thinning brown hair. A much shorter woman with button-round green eyes and a mole on her dimpled chin. They carried themselves with the typical Whitehall mix of arrogance and insecurity. The kind of people who spent their days at the bureaucratic coalface debating obscure policy points, plotting and stabbing one another in the back.

The diplomats introduced themselves to Mallet, then took Seguma to one side. The guy with the bird's nest hair sat with his knees crossed, gesticulating, talking animatedly, while the woman with the dimpled chin handed over documents for the president to read. It was clear that they were calling the shots. *This is how it's going to work*, they seemed to be saying. Seguma stayed tight-lipped throughout. He wasn't in any position to argue. A few hours ago his closest adviser had been thrown to his death. The people he was dealing with were deadly serious. He wasn't about to haggle over the small print.

Then a smartly dressed official entered the lounge and announced that the jet was ready to depart. He led the party through the gate towards a waiting Renault minivan. They clambered inside with their bags, the Renault bowled across the skidmarked tarmac stand to a Gulfstream G650. One of the long-range jets. Capable of making the short hop from Northolt to Nice, and then on to Gabon without stopping to refuel.

They boarded and stowed their bags in the aft luggage compartment. Dimpled Chin and Bird's Nest sat upfront with Seguma.

The soldiers made themselves comfortable in the rear section of the cabin. The flight attendant was male, to Loader's obvious disappointment.

As the Gulfstream taxied across to the runway, Bowman was gripped by a growing sense of unease. They were heading into the unknown, he realised. Any number of things could go wrong. But he felt something else, too. A renewed sense of determination.

Mike Gregory had saved his career once. He'd helped Bowman to turn his life around. Took him under his wing when he'd first joined the Regiment. Now, after all these years, Bowman had the chance to return the favour.

I owe the guy, Bowman reminded himself. I'm not going to let him down. I'll do whatever it takes to rescue him.

I just pray we're not too late.

Nineteen

They spent the first hour of the flight sorting out their kit. Six had supplied them with several bags filled with weapons and equipment. Bowman and Webb changed back into the civvies they had stashed in their holdalls, then joined the others at the rear of the aircraft as they dished out the hardware. They would carry Colt Canada C8 rifles as their primary weapons, fitted with suppressors and scopes with mini red-dot sights, plus four spare thirty-round magazines apiece. Including the clip in the weapon, each member of the team had 150 rounds of 5.56 × 45 mm NATO brass. They had Glock 17 pistols as their secondary weapons, with two seventeen-round mags per person, body plate armour and webbing, military radios, a rucksack filled with first aid kits and bottles of water, ballistic helmets, two thousand dollars of bribery money in small denominations. The rest of the kit was stowed in the cargo hold, Mallet had said. The heavy firepower. Two belt-fed L7 GPMG 'Gimpy' machine guns. A Barrett .50 calibre sniper rifle in a pelican case, complete with clip-on telescopic sights, deadly at a range of up to two thousand yards and capable of punching through brickwork. An Accuracy International AWC sniper rifle in a weapon sleeve. Claymore anti-personnel mines. An M224 60 mm lightweight mortar. Frag grenades, smoke grenades, boxes of ammunition: 7.62 mm belt for the Gimpys, shells for the mortar.

The team went through the usual pre-op checks. They filled the spare magazines with ammunition, packed them into the pouches on the front of their webbing. They tested the radios. Checked their vest armour. Stripped their weapons back, inspected the moving parts, put them back together. Basic stuff. But essential. Missions had been known to fail because of faulty kit.

In the front cabin, Bird's Nest and Dimpled Chin went through a long checklist with President Seguma. They discussed the statements he would make to the world's media during the rebellion, his victory speech once he had returned to power. Seguma listened while gorging on a slap-up meal and double measures of Scotch. He appeared to have regained some of his old arrogance. Between mouthfuls of food, he described in gory detail what he would do to his enemies after the coup had been crushed. People would be thrown to crocodiles or buried alive. The diplomats smiled obsequiously. They were pushing the boat out. Indulging him. Pandering to the tyrant's every whim.

'Can you believe this bloke?' Loader muttered softly as he slid a spare magazine into one of his webbing pouches. 'We're bending over backwards to help him crush this rebellion, and all he's interested in is butchering people.'

Bowman shrugged. 'They don't call him the Viper for nothing.'

'It's immoral. He was prepared to turn his back on us, and now we're treating him like royalty.'

'London has got to keep him sweet, mate. If he had agreed to the deal with the Russians, we'd lose everything in Karatandu. The cobalt, all our commercial interests and training facilities. The lot. They'd do anything to stop that from happening.'

'Doesn't make it right,' Loader said.

Mallet overheard them and said, 'We're soldiers. We're not paid to have an opinion. Even your short Welsh arse should understand that.'

'I'm just saying, John.'

'Well, don't. Six has given us a job to do. We're doing it. End of.'

The Cell leader marched aft to consult with Webb. Casey kept her gaze fixed on the president at the far end of the cabin as he finished his Scotch and yelled at the attendant for a refill.

'He doesn't seem too concerned about his family,' she observed softly.

Bowman laughed. 'That guy doesn't care about anyone other than himself. He'd throw his family under a bus if it benefited him.'

'Why ask us to protect them, then?' said Loader.

'The only reason Seguma wants them safe and sound is because they know all the skeletons in his closet. If they're captured, it'll all spill out. His relatives have been dipping their hands in the till for years. They're just as corrupt as him.'

Casey said, 'If you feel that strongly, why did you agree to come along?'

'I'm only here because of Mike,' said Bowman in an undertone. 'He was one of the best officers they've ever had at Hereford.'

'You've had better luck than me, then,' Loader scoffed. 'Most of my officers were bleeding idiots.'

'Mike's a friend. He's in trouble, and he needs our help. That's all I care about.'

Loader finished packing the mags into his webbing, then moved over to the luggage compartment to check on the rest of his kit. Casey remained quiet for several moments as she reassembled her Glock pistol. When she was sure they were alone, she said, 'Do you really think this mission could go wrong?'

'There's a chance,' Bowman admitted. 'We're rushing in. That's when mistakes get made.'

'Six doesn't think so.'

'That's just the typical Foreign Office mindset. They're academics.' Bowman spat the word out. 'They don't know how it works in the field. They think we're a bunch of super-soldiers.'

'I hope you're wrong.'

'Me too,' Bowman said. He nodded at her. 'What's your story, anyway? How did you end up in the Cell? I'm guessing you had a nice upbringing.'

She gave him a wry smile. 'What you really mean is: What's a privileged middle-class woman like you doing here?'

'I didn't mean it like that.'

'It's fine.' She sighed. 'I'm used to it. Everyone else asks me the same question. Or they think it behind my back. Which is basically the same thing, I suppose.'

She set down the Glock, stared at it in her lap.

'I never planned on joining the army,' she went on. 'I was what you might call a geek growing up. My days were spent in the library, burying my head in books. I'd always assumed I would follow my father into teaching. Or maybe even *academia*.' She gave him a look.

'What happened?'

'I woke up one day and realised it wasn't my dream after all. Oh, I enjoyed studying and so on, but the prospect of spending my career in some stuffy corner office in a university, writing papers for obscure academic journals, wasn't for me. I decided to quit my degree and enlist.' She smiled at the memory. 'When I told my parents what I'd done, they almost hit the roof. They're both teachers, you see. We had a big argument. Some unpleasant things were said.'

'Why the army, though? You could have had the pick of any career you wanted.'

'My grandfather had served in Korea. He fought at Imjin River, with the Gloucestershire Regiment. He never said a word about it until one day I sat down with him and asked him for the full story for a paper I was working on. He talked for hours. A whole afternoon. For some reason, that story stayed with me. That idea of being part of something bigger than myself, you know? So I thought, why not join the army?'

'It's as good a reason as any,' Bowman said. 'I've heard worse.'

'I'm sure.' She sat upright. 'Anyway, the army proved the making of me. I realised I was much stronger than I'd assumed. One thing led to another, and here I am. I've never regretted my decision. Although my father and I don't talk anymore.'

Bowman tried to think of something comforting to say. 'I'm sure your old man is proud of you. Even if he won't say it.'

Casey smiled sadly. 'Somehow, I doubt that's true. Nothing I do will ever be good enough for him. In his mind, I'm just the pig-headed daughter who threw away a promising future just to piss him off.' She angled her head at Bowman. 'What about you? What made you enlist?'

'I grew up in a rough area,' Bowman said. 'Everyone was in a gang or knew someone involved in one. I had a choice between the army, or a life of crime. I chose to fight.'

'Smart choice.'

'I reckoned so at the time.'

'What about your parents? Siblings?'

'Mum and Dad have been dead for years. The cancer took my mother when I was seventeen. Dad joined her a year later. Heart attack. I've got a sister, but we're not really in touch these days,' he added, remembering the promise he'd made to Mallet back at the interview in London.

Casey paused and bit her lower lip. 'The others told me about your family,' she said. 'What happened to your wife and little girl.'

Bowman lowered his gaze to the floor. He thought again about the blood. The bodies. For a fleeting moment, he saw them lying on the kitchen floor. The way he'd discovered them when he came home from the job. Amy with the bullet hole in her head. The wide gash in his daughter's throat. He saw, too, the face of the man responsible. The Albanian mobster. His monstrous scarred face, his cruel laugh. Bowman set his jaw as a hot current of anger stirred inside his guts.

'I'm sorry,' Casey said hastily. 'It's not my place.'

'You're right,' Bowman growled. 'It isn't. And I don't need your fucking sympathy.'

Casey mumbled a hasty apology, made an excuse and left him alone. Bowman sat in silence, checking his kit, tortured by the images seared into his memory. He suddenly craved another pill. Bowman waited a while, slipped into the toilet and snuffed two of Lang's yellow pills. He felt better, but not by much. The tablets weren't as potent as the synthetic opioids he usually took. The effects wore off much more quickly. Which was a problem, he knew. He'd have to sneak off more often. One of the others might notice sooner or later.

He dropped into his seat, and then the attendant brought over food for the team. They tucked into sandwiches, crisps, biscuits, chocolate bars. Loading up on calories, because they didn't know when they'd next have a chance to eat. Bowman inhaled a BLT sandwich and a protein bar, washed it down with a cup of strong black coffee. He drank another. Soon, a leaden fog clouded his brain. His eyelids were heavy. Everything felt fuzzy and slow. The tiredness of the last forty-eight hours was catching up with him. Every muscle in his body demanded rest.

While the others chatted, Bowman closed his eyes. He tried not to think about his family, or the mission. Eventually the faces of his dead wife and daughter faded away. In the empty blackness of his opioid-numbed mind, Bowman found a brief respite from his torment, and he settled into a fitful sleep.

*　　*　　*

They touched down in Libreville five hours later. Ten o'clock in the evening in Gabon. The team snatched up their C8s and deplaned from the jet with the other passengers. They left their personal luggage on the Gulfstream. There was no point taking any non-essential kit with them to Karatandu. They were going into a potential firefight. Mobility and speed would be crucial. Better to keep their individual loads as light as possible. They could collect their holdalls later, once the coup had been successfully crushed and the crew got the all-clear to return the president to his country.

A couple of officials in shiny suits greeted Seguma at the foot of the airstairs. They guided the president and the two diplomats towards a waiting Lincoln Town Car. At the same time, Mallet and the rest of the team circled round to the rear of the Gulfstream to unload their kit. A Short SC.7 Skyvan twin turboprop aircraft was parked on the tarmac seven metres away from the Gulfstream. A sturdy short-distance load-lifter. Ugly but reliable. The Karatandu national flag was affixed to the fuselage and the tailfin. One of the president's private aircraft, Bowman guessed. A portly loadie in a Karatandan army uniform stood beside the lowered ramp.

As the Gulfstream engines wound down the co-pilot hurried over and opened the rear cargo hold. Webb crawled inside the space, the other soldiers formed a chain and they began transferring the kit from the back of the jet to the Skyvan: the mortar assembly and sights, the Gimpys, the .50 cal rifle, the AWC sniper rifle, the boxes of ammo and shells, the grenades, the Claymore satchels. Like pass-the-parcel. But with deadly hardware instead of birthday presents. They piled everything in the middle of the Skyvan's boxcar-shaped cabin. The loadie secured the ammo crates with netting, Mallet gave him a thumbs-up to confirm that everything had been loaded into the hold, and then the team hurried over from the Gulfstream.

As they approached the rear loading ramp, Mallet's phone buzzed. He stopped short as he read through a stream of incoming text messages.

'What's the news?' Loader shouted above the high-pitched whine of the jet engines.

'Confirmation from Six,' Mallet said. 'They've established comms with the military base at Marafeni airport.'

'And?'

'Everything's arranged. The escort is waiting for us on the ground with our transport. We'll be ready to roll out of the gates as soon as we get off the plane.'

'How many guys in the escort?'

'A platoon. Fourteen blokes.'

'Should be enough to deal with any bullshit we might encounter along the way. Checkpoints, roadblocks, rioters.'

Mallet nodded. 'We should get to the palace for midnight.'

'If it goes smoothly,' Bowman added.

'No reason it won't.'

'What about those SF teams coming in?' Casey asked.

'The SFSG and SBS guys are en route to Libya now. Due to land at around eleven o'clock our time. They'll link up with D Squadron and take off around midnight. Which is one o'clock their time. Looks like they'll reach Marafeni at around six o'clock tomorrow morning.'

'Any word on the coup?'

'Nothing yet.'

'Have they spoken to Mike?' asked Bowman.

Mallet shook his head slowly. 'He's offline.'

'Meaning?'

'Six reached out to him half an hour ago for another update. They're still waiting to hear back. Once they've spoken to him, they'll let us know.'

'Might be a blackout,' Loader suggested. 'Power shortages are a fact of life in Karatandu. If it's out, the mobile phone network will be down. Or maybe he's just busy arranging the perimeter defence.'

'Or it could mean something else,' Bowman said.

'The last time Six checked in with Mike, the capital was fairly quiet. We've got no reason to think the situation has changed.'

'If the rebels are moving in early, Mike will be in the shit.'

'We've got no proof of that,' Mallet snapped. 'The plan stays the same. We'll get in, get the family and guard them until the strike force gets in. Then we can go home and celebrate. Or in Tiny's case, get plastered and spend the night wondering what it must feel like to be over five foot tall and attractive to women.'

'Sod off, John.'

They ascended the loading ramp and strapped themselves into the seats on either side of the cabin, their C8 rifles placed across their laps and the rucksack filled with emergency kit between Mallet's feet. The tailgate closed, the twin engines hummed. The Skyvan taxied across the runway, catapulted forward, and suddenly they were climbing into the murky night.

No way back now.

Sixty minutes later, they landed in Karatandu.

Twenty

A hot breath of wind hushed across the runway, thrusting through Bowman's hair as he stepped off the loading ramp. Shortly after eleven o'clock at night in Karatandu. The western coast of Central Africa. The heat was oppressive, like being smothered in a hot towel. The air was thick with the smell of hard rain, mixing with the potent tang of jet fuel and the faint whiff of woodsmoke. Apricot lights shimmered in the impermeable darkness beyond the airport perimeter. To the north of the tarmac stand, a hundred and fifty metres away from the Skyvan, stood a decrepit terminal building. A sign was draped above the entrance: WELCOME TO KARATANDU, THE NEW HOPE OF AFRICA.

The rest of the team glided down the ramp as a pair of soldiers marched quickly over from a tented encampment behind a chain-link fence, to the east of the terminal. A lanky, long-necked guy with a shaven head, and a squat man with a badly pockmarked face. They were dressed in loose-fitting camo fatigues, with short-sleeve jackets and AK-47 assault rifles slung over their shoulders. They stopped at the rear of the Skyvan and cast their eyes over the five Brits. Both of them seemed agitated, thought Bowman. Unnerved. The soldier with the pockmarked face kept glancing around, gripping his AK-47 tightly, as if expecting an attack at any moment. Lanky jutted his chin out at Mallet.

'You're the team from London, yes?'

'Aye,' Mallet said. 'That's us.'

'Come with us. Major Mavinda is waiting for you.'

He walked stiffly off in the direction of the tented area, Pockmark hurrying along at his side. Mallet turned to the others.

'Tiny, Alex, Patrick. Stay here and watch the heavy kit. Josh . . . come with me.'

Bowman hurried alongside Mallet, leaving the three others behind as they followed the Karatandan soldiers towards the chain-link fence. On the far side of the tarmac stand, a long queue of civilians snaked out from the terminal entrance towards an ancient-looking Boeing 737. Most of the passengers appeared to be local, weighed down with their worldly possessions, clutching plastic shopping bags and backpacks and bulging suitcases. Men argued with one another. Mothers berated their screaming children.

'Looks like they're in a big rush to get out,' Mallet said.

'Not just them,' Lanky said. 'Anyone who has the money is trying to leave Karatandu.'

'Can't blame 'em,' said Bowman. 'I'd be doing the same thing in their shoes.'

Lanky led them through the gate into a wide open-sided tent. They waited outside while Lanky approached a heavily built officer wearing a red beret. A haze of cigarette smoke hung like a curtain in the air. Soldiers lazed around the tables and chairs. Bowman counted at least thirty of them. Some smoked or drank from plastic bottles filled with some sort of local brew. Others played card games on upturned ammo crates. Two soldiers watched porn on a laptop. Much of their equipment seemed to be in poor condition. Bowman saw rusted AK-47s propped against tables or lying on the dirt floor. The men cut a slovenly appearance. One of the guys wore his water bottle upside down.

'Let's hope these lads fight better than they look after their kit,' Bowman muttered.

Mallet said, 'We're not looking for first-rate soldiers. Just guys who can help us out if it goes noisy.'

Bowman looked up as the officer in the red beret strolled over. He was hard-faced and big all over, like an athlete gone to seed, thick fat layered on top of hard muscle. Small round pupils peeked out from beneath his low drooping eyelids. His lips were curled upwards into a permanent sneer. He had the same tribal markings on his cheeks as the bodyguards in London, Bowman noticed.

The man offered a meaty paw.

'Major Julius Mavinda, commanding officer of the Marafeni airport garrison.'

Mallet shook his hand. 'John Mallet. This is my colleague, Josh Bowman. We've been sent here to safeguard the president's family and key members of the national government.'

They were in a powerful hurry to get to the family. There was no time to waste shooting the breeze with the Karatandan major and his vicious-looking soldiers.

Mavinda nodded. 'We've received our orders. My men are ready to accompany you to the palace. I'll be leading the escort personally. But we must proceed with caution. Considering the latest news.'

Bowman caught a glimmer of anxiety in the major's eyes.

'What news?' he asked.

Mavinda nodded at a soldier operating a radio set across the tent. 'We've had multiple reports of gunfire.'

A cold feeling prickled the back of Bowman's neck.

'Where?' he asked.

'Many places,' Mavinda replied. 'An army barracks fifty miles south of here. A police station in Akbeni, in the west. An armoury in the same area.'

Mallet said, 'Did they give any more details?'

Mavinda scratched his jaw. 'All we have been told is that there are reports of possible disturbances in other parts of the country. It looks like the KUF paramilitary forces are responsible. General Kakuba's men.'

'That's it? Nothing else?'

Mavinda shrugged. 'That's all I know.'

'When did you hear this?'

'An hour ago.'

'What about the capital?'

'I don't know. We have tried to contact the other bases and police stations, but no one is answering.'

'Shit,' Bowman said under his breath. 'It's started.'

Mallet inhaled sharply. 'How long will it take to get to the capital, Major?'

'Forty minutes, if we take the most direct route.'

Bowman glanced at his G-Shock: 23.12 hours. *If we leave now, we'll reach the palace just before midnight.*

'We'll have to get moving at once,' Mallet said. 'Major, you'll need to get us to the palace as fast as possible.'

Mavinda gave a hesitant nod.

'We will follow our orders, of course. It will be a great honour to help protect the family of President Seguma. But we must be careful. There is a chance we will run into the Machete Boys along the way.'

'Who the fuck are they?' said Bowman.

'A splinter group,' Mavinda said. 'They're aligned with the KUF. But they're more like a gang than professional soldiers. They wear *gris-gris* charms to protect them from bullets. Most of them are more interested in drinking and taking drugs than overthrowing the government.'

'If you think that's scary, you should see Glasgow on a Saturday night,' Mallet said.

Mavinda looked steadily at him. 'The Machete Boys are no joke. They got their name because they offer their victims a choice: T-shirt or shorts. If you tell them shorts, they hack off one of your legs with their machetes. If you ask for a T-shirt, they cut off your arm.'

'Are we likely to run into these nutters?' asked Bowman.

'It's possible. They've been causing us trouble lately, ambushing the roads, kidnapping civilians, executing our troops. If there's trouble in Marafeni, they'll be involved.'

228

'Don't worry, Major,' Mallet said. 'If we get into a contact, me and the guys will have your backs.'

Mavinda nodded again, but the look in his eyes betrayed his unease. Bowman didn't blame him. It wasn't a question of cowardice. The major seemed like a brave guy. But he clearly wasn't thrilled about getting into a scrap with a load of drug-induced rebels. *I know the feeling*, Bowman thought.

This could all go badly wrong, and we both know it.

'You're better off coming with us than staying here, anyway,' Mallet added.

'Why is that?' asked Mavinda.

'Sooner or later, General Kakuba's forces will attack this place. The airport will be one of their primary targets. They'll hit it with everything they've got. You won't want to be here when they rock up.'

The major stared at him in alarm.

'We need to get moving,' Mallet said. 'Where's our transport?'

Mavinda cocked his chin at the open side of the tent. A white Toyota Land Cruiser rested on the asphalt, next to a trio of four-door Toyota Hilux pickups and a larger Unimog truck.

'You will take the Land Cruiser. I'll lead the way in one of the Hiluxes. The rest of my men will follow in the Unimog.' The big major stared at them in turn. 'You will stay close to us, OK? Once we leave, we don't stop for anything.'

'We know the drill, pal. Just get us to that palace.'

'I'm telling you this for your own safety,' Mavinda replied firmly. 'Trust me, you don't want to get captured by the Machete Boys. They will show you no mercy. Especially the woman.'

He nodded at Casey.

'They try anything, they'll get slotted,' Bowman said.

Mallet waved an arm at the Skyvan. 'We've got some hardware on the plane. We'll need a hand unloading it.'

'My men will take care of it.'

229

The major about-turned and barked an order at his men in a jumbled mix of English, French and the local patois. Lanky, Pock-mark and a young guy with a toothbrush moustache dashed across to the Hilux. Mavinda hastened after them, shouting a string of orders at his men before he jumped into the front of the pickup truck. Ten more guys snatched up their AK-47s, utility belts and other bits of kit and sprinted across to the Unimog. Eight of them climbed into the benched seating area at the back. The other two guys sat in the cab upfront. The rest of the soldiers stayed back in the tent, smoking and watching porn.

Bowman and Mallet hurried over to the Land Cruiser parked to the side of the tented area. Bowman slid behind the wheel, found the keys in the cupholder. He gunned the engine and led the con-voy across the tarmac stand to the Skyvan. He pulled up beside the aircraft and left the engine running while Mallet filled in the others on the situation. The disturbances elsewhere in the coun-try, the possibility of running into the Machete Boys. As he talked, several soldiers dropped down from the Unimog. They ran over to the Skyvan and started lugging the heaviest equipment over to the back of the truck. The soldiers worked fast, roared on by Mavinda. They loaded the 7.62 mm ammo boxes first, then the mortar base plate and cannon, the sight box. The five boxes of mortar shells. Mallet and the others dumped the remaining pieces of kit in the back of the Land Cruiser. They would carry their rifles with them in the vehicle for easy access. No one knew what would be waiting for them on the way to the capital.

After they had transferred the last items from the Skyvan, Mal-let gave a signal to Mavinda in the front pickup. The major bel-lowed an order at his men, they scrambled back into the Unimog, and then the convoy started down the road towards the airport entrance. The Hilux in the vanguard position, the team in the Land Cruiser in the middle of the column, the rest of the platoon in the Unimog at their six.

Bowman stuck close to the Hilux as it motored towards a crude army checkpoint situated at the main entrance to the airport. A long column of vehicles jammed the opposite lane in front of the checkpoint. As they raced past, Bowman saw three soldiers yanking an elderly man from behind the wheel of his knackered car. A woman pleaded with one of the soldiers, screaming, while his two muckers mercilessly beat the old-timer with their wooden sticks.

'Looks like half the bloody country is trying to get out,' Loader said.

Casey glanced anxiously at the long line of vehicles. 'Maybe the situation is worse than we think.'

'Something has got these people worked up,' Bowman said.

'Could just be the general unrest,' Mallet said. 'We don't even know for sure that the coup has kicked off yet. Not for sure.'

'What about those reports the major mentioned?' asked Loader. 'All them disturbances.'

'Unverified. Could just be a group of rebel fighters getting ahead of themselves.'

Bowman thought for a beat, then shook his head.

'If it was one isolated incident, maybe. But we're looking at three separate attacks across the country. And those are just the ones we know about. Something is definitely going down.'

'Why would the rebels start the coup ahead of schedule?' Casey wondered. 'Six said they wouldn't go in until first light.'

Bowman said, 'The Russians will have heard about Lang's death by now. They'll know it wasn't suicide. They'll assume it's somehow linked to the coup. Which means they'll want to speed things up. Alert their partners in the KUF and trigger the takeover, before anyone can stop them.'

'We've still got time,' Mallet replied. 'You heard what the major said. The disturbances are in the south and west of the country.'

'For now. Those other targets might not hold out for long.'

231

'If they haven't been captured already,' Casey said. 'Those reports are at least an hour old. The situation might have changed by now.'

'Nothing we can do about that,' Mallet said. 'All we can do is focus on the mission.'

Bowman tensed his grip on the wheel so hard his knuckles shaded white. He looked over at the illuminated console display: 11.21. Less than forty minutes to the palace.

Not far to go now. Not far at all. *In less than an hour*, Bowman thought, *I'll be reunited with my old friend.*

Mike Gregory had my back once.

Now he needs mine.

I just hope we get there before the rebels.

Mallet tapped out messages on the phone as they continued north towards Marafeni. He pinged off another text to Six and then Casey said, 'We should stick the radio on. Tune in to the state radio station. Might tell us what's going on in the city.'

'Good plan,' said Mallet. 'Better than listening to Tiny's sad voice.'

'Fuck off, John. You're just jealous. The ladies love a bit of the old Welsh accent.'

'They're not after you for your good looks or your wealth, Tiny. That's for fucking sure.'

Mallet fiddled with the touchscreen while Bowman kept the Land Cruiser hard on the heels of the Hilux. He pressed an arrow key on the console screen, and the vehicle suddenly filled with a harsh burst of static. Mallet tapped the arrow again, scanning through the radio frequencies, found nothing but silence. They were in some sort of dead spot, Bowman guessed.

They carried on north through the African night. The road twisted past abattoirs and nature reserves and several small villages, the ground dimly illuminated in the bright wash of the convoy's headlamps. The star-pricked sky was as black as an oil spill. Civilian cars streamed past, racing towards the airport to the south of Marafeni. Others were making their way on foot along the roadside. Bowman glanced again at the time and felt his heart start to beat faster inside his chest: 11.34. Less than half an hour until they hit the palace.

Almost there.

Two minutes later, the radio sparked into life.

Music spilled out of the Land Cruiser's speakers, faintly at first. Mallet turned the knob, dialling up the volume. A hymn-like orchestral tune was playing. It sounded oddly familiar. Bowman was sure he'd heard it before, but he couldn't instantly place it.

Loader frowned. 'Is that thing tuned in to the right station?'

Bowman squinted at the console. 'This is the state radio, mate.'

'Then why the fuck are they playing classical music?'

'It's not classical music,' Mallet said. 'It's the Russian national anthem.'

Loader stared at him. The Welshman wore a look as if someone had just slapped him across the face.

'Are you sure?' he asked.

Mallet said, 'A few of us did some joint-training exercises with Spetsnaz. In the nineties. Before the country became a mafia state. They'd play that anthem all the time. I'd recognise it anywhere.'

Casey went pale. 'Then that means—'

'Aye,' Mallet said. 'The rebels must have taken over the broadcasting house.' His shook his head. 'We're too late. The bastards are already inside the capital.'

Twenty-One

The anthem played on for a couple of minutes, reaching a crashing crescendo before it faded to silence. Then a hoarse male voice spoke in broken English. The man announced himself as General Moses Kakuba, leader of the armed wing of the Karatandu United Front. The despotic reign of President Seguma was over, Kakuba said. He declared that the KUF had taken control of the main army bases and police stations around the capital and called on the remaining troops to stand down. He cycled through a list of grievances as long as Bowman's arm. He droned on about government corruption, undemocratic institutions, cronyism, torture, the unlawful use of force against protestors. The colonel proclaimed the dawn of a brave new era for the people of Karatandu, together with their Russian allies. A new Marxist government was now being formed, he said. A three-man military junta led by General Kakuba himself. There was the usual promise of free and democratic elections to follow, once the situation had been stabilised. Peace would come to Karatandu. There would be many new hospitals, schools, jobs for everyone. A better life. He was making more promises than a personal injury lawyer.

'Loves the sound of his own voice, doesn't he?' Loader said.

'This is bad news,' Webb said. 'Very bad.'

Mallet turned down the volume, reached for his phone.

'I'll call Six. Tell them what's going on. They'll have to get a message over to the main strike force. Those lads need to know what to expect before they land.'

Casey was silent for a moment. 'If the KUF are in the capital, it won't be long before they attack the palace.'

'Or they might be there already,' Webb said.

'We don't know that. Not for sure,' Mallet said.

'Why else isn't Mike answering his phone?'

Mallet tapped open the messaging app and dialled the most recent number. The Voice answered immediately. He filled them in as the convoy hurtled north towards Marafeni. The reports of gunfire elsewhere in the country, the radio broadcast by General Kakuba. The likelihood that the rebellion had already spread to at least parts of the capital. Then the Voice took over the conversation. Mallet listened in silence, his frown lines deepening, forming trench lines across his brow. He asked a couple of questions, hung up.

Then he said, 'Six has been monitoring the situation in Marafeni. The situation is worse than we thought.'

'What did they say?' asked Casey.

'They've picked up widespread reports of violence in and around the capital. Gunfire. Looting. Killing. Buildings being torched.'

'Christ.'

Mallet said, 'That's not the worst of it. Rebel forces have released hundreds of inmates from the main prison. Political prisoners, activists, murderers, petty thieves. They're out on the streets, tearing it up. Six has heard that the Machete Boys are joining in the fun too. It's chaos out there. A free-for-all.'

'Shit,' said Loader.

Webb's face crumpled in puzzlement. 'Why would Kakuba and his men attack the capital before the airport? These guys normally go for the major roadheads and airheads first.'

Mallet said, 'They might have a different strategy. They could be trying to coerce the airport garrison into surrender. Now they've got control of the airwaves, they can send out messages to the troops, telling them it's over, they're fighting for a lost cause, all that bollocks. Which might persuade the garrison to lay down their arms. They could take the airport without firing a shot.'

'Would that work?'

'You saw the looks on the faces of those guys at the airport. They're not keen to get into a scrap with the enemy, not if they can help it. If they think the game is up, they'll give in.'

'Whoever is advising them rebels knows what the fuck they're doing,' Loader said with grudging admiration.

'It's the Russians,' said Mallet. 'Those bastards know how to fight.'

Bowman thought back to what Lang had told them in Monte Carlo.

They're sending in some guys.

Military advisers.

Special Forces. Big blokes with guns.

Ten or twelve guys at most, he figured. Veteran SF operators. Calling the shots, directing the KUF paramilitary force in battle. What the military theorists liked to call a force multiplier. The Russians would have been on the ground for weeks, probably. Drilling the rebels in fire-and-move tactics, suppressive fire, using the dead ground to advance unseen on an enemy position. Nothing complicated. But highly effective. A few core tactical principles, good instructors and an intensive training package could transform a group of ragtag rebels into a cohesive, disciplined fighting unit.

If we come up against those guys, we're knackered.

He said, 'Still nothing from Mike?'

Mallet grimaced and shook his head. 'It's been hours since they've heard from him.'

'Could mean anything,' said Loader.

'Aye,' Mallet replied. 'But it doesn't look good.'

Loader said, 'If he is under attack, let's hope he can hold them rebels off for a while.'

'Mike won't give up that easily,' Bowman said. 'He's got forty guys with him from the Presidential Guard, remember. The best troops in the country. And the palace is in a good defensive position. He should be able to hold out until we can relieve the pressure.'

'So why isn't he answering?'

'We'll find out soon enough,' said Mallet.

They raced on. Bowman kept glancing at the clock, counting down the time and the distance to the palace in his head. Eighteen minutes to go. Seven miles. Almost there. They were passing through the outskirts of the city. Bowman saw tin-roofed shacks, crude dwellings, gleaming new mosques. Mountains of rubbish festered along the sides of the road. The streets were dark and empty. Everyone had locked themselves indoors to wait out the fighting. Like the moment the outlaws rode into a town in the Wild West. No one wanted to get caught in the crossfire.

They continued west until they hit the main bridge across the Karatandu River. Bowman stuck close to the Hilux as the convoy raced across towards the centre of Marafeni. Mallet strained his eyes, scanning the ground ahead. The three other operators in the back of the Land Cruiser stared out of the windows with taut expressions, gripping their rifles. They drove on for another quarter of a mile, and then Casey shot forward and pointed through the windshield.

'Look,' she said.

Bowman squinted, his eyes struggling to pick out details in the oily dark. Then he saw them. Three lifeless bodies lay sprawled across the bare dirt ground in front of a food market, their torn clothes stained red. A pack of feral dogs licked at the blood pooling beneath them. A fourth man was slumped face down in a puddle of stagnant water. At the far end of the street a taxicab had been torched. Several more fires raged in the distance to the west. In the orange glow of the flames, Bowman spied bands of looters darting in and out of damaged shopfronts, stealing whatever they could find. Across the road, a couple of kids in football shorts were tugging off the boots from the corpse of a policeman.

'Looks like Six was right,' said Loader. 'This is fucking carnage.'

The passed another large group of rioters, but none of them bothered the convoy. They had other priorities. They weren't looking to get themselves killed in a contact with a bunch of heavily armed soldiers. A pair of tattooed convicts broke away from their mates and started towards the Land Cruiser, sensing new victims. They caught sight of the hardened faces inside, the weapons they were packing, and quickly retreated. Casey watched them skulk off down the street in search of easier prey.

'Where are all the rebels?' she asked. 'All we've seen so far are looters and escaped prisoners.'

'They must have moved on,' Mallet said.

'To where?'

'The other targets. Mobile transmitters, barracks, border crossings. General Kakuba and his Russian mates will want to gain control of the country as soon as possible. Before the president's troops can regroup.'

'Or they might be at the palace,' Bowman said.

Loader grunted. 'If they are, we'll hit them fucking hard. With the firepower we've got, we'll go through them like a dose of salts.'

The convoy rattled on through the main commercial district. Bowman fought to stay alert in spite of his growing exhaustion. The few hours of kip he'd had on the jet had been his only chance to rest in two days, and he wondered how much longer he could push on before it affected his performance. *Another six hours*, he told himself. *That's all. Get to Mike and the family, secure them until the reinforcements show up. Then you can rest.*

He glanced down at the satnav. *We're a mile from the presidential palace. Not far to go now.*

As they neared the city centre, Bowman saw more signs of the violent uprising. Dead bodies littered the streets. Some of the victims had been hacked to pieces. Several others were missing arms and legs; blood gushed out of ragged stumps. Gangs of escaped convicts in bright-orange overalls roamed the city, armed with clubs or machetes. Directly ahead, the Hilux rocked as it drove over a corpse in the middle of the road. Bowman wrenched the steering wheel to the right, swerving to avoid the dead body rolling in the dirt.

'What the fuck are these guys playing at?' Loader growled in the back seat. 'We're supposed to be protecting this lot, not mowing them down.'

'Not our concern,' Mallet said coldly. 'We're here for the family. That's it.'

'Guess the major wasn't kidding when he said they wouldn't stop for anything,' Webb said.

The convoy stuck to the backstreets, avoiding the main thorough-fares. After several quick turns they hit the government district on the western side of Marafeni. The downtrodden huts were replaced by crumbling colonial villas and modern-looking office blocks. The wealthier part of town. But only just. There were signs of decay here, too, in the cracked pavements and potholed roads, the neglected gardens.

Bowman checked the console again: 23.55. *A few more minutes until we hit the palace.*

The convoy slung a left past the German Embassy and hit down a wide street lined with restaurants and state banks. Two hundred metres further to the west was the presidential palace. From a distance, in the semi-darkness, Bowman couldn't pick out many details. There was an outer guard post, an inner gate. A high security wall surrounded the compound with guard towers spaced at regular intervals. Beyond the wall stood the palace itself, as white as icing sugar on a cake.

Two bodies were slumped on the ground next to the guard post. Dressed in the uniform of the Presidential Guard.

'Shit,' Loader muttered.

Bowman felt his stomach drop.

We're too late.

The convoy cautiously passed the outer guard post and started down the driveway. It ran on for a hundred metres towards a wide carriage circle in front of the presidential palace. Which looked like a renovated colonial villa, with a porticoed entrance, surmounted by a pediment with the Karatandan coat of arms in the middle: a lion and a snake locked in a fearsome struggle in front of a pair of crossed spears, below a plentiful fruit tree. A gold dome rested on top of the roof. The palace was situated at the northern side of the compound, backing on to the ocean. To the south, eighty metres away, Bowman saw a couple of smaller buildings. From the maps he'd studied at Nice, he knew that these structures housed the guard barracks and servants' quarters. A service road ran from the barracks to a secondary gated exit in the south-eastern corner of the compound.

The palace grounds were strewn with abandoned equipment: body armour, helmets, canteens, boots. And dead bodies. Bowman counted at least half a dozen of them, their shapes faintly visible in the glow from the security lights. They were all dressed in the dark-grey uniform and green berets of the Presidential Guard.

'Jesus . . . ' Loader said. 'What the fuck happened?'

The rear brake lights on the Hilux suddenly flared as the pickup halted. Bowman quickly stamped hard on the brakes, the Land Cruiser skidded and lurched to a stop half a metre behind the Hilux. To their rear, the Unimog driver had also stopped.

'What are those idiots doing now?' Loader said angrily.

Bowman didn't reply. Beyond the red ghost-like flare of the Hilux brake lights, he spied movement. Fifty metres away. Four figures, near the entrance to the palace.

Not members of the Presidential Guard.

Not friendlies.

The Machete Boys.

Twenty-Two

It took Bowman half a second to identify the four figures at the entrance to the palace. They were dressed in a strange mishmash of cargo shorts, athleisure and brightly coloured T-shirts, their AK-47 rifles slung casually over their shoulders. Therefore, not soldiers or police. All four men wore amulets around their wrists. Animal paws hung from chains draped around their necks. They had small leather pouches tied to ropes around their waists, their chests, their biceps. Presumably containing coins or buttons or other magical items.

Gris-gris, Mavinda had said. Good luck charms. Worn by the Machete Boys to protect them from bullets and other dangers.

A splinter group. More like a gang than soldiers.

Three of the Boys were hauling loot out of the palace. One guy in a replica Portugal football jersey carried a bronze bust the size of a bowling ball. A second man with a red bandana tied around his head gripped the gilt frame of an oil painting. Next to him, a third bloke in a garish pink T-shirt was lugging a wooden chair. They carried their stolen treasure over to a battered truck parked at the eleven o'clock position on the carriage circle. A fourth kid, no older than sixteen or seventeen, bare-chested and wearing flip-flops, leaned against the side of the truck, swaying drunkenly as he swigged from a bottle of whisky.

The guy with the bandana caught sight of the convoy in the driveway. He stopped dead and shouted at his mates, and then Pinkie and Portugal dropped the loot they had been carrying, and Flip-Flops wheeled round to see what they were looking at.

The four Machete Boys had a sudden decision to make. The biggest decision of their lives. Possibly the last, depending on the outcome. They could stand and fight. Or they could turn and run.

The rebels unslung their assault rifles. Going for the first option. Brave, but stupid.

In the Land Cruiser, Casey reacted fractionally quicker than the rest of the team. She flipped her door open, jumped down and raised her Colt rifle at the Boys. 'Put your guns down! Hands in the air!'

The Boys ignored her. They had already made up their minds. They weren't going to abandon their goods. They were going to stand and fight.

Bandana and Portugal let rip first, firing from the hip as they emptied a couple of wild bursts at the Land Cruiser. Three rounds missed the target completely, slapping into the tarmac eight or nine inches short of the wagon. Two other bullets struck the grille in a shower of flying sparks. A sixth round glanced off the body-work near Casey, forcing her to dive for cover behind a statue of the president, two metres to the right of the driveway.

Then Pinkie discharged a third burst. Slower reactions, but a marginally better marksman. Two bullets glanced off the ground at the spot where Casey had been standing a moment earlier. Another round ricocheted off the statue, taking off a chunk of the president's face.

In the Land Cruiser, Mallet, Bowman, Loader and Webb instantly snatched up their rifles. They didn't need to communicate with one another. There was no time for a debate, anyway. They knew exactly what to do.

Engage the targets. Neutralise the threat.

The three soldiers leaped out of the wagon. Bowman and Mallet took up positions behind the front side doors, using them as cover. Behind them, Loader and Webb shielded themselves behind the two rear passenger doors. A brief glance at his six o'clock told Bowman that the Karatandan soldiers were still bottled up in the back of the Unimog. Awaiting orders from Major Mavinda, presumably.

In the next half-second the Boys opened fire on the Hilux. Rounds hammered against the pickup bonnet in a piercing din. Two rounds struck the windshield, spider-webbing the glass. Mavinda and his deputies made no attempt to debus. Illogical. But an instinct thing. *We're safer inside than out.* Through the rear windshield Bowman glimpsed four heads ducking down as another vicious torrent of incoming rounds peppered the truck.

Four seconds had passed since the first shot had been fired.

Bowman held his weapon in a steady two-handed grip, the telescopic stock tucked against his right shoulder as he coolly lined up the holographic sight with Bandana. He aimed for the midriff. The best target. The percentage shot. Like buying tech stock. Obvious, but lucrative. A 5.56 × 45 mm round could do a serious amount of damage to a person's torso. Enough to put Bandana and his mates out of the game.

The Boy was still spraying rounds at Hilux when Bowman pulled the trigger.

Two rounds flamed out of the muzzle in quick succession, thumping into Bandana's upper chest. The lucky charms didn't save him. His head snapped back and he did a kind of drunken pirouette before he dropped. Bowman plugged him twice more as his body belly-smacked against the blacktop.

A metre to the right, Portugal did the dead man's dance as Mallet emptied three rounds into his stomach. The two other Boys panicked and ran towards the palace entrance. Rapidly reconsidering the power of their charms. A couple of muzzles flashed in Bowman's peripheral vision as Loader and Webb gave them the double-tap treatment. Doing the business. Bullets thumped into Flip-Flops and Pinkie, tearing through their upper backs. The pair of them fell to the ground a few metres from the truck.

Seven seconds since the fight had started.

Four dead Boys.

Shadows flitted in and out of the trees studding the lawn at Bowman's ten o'clock. More looters were scampering out of the palace, alerted by the sound of gunfire. They dashed out of side exits and windows, carrying strips of copper wire, light fittings and bits of furniture and laptops as they scuttled south across the compound. None of them appeared to be armed, but Bowman put an automatic burst down in their direction anyway. Sending a clear message. *Stay away.* The figures scurried through the gate and disappeared into the shadows.

Mallet shouted, 'Move yourselves! Get inside! Find the family!'

The team broke forward. Casey picked herself off the ground and caught up with Bowman and Webb as they ran up the drive and past the carriage circle, making for the entrance. Mallet left them and darted over to the Hilux, bellowing orders at Major Mavinda. Shouting at him to get out and order his soldiers to throw up a cordon around the palace.

A warm salty breeze gusted in from the sea, whipping past Bowman as he bounded up the steps to the portico. Loader ran alongside his comrade, breathing hard. Webb and Casey were a couple of paces further back. Bowman could hear their equipment clinking as they raced past the dead Boys. The four soldiers ran past the columns and swept into the palace foyer. Weapons up, covering one another.

Bowman quickly orientated himself as he stepped into a marble-floored reception. There was a courtyard at the far end, he saw. Corridors to the left and right. The palace had been trashed by its latest visitors. Broken glass and spent jackets scattered the floor. Bullet holes studded the walls. Priceless artworks had been cut out of their frames. Other items had been discarded by the thieves in their haste to escape. Books, framed photographs, an ocean of paperwork, various trinkets. One or two wall lights still flickered. The remainder had been torn out of their sockets.

Bowman and Loader moved quickly across the reception, index fingers feathering triggers. They tacked right, moving down the corridor leading towards the banqueting room. Webb and Casey leaped up the stairs to clear the private quarters on the first floor.

As Bowman moved down the corridor, he tried to recall the faces of the president's family. His wife Christel, his three kids. His brother, Francis Seguma. His sister-in-law. Their twin daughters. He'd seen them pinned to the display board back in the Shed. Twenty-one hours ago. Another lifetime. Before the briefing with the Voice, the arrest in Monte Carlo.

His heart was beating frantically as he barged into the staff kitchen. He didn't know what they would find inside the palace. But he feared it wasn't going to be good news. The Machete Boys weren't professional soldiers. They wouldn't have risked ransacking the palace unless they were sure the fighting was over. And that could only mean one thing.

The rebels have already wiped out the family.

They're dead.

They cleared each room rapidly, arcs swinging from left to right, looking for enemy targets and friendlies, moving with the speed and controlled aggression of elite operators. They checked the kitchen, the pantry, the banqueting room, the music room. Then they crossed the reception and cleared the offices and the grand meeting chamber on the south side of the ground floor.

Every room had been stripped bare of its valuables. Cupboards had been emptied. Drinks cabinets raided. Carpets ripped up. Furniture broken up or stolen. The looting parties had been extremely thorough. Anything they couldn't take with them had been damaged or destroyed. But there was no sign of the family, or Mike Gregory, or the other members of the Presidential Guard.

There's no one here. Just a handful of slotted guards.

'Where is everyone?' Loader rasped.

They hurried back down the corridor towards the reception area. From upstairs Bowman could hear the stomp of boots on carpet, Casey and Webb shouting, 'Clear!' to one another as they rapidly searched through the rooms on the first floor.

Only one floor left to clear.

'Come on!' Bowman roared as he cantered across the reception. Glass shards cracked like ice underfoot as he sprinted back down the corridor to the right. Loader ran after him, and they crashed through an unmarked door leading down to the basement level. A secret network of emergency operation rooms ran underneath the main house, Bowman recalled from the layout. Somewhere for the president and his entourage to bunker down if they came under attack.

He raced down the corridor, past the exposed pipework and ducts, past the ammo crates stacked against the bare walls. They ducked in and out of the various storerooms, the admin offices, the living quarters. The private cinema. The games room.

Empty.

So where the fuck is the family?

Bowman swung back into the corridor and made for the door at the far end. The last room to check. The president's private library. Which also housed the palace broadcasting equipment. Bowman remembered something from the briefing about Seguma's family issuing hourly radio broadcasts from the same room. Imploring the soldiers to stay loyal to their great leader.

He crashed through the door, stumbled and almost tripped over the corpse of a palace guard. The man lay on the floor, his dead eyes as wide as golf balls. His lower jaw had been completely blown away. Bowman stepped around the slotted guard, dread flooding his guts as he pushed into the room. He looked up. Turned to his left.

Then he saw the bodies.

Twenty-Three

Bowman stopped cold just inside the room. He was looking at a tangled mass of limbs and torsos. Five guys and two women. Two other victims, dressed in the uniform of the Presidential Guard, were sprawled on the carpet beside a desk. There was a presidential seal on the wall behind the desk and a cluster of lighting equipment and camera tripods and cables. The other seven corpses all wore civilian clothing. Dark suits for the men, skirts and blouses and heels for the women. There was blood everywhere.

Bowman lowered his weapon and approached the victims. The hot stink of gunsmoke and blood clung to the air, thickening in his nostrils. He dropped down beside the dead civilians. Some of them appeared to have been mutilated beyond recognition. One guy had been shot in the face, seemingly at point-blank range. The killers had taken their time. Bowman saw a woman with her eyes gouged out. A man with his throat slashed open. A yawning gash of cartilage and tissue glistened beneath his slackened jaw.

The second time in his life he'd walked into a murder scene.

'It's the family,' Loader said between ragged draws of breath. 'They've been murdered.'

Bowman stared at them in silence, his jaw tightly clenched. He didn't immediately recognise any of the victims from the photographs in the Shed. But it was hard to be sure. He'd only glanced at the snaps on the wall for a few seconds. The early hours of yesterday morning. Another lifetime. And some of the faces were horribly disfigured.

'I don't know, mate,' he said. 'It might be them.'

'Who else could it be? The family are the only civvies we're expecting to find here. We're too fucking late.'

Bowman ran his eyes over the corpses. Something about the scene didn't make sense. 'I don't see any kids.'

'So what?'

'The president said we'd find his wife and children here. His youngest kid is only a few months old. His brother has a couple of twin girls. If this lot are his relatives, where are the children?'

'What difference does it make?' Loader said. 'The family has been massacred.'

He left the room and hurried upstairs to fetch the others. A short time later there was an urgent patter of footsteps in the corridor. Mallet and Mavinda entered the room, stepping awkwardly around the guard with the missing jaw. Loader followed them inside with Casey and Webb. The major took in the scene, then knelt down and examined the bodies. He inspected each of them quickly, stretched to his full height and gave a slow shake of his head.

'These are not members of Mr Seguma's family,' he announced.

Loader's brow dropped. 'Who are they, then?'

Mavinda gently tapped his foot against the nearest body. 'This one is the education minister. This one, over here, is the minister for agriculture,' he added, indicating the guy with the bullet hole in the middle of his forehead. 'Or was, I should say.'

'And the others?'

'Two others are cabinet ministers. The rest are staffers. Administrators. Nobodies.'

His voice was callous, cold.

'What about the first floor?' Bowman asked. 'Anyone up there?'

'All clear,' Webb replied.

'The barracks?'

Mavinda said, 'Some of my guys are searching it as we speak. But it looks like they're empty.'

Loader stared at the major. 'So where the fuck is the family?'

'Maybe the KUF has taken them hostage,' Bowman said, thinking fast.

'Why would they do that?'

'General Kakuba could use them as bargaining chips. He could threaten to execute the president's wife and kids immediately unless he agrees to step aside.'

Webb made a pained face. 'If that's true, we're finished.'

'We've got a live one here!' Casey called out.

The others ran over. She was kneeling beside one of the guards. A skinny hollow-cheeked guy with long bony hands and eyes set deep in their sockets. He had the drowsy, comatose look of the almost-dead. Waiting for the light to appear at the end of the tunnel. His lips were cracked. His breath escaped his lungs in shallow, erratic rasps. Bowman glanced down at the man's wound. The man had been drilled through the guts. The lifeblood was oozing out of him, drenching his shirt and groin.

His lips moved slightly, making a feeble sound. He repeated the same word over and over.

'What's he saying?' Loader asked.

'He is asking for water,' Mavinda said.

Mallet turned to him. 'Give him your canteen, Major.'

'This man is dying. It is pointless.'

'Do it.'

Mavinda reluctantly unhooked his bottle from his belt and pressed it to the guard's lips. The man drank greedily, water dribbling down his chin. He swallowed another mouthful and groaned in pain. Then he said a few words to Mavinda in a tongue Bowman didn't understand. It sounded similar to the language the president's bodyguards had used when speaking to each other, back at the royal wedding.

'Ask him what happened here,' said Mallet.

Mavinda jabbered at the guard. The man winced and said a few words in reply. Then Mavinda translated.

'He says the enemy attacked two hours ago. They came out of nowhere. A hundred of them.'

'What happened to the rest of the Presidential Guards?' Loader said.

Mavinda related the question. The guard wetted his lips again before making his reply.

'Many of his brother soldiers chose to flee, when they saw the rebels approaching,' the major said. 'Only a few remained. They were cut down in a matter of minutes.'

'By the Machete Boys?' Mallet asked sceptically.

Mavinda shook his head. 'KUF paramilitaries. General Kakuba's men.'

'KUF?' Loader frowned. 'But those guys we dropped upstairs were from the Machete Boys.'

'They're just scavengers,' Mavinda said. 'They wouldn't have the skill or discipline to attack the palace. Only the KUF are capable of such a thing.'

'Looks like they made short work of the opposition here,' Mallet observed.

'Do they wear lucky charms as well?' Loader joked.

Mavinda's expression was deadly serious. 'The KUF are the closest thing the rebels have to a professional fighting force. Many of them deserted the army with General Kakuba. They even dress like soldiers.'

'They must be the ones being trained by the Russians,' Webb said.

Mavinda stared at him with raised eyebrows. 'Russians?' he repeated.

'They're supporting the rebels,' Mallet said. He told Mavinda about the military advisers, the Kremlin plot to back the coup.

'The Russians have chosen a dangerous ally,' Mavinda said after he'd finished. 'General Kakuba is a terrible man. He has attacked many villages in Karatandu. His soldiers rape, kill and loot anything they can find, then burn the villages to the ground. They say he eats the livers of his defeated enemies.'

'Let's hope we don't bump into that fucker,' Loader said.

Mallet said, 'What happened to the president's family? Ask your man.'

The major relayed the question to the wounded guard. He responded in a croaking whisper, then coughed up a gout of blood.

'He says they managed to escape,' Mavinda said after the man stopped talking. 'Through a service exit.'

'He's sure?' Casey asked.

'The family fled before the KUF rebels could get into the compound,' Mavinda said. 'This man says he is certain of it. The senior ministers tried to flee through the same exit, but the rebels cut them off and herded them into this room with the remaining guards. Then they executed them, one by one. The staff pleaded with their captors to spare them, but General Kakuba did not care. Some of his men were laughing when they tossed grenades at the victims.'

Casey suppressed a shiver. The man said something else. Mavinda's face clouded with unease.

'What is it?' Bowman demanded.

'He says Mr Gregory is with the family as well. He helped them to safety.'

'Mike? He's with the family?'

'Yes.' There was a hint of trepidation in his voice. The major gave him a wary look. 'You know him?'

'He's a good friend of mine,' said Bowman.

'Where did they go?' Mallet interrupted. 'Ask him, Major.'

The guard was drifting out of consciousness now. He muttered something inaudible. Mavinda told him to repeat it. The man mustered one last reserve of strength, lifted his dimming eyes to the major.

'Rogandu,' he said. 'Rogandu.'

His head dropped. His breathing faded to a faint murmur.

Mallet turned to the major. 'What's this Rogandi gaff your man is talking about?'

253

'*Rogandu*,' Mavinda corrected. 'It's a small village. The most eastern district in the country.'

'Why would the family leg it there?'

'There's a private estate near the village. A few miles to the north. One of Mr Seguma's friends built the place. It was intended as a gift to the president.'

Bowman said, 'Who's the friend?'

'A Canadian. Mr Camby. He's responsible for all public transportation in Karatandu. A very lucrative position. He paid for the mansion in Rogandu, but it really belongs to Mr Seguma.'

'Must be good mates,' Mallet noted. 'Not everyone has a friend who builds them a fucking palace for free.'

'Mr Camby owes his fortune to his friendship with Mr Seguma. It's in his interest to keep the president happy.'

'Is that where we'll find his wife and kids?'

Mavinda thought for a moment. 'Makes sense. Rogandu is isolated, far from the capital. Mr Seguma hasn't stayed there for several years. They say the place has fallen into disrepair these days. I can't think of a better place to hide.'

'It's a lot safer than staying in the city,' said Loader. 'What with the Machete Boys running around chopping people up.'

'How far is it from here?' asked Webb.

'A hundred and fifty miles. Four hours, if you stick to the main road. Less, if you take the short cuts.'

Mallet said, 'Will the rebels know about this place?'

'Everyone knows about Rogandu. It is the worst-kept secret in the country.'

'In that case, we can assume the enemy will be heading for the mansion soon,' Casey said.

'Then we're fucked.' Loader threw up his hands. 'They've got a head start on us. Even if we leave now, we'll be lagging behind. They'll get to the residence before us.'

Mallet shook his head firmly. 'There's a chance we can get there first.'

Loader threw him a doubtful look. 'How'd you figure that, John?'

'The president owns a load of other residences around the country. The rebels will assume the family has fled to one of those other homes. They'll be busy searching them all. That should buy us time to get to the jungle estate before them.'

'You might be wrong,' said Casey.

'What's the alternative? Either we go to Rogandu, or we throw in the towel. Unless anyone has got a better idea?'

'We'd still have to get there fast,' Webb argued. 'It won't take the KUF long before they figure out where the family is hiding.'

Mallet swung back round to the major. 'Do you know where to find this mansion?'

'Of course,' said Mavinda. 'I've been there many times. No one knows the route better than me.'

'How fast can you get us there?'

'Three and a half hours. Maybe less.'

'Any checkpoints along the way?'

'We can get you there safely.' Mavinda pressed his lips together. 'But how do you expect us to hold out against the KUF if they attack us? I have only one platoon under my command. They cannot defend against General Kakuba's men.'

'They won't have to,' Mallet said. 'If we leave now, we'll get to the mansion before four o'clock. Ninety minutes before first light. There's a strike force coming in to take back control of the country. Two hundred Special Forces operators. They're due to get in at six o'clock. We'll only have to guard the family for a couple of hours before they arrive.'

'What if they are late?'

'They won't be,' Mallet said. 'They're scheduled to fly down from Libya as we speak.'

'You think they'll succeed?'

'It's the Regiment. We don't do failure.'

'The rebels are determined. They won't give up without a fight.'

'Neither will we.' Mallet flashed a savage grin. 'Trust me, Major. By the time the sun comes up, the rebels will be wishing to fuck that they had stayed tucked up in bed tonight.'

There was a look of steely determination in the Scot's eyes as he spoke. The major drew strength from it and relaxed slightly. A question hesitated on his lips. 'You say you have a direct line to Mr Seguma.'

'Aye.'

'Don't forget to mention my name to him, OK? Tell him Major Julius Mavinda did not let him down, in his hour of need.'

'Major, when this thing is over, you'll be a colonel before long.'

Mavinda puffed out his chest, perhaps imagining shiny new medals pinned to his breast.

He said, 'I'll give the order to my men.'

'We'll need more fuel,' Bowman pointed out. 'The Land Cruiser won't get us as far as Rogandu. Not without a top-up.'

Mavinda said, 'We have some spare jerry cans. In the back of the Unimog. Take what you need. Sergeant Nakamba will help you.'

Mallet turned to his team. 'Tiny, take care of it. The rest of you . . . get your shit together and get back into the vehicles. We're on the road again in five.'

'What shall we do about him?' Casey indicated the guard.

Mallet dropped his gaze to the dying man. His breathing had reduced to a faint murmur. Dark blood pumped steadily out of his stomach wound.

'We should put a bullet in his head,' Mavinda said. 'Put him out of his misery. Best thing for him.'

'No.' Mallet looked up and turned to Webb. 'Give him a couple of morphine shots from the emergency kit. That's the least we can do for this poor bastard.'

Mavinda clicked his tongue. 'A waste. It would be easier to shoot him.'

'He gets the shots,' Mallet snapped.

'Your choice.'

He walked out of the room. Casey's gaze lingered on the massacred civilians for a beat. 'I thought the Russians were directing the coup,' she said.

'They are,' Mallet replied.

'But the guard didn't say anything about Russians being involved in the assault. We haven't seen them on the streets. Where are they?'

'They'll stay in the shadows. They won't be doing the actual fighting.'

'Why not?'

'It would make the Kremlin look bad. Assisting a band of rebels to destabilise a central African government. That's too much, even for Moscow.'

'Especially if they lost,' Bowman added. 'The Russians would be embarrassed. They'd have to deal with the prospect of their own guys being taken hostage. There's no way they'd want to risk that.'

'So they'll just stay in the background, giving orders?' asked Casey.

'More or less.'

Mallet looked up at her.

'Don't underestimate these fuckers,' he said. 'They might operate in the shadows, but they're just as lethal as if they were out there doing the shooting. They're doing exactly what we do on team jobs. Training up a foreign force, showing them how to kill the enemy. We won't be trading any bullets with them, but the Russians are our main enemy in this fight.'

He stood up straight and nodded at the others.

'Get back to the wagon. We're leaving for Rogandu at once.'

Twenty-Four

They took the back roads out of Marafeni. The major and his three deputies led the way in the Hilux. Then the Cell team in the Land Cruiser. Then the ten other guys in the platoon in the Unimog. Mavinda guided the convoy north from the palace, past the rows of foreign embassies and terracotta-roofed high commissions. Tendrils of smoke trickled upwards from behind several of the compound walls. The mood was tense. Bowman could feel it in the air. Bands of marauders prowled the city, smashing up storefronts, clubbing people to death. Several of the Machete Boys were passed out drunk in the streets. Three of them were celebrating in front of a hostel, jeering wildly as they loosed off rounds into the air. They scarpered for cover at the first sight of the approaching convoy.

'Look at this lot,' Loader said as they passed the hostel. 'Running around like headless chickens. We could drop these idiots in their sleep.'

'They're not the ones we have to worry about,' Mallet said. 'It's the KUF rebels under the command of the Russians. General Kakuba's men. They'll be a different proposition.'

'Would they really be much better than this mob?'

'You've worked on training teams before, Tiny,' Bowman said. 'All they need is a handful of elite warriors to take charge, drill them and instruct them in some basic manoeuvres, and they'll be a tough opponent for anyone.'

Loader grunted his agreement.

'How many guys are we talking about?' asked Casey.

'A dozen Russians,' Mallet guessed. 'They'll be spread out across the country with units from the KUF. Kakuba's best men. Three or four hundred rebels, I'd say. One group in the capital, another to take the airport, a third to secure the borders. A fourth to seize the mines. That's the way I'd do it. With the Russians pulling the strings, they could have the coup wrapped up in a matter of hours.'

'Not once D Squadron and the other SF teams get in. They'll send the twats packing,' Loader said. 'All we've got to do is make it to Rogandu, protect the family, and it's job done.'

No one replied. Casey stared out of the window at the burning buildings, the mutilated corpses dumped at the side of the road.

'What's the plan once we get to the mansion?' she asked Mallet.

'We'll link up with Mike Gregory, secure the family, sort out the defences around the estate. Then wait for the reinforcements to come in.'

She inclined her head slightly. 'Do you think we're in for a fight?'

'Anything's possible. But General Kakuba and his men won't be heading to Rogandu, not immediately. It'll take them a while to search the president's other homes. By the time they arrive at Rogandu, we'll be getting a brew on.'

'The timing is tight,' Bowman said. 'If there's a delay, we're fucked.'

Loader said, 'I think we can handle a few poxy rebels.'

'We're down to the bare bones, mate. We were counting on those forty lads from the Presidential Guard to bolster our numbers. If Kakuba attacks us in force, we're gonna be up against it.'

'We won't have to wait there for long,' Mallet said. 'A couple of hours, max.'

They continued north until they were within sight of the port and then navigated east, steering well clear of the obvious targets. Police stations, army barracks. Radio stations. The president's numerous residences. Anywhere the rebels might be gathered in large numbers. Mavinda took them on a winding route out of the city, through narrow roads lined with shanty huts and modest dwellings partially hidden behind graffiti-decorated breeze-block walls. The darkened streets were heaped with mounds of rubble and chopped timber and plastic bottles.

As they bulleted east Mallet put in another call to the Voice. He got no answer, left a long message, filling the Voice in on the current situation. The massacre at the palace. The family's flight to the country pile in Rogandu. The new plan. He asked for an update on D Squadron and the other elements of the strike force: SFSG, the SBS. He told the Voice to get hold of Mike Gregory, if possible. Let him know that the team was on the way. He hung up, plugged the phone into the cigarette lighter receptacle and left the handset on charge.

They crossed a small bridge over the Karatandu River and skirted around the fringes of several outlying villages, avoiding the main highway. The only stretch of paved road outside the capital. The most obvious route to Rogandu, the major had explained. But slower and less direct than the country tracks. And much more dangerous. The rebels might have ambushes set up on the main routes, he said.

The road soon degraded into a rough track, the lights from the smaller settlements shrank to dots, and suddenly they were pushing through the Karatandan countryside. The slums and ruined colonial villas gave way to a seemingly endless sprawl of lowland plains and claustrophobic forest, the muddied track slithering like some giant black snake beneath the gloom of the canopy. The Hilux rocked along in front of them, headlamps cutting through the pitch-black night.

Mallet tried to get hold of Six again. But they were in a sparsely populated area. The signal was terrible. Non-existent. He gave up after the fourth attempt and settled back into his seat as the vehicles steered deeper into the jungle. Bowman glanced over at the bluish digital glow of the console display.

02.00 hours. A hundred miles from the mansion near Rogandu. Two hours to go.

Two hours until I can pop another pill.

Bowman was flagging badly now. It seemed as if epochs had passed since he'd last slept. He found it hard to concentrate on the road. His vision was juddering, the Hilux kept slipping in and out

261

of focus. The world had a weirdly dreamlike quality to it. To make matters worse, the cravings were beginning to sneak up on him. The air con in the Land Cruiser was on full whack, but Bowman was sweating beneath his webbing and plate armour. He felt the ache deep in his muscles, a sharp scissoring pain shooting through his body, tingling in his fingertips and toes. Five hours since he'd dropped a pill. Too long. His mistake.

Another two hours until we get to the mansion, Bowman thought to himself. *Four o'clock in the morning. Keep pushing on. Hang on until we get there.*

Then you can drop a couple of Lang's magic pills.

The road was empty. They saw no other cars on the road, no gangs of rebel soldiers or pedestrians. An hour later, the forest began to thin out. The convoy trundled on for another ten miles, past pockets of mangrove swamp and impoverished fishing villages clinging to the banks of the river. Mallet checked his phone for a signal. Still nothing. Webb and Loader dozed in the back seat. Casey sat wedged between them, alert, tense, on edge.

The jungle ended abruptly. Like a curtain being lifted from a stage. One minute they were driving through the swampy suffocating dark of the forest. The next they were leaving the treeline behind them and rolling across a low grassy plain, so flat you could play billiards on it. A quick glance at the console told Bowman that they were less than half an hour from the target location. *We're getting close to Rogandu now.*

Mallet checked his phone again, got a weak signal and dialled Six. He waited several long beats. Then he hung up, swore under his breath and sent a brief encrypted message.

'Still no answer,' he said.

Bowman shot him a look. 'Why aren't they picking up?'

'Fuck knows. Could be anything.'

'Maybe they're busy briefing the strike force,' Casey said. 'Giving them the latest intelligence on the rebellion.'

'It's half two in the morning in London. They might be off getting pissed on espresso martinis as far as I know.'

Loader said, 'It ain't like Six to go silent. Usually, you can't stop that lot from gassing off.'

'We can't worry about that now. Keep driving. I'll try them again once we reach the mansion.'

Bowman stuck close to the Hilux. Behind them, the Unimog headlamps burned like halos in the rear-view mirror. The convoy steered away from the river and cut south across the plain. Fifteen minutes later they hit Rogandu.

There was nothing to announce the village. It simply emerged from the darkness, a handful of unlit streets laid out in a rough grid and set in the middle of a barren, dusty landscape. They passed rickety shacks and wattle-and-daub huts, run-down farms. The minaret of a mosque towered like a lighthouse above the dwellings. Bowman looked round but saw no signs of activity. The dead hours. Everyone would be asleep. Maybe the locals didn't even know about the rebellion yet.

They reached a T-junction south of the town and slewed left on to a modern metalled road running east towards the mountains. They were only a mile from the country residence now, Bowman realised. The road had been built at the request of the mansion's owner, probably. The building had been intended for the use of Mr Seguma. Therefore, it would need excellent transportation links, fit for the president. Unacceptable to expect the head of state to travel in the same discomfort as his impoverished people.

They drove past a densely wooded area on their right. A scattering of farms and tin huts and unfinished buildings on their left. The Hilux made a sharp right and bombed down a single-lane approach road leading south between the two dense sprawls of woodland. The convoy continued on the approach road until they broke clear of the forest, and then Bowman caught his first glimpse of Seguma's country residence.

At four o'clock in the morning, in the gloom before first light, he couldn't see much. There was a whitewashed three-storey mansion set in the middle of a large parcel of land, at the end of a long front driveway. Lights glowed in several of the ground-floor rooms. Bowman spied a smaller one-storey building to the left of the mansion. Some sort of guest house, perhaps. A stone archway towered like a triumphal arch above the entrance to the driveway, two hundred metres beyond the treeline.

'Seems quiet enough,' Loader observed. 'Looks like we got here in time.'

'Only one way to find out,' Mallet said.

The Hilux slowed as it neared the sentry box to the left of the archway. Two Presidential Guards stepped forward, raising their AK-47 rifles at the pickup truck and shouting for the driver to stop. The Hilux slammed on the brakes just short of the driveway, the rest of the convoy ground to a halt, and then the older guard approached the pickup while the second guy kept his rifle trained on the Land Cruiser. He looked young and bug-eyed with fear. The rifle visibly trembled in his grip.

'Bit nervy, ain't they?' said Loader. 'Like they're one step away from doing a runner.'

'These lads have just seen most of their muckers get carved up and shot,' Mallet replied. 'They're bound to be jumpy.'

There was a swift exchange between Mavinda and the older guard. Mavinda pointed to the vehicles behind him, gestured at the mansion. The guard back-stepped from the Hilux and barked an order at his comrade. The bug-eyed soldier. The latter relaxed his stance and lowered his rifle, waved them through the gate.

The convoy passed under the huge archway in single file, the Hilux leading the way. The driveway dipped down slightly, then rose on a gentle incline and hooked around a fountain surmounted with a bronze eagle. The estate looked neglected, thought Bowman. Weeds poked through the cracks in the blacktop. The lawn was dotted with crumbling statues and withered trees. There was a half-derelict pagoda to the left of the drive, overlooking a rancid pond. An ornamental garden to the right, sloping down towards an irrigation ditch. The mansion itself looked like it had seen better days. The marbled columns were dulled and weathered. Sections of the ornate parapet were badly damaged. The once-gleaming white façade had buckled and flaked away in places, revealing the crumbling brickwork beneath.

'This place is frigging huge,' said Loader.

'Almost big enough to house your entire family, Tiny,' Mallet said.

'Piss off, John. I ain't got that many kids.'

'Depends on your definition of "many", I suppose. What are you up to now, anyway? Twelve, thirteen?'

'Eight,' Loader replied. 'But we're expecting in June. A boy.' His face swelled with pride.

'That's the first I've heard of it,' said Mallet.

'You didn't ask.'

Mallet looked back at him. 'What do you think I am? Your fucking therapist? I've got enough on my plate without trying to keep on top of your ever-growing brood.'

Loader looked hurt. Mallet grinned at him.

'Cheer up, Tiny. I'm just joking. Congratulations.'

'Thanks, John.'

'Let's hope he doesn't inherit your looks, eh?' he went on. 'Otherwise the poor sod will have even less luck with the women than your sorry arse.'

The convoy pulled up behind a trio of mud-spattered Land Rover Defenders parked in front of the mansion. Bowman killed the engine, the team got out, Major Mavinda and his three subordinates climbed out of the Hilux, and then the rest of the platoon hopped down from the back of the Unimog.

Two more soldiers stood guard at the entrance. They stepped aside as a stumpy, bull-necked officer strode out of the mansion and made a beeline for Major Mavinda. He seemed to know Mavinda. Bowman sensed an easy familiarity between the men as they greeted one another. They swapped a few lines in the local lingo, and then Mavinda introduced the stumpy officer to the Brits.

'This is Colonel Joseph Lubowa,' he said. 'Commander of the Karatandu Presidential Guard.'

'John Mallet.' He extended a hand, indicated the others. 'This is my team.'

Lubowa shook his hand limply. 'You're lucky my men didn't kill you, Mr Mallet. They saw your headlights approaching and thought you might be the Machete Boys.'

'Are they in the area?' said Bowman.

'Not yet. But they will be, soon enough. We've heard reports of fighting in the nearest big town. Farangi. Thirty miles from here.'

'Closer than we thought,' Loader muttered.

Colonel Lubowa regarded the new arrivals. A look of disappointment crossed his face.

'Is this all of you?' he asked.

'This is everyone,' Mallet said.

Lubowa shrugged. 'Then I suppose it will have to do.'

'Where's the family, Colonel?'

'Inside. Mr Gregory is guarding them.'

The two Karatandan officers shared a meaningful look. Bowman thought he saw a nervous expression edging across Mavinda's face. He wondered about that.

'Are they OK?' Mallet asked.

'Mr Seguma's family is safe. A few of them have minor injuries, cuts and bruises, but nothing serious.'

'When did you get here?'

'Two hours ago,' Colonel Lubowa replied. 'About two o'clock.'

'How many guys have you got guarding this place?' said Loader.

'Four. These two men, the two on the gate. And Mr Gregory, of course.'

'No one else escaped the palace?'

'No.'

Mallet said, 'We'd better go and brief Mike.' He half turned to Mavinda. 'Tell your men to start unloading their kit. Check their weapons too. Make sure they're ready for a scrap.'

He spoke to the major in a stern tone. Establishing authority. *We're in charge now. This is what we do.* Mavinda didn't argue. He just nodded at his subordinates. Toothbrush, Lanky and Pockmark marched over to the Unimog, bellowing orders at the squaddies.

'Follow me,' Lubowa said.

He led the Cell team and the major towards the entrance. Bowman wearily brought up the rear with Loader, a tight feeling in his chest as he glanced round the estate.

'Better hope those reinforcements aren't running late,' he murmured.

Loader glanced at his mucker. 'Don't tell me you're getting twitchy about a few junkie scavengers who can't shoot properly. We've handled tougher enemies than that in the Regiment.'

Bowman shook his head. 'It's not that.'

He swept a hand across the estate.

'Look around you, mate. There's a lot of dead ground here,' he added. 'Those ditches, the depressions. Plenty of cover for the enemy to hide.'

'I don't think the Machete Boys will understand the principle of using dead ground to advance, Josh. They're a bunch of junkie scavengers.'

'Maybe not them,' Bowman admitted. 'But any decent rebel force that's switched on will know what to do. They could use that cover to get right in among us. And if that happens, we're in fucking trouble.'

Twenty-Five

They crossed the marble-pillared porch, passed the two guards posted on the front door and entered a large central atrium garishly decorated in gold and ivory. A nine-foot-tall bronze sculpture of Ken Seguma dominated the middle of the floor space. The atrium was filled with a chaotic arrangement of artwork: Greek statues, Renaissance paintings, ceremonial masks. Colonel Lubowa guided them off to one side, down a long corridor adorned with gilt-framed mirrors and crystal chandeliers. At first sight, everything looked impressive. But the fittings were as worn and tired as the exterior. Damp patches stained the walls. The arms on some of the chandeliers were broken or damaged. Everything looked in need of a lick of paint.

Lubowa led them to the end of the corridor, turned right, then walked down a shorter hallway. Bowman saw peeling silk wallpaper, a faded ceiling mural. At the far end, the room opened up into a lavishly furnished salon. There was a bar to the right, with a row of leather-seated stools and a rack of spirit bottles mounted to the wall. A white Steinway grand piano. At the back of the room, a set of French doors led out to a terrace overlooking a swimming pool set at the foot of the sloped rear garden. The sound of chirping crickets drifted through an open window.

Eight figures sat at a pair of giltwood tables on the left side of the room. At the nearest table, Bowman saw a short, stout woman in her late thirties. She wore a pair of half-moon glasses and a bright-green dress intricately patterned with strange shapes and symbols. Bowman recognised her from the photos he'd seen back at the Shed. Christel Seguma. The tyrant's third wife. She was dandling a screaming infant on her knee. Next to her was a wide-hipped woman in her fifties with a traditional Karatandan head cloth covering her hair. A slight, well-groomed man was seated beside the two women. He was dressed in a silk tunic embroidered with gold. The brother and sister-in-law.

The other four children sat cross-legged on the floor around the second table. Two boys aged around nine or ten. The president's sons, Bowman presumed. And a pair of twin girls. The brother's children. They were younger than the boys. Five or six, maybe. A few years older than Sophie had been when her killers had cruelly ended her life. The twins were dressed in matching yellow dresses, the boys in dapper suits. One of the girls held a cuddly toy bear. The boys were playing a game on an iPad, arguing over whose turn it was to go next. They seemed oblivious to what was going on around them. Which was probably for the best.

A ninth figure walked up and down the terrace. A tall hard-bodied guy with an unkempt beard, holding a clamshell phone to his ear. Bowman caught sight of his face through the glass.

Mike Gregory.

The ex-OC of B Squadron ended the call and stepped inside. He marched straight over to the team and looked them over before his eyes settled on Bowman. A grin cracked his leathery ex-soldier's face.

'Josh. My God. It's really you.'

'Mike.'

They shook hands. Mike Gregory looked leaner than Bowman remembered. As if he had aged backwards. He had the sinewy, supple build of someone twenty years younger. The kind of physique earned by a lifetime of hard work in the field. Only his face seemed to have got older. His skin had the texture of petrified wood. His beard was more grey than brown.

Gregory turned to greet the rest of the team. 'John, Tiny. Good to see a couple of old Hereford faces.'

'Likewise,' said Mallet. He introduced Webb and Casey, the major. Gregory smiled at them with evident relief.

'I was starting to think you guys wouldn't make it,' he said. 'How the devil did you know where to find us, anyway?'

Bowman told him about the dying guard at the palace. The dismembered bodies. Gregory listened impassively.

'That's General Kakuba for you. His men are a bunch of cold-blooded killers. They're not interested in politics or ideology, whatever he might say on the radio. Those scum just want to murder people.'

'Looks like you made it out just in time,' Mallet said, tipping his head at the family.

'We very nearly didn't,' Gregory replied with a grimace. 'The rebels took us by complete surprise. Another two or three minutes and we would have been trapped inside with the rest of those poor buggers.'

'They were directed by the Russians,' said Bowman. 'Their guys were calling the shots on the assault.'

Gregory nodded. 'I'd figured as much.'

'Have you spoken with Vauxhall?' Mallet said.

'Not since before the rebels attacked the palace. I tried raising them on the way over, but coverage is patchy in the jungle.'

'We noticed.'

'Signal is better here, at least.' Gregory scratched his beard. 'There's a cell tower in the local village. Installed on Mr Seguma's orders a couple of years ago. I left a message for Six shortly after we got here. But I haven't heard back.'

'Same for us. They're not answering.'

'Any idea why?'

'Not a fucking clue. Trying to second-guess that lot is a pointless exercise. May as well gaze into a crystal ball.'

Gregory pursed his lips. 'Perhaps they're working out how to respond to the latest developments.'

Loader's face worked itself into a heavy frown.

'What developments?' he asked.

'Haven't you heard? The KUF have seized control of Marafeni airport.'

Mavinda's eyes went so wide they looked as if they might tumble out of their sockets. 'That can't be. We were there a few hours ago. I've got two platoons guarding it.'

'You did, Major. Not now.'

'Are you sure about this?' asked Mallet.

'I'm afraid so, John.' Gregory held up his clamshell phone. 'I've just been speaking with Brigadier Ikouma. Commander of the Karatandan Army. He's received several reports from one of the garrisons near Marafeni. The rebels captured the airport an hour ago.'

'But that means they must have taken full control of the capital,' Bowman said.

'Worse than that, I'm afraid. According to the brigadier, General Kakuba's forces have closed off the borders and taken over the major crossing points. No one is allowed in or out. Which means the KUF have assumed de facto control of the country.'

Loader's eyes bulged with shock. 'Those bastards have been busy. They're moving fast. A few more hours and they'll have the coup wrapped up.'

'It's the Russians,' Mallet said. 'They're a game changer. The smart money says they were the ones directing the attack on the airport.'

'We should notify Six,' said Casey. 'Tell them about the airport. The teams coming in will have to find an alternative place to land.'

Gregory said, 'There's a private airfield twenty miles up the road. President Seguma had it built for his family, to make it easier to jet in and out of here. Some of the guys could land there.'

'I'll let Vauxhall know,' said Mallet. 'Where's the brigadier now?'

'Holed up in an army base in the north. With a few of his loyal men.'

'And the rest of his troops?'

'Scattered around the country. Some of them have dispersed or surrendered to the rebels. The rest are barricaded up inside their bases.'

'Why aren't they out taking the fight to the rebels?' Loader asked.

'They're waiting to see which way the wind blows. They won't want to risk their lives if they think it's a lost cause.'

'Fucking great,' said Loader. 'The local squaddies are worried about getting clipped, so they're leaving us to deal with the mess instead. It's nice to know they're up for a scrap.'

'It is what it is.'

Casey said, 'Have you had any trouble from the rebels?'

'Not a sniff,' replied Gregory.

'They'll come,' Mallet said. 'They have to. General Kakuba won't rest as long as Seguma's wife and kids are still at large. They're too much of a threat to his credibility.'

His phone suddenly hummed into life. He wandered off to take the call, talking in a low voice to Six while the others waited near the bar. The infant was still crying despite his mother's best attempts to calm him down. The two boys were engrossed in their iPad game. The president's brother drank from a plastic bottle of water and touched a graze on his head. His wife, the president's sister-in-law, stared off into nowhere, lost in her thoughts.

Gregory planted a hand on Bowman's shoulder and smiled.

'It's bloody good to see you, Josh. You look well.'

'You too,' said Bowman. 'Shame it's not under happier circumstances.'

'Yes.' He smiled ruefully. 'Still, I'm glad you're here. Nothing like the sight of one of my old B Squadron hands to warm the heart. How is your sister these days? Hayley, isn't it? And your niece?'

Bowman stared at him in amazement. But he shouldn't have been surprised. Gregory had always taken a keen interest in the lives of his men, Bowman reflected. Unlike some of the

Ruperts, he'd displayed a genuine fondness for the soldiers under his command.

'Fine, thanks,' he said. 'They're just fine.'

'So you're with the Cell these days,' Gregory said. 'John's unit.' Bowman nodded. 'I'm pleased for you. I always rated you as an operator. One of the toughest guys I ever had the privilege to fight alongside.'

'Thanks, Mike.'

Gregory attempted a slight smile. 'Perhaps once this is over, I can convince you to come and work for me. I could use a good man to help run this show. And the money's good. Very good.'

'We've got to survive the next few hours first.'

'This rebellion won't last,' Gregory replied darkly. 'The rebels might be winning right now, but once the reinforcements arrive, we'll put the bastards to the sword. Then we'll round up the ringleaders and teach them a lesson they won't ever forget.'

'And the Russians?'

'They'll abandon General Kakuba, once they realise the game is up. Mark my words. No one will dare to challenge Mr Seguma in the future. I'll make damn sure of it.'

There was an icy coldness to his voice that surprised Bowman. In the corner of his eye, he glimpsed Major Mavinda shifting uneasily on the spot. The Karatandan officer seemed almost wary of Gregory. Which struck Bowman as unusual. He remembered, too, the apprehensive look he'd seen on the major's face in the palace basement when Bowman had mentioned Gregory's name.

What's he afraid of? Bowman wondered.

Mallet hung up and strode back over to the group. He looked worried. The skin was pulled so tight across his face it looked like it might snap. He cleared his throat.

'That was Six,' he said. 'We've got a problem.'

'What is it?' Loader asked.

'They've heard from the base in Tripoli. The strike force is running behind schedule. One of the Hercs went tech before take-off. Some sort of engine trouble, they reckon.'

A frigid silence descended over the room. Casey looked startled. 'When did they leave?'

'Two hours ago. Just after two o'clock our time.'

Bowman checked his G-Shock: 04.09. He thought: *It's a six-hour flight from the squadron base in Libya to Karatandu. Which means they won't land in-country until around eight o'clock.*

We're gonna be on our own for the next four hours. At least.

Webb said, 'What about the other elements of the strike force? The SBS and SFSG?'

'They had to wait on the ground until D Squadron was ready to depart. Orders from the head shed. They were adamant that the teams came in together, or not at all.'

Casey said, 'But why not send the other teams in ahead of D Squadron? It doesn't make sense.'

'That's not how the Foreign Office sees it,' Mallet said. 'As far as they're concerned, the priority is a smooth operation with no friendly casualties. They don't want coffins coming home draped in Union Jacks. That means a coordinated attack, maximum fire-power. They're not going to sanction a staggered assault.'

'What if the rebels attack before they arrive?'

'We'll do what we do best,' Mallet replied. 'Fight.'

'The rebels will take hours to get here, anyway,' Loader said. 'They'll be busy securing the rest of the critical infrastructure right now. Scouring the president's other homes. They won't hassle us for a while.'

'The Machete Boys aren't far away,' Casey reminded the others. 'They're at Farangi, according to the last reports. Thirty miles away.'

'Even if they hit us, the odds are still in our favour,' Loader argued. 'We've got the Gimpys, the .50 cal, the mortars. That's more than enough hardware to hold the Boys off.'

'Tiny's right. For once in his life,' Mallet said. 'The situation isn't ideal, but it's nothing we can't handle.'

'And if they hit us hard?'

Gregory's powdery blue eyes twinkled. 'Then we'll give the bastards hell.'

Mallet checked his watch. 'It's first light in eighty minutes. There's a decent chance that the rebels will hit us then. We'll need to get the defences sorted out before they turn up.' He nodded at Gregory. 'How many lads have you got, Mike?'

'Six. Myself, the colonel, the two guys watching the gate and the two on the front door.'

Mallet made a quick mental calculation and nodded. 'That gives us twenty-five soldiers in total. Fourteen in the platoon under the major, your guys, plus my lot.'

'It's a good number,' Loader said.

'Against a few small groups of Machete Boys,' Bowman said. 'But if General Kakuba's men and his Russian mates turn up, it'll get hot.'

'That's a big fucking "if". That mob has only just finished capturing the main airport. They're hours away.'

Mallet rubbed his temples and turned to Mavinda. 'What fire-power have you got with you, Major?'

'We have AK-47s. Grenades. Browning pistols.'

'Anything heavier?'

Mavinda nodded. 'Two FN machine guns.'

'Ammo?'

'Plenty. Twelve hundred rounds of belt apiece.'

'That'll do.' Mallet addressed the two Karatandan officers. 'Major, Colonel, your guys will be posted around the perimeter of the building, covering individual sectors of fire. My guys will take up positions on the rooftop. Mike, you'll direct one of the GPMG teams on the ground.'

Gregory grinned. 'It'll be just like the good old days in the Regiment, John. Lobbing mortars and whacking the enemy with Gimpys.'

'Aye. Except this time, we've got no air support to dig us out of the shit.' The two veterans shared a smile, and then Mallet said to Mavinda, 'We'll need shovels to dig the mortar and fire pits. Petrol, too. Whatever you can spare from the Unimog.'

'What for?' Mavinda asked.

Mallet waved a hand in the general direction of the front entrance. 'We'll need to burn any trees or shrubs around the stronghold. The rebels might use any of it as cover when they attack.'

'There's a storeroom next to the garage,' Gregory explained. 'That's where the gardening tools are kept. You should find everything you need in there.'

Casey said, 'What about the family? We can't just leave them here.'

'Alex has got a point,' Loader said. 'It ain't safe for them in this room. Not when the rounds start flying.'

Mallet thought for a moment. Then he turned to Gregory. 'Is there a strong room anywhere in this place?'

'Afraid not,' Gregory said.

Mallet nodded at Loader and Bowman.

'Tiny. Search the house. Find a secure location. The safest room in the building. Somewhere with thick walls, preferably no windows. Stick the family in there.' He swung back round to Gregory. 'Is anyone else inside the building? Grounds staff?'

'There's a housekeeper,' said Gregory. 'A couple of maids and a gardener. They're in the staff kitchen for now.'

'We'll put them in the same room as the family. They can keep Seguma's rellies company until this thing is over.' Mallet's cold blue eyes rested on Bowman. 'Stay here until Tiny has found a safe place for the family. The rest of you, follow me outside. We'll start organising the defences. Questions?'

He looked round the bar. No one raised a hand. The other four members of the team stared back at Mallet with looks of grim determination.

'Get to work,' he said. 'There's not a moment to lose.'

Twenty-Six

The soldiers sprang into action. Bowman and Loader stayed behind while Mallet hurried out of the room with Casey and Webb. Gregory, Lubowa and Mavinda followed in their wake as they raced towards the front of the stronghold to begin organising the defences. The president's brother and his wife watched the departing soldiers, their faces taut with fear and confusion. Seguma's wife soothed her infant son, shushing in his ear. The twin girls gazed at Bowman and Loader with shy, curious expressions as they approached the table.

'Ma'am.' Loader addressed the president's wife, Christel Seguma. He waved a hand at Bowman. 'This is my colleague, Josh. He's going to wait here with you for a bit.'

'Why?' The brother spoke up. The smartly groomed guy in the embroidered silk tunic. Francis Seguma. The vice-president. 'What's going on?'

'We need to move you and your relatives to a more secure part of the house, sir,' Loader replied softly. 'Josh will stay with you while I search the house for a good place for you to shelter in.'

'Are we expecting trouble?' asked the president's wife.

'It's a possibility, ma'am. But if there is any shooting, me and the lads will take care of it. You won't come to any harm.'

Francis Seguma let out a bitter laugh. 'That is what Colonel Lubowa told us at the palace. He vowed to protect us from these . . . these animals. And look how that turned out!'

'It'll be different this time, sir,' Bowman said. 'Help is on the way.'

'You expect us to believe that?'

'It's the truth, sir.'

'And what are we supposed to do until then? Hide like cowards while these scum attack us?'

'It's for your own safety.'

The brother folded his arms. 'Unacceptable. I demand to speak to my brother. We should be leaving the country while we still can, not waiting for these treacherous dogs to hunt us down.'

'It's too late for that, sir,' Loader said. 'The rebels have closed off the borders. We're stuck here.'

Bowman was drowsy with tiredness. The fog in his mind was thickening. He tried to close his mind to it. To the sweats and the cravings, the intense cramping pain in his guts.

He said, 'This isn't up for debate, sir.'

'Why can't we stay here? This seems perfectly safe to me.'

'Right now, maybe. But when the rounds start coming in, these windows won't protect you. Trust me.'

The brother stared at him, fear gleaming in his eyes. He sighed.

'Very well,' he replied. 'We will do as you wish. But if anything happens to my wife and daughters, or my brother's family, I will hold you personally responsible.'

'We'll keep 'em safe, sir,' Loader said, gently. 'You have my word.'

He left the room and started down the corridor, leaving Bowman to guard the family. Francis Seguma and his wife were having a heated discussion while the president's wife tended to her baby. The boys seemingly took no notice of their mother. Their eyes were glued to the garish images on the tablet screen. They were playing a cartoonish shoot 'em up. There was lots of tinny gunfire and zombie howls, and jaunty music.

One of the twin girls cautiously approached him. Francis Seguma's kids. Her eyes were as round as saucers. A hollow feeling formed in his stomach and he found himself thinking about his little girl. Her infectious giggle. The cheeky look in her eyes. The way his heart would burst with joy whenever she smiled at him.

His life and joy. Snatched away from him.

Murdered.

The girl who wasn't his daughter held out the fluffy toy bear towards Bowman. Like a peace offering.

'This is Leo,' she said in perfect English. 'He wants to say hello.'

Bowman bent down and attempted a smile. 'Hello, Leo.'

The girl leaned in close to the bear and furrowed her brow, as if listening to some whispered remark. Then she looked up at Bowman with a deeply serious face.

'Leo wants to know if you'll be his friend.'

'Of course,' said Bowman. 'I'd be honoured.'

'What's that?' She leaned in again. Lifted her big round eyes to Bowman and pouted.

'Leo says you look sad,' she said.

'Does he?'

She gave an exaggerated nod, in that excited way all small children nod, at the age when the whole world seems impossibly new. 'He says you have sad eyes.'

'Well, you can tell Leo not to worry. I'm just fine.'

The girl spoke softly into the bear's floppy ears. Then she leaned towards Bowman and lowered her voice to a conspiratorial whisper. 'Do you want to know a secret?'

'Go on.'

'Leo gets sad sometimes too. Especially when he doesn't have any honey.'

'Is that so.'

She nodded eagerly. 'Leo says it's OK to be sad. Just as long as it's not forever.'

'Leo's a smart bear.'

'Oh, yes. He's the smartest.'

The president's sister-in-law called out to the girl. The middle-aged woman with the wide hips and the colourful head cloth. 'Marie! Come here!'

The little girl smiled at Bowman, then ran over to her mother, gripping Leo tightly in her right hand. Bowman stood upright and felt a hot pain scratching inside his skull, drilling into his temples. He'd been able to ignore the cravings for the past two hours, but now they came back with a vengeance. His fingertips felt as if someone had taken a blowtorch to them. Sweat percolated down his spine. His stomach churned. He needed to get some pills into his exhausted body. Before he collapsed with fatigue.

He started towards the door.

'Wait here,' he ordered the family.

'Where are you going?' the brother demanded.

'I'll be back in a minute.'

He snuck out of the salon and paced back down the silk-wall-papered corridor. He started pushing open doors, searching for a toilet. One door led into a gym. The second led into a dining room. He got lucky with the third door on the left. Entered a bathroom with more gold in it than a Swiss bank. The toilet seat was gold-plated; so were the taps and the toilet roll holder. Bowman locked the door, propped his rifle against the tiled wall, tipped two pills into the palm of his hand and ground them up in the crusher. He figured it would take Loader several minutes to work his way through the mansion. He'd want to scope out the first floor, the rest of the ground floor rooms, the basement. The guy would be checking for entry and exit points, looking at the security of the doors and windows, the proximity to likely firing positions.

I've got time. A minute to get my head right, before things go noisy. That's all I need.

He snorted up the finely ground opiate dust and felt a sharp searing pain in his nostrils, as if he'd inhaled broken glass. In another few minutes he'd get the electric buzz, the warm fuzzy feeling would flood through his body and the pain would fade away. For a brief while, at least. That was why he'd first got hooked on the pills. People assumed you took drugs to get high, but that wasn't the point, not really. Bowman wasn't looking for euphoria. He wasn't looking to feel anything at all. The opioids gave him that. They took him to a place beyond pain. A place where he didn't care about anything. Where the grief couldn't hurt him.

Bowman tucked the pill container back into his trouser pocket. He ran the cold tap and splashed freezing water on his face, shocking himself out of his lethargy.

Then he heard a woman scream.

The echoing boom of gunfire.

Bowman snatched up his Colt rifle, flung open the door and sprinted back down the hallway to the bar. He heard two more gunshots, a chorus of demented cries, muffled by the sound of the blood rushing in his ears, the hammering of his heart against his breastbone. The fatigue melted away as he charged into the bar, weapon raised, and then his eyes locked on the rebel.

The man stood a couple of paces inside the room from the terrace. A stick-thin guy with an assortment of good luck charms draped over a threadbare Elvis Presley T-shirt. His AK-47 was trained on the terrified figures scrambling for cover across the room. Bowman saw the president's brother lying in a pool of blood, a triangle of bullet holes in his chest. His wife, the president's sister-in-law, shielded the two boys with one arm, her other wrapped around the wailing hysterical form of one of the twin girls. Seguma's wife was curled up in a tight ball, hugging her screaming baby tight to her chest. As if she could protect the boy from the stopping power of a 7.62 × 39 mm bullet.

Then Bowman saw the other girl.

Marie.

She lay limp on the floor, blood oozing out of her belly and head. Her dead hands clutching her blood-splashed toy bear.

In the same frozen moment, Elvis spotted Bowman crashing into the room. He turned towards the new threat and fired. The AK-47 barked. Bowman tucked into a roll and shifted to the right as the rebel let off a three-round burst, shooting from the hip. The rounds thudded into the wall six or seven inches above Bowman, putting holes in the president's personal photo collection. Bowman came up from the roll in a rapid blur, then angled his weapon at the rebel. No time to properly aim. He just centred the barrel on Elvis's mass and pulled the trigger twice.

The rounds smacked into Elvis in a quick one-two. The first nailed him in the crotch, shredding his balls. The second bullet plugged him in the chest. His vital plumbing. The rebel let out a pained grunt as he toppled backwards. He crashed against the door and landed on his back, his weapon clattering to the floor beside him.

Bowman stood rooted to the spot, unable to move, staring help-lessly at the girl. He heard voices in the corridor.

A moment later, Loader charged into the room ahead of Mallet. Casey, Webb, Gregory and Lubowa ran in after them, weapons drawn. They caught sight of the two bodies and froze. The president's sister-in-law ran over to her dead daughter, howling in grief and anguish. The two boys hugged their mother, tears streaming down their terror-stricken faces. The other girl screamed for her dead father.

Loader dropped down beside the bodies and checked them for pulses. Shook his head slowly.

'What the fuck happened?' he demanded.

'Bastard snuck in from the terrace,' Bowman said. He felt sick, had to force the words out. 'There was nothing I could do . . . '

'Just the one?'

Bowman nodded.

'Must have been a lone raider,' Webb said.

'Or a scout for the Machete Boys,' said Mallet. 'Sent here by his mates to see if the place was worth looting. He would have spotted the lights.'

'How the fuck did he get in?' Loader said.

'This place is surrounded by a chain-link fence,' said Gregory. 'It's not in the best condition. There are gaps in it. He must have snuck through one of them.'

'He left us!' the sister-in-law shouted between her pained sobs. She pointed an accusatory finger at Bowman. 'He wasn't here! He should have stopped that man!'

Mallet stared at him, the blood draining from his face. 'Where the fuck were you, Josh?'

'The bathroom,' Bowman replied falteringly. 'I . . . I was gone for a minute. Not even that.'

'I don't give a fuck if it was ten seconds. You shouldn't have left them alone.'

'I didn't know . . . ' Bowman choked up. 'I thought it was safe.'

'You thought fucking wrong.'

'I thought you men are supposed to be professional,' Lubowa said.

'We are,' Mallet snapped back. He glowered at Bowman. 'Most of us.'

Bowman gripped the rifle so hard he thought it might break apart in his hands. A father and his young daughter had been killed. His own fault. He'd fucked up once before, fifteen years ago. Back then, his mistake had cost the lives of his own family. Sophie. Amy. Now he had the blood of two more innocents on his hands.

You should have been protecting them, the voice at the back of his head told him. *Watching for threats.*

Instead, you were shoving drugs up your nose.

And now two people are dead.

'Get some men out there,' Mallet ordered Colonel Lubowa. He gestured towards the grounds overlooked by the terrace at the rear of the estate. 'Cover the treeline before any other fucker gets the same idea. If they see anything moving that's not friendly, drop it.'

Lubowa shot Bowman a scolding look before he hastened back down the corridor.

'You two.' Mallet addressed Casey and Webb. 'Back to work. Get those defences in shape.'

Once they had left the room, he swivelled his gaze round to Loader.

'Did you find a safe room for the rest of the family?'

He nodded quickly. 'The wine cellar. They'll be safe down there, John. Only one way in or out. Strongest point of the house.'

'Take this lot down there now,' Mallet said, indicating the family. 'Tell the colonel to stick one of his guards in the cellar with them. Make sure he understands not to leave them under any circumstances. Tell him not to answer the door until the fighting is over.'

'What about the girl? The president's brother?'

'Get them out of this room. I don't care where. Just get them out of here.'

'This means trouble.' Loader sucked in a deep breath. 'The Machete Boys will know where to find us now. They'll figure it out, once they realise their mate ain't coming back.'

'Not just them,' said Gregory.

Casey looked up at him. 'What do you mean?'

'The Boys and the KUF are allies,' Gregory explained. 'The Boys will alert General Kakuba's men as soon as they know where we are. They'll want to pass on the message.'

'Bloody great,' Loader muttered.

Mallet's hard blue eyes lingered on Bowman. 'You. Sort your fucking head out. Give Tiny a hand. Then get outside and help the others.'

He marched out of the room, rifle at his side. Gregory followed him. Loader gently pulled the sister-in-law back from her dead daughter, Bowman ushered the boys and the other twin girl to their feet. Seguma's wife gathered her belongings, and then Bowman and Loader ushered the family down the hallway. The children wept softly, the sister-in-law made a deep keening noise in her throat.

They reached a door off to one side of the central atrium and descended a spiral staircase to the basement. Loader led them down a cobwebbed corridor, past a plain metal door, into a spacious wine cellar with a vaulted ceiling. Rows of wine bottles were arranged in timber racks, the necks coated in a patina of dust. Boxes of wine yet to be unpacked had been stacked against the walls. In one of them Bowman glimpsed a set of electric cattle prods. He wondered what they were doing in the cellar. A mistake, probably. One of the household staff putting the wrong package in the wrong place.

The family sat around the oak table in the tasting area. Bowman jogged back upstairs, and left Loader to watch over the family while he fetched the staff. The two maids, the chef. The gardener. He led them down to the basement. Left them with the family, hurried back up to the ground floor and ran outside. He beckoned over one of the presidential guards, led him into the cellar. Loader told the guard not to leave the room, no matter what. He made sure the guard understood his job, demonstrated the knocking code they would use when it was safe to emerge. Then he stepped out into the corridor with Bowman, closing the door behind them.

'What the fuck was that all about?' Loader hissed.

Bowman kept on walking. 'Don't know what you're talking about, mate.'

'Yeah, you do. Upstairs. Leaving the family alone. What were you thinking?'

Bowman stopped and rounded on his mucker.

'Have you got something you want to say to me, Tiny?'

Loader gritted his teeth. His face seethed with rage. 'You've lost your edge. You're a joke. That girl's dead because of you.'

Bowman half-closed his eyes. 'It was a mistake. I didn't know that shooter was out there. No one did.'

'Don't take the piss. I've heard the stories doing the rounds at Hereford.'

Bowman tensed. 'What stories?'

'Everyone knows you ain't the soldier you used to be. All the lads at camp have been saying the same thing. They reckon you've got sloppy. Turning up late for briefings, losing bits of kit, getting the basics wrong. I didn't believe them at the time, but now I'm beginning to see what they meant.' He wrinkled his nose at Bowman, as if he carried a bad smell. 'John should never have recruited you to the Cell.'

'Those lads should mind their own business. And so should you, Tiny.'

'Fuck off, Josh. We're about to get hit by a swarm of rebels. This is no place for a washed-up Blade. Christ, we can't even rely on you to guard a few civvies.'

'I've got what it takes,' Bowman insisted.

'Bollocks. This ain't the first mistake you've made on this op. Is it?'

Bowman said nothing.

'Patrick told us about what happened in Monte Carlo,' Loader went on. 'Raiding Lang's medicine cabinet when you should have been doing a bog-standard room clearance. Almost blowing your cover story with the concierge. And to top it off, you're bang out of shape. You've been sweating non-stop since we left London. I've seen slop jockeys on Selection in better condition than you.'

'It's not what you think,' Bowman said.

'How's that, mate? Because from where I'm standing, it looks like you're a fucking liability.'

Bowman stared at the floor for a long beat, trying to find the words. Ashamed to look his friend in the eye. Ashamed of himself, his failure to protect the little girl. Then he sighed and looked up at his old Regiment mucker.

'I've got a problem. A habit. A bad one.'

'What is it? Booze?'

Bowman shook his head.

'Gambling, then? You spunked all your hard-earned cash down at the bookies, is that it?'

'No, mate. Nothing like that.'

'What, then?'

'Opioids,' Bowman said. 'I'm dependent on opioids.'

Loader jerked his head back in surprise. 'What, like smack?'

'I've never touched heroin. And I don't inject. It's just pills.'

'Like painkillers, you mean? Them ones you get on prescription?'

'Sometimes. Mostly it's synthetic tablets. From China. They make them in illegal factories over there. Red Lights, Jumping Jacks, Cookies, Space Dust. That's what they're called on the street, anyway, I don't know their real names. I get a regular supply through a trusted contact. A friend of mine from back home. He's my connect.'

It was out there at last. His secret. Bowman felt something heavy lift from his chest. Loader looked at him in stunned silence. 'How long has this been going on for?'

'Ten years.'

'You've been an addict for a fucking decade?'

'Not all the time. There are periods when I've been clean. Sometimes I've been able to get by with the odd pill or two. Other times, it's worse than that. It gets out of hand. Then the drugs start controlling your life.'

'Like now.'

'I guess so.'

'That's why you left the family up there? To pop some pills?'

Bowman nodded, burning with shame. He hated himself in that moment. Despised what he had become. 'Yes.'

Loader stared at him in shock and disbelief. 'Why'd you do it, mate? Why get hooked on that shit in the first place?'

Bowman exhaled deeply. 'You know about my family. What happened to them, back when I was in the Met.' Loader nodded. 'It was my fault,' Bowman said. 'They died because of me, mate.'

Loader's eyebrows pinched together. 'I thought they were murdered by the Albanian mob?'

'Those bastards did the killing. But I was the one who put their lives in danger.'

He looked away, lips trembling, fists shaking with impotent rage. Loader waited for him to go on.

'I was working undercover at the time, see. A long-term job. We were trying to penetrate a gang of ex-cons based in Essex. But the real target was the Albanian mobsters they were doing business with. The Hoxha clan. The older brother, Agon, was the boss of the outfit. They were involved in a lot of the big cocaine shipments coming in from Europe.

'I spent months trying to earn their trust. It was hard work, hanging out with a bunch of sick gangsters all day long, sticking to my cover story, making sure I didn't slip up. But it was worth it. All the int I gleaned I passed back to my handler at the Met. She was the only one who knew my true identity. That was the arrangement. No one else was supposed to know anything about me.

'Eventually, Agon Hoxha invited me to a high-level meeting with the clan. A major arms-trafficking deal they wanted to discuss. I thought that was the big breakthrough. I'd go to the meeting and get enough intelligence to put the Albanians and their Essex business partners away for life. That was the plan, at least.'

'What happened?'

'Someone had tipped off the Albanians about me.'

'Who?'

'A bent copper. Agon Hoxha had him on the payroll. He'd managed to uncover my identity, piecing together scraps of information from the file. The Albanians found out and planned to lure me into a trap. Put one in the back of my head and dump my body in the Thames.'

'How did you get away?'

'I was on my way to the meeting when I got a message from my handler, telling me to get away immediately. I managed to escape,' he added, his voice strained with grief. 'But when the Hoxha clan couldn't get to me, they took revenge on my family instead.'

Tears welled in Bowman's eyes at the memory. He struggled to go on.

'I found them at home. I'll never forget that scene. There's not a day goes by when I don't think about it. They took my wife, tied her up and carved a clown's smile on her face from ear to ear. Then they slit my daughter's throat and let her bleed out on the kitchen floor. Made my wife watch the life drain out of our beautiful little girl. Then they blew Amy's brains out. Left them there for me to find, like some sick present.'

'Christ, mate. I'm sorry.'

'Not your fault.'

'I know. But still.' Loader hesitated. 'Didn't they arrest the bastards who did it?'

'There was a big investigation. We all knew who was responsible. Everyone wanted to nail them. It wasn't for a lack of trying. But the Crown Prosecution Service felt the case was too weak. Too many flaws, not a reasonable likelihood of a conviction.'

'Jesus. I didn't know that part of it.'

Bowman sighed and said, 'What happened, it messed with my head. Nothing could shut out the pain. I couldn't sleep, couldn't think. Then someone offered me a pill. Said it would make it all go away. That's how it started. I used the pills for a few months, cleaned up my act and joined the army. Did my time in SFSG, passed Selection. Everything was rosy. I managed to stay off the pills. For a while.'

'Why'd you get back on it?'

'Iraq. All that high-intensity warfare. You remember what it was like out there, mate.'

Loader nodded with feeling. 'Yeah, I do.'

'I was stressed, exhausted. Burning the candle at both ends. Some of the guys we were working with in Delta Force were using a cocktail of drugs just to get from one day to the next. So I got back on the stuff again. Since then, it's been on and off. Sometimes I'm clean. Sometimes not.'

'Iraq was a long time ago,' Loader countered. 'You can't blame it on the war. We were all there. Not all of us turned into fucking junkies.'

'You don't understand, Tiny. No one plans on becoming an addict. But once you get hooked, it turns into an obsession. Getting pills, making sure you've got enough to last the day, it's all you care about.'

'That's what has been on your mind since we left London?' The anger in Loader's voice was so sharp you could cut glass with it. 'When you can get your next high?'

'It's not about that, mate. I'm taking this stuff to feel normal. That's it.'

'So kick it. If it ain't about getting high, stop doing it.'

Bowman shook his head. 'If I went cold turkey, I'd get the shakes. You don't know what that feels like. It's the worst thing in the world. I can't even begin to describe how much it hurts. Addicts – people like me – we'd do anything to avoid withdrawal.'

Loader looked closely at him. 'How bad is it right now?'

'I've been in darker places.'

'Are you sure you're up for this?'

Bowman said, 'I've got pills. Enough to last me the rest of the day. As long as I get a regular hit, I'll be able to function.'

'That's not what I asked.'

'I can handle the firefight. I won't let anyone down.'

Loader stared at him for a long moment. There was anger in his eyes, but something gentler, too. The concern of an old friend.

'You can't go on like this, Josh.'

'I realise that.'

'We shouldn't even be having this discussion. I should go straight to John with this. He'd hit the roof if he found out.'

'Somehow,' Bowman said, 'I think he already knows.'

Loader's face screwed up. 'Why would John bring you on to the Cell, if he thought you had a drug problem?'

'I don't have a clue. But there's something about the way he talks to me. Like he sees right through the bullshit.'

'John don't miss much,' Loader agreed. 'But he might see things differently if he found out you were snorting pills when you should have been protecting the family. He'd boot you off the Cell.'

'You're probably right. And I'd deserve it.' Bowman's head hung low. 'I'm sorry as fuck about what happened to that girl and her old man, believe me. I'll never forgive myself for that. But I'm going to get better. I promise.'

Loader looked at him, tight-lipped, his eyes as narrow as knife slashes.

'Why should I believe you?' he asked after a beat.

'I've kicked the pills before,' Bowman said. 'I can do it again. As soon as this op is over, I'll go clean.'

'You could start now.'

'I can't, Tiny. I'd get the shakes if I tried. I'd be no use to anyone in a firefight then. But if you give me a chance, I'll get my head sorted once we're out of here.'

Loader kept on staring at him. His face was a picture of indecision. Torn between his loyalty to Mallet and his sympathy for an old friend. Then his face appeared to relax, and he tapped a finger against his chin.

'I've heard about these ceremonies,' he said. 'Down in Peru. People go there to take ayahuasca. My missus told me all about them. Mary's always reading the news. Got a brain on her, she does,' he added proudly.

'I don't follow. What's that got to do with opioids?'

'Mary reckoned a lot of addicts go to these ceremonies. To cure themselves. Drug addicts, alcoholics, all kinds of people. Cleanses your body or something. I didn't understand it myself. But you might want to look into it. Once we're out of here, like.'

Bowman smiled at his mucker. 'Thanks, Tiny.'

'Don't thank me just yet. I'll keep this between us for now. But if you can't get your habit under control, I'm going straight to John.'

'It won't come to that,' Bowman said. 'I'm not gonna let this beat me.'

'I hope not.' Loader flashed a cheeky grin. 'After all, if you get kicked off the team, who's going to be my wingman?'

'With your crap dance moves, Tiny, the only thing you're at risk of pulling is a muscle.'

Loader laughed. 'Come on, you Cockney bastard. Let's go.'

They turned and headed for the stairs.

04.38 hours.

Fifty-two minutes until first light.

Twenty-Seven

They stepped out to a hive of frenetic activity. Teams of Karatandan soldiers were toiling away in the eerie predawn. Four of them worked in pairs, digging gun pits in the lawn either side of the eagle-topped fountain. One other guy hacked at the trunk of a palm tree. His mate bucked another felled tree into six-foot-long logs using a petrol chain-saw. A third soldier lifted up one of the logs and hauled it over to the nearest gun pit. He stacked it beside the heaped soil at the edge of the hole. Another soldier began covering the timbers with the backfilled earth, compacting it with the flat head of the shovel. The wood and soil would create an area of frontal cover strong enough to stop a small-calibre round. Further to the east, a hundred metres away, two other Karatandan soldiers were stacking garden rocks and stones from the pagoda around the rim of their shallow trench. Creating a classic mur-der hole. The guys would leave a gap in the rocks wide enough to stick their rifle barrels through, allowing them to cut down the enemy with-out exposing themselves to incoming rounds. The remainder of the local troops were hastily clearing the fields of fire across the ground on the north side of the estate, burning down trees and bushes.

Mallet stood beside the soldiers at one of the half-finished fire pits, bellowing at them. 'Call that a fucking pit? I've seen puddles deeper than that. Keep digging.'

He caught sight of Bowman and Loader and beckoned them over. Mallet scowled at them both. 'Where have you two idiots been?'

Loader started to reply but Mallet cut him off with a wave of his hand, chopping air.

'Save your breath.' He thrust an arm at the irrigation ditch run-ning north to south beyond the garden wall. 'Set up the Claymores over there. That ditch is the most vulnerable area of the estate. If the rebels cut through the fence, they could use it to crawl right up to us.'

'Like the battle of Little Bighorn,' said Bowman. 'When the Plains Indians used the dead ground to advance on the cavalry.'

'Exactly. Except Custer didn't have a couple of Claymores to play with. We do. So let's fucking use them.'

'Where are the other guys?' asked Loader.

'Alex is on the mortar with one of the major's lads. The others are on the roof. Patrick has got the AWC. You two will operate the Gimpys. I'll be up there as well with the .50 cal. Between us, we'll cover the approaches to the stronghold.'

'What about Mike?'

'He's got one of the spare radios. He'll cover the front of the stronghold with one of the platoon's Gimpys. If the rebels manage to cut through the fence, he'll take them down.'

'And the local troops?'

'We're posting four other guys at the front. Two on top of the guest house, two others in a pit to the east. Four others in defensive positions guarding the west flank. The major will man the second platoon Gimpy in the gun pit to the rear. If they start taking rounds from any rebel forces from that direction, he'll let us know.'

'Better that way,' Loader said. 'The last thing we need is a blue-on-blue.'

Bowman nodded in agreement. The men in Mavinda's platoon seemed brave enough, but they weren't trained to an elite level. Giving them designated sectors of fire lessened the chances of an inexperienced soldier accidentally slotting a friendly.

'Get a move on,' Mallet says. 'Once you've got those Claymores rigged, give us a shout. There's still lots to do before we're ready.'

He gave them his back and marched over to the soldiers at the gun pit. Bowman and Loader left the porch and sprinted across the driveway to the Land Cruiser. They grabbed the satchels containing the two Claymores from the boot and ran at a brisk clip towards the western garden. Casey was kneeling beside the mortar pit in front of the ruined wall on the north side of the garden. The second guy on the mortar team, the lanky Karatandan sergeant, sat next to her. They worked together, Lanky emptying the shells from their boxes, Casey taking the pin out of the nose of each projectile and lining them up at the side of the mortar cannon. Prepping them for the fight.

Bowman and Loader hastened past them, ducked around the corner of the garden wall. They climbed down into the southern end of the drainage ditch, crawled forward twenty metres, stopped and placed the charges facing out towards the northern end of the ditch.

'Line them up here,' Bowman said. 'We'll turn this area into a massive IED.'

They carefully removed both mines from their bandoliers, flipped out the scissor legs and planted the Claymores in the grass, sighting them down the ditch. They screwed the blasting caps into the detonator wells, sprinkled grass and leaves over the mines to camouflage them, rechecked the sights. Then Bowman and Loader unwound the coils of electrical wire and retreated around the wall, back towards the mortar pit. They made sure the safety bails were flipped up on their firing devices, then connected the electrical wires to the clackers.

'You triggered one of these before?' Loader said to Casey.

She gave him a long hard stare. 'Take an educated guess.'

'Just checking.' He indicated the clackers. 'The safetys are on. Don't fire them until one of us gives the word from the rooftop. We'll need to nail as many of the enemy as possible. No point wasting them on one or two attackers.'

'Got it.'

She set the clackers down beside the cannon, went back to setting up the mortar. Loader grinned.

'That'll give those fuckers a nasty surprise,' he said to Bowman.

Bowman glanced back at the ditch. The Claymores would repel any rebels attacking from the dead ground to the north of the garden. As soon as the enemy neared the southern end of the channel, Casey would detonate the mines, annihilating them in a lethal torrent of steel balls. Anyone caught in the blast radius would be torn to pieces.

'Tiny! Get the rest of the Gimpy ammo on the roof.' Mallet yelled at them from across the front drive. 'Josh, start putting down some range markers for the mortar and sniper teams.'

Loader bounded back over to the Unimog. He started unloading the remaining boxes of 7.62 mm belt for the Gimpys, garlanding the linked brass around his neck. Meanwhile Bowman tapped the pressel switch on his webbing and raised Webb on the tactical radio. The latter was on the mansion rooftop, scanning the estate through the Schmidt & Bender Mark II variable sight attached to his rifle.

The two soldiers worked together, Bowman pacing out various distances from the stronghold and setting down visual markers, then reporting them back over the comms to Webb, who then made notes of the ranges with a pencil and paper. Creating a series of reference points for the guys on the roof to help determine the distance to the target. Bowman paced out fifty metres, set down a large rock from a water feature in the garden. He placed more markers at fifty-metre intervals, all the way to the fence, and then the treeline. Which was five hundred metres from the mansion. The demarcation line for the mortar. Everything between that line and the two-hundred-metre mark was mortar-lobbing territory. Anything shorter than that would land dangerously close to the defenders.

If we have to start putting down rounds at that range, thought Bowman, *the enemy will have breached the estate.*

And we'll have our backs to the fucking wall.

He laid a final marker at the edge of the clearing, then jogged around the estate, checking the condition of the perimeter fence. Looking for any weak points or gaps big enough for a human to sneak through. He deposited stones beside the largest gaps, so the defenders could easily concentrate their fire on those areas.

He didn't feel tired now. Adrenaline was taking over, juicing his bloodstream, boosting his fatigued body. Adrenaline, and the iron will to win that lived within all SAS men.

The odds of the team getting attacked in the next few hours were high, Bowman knew. The Machete Boys would expect their scout to return from the mansion shortly. Once he failed to report back, the Boys would come looking for him. And they would be ready for a scrap.

So will we, thought Bowman. *We're preparing for the fight of our lives.*

He hurried over to the Unimog to unpack the remaining boxes of 7.62 mm belt. The soldiers under Mavinda's command were frantically burning down vegetation or piling earth on top of logs around the fire pits. To the east, two men from the Presidential Guard carted an aerial ladder over to the guest house. One of the guards held the base while the second raised the fly section until the top rung drew level with the guest house rooftop. They braced the ladder against the façade and started scaling towards the roof to set up another firing position.

At the front of the mansion, Gregory and the Karatandan soldier with the toothbrush moustache were preparing one of the platoon's FN machine guns in a fire pit. The weapon looked essentially the same as the Gimpys used by the Cell. But older, battered and rusting, with a scratched wooden stock.

Mallet checked his watch and shouted across at Bowman. 'That's it! We're going topside. Hurry the fuck up!'

Bowman ripped open the lids from the last three boxes of GPMG ammo. He draped the gleaming belts around his neck, snatched up his rifle, and hastened towards the mansion with Mallet. They ran up the grand staircase, hit the second-floor landing and passed down a hallway lined with portraits of Seguma in various heroic poses: riding a horse, Seguma the hunter posing with a dead lion, Seguma in uniform inspecting the troops. They barged through the emergency fire exit, climbed a dank stairwell and cannoned through the door at the top.

The rooftop was a chaotic cluster of satellite dishes, antennae, solar panels and air-conditioning units. Rubbish and gravel littered the ground. The other members of the team had taken up firing positions along the decorative stone parapet. Loader was covering the eastern approach to the stronghold with one of the two GPMGs. Webb had a spot on the north side overlooking the ground to the front. He was in a kneeling stance, aiming his AWC rifle through one of the perforated gaps in the parapet wall. As well as the heavy weaponry each man also had his primary rifle, pistol and several frag grenades. A massive amount of firepower.

Let's pray we don't need to burn through it all.

'Get on the other Gimpy,' Mallet ordered. 'Move!'

Bowman ran past the central skylight and darted over to the second GPMG resting on the floor next to the west-facing parapet. Mallet made for the .50 cal rifle along the southern wall, covering the rear of the estate. Bowman laid out the belts of 7.62 mm ammo he'd carried up from the Unimog, placing them on top of the seven other belts heaped next to the Gimpy. Two hundred rounds per belt. A total of two thousand bullets.

Bowman knelt beside the Gimpy, cocked the bolt on the side of the receiver and engaged the safety. He popped open the top cover, lifted up the belt of 7.62 mm from the top of the pile and inserted the end of it into the feed tray. Closed the cover. Glanced at his watch.

Sixteen minutes until first light.

'See anything, Patrick?' Loader said.

'Nothing,' Webb replied calmly. 'It's all clear out there.'

'Where do you think they'll hit us, John?' asked Bowman.

'The front,' Mallet said. 'It's the most obvious route into the estate. No gate. If they're going to attack us, that's where the bastards will probably come from.'

'They're not military geniuses, Josh,' Loader said dismissively. 'We're dealing with the Machete Boys. A bunch of pissed idiots. They're not gonna sneak up on our flanks.'

'Alex? You OK down there too?' Mallet said into his mic.

'This may come as a huge surprise to you guys,' Casey said, 'but I'm doing just fine.'

'Don't start putting down rounds with the mortar until I give the order. Stick to your rifle for now. We want to save the heavy stuff until they start coming at us en masse.'

'Do you want to tell me how to use a gun as well?'

Mallet laughed.

Casey said, 'Don't worry about me, guys. Look after yourselves.'

Bowman rested the Gimpy on top of the stone parapet and scanned the ground to the north-west. In the murky half-light before dawn he could make out the ornamental garden below, the mortar pit beside the crumbling wall on the northern edge of the garden. The irrigation ditch to the north of the garden wall, with the two Claymores planted at the bottom of the trench. Further west a pair of gun pits guarded the flank. In the far distance, Bowman could just about see the outline of a clump of trees.

Everyone watched and waited.

Eleven minutes until first light.

'Still quiet,' Webb said.

'Won't stay that way for long,' Loader said. 'The Machete Boys will know we're here. The only question is when they're going to hit us. And how hard.'

They continued watching. Mallet checked his phone for messages from Six. Loader ran downstairs to get a brew on. He came back a short while later with a two-litre coffee flask, cups, loaves of bread, a bag of apples. The team helped themselves to mugs of hot black coffee while Webb observed the front approach road. Occasionally, he would get tired of peering through the scope and look up, scanning the ground with his naked eye. The treetops were alive with the predawn chorus of birdsong and primates, announcing the coming of the new day.

Maybe our last, Bowman thought.

Six minutes before first light.

'Anything, guys?' Loader called out.

'Nothing,' Webb replied.

'Same,' Mallet said.

'Any word on those inbound Hercs?' Bowman asked.

'On their way. No change. Still due to land at eight o'clock.'

Bowman checked his watch: 05.25.

There's a long way to go yet, he thought.

'Where will they land?' Loader asked. 'The main airport is out of action.'

'They'll fragment,' said Mallet. 'SFSG and the SBS detachments will head for an RV in the north of the country. They'll retake the airport and secure the infrastructure in and around the capital. D Squadron will land at the private airfield up the road. Twenty miles from here. Which is good news for us. Means they'll get here sooner.'

'How long will that take?'

'Depends,' said Mallet.

'On what?'

'The situation on the ground. The guys might run into an ambush on the way over here. Or they might hit an IED. Any number of things could slow them down.'

'Or the rebels might attack the airfield,' Webb said.

'Not likely. There's a military contingent based at the airfield. Two platoons. They're under orders to protect the airstrip at all costs.'

'What about air support?' Bowman asked.

'I've asked the question. It's a hard no,' Mallet said. 'Nothing in the area. No fast air. It's just us.'

'This op just keeps getting better and better,' Loader grumbled.

'We've still got the upper hand. We've got the high ground, the hardware. A few hours from now, D Squadron will fly in and roll through the enemy.'

'As long as they get here before the KUF, I'll be happy. General Kakuba sounds like an evil bastard.'

Mallet said, 'We've had no reports of KUF paramilitary activity in the area. As far as we know, the only rebels nearby are the Machete Boys.'

A few minutes later, the first pale glimmer of light fringed the horizon. Gradually, the darkness lifted. Bowman sipped coffee and glanced round the estate. He could see the ground to the west more clearly now. The distant trees resolved themselves into a dense palm grove. There was another grassy field to the east of the stronghold leading towards an orchard. He saw the blackened stumps of burned-down trees and bushes at the front of the mansion. The thick woodland a hundred metres north of the clearing. In the far distance he spied a chain of hogbacked hills shaped like the knuckles of a clenched fist, silhouetted against the lightening sky.

A minute passed.

Then another.

Then Webb said, 'I've got movement.'

'Where?' Mallet said.

'The farms across the main road,' Webb replied.

'Rebels?' asked Bowman.

'Civilians. Unarmed. Men and women, some kids. A big group of them.'

'What are they up to?' asked Loader.

Webb said, 'They're running into the interior. Moving fast. Looks like they're expecting trouble.'

'They must know something we don't,' Loader said.

'It's the rebels,' said Bowman. 'They must be on the way.'

'Why aren't these people staying hidden indoors?'

'This isn't a spectator sport, Tiny. They won't want to stick around when the shooting starts.'

Mallet tapped his pressel switch. 'Mike, Alex, Major. Heads-up. The locals are scarpering. We're about to get engaged.'

Webb kept the AWC trained on the ground to the north of the mansion. The others scanned the flanks and rear. Bowman tightened his right hand around the GPMG grip. The pain between his temples had faded. He wasn't thinking about the pills anymore, or how long until his next hit. Every fibre of his being was concentrated on the imminent battle.

Then Webb said, 'Enemy movement. On the approach road. There's a technical with them. Coming this way.'

'Move!' Mallet shouted.

The others swiftly converged on the north side of the parapet. Bowman and Loader stood with their GPMGs resting on the top of the stone capping, either side of Mallet. The latter dropped to a prone firing position and poked the .50 cal barrel through an opening in the parapet. Bowman peered through the Gimpy scope and saw the stone archway at the far end of the front drive, four hundred metres to the north of the stronghold. He saw the clearing beyond. The dark mass of woodland either side of the approach road, screening the main road from view. He concentrated on that area, straining his eyes.

Then he saw the technical. Which was basically a battered pickup truck with a machine gun mounted on a tripod on the rear platform. The distance from the rooftop to the vehicle was something like six hundred metres but Bowman could clearly identify it. He saw the gun mounted on the back, the gunner. The technical was crawling along at walking speed towards the stone archway.

Two groups of rebels were moving forward in the shadows either side of the truck, staying close to one another. A safety in numbers thing, Bowman guessed. He couldn't see their faces at this distance, but he could easily distinguish their shapes through the GPMG sights. The driver had killed the technical's headlights to reduce their visibility.

Loader said, 'The Machete Boys?'

'Looks like it,' said Webb. 'Three of them are wearing lucky charms.'

'They won't be feeling so lucky in a few minutes.'

'Do you see any weapons, Patrick?' said Bowman.

'Most of them are carrying AK-47s. A few have got pistols or knives.'

Mallet hit his pressel switch and spoke into his throat mic. 'We've got incoming rebels. Approaching the archway. Don't fire unless I give the order.'

'Roger that,' Gregory said.

'Roger,' said Casey.

Mallet scoped out the enemy with the .50 cal. 'Tiny, on my signal you take the guys on the left of the technical,' he said. 'Josh, drop the fuckers on the right. We'll deal with the technical.'

Bowman exhaled and kept his cross hairs fixed on the rebels. Dawn burnished the sky, a ribbon of orange rising above the distant hills. The shapes to the left and right of the technical grew more distinct as they neared the clearing. Bowman understood why Mallet wanted to wait. If they fired too early, the Boys would scatter into the woods. Better to hold their fire until they had broken beyond the trees. Once they were in the open ground, there would be nowhere to hide.

'How many guys have you got eyes on, Patrick?' Loader asked.

'Thirty,' said Webb. 'Two more in the technical. One driver, one on the back manning the machine gun.'

'A small unit for an assault.'

Bowman said, 'They're not expecting a big fight. They probably think they've only got to deal with a few guards.'

'Patrick, I'll go for the engine,' said Mallet. 'You take out the driver and the guy on the back.'

'OK.'

Bowman lined up the wire cross hairs with the cluster of figures to the right of the technical. A series of horizontal lines marked the vertical axis of the graticule. To help the shooter compensate for things like bullet drop and gravity. As Bowman looked on, the technical crawled past the treeline and reached the clearing.

The rebels swarmed forward either side of the vehicle. There were no guards at the sentry box to the side of the archway. They had been deliberately withdrawn to one of the gun pits at the rear of the stronghold. Part of the trap the team had set, designed to lure the enemy into a false sense of security. The Machete Boys would see the abandoned guard post and think the building was poorly defended. They wouldn't spot the soldiers on the rooftop, not at this distance.

Not until it was too late.

'Wait,' said Mallet.

The last of the rebels glided past the treeline. The men in both columns were closely grouped together, Bowman noticed. Which was a big mistake. A professionally trained unit would have advanced to the target in a loose formation. Massed ranks of infantry were easier to cut down than individuals spaced far apart from one another.

The Boys cantered on alongside the technical as it came bouncing down the approach road towards the archway. Then they broke across the clearing. They moved five metres beyond the treeline. Then ten metres. Fifteen.

Twenty.

Mallet waited another second.

Then he pulled the trigger.

Twenty-Eight

The gunshot thundered across the breaking dawn.

Bowman looked through his scope as the half-inch-thick round struck the front of the technical, cratering the radiator and the cylinder block, killing the engine. Which was the smart move, from a tactical point of view. Kill the vehicle first, instead of the guys on foot. Disable the main threat. Specifically, the machine gun mounted on the back of the technical. Bowman couldn't identify the weapon from this distance, but he assumed it was a DShK or similar. Something Russian, in the heavy machine-gun family, with an effective range of about two thousand metres. A much more serious threat than the AK-47 rifles the foot soldiers were packing. The team didn't want to be on the receiving end of a burst from the technical.

The pickup jerked to a sudden stop in the middle of the clearing. Smoke gushed out of the sides of the bonnet. Bowman heard a sharp *ca-rack* as Webb took aim and fired the AWC. The smaller calibre sniper rifle. Chambered for the 7.62 × 51 mm NATO round, lethal up to a range of eight hundred metres. The bullet starred the front windshield, killing the driver before he could debus. Webb cocked the bolt in one smooth motion and fired a second time. The rebel on the back of the truck tumbled away from the machine gun. Three quick shots and the technical was out of the fight.

The thirty Machete Boys either side of the truck froze.

The suddenness of the attack had shocked them. Like getting punched in the face by a stranger in the street. They were experiencing sensory overload. Three of their mates had just been wiped out in a few seconds. No one knew what to do. The Boys had no plan B. They had walked straight into an ambush. Everything had gone to shit.

'Open up with the Gimpys!' Mallet shouted. 'Now!'

Smoke was still pouring out of the engine block as Bowman aimed at the close grouping of rebels to the right of the knackered technical. His left hand rested on top of the GPMG's plastic stock, his right clasped the grip, creating a stable firing platform. A few metres away, Loader was standing in front of the parapet wall, pointing his weapon at the massed group of figures to the left of the stationary pickup. No need for the operators to shelter behind the parapet itself. The Boys were going to get dropped before they could loose off any rounds. No more than two seconds had elapsed since Mallet had fired the first round from the .50 cal.

The rebels were thirty metres from the perimeter fence. Seventy metres from the wooded area to the north. No man's land.

The kill zone.

Bowman fired.

A gout of flame spewed out of the Gimpy snout. Spent link and cartridges pinged out of the ejector on the right side of the receiver, tinkling against the cement floor as Bowman emptied two bursts at the Boys to the right of the technical, cutting down five of them in a storm of hot lead. At his nine o'clock, Loader was letting rip with the second Gimpy, poleaxing the rebels to the left of the approach road.

Both soldiers fired again. Two more five-round bursts apiece. The industrial *duh-duh-duh* of the machine guns filled the air. The bullets tore through the targets at a downward angle and punched through the guy immediately behind them before they smacked into the soil, flinging clumps of dirt into the air. Every fifth round was a red tracer, to help the shooters see where the bullets were falling. Several of the tracers on both sides of the truck ricocheted off the ground and fired upwards into the lightening sky, like rockets at a firework display.

More than half the targets in both groups were dead on the ground. Sixteen or seventeen bodies.

The surviving Boys instantly scattered across the exposed terrain. Running in different directions in a frantic search for cover. Every man for himself. Bowman heard the clipped report of the AWC, the deeper boom of the .50 cal as Webb and Mallet joined in with the fighting. They were taking down opportune targets while the two GPMGs dealt with the larger groups. One guy in an animal-print jacket and shades leaped onto the rear of the technical in a desperate attempt to take control of the machine gun. The AWC ca-racked. The man toppled backwards from the gun, limbs flailing as he dropped to the ground. To the left of the technical, another rebel wearing a beanie hat started to raise his AK-47 at the stronghold. The .50 cal boomed, the man's head exploded in a bright-red spray.

The remaining stragglers fled towards the cover of the treeline, running as fast as their legs could carry them in their desperation to escape the killing ground. Mallet shot one guy in the back as he legged it across the road. The remainder disappeared into the woods to lick their wounds before the defenders could rip them to shreds.

Bowman stopped firing. So did the others.

The fight had lasted no more than ten seconds. He counted more than twenty bodies on the ground in the clearing. Which was more than two-thirds of the attacking force. The Boys hadn't even had the chance to loose off a few rounds at the stronghold. They had been crushed. Annihilated. The definition of a one-sided victory. Like a football team racing into a five-nil lead before half-time.

Bowman focused on the treeline in case any of the surviving Boys came back for another go. But the ground remained quiet. No rebels came charging out of the woods.

'That should shut the bastards up,' Loader said after several moments.

Mallet stared at the dead in the clearing and nodded slightly. 'For a while, aye.'

'You think they'll come back?' asked Webb.

'They have to,' Mallet said. 'They'll know the president's family are inside now. The Machete Boys will work that out pretty fast. They'll be better prepared next time.'

'They'll want to avenge their dead mates, too,' Bowman said.

'Let 'em try,' Loader said with a snort. 'They haven't got a clue when it comes to tactics. We could slot these jokers in our sleep.'

'Everyone OK down there?' Mallet asked over the radio.

Three OKs came back. First Casey, then Gregory, then Mavinda. Mallet briefly updated the major on the situation at the front of the stronghold. The brief skirmish with the Machete Boys. Their ragged retreat into the woods. Everyone seemed confident. No one was panicking. They had just given the enemy a licking without taking casualties of their own. And they had a stack of ammunition left to expend. Bowman rubbed his aching, tired eyes and looked down at his G-Shock: 00.44. More than two hours until D Squadron was due to land at the private airfield.

Mallet was squinting at his damaged phone screen.

'Anything from Six?' Loader said.

'No news,' Mallet said back. 'The airfield is still clear. D Squadron's still due to arrive at eight o'clock.'

'Any reports of KUF rebels in the area?' Bowman asked.

'Not as far as we know.'

Webb looked at him with a serious expression. 'Do you think they might come here?'

Bowman shrugged. 'Mike told us the KUF and the Machete Boys are allies. The Boys are bound to alert General Kakuba. For all we know, his men might be on their way already.'

Mallet tore off a piece of bread, popped it into his mouth. 'If those guys were nearby,' he said. 'We'd know about it. Six would have sounded the alarm.'

Webb gazed out across the treeline, eyes narrowed, searching for any sign of movement among the shadows.

'How long until the Boys come at us again, do you think?' he said.

'Half an hour,' Mallet said. 'Maybe a little longer. They'll probably wait for their mates to turn up before they have another crack at us.'

'Bastards will want to get some booze in their system and all,' Loader chipped in. 'We've just given them a serious fright. They'll need some Dutch courage to get over it.'

Bowman looked from the abandoned technical to the stone archway at the front of the estate. A thought slowly taking shape.

'We should block that archway with that technical. Seal off the estate from the approach road. Stop any vehicles from getting through.'

'How?' asked Loader.

'We can use one of those Land Rovers we saw parked out front.' Bowman pointed to the entrance. 'Hook the winch around the technical and drag it over. That would make a decent barrier.'

'Good idea,' Mallet said. 'Go down there and sort it out.'

'I'll need some help.'

'Get a few of the major's men to lend a hand. We'll stay on the rooftop and watch for enemy movement. If we see anything, we'll let you know. And make it quick. Those fuckers will be back soon enough.'

* * *

Bowman raced across the rooftop to the fire exit. As he hurried down the stairwell, he raised Mavinda on the radio and told him to send over half a dozen guys to meet him at the front of the estate. He ran down the second-floor corridor, past the heroic paintings of Seguma. Down the staircase. Through the front door.

The six Karatandan soldiers were waiting for him on the steps. Toothbrush, Pockmark and Lanky. Plus three others. Bowman led

313

them over to the three mud-caked Land Rover Defenders parked to the left of the entrance. He got into the lead Defender with Toothbrush and Pockmark. The other four climbed into the second wagon. There was no need to mess around looking for the keys. Gregory had confirmed that they had been left inside the vehicles. Bowman gunned the engine and swung away from the mansion. He sheered around the grotesque fountain, the second Defender close behind as he sped towards the front of the estate four hundred metres away.

Bowman pulled up a few metres short of the stone-built archway, with the vehicle facing straight down the throat of the approach road. The second Defender halted two metres to the rear. Bowman left the engine running, engaged the parking brake and got out with Toothbrush and Pockmark. The four Karatandans debussed from the other Defender. They gathered around as Bowman gestured towards the clearing littered with the dead Machete Boys.

'Spread out across there,' he said. 'Get into firing positions. You see anyone coming through that treeline or down the road, you shoot. Don't hesitate.'

Toothbrush led his muckers across the clearing, dodging the broken bodies. Half of the soldiers fanned out and took up positions facing out to the woods. The others cleared the stretch of blacktop between the technical and the archway, dragging several corpses into the long grass either side of the road. Bowman circled round to the front of the Defender. He grabbed the metal hook from the end of the winch rope and walked the cable over to the technical, unspooling it from the drum. He looped the cable around the roll bar on the front of the truck, tested it, then jogged backed over to the Defender. Then he released the lever on the side of the drum and started winching in the technical.

The cable tensed as it hauled the pickup towards the stone arch. Bowman reeled in the winch wire until the technical was four metres from the arched entrance. He engaged the lever again, cupped his hands as he called out to the soldiers.

'One of you, over here!' he yelled. 'Get inside the truck!'

Pockmark broke away from his mates and dashed across to the technical. He pulled open the door on the side of the front cab, dragged out the slotted driver, slid behind the steering wheel.

'Yank the wheel hard to your right,' Bowman shouted at him. 'Keep it turned until we've brought the truck side on.'

Bowman released the winch lever again. At the same time Pockmark spun the wheel round, turning the pickup away from the archway so that the winch hauled it in at an angle. Bowman kept winching until the technical was broadside with the arched entrance. He pulled the lever, unhooked the end of the cable from the roll bar and walked over to the truck. Pockmark dived out of the cab as Bowman clambered on top of the rear platform. He climbed over the slotted rebel next to the mounted machine gun and wrenched up the carry handle on the side of the weapon, detaching the barrel. He quickly dismantled the other working parts, the guts of the gun. Then Bowman clipped the winch hook to the bipod welded to the platform floor, hopped down from the truck, hurried back through the entrance and dumped the barrel and the other working parts in the back of the Defender.

'Get over here!' Bowman shouted at the soldiers. 'Now!'

Toothbrush hollered at his men. They scurried back from their defensive positions and linked up with Pockmark beside the truck.

'Get round to the far side,' Bowman said, pointing to the truck. 'As soon as I give the word, start pushing it towards the Land Rover.'

The men slung their weapons over their shoulders as they lined up along the far side of the truck. Hands planted firmly against the bodywork. Waiting for the signal from Bowman.

He hit the lever. The winch started to wind in.

'Push! Put your backs into it!'

The soldiers shoved their collective weight against the technical. The winch motor groaned under the strain. The truck rocked heavily on its wheels. Bowman thundered at the men, roaring them on. The soldiers pushed once more, and then the pickup came crashing down, landing onto its side between the archway pillars, the exposed chassis facing out towards the clearing. The dead Boy tumbled out of the rear platform and fell to the ground in a bloody heap. Bowman pushed him aside, untied the winch cable from the machine-gun bipod, released the lever, paid in the rest of the wire, then secured the hook on the front of the Defender.

'Push again!' he shouted. 'Flip it over!'

The soldiers bent to the task, groaning with the effort as they pushed against the wheels. Toothbrush urged his colleagues, they gave it one last big shove, and the technical tipped over onto its roof, crushing the dead rebel beneath it. Bowman paused briefly to admire his handiwork. The upended truck blocked the archway leading to the front drive. It wouldn't stop the rebels from slipping through the entrance on foot. But it would prevent any enemy vehicles from bombing straight down the access road and into the estate.

'We're out of here,' Bowman bellowed at the soldiers. 'Back to the wagons!'

The soldiers slipped through the small gaps either side of the technical and bundled back into the two Defenders. Pockmark and Toothbrush jumped back into the wagon closest to the archway, Lanky and the others got into the second Defender. They U-turned across the front lawn, tyres churning up the dry earth, then shot back down the driveway towards the mansion. They pulled up behind the Unimog near the front steps. The men got out again, Bowman grabbing his rifle as he leaped down from the vehicle. He ran for the front door while the Karatandans sprinted over to the gun pits.

The sun was coming up fast as Bowman emerged to the rooftop. He weaved past the skylight and the maze of satellite dishes, crouched down beside his GPMG on the west side of the parapet.

Mallet and Loader had taken up spots across the eastern flank and rear. Webb observed the north side of the stronghold.

Bowman set down his rifle, helped himself to a glug of water from one of the plastic bottles. He hefted up the Gimpy. Looked out to the north-west. He saw the garden, the ruined wall, the irrigation ditch. The scrubland. The tall grass beyond the chain-link fence. The palm grove to the west. The landscape was utterly still. No movement. Nothing except the rustling of the palm fronds in the gentle morning breeze.

'You see anything?' he asked.

'Nothing,' Webb said. 'It's dead quiet.'

'They'll hit us soon,' Bowman said.

Webb looked up and blinked, resting his tired eyes. 'Reckon they'll attack us the same way?'

'I doubt it,' Mallet said. 'Even the Machete Boys aren't that thick. They'll want to try something new after seeing their mates get clobbered.'

'There might be more of them, too,' Bowman added. 'Any rebels in the area will want to get in on the action. They'll be all over this place like flies on a turd.'

Loader said, 'So what? We're up against a load of amateurs. Probably high as kites by now.'

'As long as D Squadron doesn't run into trouble.'

'Mike's in contact with the platoon guarding the runway,' Mallet said. 'They've not had any reports of enemy activity yet.'

'We'll get through this,' Loader said confidently. 'Everything's sound, boyo. We've got nothing to fear.'

Bowman checked his watch.

06.05.

Two hours until D Squadron was due to arrive.

We'll be out of the shit soon.

They watched and waited on the rooftop, scanning the various approaches to the stronghold. Mallet checked in with the guys on the ground. Gregory was in constant contact with the private airfield, feeding information back to the team on the roof. Casey and Lanky were standing by with the mortar. Mallet got on the phone to Six, letting them know they had been in a skirmish with the Machete Boys and expected another attack soon.

Mavinda's voice carried over the radio net. 'Message from one of the garrisons outside the capital,' he said. 'They've got reports of a large rebel force leaving Marafeni airport.'

Bowman automatically tensed. 'KUF?'

'Got to be,' said Webb. 'They're the ones who captured the airport.'

'When was this, Major?' Mallet asked.

There was a pause before Mavinda replied. 'An hour ago.'

'How far is Marafeni airport from here?'

'Three hours, give or take.'

'Then the KUF could be on their way here now,' Bowman said, knotting his brow. 'They could be here in a couple of hours.'

'Or they might be moving on to another target. The mines, the port. One of the garrisons. We don't know where they're going.'

Before Bowman could respond, Webb called out to the team.

'Enemy vehicles, inbound,' he said as he scanned the horizon. 'Coming from the north-west.'

Bowman narrowed his eyes in the direction Webb was looking. In the distance, a mile or so away, he could make out the tiny settlement at Rogandu, the T-junction leading south towards the main metalled road. The faintest puff of dust clouds swirled high above the treeline.

'How many, Patrick?' Mallet said.

'I see three of them. One technical. Two pickups. Guys on the back. Looks like more Machete Boys.'

'The bastards want another taste,' Loader said.

Mallet talked into his throat mic. 'Guys, looks like we've got more rebels coming our way. Hold your fire until I say otherwise.'

For the next several minutes more rebels arrived in dribs and drabs. Two pickup trucks, then another three civilian cars. They came bombing in from the village to the north-west, spewing up clouds of grey-brown dust as they RV'd with the surviving gang of rebels sheltering behind the woodland to the north.

Webb kept a close eye on the enemy, reporting their movements and numbers. Bowman, Mallet and Loader surveyed the other approaches to the stronghold. Looking to see where the rebels would hit them next.

Twelve minutes passed.

Bowman figured the rebels were psyching themselves up for the next attack. Pouring booze down their throats, smoking the local ganja, egging each other on. Their mates had been pasted. They had been personally humiliated on the field of battle. Pride was at stake. They would be itching to get their revenge. They would be feeling bullish about their chances of victory, now that their ranks had been bolstered.

Won't be long now, he thought.

Four more minutes crawled past.

Then Webb said, 'I see them! The treeline! Here they come again!'

Twenty-Nine

Bowman ran over to the northern side of the parapet. He propped up his GPMG barrel on the stone coping and centred the sights on the woods beyond the body-strewn clearing. Loader took up a spot to the right with the other Gimpy. Mallet went down to a prone firing position between the two soldiers, aimed the .50 cal barrel through a hole in the decorative stonework. All four of them targeted the treeline on the north side of the clearing.

Bowman saw the figures at once. A throng of Machete Boys, clearly visible in the thin light of the early dawn, creeping forward from the wooded area to the left of the approach road. Maybe another thirty guys, he estimated. They were moving in a rough line formation, three ranks deep, staying low as they crept towards the entrance. Bowman swiftly grasped their intention. The Boys were hoping to sneak up to the archway using the natural cover available. They would slip through the gap between the upturned technical and the stone pillars, then spread out across the estate, taking on the defenders in detail. *Not a terrible plan*, thought Bowman. *Not as foolish as strolling up the approach road in massed ranks.*

But still a bad idea.

One of the Boys in the front rank had an RPG resting on his shoulders. A skinny rebel wearing a trapper hat, a rope of *gris-gris* charms tied like a belt around his waist. The others were armed with AK-47 rifles or machetes, or both. They were five hundred metres from the stronghold now. A hundred metres from the fence.

'What's the plan?' said Bowman.

Mallet rolled his tongue around his mouth and spat.

'We'll let the buggers get through the archway,' he said. 'Once they're inside, Patrick will take down the fucker with the RPG. As soon as he's down, you're free to go.'

Mallet relayed the orders over the mic. Bowman tracked the enemy as they advanced stealthily across the clearing. They were moving in a loose group, crouch-walking through the tufts of long grass to conceal their approach. He watched as the front rank of rebels picked their way past their slotted comrades and reached the archway. They waited for the rest to catch up, then slipped through the gaps either side of the technical.

Bowman felt his pulse quickening as he centred his sights on the enemy. The rebels shuffled past the overturned truck blocking the road and spread out across the estate in a ragged line. The guy in the trapper hat motioned to the others to hurry up. Only four hundred metres separated them from the stronghold and the president's family. Revenge was on the cards. The Boys thought they were going to win.

Bowman said to Loader, 'I'll take on the guys to the left of the group. You aim for the rebels on the right. We'll work our way in and meet in the middle.'

The last of the rebels stole through the archway.

'Nowhere for the bastards to go now,' Loader said eagerly.

Mallet said, 'Patrick, do you see the bloke with the RPG? The guy in the trapper hat?'

'Got him,' Webb said.

'Wait for my signal. As soon as I give the word, take him out. Then the two Gimpys can get to work.'

Bowman locked his sights on the Boys. They were as strangely dressed as the men he'd seen outside the presidential palace. One rebel wore a zebra-print jacket. Another had a rusted steel chain wrapped around his neck, like some oversized necklace. The guy to his left wore an animal headdress. A fourth man had a pair of ivory tusks draped over his shoulders. Their bodies were festooned with amulets and pouches containing their good luck charms.

The Boys were five metres inside the estate now, shuttling down the front drive in a disorganised rabble as they stole past the weeds and the burned-down trees. One rebel drew his machete and raised it above his head, encouraging his mates forward, like an officer on the Western Front.

Six metres beyond the entrance.

Eight.

'Now,' Mallet said.

Bowman heard a splintering hollow crack as Webb fired a single shot from the AWC. He didn't see the guy in the trapper hat drop. Bowman was focused on the main cluster of rebels. But he knew Webb had hit the target because Mallet was suddenly shouting, 'That's it! Let them have it!'

Bowman gave the rebels a five-round squirt from the Gimpy. Loader unleashed a burst at his targets in the same beat. The machine guns roared, chewing up the enemy. Bowman saw the guy in the zebra-print shirt go down, and the Boy with the headdress, the guy with the steel chain. They went down one after the other, like pins in a bowling alley. The rebels didn't stand a chance. Not against the combined firepower of the GPMGs.

A handful of rebels managed to survive the initial killing frenzy. Some of them broke to the left and right, fleeing across the open ground, diving behind any scraps of cover they could find. Two guys in matching red headscarves dropped to the grass and let off a couple of quick bursts at the rooftop. But it wasn't accurate fire. They were reacting on instinct, firing in the vague direction of the opposition. Shooting because they felt they needed to, because they were confused and afraid. Bullets slapped into the parapet some-where off to Bowman's right. The bee-like buzz of a bullet several inches above his head. He fixed his cross hairs on the headscarf twins and hit them with a blast from the Gimpy. They disappeared in a spray of blood and guts.

Bowman was dimly aware of several muzzle flashes from the gun pit beside the pagoda. The Karatandan soldiers were getting ahead of themselves, putting down rounds on the rebels.

'Cease fire!' Mallet thundered over the radio. 'Tell your men to cease fire, Major! You're wasting rounds. Leave them to us!'

By now, five seconds into the skirmish, at least twenty of the attackers were dead. Bowman and Loader swept their GPMGs from left to right, tearing up any surviving rebels, the mechanical patter of the machine guns punctuated by the sounds of the .50 cal and the AWC rifle. Webb and Mallet focused their fire on the archway, killing those few rebels attempting to escape back to the clearing. The remaining Boys fell back from the entrance and tacked left or right, looking for another way out. They ran straight into the hail of murderous gunfire from the two Gimpys.

Mallet called out across the roof, directing the GPMGs towards a section of the fence to the right of the arch. Bowman slid his weapon across, saw three figures trying to scale the chain-link fence in a futile effort to escape the massacre. Before he could open fire the earth suddenly exploded around the rebels as Loader cut them down with two controlled bursts. They dropped to a bloodied heap at the foot of the fence.

'Two more rebels in dead ground,' Webb shouted over the cacophony. 'Three posts to the left of the archway.'

Bowman arced the Gimpy back across to the spot Webb had identified and fixed his sights at the swale a few metres south of the fence. He waited a beat. Two heads popped up from the grassy trough, like meerkats looking out from their burrows. Bowman fired. Flames burped out of the muzzle. Spent brass dinked against the cement floor. The rounds thumped into the rebels. Their jolting bodies fell back into the swale.

'Got them,' Bowman said.

Ten seconds in. Four rebels left. Four panicked silhouettes. Loader plugged two of them as they crawled towards a dip in the ground in front of the fence. One rebel was hit in the neck by the AWC as he attempted to climb over the technical blocking the archway. A Boy in a white string vest bolted past his mate as he ran for the gap between the truck and the archway pillar. Another boom erupted as Mallet aimed the .50 cal at the fleeing figure. The back of the rebel's head exploded in a red mist. He fell forward and face-planted on the ground beside the technical, kissing the blacktop.

The firefight had lasted twelve seconds.

Bowman scanned the killing ground. The grass was thickly carpeted with the mangled dead. Thirty slotted rebels. None of the bodies showed any signs of life. He wasn't surprised. The GPMG had a rate of fire of 650 rounds per minute. No one could survive an onslaught from two well-aimed Gimpys.

Loader lifted his gaze from his weapon. He stared across the parapet at the archway and shook his head in astonishment.

'Jesus. Now I know what people mean when they talk about a turkey shoot.'

'So much for the Machete Boys being rock hard,' Webb said.

'We're not out of the woods yet,' Bowman said.

'These Boys ain't gonna lay a glove on us fighting like this.' Loader sniffed. 'If they keep this up, we've got no worries. This is a piece of piss.'

'So is taking the mick out of your love life, Tiny,' said Webb.

Mallet shot them both a stern look. 'Don't get ahead of yourselves,' he warned. 'You won't be laughing if we get overrun by those bastards. Back to your positions.'

The team returned to their observation points on the other sides of the parapet. Looking out across the flanks and rear, watching for the enemy. The sun climbed above the mountains to the east, burning fiercely in the cloudless blue sky. Sweat leached down Bowman's face as he scanned the ground to the west. He suddenly remembered he was thirsty, grabbed a bottle of water from a crate near the skylight and took a long swig. The warm liquid refreshed him. Like the best pint he'd ever had. He set the bottle down, checked his G-Shock.

06.57.

Still more than an hour to go until D Squadron was due to land. Mallet called out to him.

'Get down to the mortar pit,' he said. 'See if you can bolster the defences around that garden wall. Give them two some more protection.'

'Roger that.'

'Take the RPG from that dead fucker as well,' Mallet added. 'Leave it with Alex. Might come in handy.'

'I'm on it,' said Bowman.

He ran downstairs, hurried out of the atrium and broke into a steady jog across the heat-baked ground. Bowman ran past the water fountain, past Gregory and Toothbrush in the gun pit with one of the platoon's GPMGs. He willed his exhausted body on as he continued up the front drive, his throat burning. He reached the sprawl of dead rebels ten metres from the archway, found the guy with the trapper hat next to a blackened stump of a tree. The bullet from Webb's AWC had struck the rebel through his left eye, boring deep into his skull. Instant death. There was a dark glistening crater where his eyeball should have been. Bowman rolled the man onto his front and tore off the canvas backpack containing the three spare rockets. He slung the backpack over his shoulder, snatched up the RPG launcher and cantered back down the driveway to the ornamental garden.

Casey was hunkered down beside the mortar, gazing out through a gap in the crumbling wall at the treeline. Pockmark, the other member of the mortar team, grazed on a chocolate bar while he kept an eye on the fence to the west. Casey looked up at Bowman as he dumped the canvas bag and the RPG at her feet.

'What's this for?' she asked.

'Extra firepower,' Bowman replied. 'Compliments of the Machete Boys.'

One of her eyebrows hitched up. 'Do you think we'll need it?'

'We're not likely to get hit again,' Bowman said. 'Not unless the Machete Boys want to send any more of their mates to their deaths.'

'Those KUF rebels won't be so easy, will they?'

'No,' Bowman said. 'But D Squadron is an hour out. As soon as they arrive, we're safe.'

'Unless the KUF gets here first.'

Bowman nodded. He pointed to the missing sections of the wall beside the mortar pit. 'We'll need to reinforce this position. Get some more stones around it. Stay here.'

He called over to Pockmark. The two men worked hastily, grabbing rocks from the loose stonework on the other sections of the garden wall, then carrying them over to the mortar pit. Casey helped them pile the stones around the base of the wall, plugging the holes. They added more rocks on top, raising the height of the wall so that it was level with their waists. Once they had finished, Bowman sprinted back across the front lawn, into the mansion and up the emergency stairwell. Out of the fire exit. Back to his OP on the western side of the rooftop. He guzzled water. Took up the GPMG. Checked his watch.

07.09. Fifty minutes until D Squadron landed.

The sun climbed higher above the hills. Bowman wiped sweat from his brow and scanned the west flank. He saw nothing except the palm grove, the long grass swaying in the faint early-morning breeze. Around him the other guys were watching their individual observation points, glancing at their watches and taking gulps from their water bottles. Mallet smoked a cigarette. Webb took a piss in the far corner of the rooftop. Loader bit into an apple and spat it out, a disgusted look on his face.

'Shit's rotten.' He threw the core away. 'Tell you what. Them guys in D Squadron had better have some good rations on them. Been ages since I had a decent meal.'

Mallet gave him a disgusted look. 'You stuffed your face on the jet, you greedy bastard.'

'A few protein bars, some crisps and sandwiches. That's hardly what I call a slap-up feast, John. I'm talking about a nice lamb roast with all the trimmings. Like what my Mary cooks. She doesn't hold back on the portions, either.' He licked his lips. 'Best food in Wales, that,' he added wistfully.

'She'd better be a good cook. She's feeding half the fucking country, what with all the kids you've got.'

Webb said, 'What's the plan once D Squadron gets in?'

Mallet said, 'No reason for us to hang around. Once we've made the handover, our job is done. We'll wait for clearance from Six to fly out. With a bit of luck, we'll be back home this evening.'

'Not a moment too soon,' said Loader. 'Give me Swansea over this place any day of the week.'

'Or anywhere that's not a war zone,' Webb added. He shook his head bitterly. 'I was told I'd be wearing civvies and carrying a PKK when I transferred to the Cell. Fighting drug barons and running surveillance jobs. Now look at us.'

Mallet laughed cynically. 'Thought you'd be used to it, Patrick. All those years you spent in the SRR and the Rifles regiment.'

Bowman looked curiously at Webb. 'You were in the Rifles?'

'Five years. First Battalion. Sniper team.'

So that's why the guy is so good with a sniper rifle, thought Bowman.

'Why'd you join them, mate?' he asked.

Webb stared evenly at him. 'I had a choice,' he said softly. 'The army, or prison.'

'Fuck me. What did you do?'

He looked away.

'Long story,' he said. 'Another time.'

'Let's just focus on getting out of here alive,' said Mallet. 'We're not safe yet. Those Boys might fancy another crack at us before they raise the white flag.'

For the next fifty minutes the team took turns keeping watch over the stronghold. They worked in pairs in half-hour rotations. Two guys on OP duty while the other two guys got some kip. Despite the exhaustion each of them was feeling, they found it impossible to switch off. They were too wired, restless. Like trying to sleep after knocking back a crate of energy drinks. Only Loader managed to get a proper rest.

Then a cry went up from the northern parapet.

'Vehicles coming this way,' Webb said.

Mallet and Loader shot up and hurriedly took up their observation points. Bowman looked beyond the treeline at his two o'clock. He saw a large dust cloud stirring close to the horizon.

'Another load of Machete Boys?' Loader asked.

Webb paused as he focused his sights on the dust cloud. 'Doesn't look like it,' he said finally.

'What can you see?' Bowman said.

'Buses,' Webb replied. 'Three of them. Look like school buses.'

Loader grunted. 'Bit fucking weird.'

Mallet said, 'Is there a school round here, Major?'

'If there is,' came the reply over the radio, 'it's the first I've heard of it.'

'More vehicles inbound.' Webb was giving a running commentary as he observed the dust cloud through the Schmidt & Bender scope. 'I see four of them. An SUV. Looks like a Land Cruiser.' He paused again. 'A pickup, two personnel trucks. Looks like a substantial force heading our way, guys.'

Bowman felt his guts drop. Mallet rushed over to the north-facing parapet and trained the .50 cal sights on the convoy.

'Army trucks?' Loader said. 'I thought the major said there's no local garrison in the vicinity.'

'There isn't,' Bowman said. 'Apart from the platoon at the airfield. And they're under orders not to abandon their posts at any cost.'

'Major, are we expecting any friendlies in the area?' Mallet said into his mic.

'Let me check,' Mavinda replied.

Webb watched the dust cloud.

Bowman and Loader scanned the flanks.

Mallet waited thirty seconds.

Then he said, 'What's the news, Major?'

There was a long beat before Mavinda replied. 'Negative,' he said. 'There are no friendly forces in the area. Repeat, no friendlies.'

'So who the fuck are these guys?' Loader wondered.

Webb said nothing.

Bowman swallowed.

Mallet said, 'They're not friendly soldiers. It's the KUF. They're here. Them and their Russian advisers.'

Thirty

Bowman looked on as the KUF convoy approached the stronghold from the west. The dust cloud migrated south as the vehicles motored past the village towards the T-junction. The convoy hit the metalled road, and the cloud promptly disappeared behind the broad belt of trees to the north-west of the estate. After a short while, Bowman heard the low distant growl of diesel engines, steadily growing louder as the rebels neared the main road opposite the estate.

'Mike, Alex. Major. We've got a large force of KUF rebels coming our way,' Mallet said. 'Get ready. We're gonna need to hit these bastards hard when they attack.'

Somewhere behind the treeline came the screech of brakes. A thick plume of dust eddied into the sky. Then Bowman heard the pneumatic hiss of bus doors sucking open, the faint din of shouts and cries carrying across the hot morning air.

'How many guys do you think they've got?' Loader asked.

'Hard to tell,' Mallet replied. 'Twenty men in each truck. Another twenty or so in the buses. We're looking at maybe a hundred rebels. Could be more.'

'Jesus.'

'You think the Russians are with them?' Webb said.

Mallet said, 'I'd bet my pension on it.'

'Let's hope they don't decide to join in the fighting.'

'They won't. The Russians will be on the ground, directing the rebels. But they won't get involved in the shooting.'

'Just as well,' said Loader. 'We've got our hands full dealing with these fuckers. The last thing we need is a bunch of Spetsnaz guys getting stuck in.'

Mallet and Webb continued watching the treeline. Loader and Bowman observed the east and west flanks.

Nothing happened for several minutes.

Bowman could guess what was happening on the far side of the woods. The Russians would be thrashing out a new plan with the rebels. Taking control of the situation. *You've had your chance,* they would be saying to the Machete Boys. *Now it's our turn. This is what we're going to do.*

They would be organising their forces, briefing them on the attack. The Russians would probably draw a rough map of the stronghold on the ground. A crude model, with a rock to represent the mansion and twigs for the surrounding fence. Branches for the treeline. Leaves for the archway. They would use it to point out features when talking the rebels through the assault. *You guys will advance from here. You'll target this sector.* Helping the soldiers to visualise the plan.

Still nothing happened.

'Guys, have you seen anything?' Mallet asked twelve minutes later. 'Any movement around the flanks?'

'Not a thing,' Bowman said.

'Same,' Loader said.

'Major, what's the situation at the rear?' Mallet asked.

'All quiet here,' Mavinda reported.

'The bastards are up to something,' Loader said.

'Any word on D Squadron landing at that airfield?' Bowman said. 'They should have landed a few minutes ago.'

'Checking in now,' Mallet replied.

He kept one eye on the woods while he dialled the Voice. He spoke in a terse tone as he told Voice about the arrival of the rebels. He described the size of the enemy force, the direction they had travelled from. The information would help D Squadron to plan their route to the stronghold, so they wouldn't run straight into the enemy. He told the Voice to make sure D Squadron hurried the fuck up.

'D Squadron has landed,' he said as he hung up. 'They're on the way.'

'Have we got an ETA?' asked Loader.

'Could be anytime. Depends what's waiting for them lads en route to this place.'

Bowman felt his guts stir. *We're relying on D Squadron to get here fast*, he thought. *But if they run into a rebel ambush or hit a landmine, if they get held up for whatever reason, we're done for.*

The voices behind the treeline went silent. Bowman heard nothing except the faint whisper of the wind moving through the long grass, the gentle swishing of leaves. He surveyed the palm grove intently, waiting for the first sign of the enemy. Behind him, the other guys were spread out across the rooftop, watching their separate OPs.

'Rebels approaching,' said Webb. 'Three of them.'

'Where?'

'Treeline, due east of the approach road.'

Bowman scrambled across the rooftop with Loader. They joined Mallet and Webb along the parapet, aimed their weapons at the dead ground to the south of the wooded area. A moment later, Bowman laid eyes on the rebels.

The three rebels were scuttling across the clearing towards the chain-link fence to the right of the archway. One of them wore a purple basketball shirt. Another sported an orange cap. The third guy was dressed in a gilet and a female blonde wig. He carried a pair of bolt cutters in his left hand.

'Machete Boys,' said Webb.

'Must be the dregs,' Mallet said. 'The guys we didn't wallop first time round.'

Bowman squinted at the treeline. 'Looks like they're alone,' he said.

'Why haven't they got any support?' Webb asked.

'Them idiots must have a death wish,' said Loader. 'Either that, or they're pissed out of their minds.'

'Patrick, wait until they get closer,' said Mallet. 'As soon as I give the word, I'll slot the bloke in the wig. You drop the others.'

They watched the rebels as they drew closer to the fence. The guy in the blonde wig was trailing a couple of paces behind his comrades, increasing his stride in a bid to catch up with them. He was almost level with the other rebels, fifteen metres from the fence, when the .50 cal exploded.

The man jerked, as if he'd run into a clothesline. He was still falling away as Webb fired two quick shots at the other targets. The guy in the basketball shirt, the guy in the orange cap. They were both dead before they hit the ground.

'Keep your eyes on the front,' Mallet said. 'There might be more of the fuckers on the way.'

Bowman and Loader scanned the woodland on the left side of the approach road, looking for movement in the narrow gaps between the trees. Webb and Mallet watched the patch of ground to the right. But no one emerged from the woods. The ground outside the estate was eerily quiet and still. Mallet got on the open radio and briefed the team on the ground.

'What was that about?' Gregory asked. 'Why would the Russians send those guys to their deaths?'

'They're testing us,' Mallet said. 'Probing for weak points. They want to know if we've got eyes on the perimeter fence.'

Gregory was silent for a beat.

'They're going to hit us soon, then.'

'Looks that way,' Mallet said grimly.

'Reckon we're in for a proper fight this time, guys,' Loader said. 'These Russians ain't stupid.'

'No. They're not.'

'Do us a favour, John,' Gregory said over the comms.

'Aye, what's that?'

'Leave some of the enemy for us this time. You bastards have had all the fun up there.'

Mallet laughed drily. 'Be careful what you wish for.'

The stillness continued. Bowman and the rest of the rooftop team searched the treeline for the enemy. Every few minutes Mallet checked in with the team on the ground to see if they had spotted anything. Time inched past. Like a sports team watching the clock and finding out they were only three-quarters of the way through a gruelling match. Bowman sipped bottled water, squinted at his G-Shock.

08.12.

He looked back at the woods.

In the distance, a single shot rang out.

'What the fuck was that?' Loader asked.

Then the fence exploded.

Bowman glimpsed the split-second pulse of orange flame in the north-west corner of the estate. Then came a deafening bang as a pall of smoke spread outwards, engulfing the chain-link fence in a teeming mass of earth and debris. Acrid smoke bubbled upwards, mushrooming into the early morning sky.

Amid the chaos, Bowman saw that four sections of the steel mesh had disappeared. A forty-metre-long stretch. Only a single scorched post remained standing.

'Fuckers have planted charges!' Loader yelled.

Bowman stared in shock at the breach, his stomach knotting. *The KUF rebels must have crawled right up under our noses*, he thought. *We were busy watching the forest, waiting for more rebels to appear, while they were rigging up the fence with explosives. It wouldn't have taken much to bring the fence down. An ounce of PE on each post would have done the trick. The gunshot must have been the signal for the team to detonate.*

These guys are good at fieldcraft. They had a plan to distract us from the breach and it worked perfectly.

He glanced quickly round the rooftop, wondering if the rebels had sent any more teams to sneak around the flanks or the rear.

His heart was beating so hard it threatened to burst out of his chest.

We're about to get hit hard.

'I see them!' Loader bellowed. 'They're coming!'

Bowman swung back round. He gazed out across the northern fringe of the woods. As the smoke cleared, he saw a long line of figures charging out from the treeline. He counted roughly sixty of them. They were spaced widely apart and decked out in olive-green T-shirts, military jackets, dark jeans. Some wore black berets or armbands. Two rebels in each group brandished large machine guns with bipods mounted to the barrels and metal ammunition boxes attached to the underside of the receivers. Bowman had seen such weapons before. PKMs. Manufactured in Russia. Similar to the Gimpys, and just as deadly.

Webb and Mallet scrabbled over from the other end of the parapet wall. They dropped down and went into prone firing positions beside Bowman and Loader in the north-west corner.

'Alex!' Mallet roared. 'Start lobbing mortars on the treeline! Fire for effect!'

The rebels charged across the exposed ground. Then Bowman heard the hollow pop of the mortar firing as Casey and Lanky got to work. The bombs crashed down on the ground in front of the treeline with a series of explosive crumps, vaporising half a dozen rebels towards the rear.

'Pull back twenty metres,' Mallet ordered. 'Fire for effect.'

Smoke veiled the clearing. More bombs fell on the area close to the rebels, churning up the soil. The ground was starting to look like something out of the Western Front. Metal shredded a trio of rebels on the left of the line, taking them out of the fight. The others held their nerve and ran on towards the breach. Determined not to lose the momentum of their advance, in spite of the death raining down on them from above.

These guys are different to the Machete Boys.

They're motivated. Trained.

Bowman emptied a couple of bursts at the figures gaining ground towards the stronghold, clipping one rebel as he weaved past an exploding mortar. The defenders kept up their furious rate of fire but the rebels were spread out more thinly than the Machete Boys, reducing the effectiveness of the Gimpy bursts, forcing Bowman and Loader to drop individual targets instead of multiple opponents.

A hideous scream cut through the air as another mortar shell tore into the enemy ranks, ripping four rebels to pieces. Their comrades didn't stop. They ran on through the explosions and the gunfire, like soldiers charging across no man's land a hundred years ago. The rebels were now less than forty metres from the destroyed section of the perimeter fence. Mallet got on the team radio again, shouting to make himself heard above the deafening crump of the mortar shells.

'Pull back, Alex! Twenty metres! Fire for effect!'

As the rebels drew nearer two men in camouflaged ghillie suits promptly stood up from the grass. They quickly moved forward, joining the rest of the attackers. So that's how the rebels managed to plant the charges, Bowman realised. The men in the ghillie suits would have inched across the clearing to the detonation points while the defenders had been busy watching the trees. With their camouflaged outfits, they would have easily blended in with the surrounding greenery. Once the rebels had placed the charges, they would have retreated to a safe point outside the danger zone, then waited for the signal to detonate.

We're dealing with pros here.

In the next instant, the rebels poured through the fence line and separated into three loose assault groups spaced twenty metres apart. The groups on the left and right of the line swiftly disappeared from view as they dropped into a shallow depression. Mallet was shouting into his mic, telling Casey to pull the range back to the four-hundred-metre mark. More shells smashed into the area where the fence had once stood, hurling wads of incinerated soil and torn bodies into the air.

Then Bowman saw the middle assault team moving forward. Dozens of muzzle flashes suddenly lit up across the depressions as the two flanking groups opened fire at the rooftop.

'Stay the fuck down!' Mallet hollered.

Bullets zipped narrowly overhead, spattering into the wall behind Bowman, gouging out chunks of masonry. Through a slender gap in the parapet he saw the rebels in the middle assault team go static at a baseline four metres ahead of the depression. Tongues of flame licked out of their weapon muzzles as they started putting down suppressive fire on the rooftop. The assault group on the right flank advanced four metres, drew level with the middle team, then half disappeared into the ground cover. The front two assault groups took over the fire-support role, aiming at the parapet while the third team ran forward and hit the same baseline as their comrades.

The rebels are pepper-potting, Bowman realised. *Fire-and-move tactics.* They were advancing incrementally, one group moving forward while the two others covered them with sustained fire. The most efficient way of moving across exposed ground. Two of the teams could engage their opponents at all times, forcing them to keep their heads down while their muckers rushed ahead to establish a new baseline.

'This isn't a rebel force,' Loader shouted. 'It's a fucking army. These guys are trained soldiers.'

Webb yelled at Bowman, drawing his attention to the group of rebels to the left. Bowman shifted round on his belly, shoved the Gimpy barrel through a small aperture in the parapet. He aimed at the assault team as they ran forward, hit them with a couple of short bursts moments before they disappeared behind a dip in the ground.

'Go right, go right! Rebels moving!' Webb shouted.

Bowman slid round to a new firing position. The team on the opposite flank was now breaking forward. He put in three more bursts, saw the tracers punching into the rebel ranks, reached the end of the belt.

'Changing mag!'

He yanked the bolt back, flipped open the top cover and cleared the freed tray. Then he grabbed a fresh belt from the stack, replaced the cover, stared down the sights. Webb bellowed at him to go left. Bowman saw the middle fire team emerge from cover and opened up on them, killing two more rebels before they went static again.

The guys on the rooftop were communicating with one another constantly. Giving orders, making sure that every member of the team knew exactly what they were doing. Webb and Mallet were shouting out enemy movements to the two guys on the Gimpys, directing them on to target and taking out key individual figures. Anyone rallying the troops or whose body language suggested they might be a senior officer. The quickest way to win the battle, Bowman knew. Take out the commanding officers.

Mavinda's voice sounded in his earpiece.

'Enemy attacking from the west flank,' he said. 'Machete Boys. Forty of them.'

Bowman glanced across his shoulder. Through the gaps in the western parapet, he caught sight of the line of Boys swarming forward, firing on the gun pits on the west side of the garden. The ragtag leftovers of the earlier assaults.

Loader was looking in the same direction. 'Where the fuck did they come from?'

'Must have snuck in through the fence.'

'Shit. Just what we bloody need.'

The Boys were the sacrificial lambs, Bowman realised. Sent in by the Russians to draw the defenders' fire away from the main attack. They weren't crucial to the plan. If they got within close proximity of the stronghold, it was a bonus. If they failed, it didn't matter. They would still tie the opposition down.

'The Russians know what they're doing,' Loader growled.

Mallet spoke into his mic.

'Major, tell your men on the west to concentrate on the Machete Boys. Whatever you do, keep them from the stronghold. We'll take care of the enemies to the front.'

The defenders were constantly shifting firing positions, targeting each assault group as they advanced four metres before going to ground again. Then the team switched their aim to the next group breaking cover. Loader fired at them with short spurts from the other Gimpy. Webb dropped targets with the AWC. Mallet had switched to his C8 rifle for the closer-range stuff. But the barrage of rebel gunfire was unrelenting. Dust and masonry whipped up around the men on the rooftop. With all the shit flying past them, Bowman and the others found it harder to aim. The rebels were now twenty metres inside the estate, edging forward slowly but steadily. Like the tide creeping in.

In the tail of his eye, Bowman glimpsed several rounds smacking into the northern garden wall as some of the rebels trained their fire on the mortar pit. A few others aimed at the gun pits scattered across the front of the stronghold. But the majority targeted the GPMGs on the rooftop. Bowman felt the hot carriage of air as a bullet winged past him and glanced off the generator.

'Jesus,' he said.

'This is nothing like the last attack,' Webb said.

'Tell me about it,' Loader shouted. 'These guys actually know how to fucking shoot.'

Mortars splashed into the soft ground around the rebel groups. A few men were torn apart by the bombardment, but most were sheltered behind the dips in the ground. Bowman saw an orange flash below the parapet as Gregory opened up with the platoon GPMG in the front gun pit. The assault teams continued to advance despite the appalling fire pouring down on them. They knew how vital it was to maintain momentum during an assault.

Bowman put in another burst at the rebels and stole a glance at the ground to the west. To his surprise, he saw that the Machete Boys were a hundred metres inside the fence and closing fast. Mallet yelled an order at Loader. The latter uplifted the GPMG and swung round to the west-facing parapet. He went prone and gave the Boys a few spurts from the Gimpy. Then he shifted back round to the north side, fired at the main group.

'We're juggling here!' he shouted. 'We're in trouble, John!'

Mallet got straight on the comms to Casey.

'Pull back fifty metres. Repeat, fifty metres,' he said. 'Hit them with some near-surface bursts.'

There was a brief pause as Casey set the fuses on the mortars to near-surface detonation. At the front of the estate, Bowman saw the middle assault group spring up from ground cover and start towards a new baseline. The two teams on the left and right flanks began putting down suppressive fire on the GPMGs on the roof-top, covering the middle team's advance. Bowman came to the end of another belt and hastily reloaded. His fourth belt. Six belts of 7.62 mm brass left.

In the next breath, he heard a sequence of dull pops as Casey launched the mortars at terrific speed. The bombs plunged to the earth and detonated half a metre above the surface. Which gave a much wider spread than an impact-burst bomb. Men screamed as a deluge of shell fragments tore through them, slashing through flesh and lacerating vitals. Three more mortars dropped into the stretch of dead ground between the front and rear assault teams, wreathing the ground in greyish smoke.

'That's it!' Loader roared. 'Fucking give it to 'em!'

With mortar shells exploding all around them, the two groups of rebels to the rear struggled to keep up their sustained fire on the stronghold. The middle assault team suddenly came under an intense hail of fire as Bowman, Loader and Gregory poured bursts into them from the Gimpys. A handful of figures peeled away from the group and fled towards the breach in the fence. One stout rebel in a beret, presumably the commanding officer, gestured frantically at his men, urging them on. Webb dropped him with a single well-placed shot. With no one to organise the men, panic swiftly set in. The remaining fighters turned and bolted.

'They're on the back foot!' Mallet roared. 'Target the other groups!'

Bowman and the others continued plugging away with the GPMGs. The two outer assault teams swiftly broke contact, running pell-mell for the breach. Half a dozen rebels were struck down, nailed in the back before they could escape the estate. The rest scrambled back across the clearing in a disorganised rabble. Mallet ordered Casey to lob in a few more mortars. Bombs pounded the clearing, throwing up clods of earth and fragging several rebels before they could escape.

With the main attack repulsed, the gunfire from the west flank quickly abated. 'Enemy retreating!' Mavinda yelled over the radio. 'The rebels are pulling back.'

Bowman looked past his shoulder through an opening in the parapet. He glimpsed the Machete Boys beating a hasty retreat across the plain.

'They won't be hassling us for a while now,' Loader said.

'Alex, are you OK down there?' Mallet asked.

'I'm fine,' she reported. 'But I'm almost out of ammo.'

'How many?'

She paused. 'Four bombs. That's it.'

Bowman said, 'It'll be harder next time. That mortar was our trump card. We've just used it. And we haven't got another.'

He looked at his watch: 08.31.

'Where the fuck is D Squadron?' Loader ranted. 'They should be here by now, for Chrissakes.'

'I'll check,' Mallet said as he grabbed his phone. Bowman looked round at the treeline and the surrounding terrain, the tension building in his chest. The minutes dragged. Like the last quarter of a football match. They were still winning, but the scoreline was much closer now. The enemy had pulled back a couple of goals. The defenders were clinging to their lead by the skin of their teeth. Hanging on, physically drained, waiting for the final whistle to blow. Bowman was running on fumes. *I don't know how much longer we can hold out*, he thought.

Mallet hung up.

'What's the news?' Bowman asked.

'Six hasn't heard from D Squadron since they landed. Half an hour ago.'

Loader checked his watch and grunted. 'The airfield's only twenty miles away. A straight run on the main road. What's taking them so long?'

'Maybe the Russians have sent out a force to ambush them,' Webb said.

'Could be,' Bowman said. 'The way they've masterminded this attack, it wouldn't be a surprise.'

Loader said, 'Whatever's holding them up, those fellas need to get a move on. Foot to the floor, like. We're in the shit here.'

'It's out of our hands now,' Mallet replied. 'Nothing we can do about it except sit tight.'

'Christ, no,' Webb said as he stared at the woods. 'It can't be.'

'What is it?' Mallet asked.

Bowman planted his left hand on the Gimpy stock and scanned the trees. At first, he saw nothing except the mortar-churned earth, the shrapnel-slashed bodies, the blood.

Then he spotted the figures charging out of the gloom of the forest, and his heart sank.

'Oh, fuck!' Loader shouted. 'There's more of them. They're coming again!'

Thirty-One

The rebels streamed forward in a loose throng, sprinting across the open ground in the same formation as the first wave. Except the second wave was bigger. Eighty or so fighters. Sixty men, plus the twenty survivors from the initial attack. The defenders on the rooftop stared at them in shock for a moment. Then their training instincts took over. Mallet shouted into his mic, screaming at Casey to pop off the few remaining bombs at the treeline. Bowman and Loader aimed through the holes in the parapet and squeezed off bursts from the Gimpys at the mass of figures flooding towards them. Mortar shells battered the clearing, killing half a dozen of the rebel fighters. The machine guns picked off a few more. The rest ran on unscathed towards the demolished stretch of the perimeter.

'I'm out of bombs!' Casey said over the radio. 'Switching to my rifle.'

'Where did this lot come from?' Loader shouted.

But Bowman already knew. The first wave had been sent in to soften the opposition up. The Russians had kept the second force in reserve, waiting behind the trees in case they were needed. As soon as the first assault had failed, the Russians would have brought these guys forward to finish the job.

In a few seconds, they're going to sweep through the gap in the fence, he thought. *And we've got no mortars left to hit them with this time.*

As he took aim, a torrent of bullets slapped into the section of parapet eight inches to his right. Bowman quickly pulled back from the edge. The rounds ate into the coping, spitting out clouds of dust across the rooftop. One bullet narrowly missed his cheek before it embedded itself in the wall behind him. Loader and Webb shrank away from the parapet as sustained bursts of gunfire accurately raked their positions.

'Who the fuck is shooting at us?' Loader yelled.

Bowman said, 'The Russians must have set up a support position. Somewhere along the clearing.'

'Whoever it is, they're getting close.'

The rounds were coming in thick and fast. They were getting hit by something heavy. Another PKM machine gun, perhaps. Or something similar. The Russians would have established by now that the main fire was coming from the top of the mansion. They would have positioned a lone shooter behind cover, with orders to put down sustained fire on the parapet to cover the main attacking force. One PKM could do the job. They were brutally efficient weapons. Effective to a range of 1,000 metres, with a rate of fire of 650 rounds per minute.

Another smart call from the Russians, Bowman thought. *They've been more than a match for us today.*

'I'll deal with the shooter,' Mallet said. 'You lot focus on the main group.'

They belly-crawled over to new firing points further along the northern side of the parapet. Mallet traded his C8 rifle for the meatier .50 cal and lay flat on his stomach, observing the ground to the right of the arch as he looked for the muzzle flash from the shooter. At their twelve o'clock, the main KUF force was pouring through the breach. They speedily divided into multiple assault teams and started pepper-potting forward. A carbon copy of the first attack.

Bowman and Loader brassed up the middle group with four rapid bursts, then backed away before a chunk of the parapet disintegrated under a savage volley of machine-gun fire. They shovelled their weapons to the left, laid flat on their stomachs, fired, scurried back. Rounds whizzed through the perforations and smacked into the low wall behind the soldiers. Loader swore as a chunk of debris tumbled down on him.

'Locate that fucker, John! We're getting hammered!'

Between the rounds coming in from the front and the north-east, Bowman and Loader were under almost non-stop pressure. With no mortars to drop and the extra fire support, the frontal assault teams were advancing with greater speed than the first wave. A few of the enemy wielded RPGs or machine guns. Several others were gripping newer Russian assault rifles with grenade launchers fitted under the barrels.

'These bastards are gonna be right on top of us in a few minutes,' Bowman shouted.

'It'll be sooner than that,' said Loader, 'if we can't put the drop on that shooter.'

As he spoke, the concealed shooter fired at them again, driving the men back from the parapet. The incoming burst was suddenly interrupted by the boom of the .50 cal as Mallet popped off two rounds at the shooter. The latter replied with a frenzied burst. Mallet fired a third time. The rebel machine gun still kept on peppering the rooftop. Mallet fired and got the dead man's click as he reached the end of the ten-round clip. He set the weapon down, grabbed his rifle. Shouted into his mic.

'Alex, stick an RPG in! Right of the arch. Corner. Engage!'

Bowman glanced down at the mortar pit, fifty metres to the north-west of the mansion. He spied Casey breaking cover from behind the rock wall, the RPG-7 launcher propped up on her right shoulder. She knelt down, took aim at the spot Mallet had identified next to the archway. Fired.

Flames gushed out of the flared opening at the back of the tube. The grenade whooshed across the front grounds of the estate and slammed into the turf next to the arched entrance, flattening the sentry box and another section of the fence.

'Throw another one in there,' Mallet said to Casey. 'He's still firing. Wallop the bastard!'

Bowman looked down. Casey was beside the mortar pit, jamming the stem of a second rocket into the tube. A handful of the

347

rebels concentrated their fire at her, spattering the nearby wall with lead. Casey held up the RPG in spite of the rounds flying past her, aimed at the archway through the launcher's flip-up sights. She fired again. The missile hissed across the front drive and smashed into the base of the archway with a crashing boom, burying the technical beneath an avalanche of rubble.

The shooter fell silent.

Then Bowman became aware of a movement at his ten o'clock, at the periphery of his vision. He saw a couple of figures kneeling beside the nearest assault team, their rifles elevated at angles as they popped off rounds from their under-barrel 40 mm grenade launchers. Aiming them directly at the mortar pit, two hundred metres away.

He screamed over the radio at Casey.

'Alex! Incoming! Get the fuck down!'

Fifty metres away, Casey turned and ran towards the mortar pit.

The first grenade fell twenty metres short, splashing into the soft grass twenty metres north of the mortar. The second detonated to the south, ten or twelve metres from the edge of the pit. Outside the kill radius of a Russian grenade. But well within fragging range. The force of the explosion lifted Casey off her feet and threw her to one side, spraying her with fragmentation as she slammed head first into the garden wall. She crumpled to the ground beside Lanky's ragged body.

Mallet instantly got on the radio. 'Alex, are you there?'

No response.

'Shit,' Webb said.

Mallet tried again.

Nothing.

Without a moment's hesitation, Loader ditched the GPMG, seized his rifle and the medical rucksack dumped near the skylight.

'I'm going down,' he said.

He set off across the roof before anyone could argue with him. Rifle in one hand and the medical rucksack in the other. He barrelled through the fire exit, disappeared down the stairwell.

'Patrick, get on that Gimpy,' Mallet ordered.

Webb snatched up the spare machine gun. He swept aside a pile of rubble blocking one section of the parapet, stabbed the barrel through the hole. Bowman refocused on the battle, looking for targets.

By now the main assault was in full swing. Less than three hundred metres separated the rebels from the mansion. From the rear of the estate came the crackle of small-arms fire, and Bowman knew the enemy must have sent a force round to that side.

They're hitting us from all angles, he realised.

We're in fucking trouble.

Immediately below, Loader sprinted out of the building.

Then Bowman glimpsed a blur of movement to his left. He jerked the GPMG across, saw a handful of rebels in the nearest assault team rising up from the dead ground. Their rifles trained on Loader. Going for the easy kill. Bowman depressed the trigger, lighting them up. Webb gave them another two bursts with the other Gimpy. More rebels kept popping into view, firing at the Welshman as he scrambled towards the mortar pit. Loader ducked and dived across the open ground, his short legs pumping madly, the earth fountaining all around him. He neared the pit and launched himself forward, diving behind the garden wall moments before a flurry of rounds thwacked into the grass behind him.

Keeping his head below the mortar pit wall, Loader deshouldered the medical rucksack and quickly checked on the bodies.

'One man down,' he said via his tactical radio. 'The lanky fella's dead.'

'And Casey?' Mallet said.

'Concussed. Taken a couple of frags in her shoulder and arm. But she'll survive.'

'We're taking incoming fire to the rear,' Mavinda screamed over the comms. 'Rebels have cut through the fence. I've got three men down.'

'Hold that line,' Mallet ordered. 'Major, don't let them get near the building.'

'What the fuck is taking D Squadron so long?' Webb snarled. 'They should've been here ages ago.'

Bowman said, 'We need to speak to Hereford. Get them to send a message to D Squadron. They need to know we're in the shit.'

Mallet reached for his phone. One last desperate call. Bowman heard the Scot shouting down the line, identifying himself to the operator in Hereford. Telling them to get in touch with D Squadron and pass on the message. *Hurry up. We're about to get overrun.* Then he hung up, retrieved his rifle and joined the others at the parapet.

The rebels were now two hundred metres inside the estate. Halfway to the grand prize. At that range, the two guys on the Gimpys didn't need sniper spotters. Bowman and Webb were simply putting down frantic bursts left and right. The defenders were fighting manically to stem back the rebel tide. Loader was firing his C8 through a hole in the garden wall. Casey lay slumped in the mortar pit, clutching her bloodied shoulder. Gregory operated the Gimpy in the gun pit to the north. The staccato crack of gunfire echoed from the ground to the rear of the mansion as Mavinda and his men engaged the enemies pouring through the back fence.

Bowman reached the end of the belt. He brushed away the piles of link and spent cartridges littering the cement floor. Grabbed another belt.

'I'm running low on ammunition,' he called out. 'Three belts left.'

'What have you got left, Patrick?' Mallet asked.

'Five belts,' said Webb.

'Ammo report,' Mallet said into his mic.

'Two belts,' came the reply from Gregory.

'Four mags,' Loader said.

'Five mags,' said Casey.

'We've got next to nothing back here,' said Mavinda. 'One box of two hundred.'

'It's not enough,' Webb said. 'We're gonna run out of ammo soon.'

Bowman briefly scanned the horizon, looking for any sign of the dust clouds that might signal the imminent arrival of D Squadron. But the skyline remained agonisingly clear. Almost fifty minutes had elapsed since the reinforcements had landed at the nearby airfield. For the first time, Bowman started to lose faith.

They're not coming. We're not going to get any help.

'Rebels at our eleven o'clock!' Webb shouted. 'They're in the drainage ditch!'

Bowman swung his weapon round, focused on the ditch running south towards the corner of the ornamental garden. The rebels on the right flank were working their way down the spine of the canal, using the dead ground to sneak up close to the house. Just as he had feared. Once they reached the garden wall, it was all over. At that point the enemy would be less than fifty metres from the stronghold.

A few more paces and they'll be in hand grenade range.

'Tiny! Enemies approaching in the ditch. About forty metres from your position,' Mallet hollered over the comms. 'Get ready to detonate those Claymores. On my signal.'

Down in the mortar pit, Loader put down a three-round burst and crawled over to the clacker, staying low to avoid the rounds whipping overhead. Enemy bullets and grenade shrapnel splintered the mound of rocks around him. On the far side of the wall, the horde of rebels in the ditch crept towards the north-west corner of the garden.

Closing in on the mortar pit.

Mallet counted down their approach to the team.

'Rebels are about thirty metres to the Claymores . . . Twenty metres . . . Fifteen.'

Bowman and Webb blasted away at the assault groups to the north.

In the mortar pit, Loader prepared to detonate the Claymore clacker. The enemy rounds were striking dangerously close to his firing point, chipping away at the rocks.

'Ten metres to the Claymores,' Mallet said. 'Five . . . Fire!'

The ditch erupted with a pair of thunderlike booms. The rebels disappeared behind a swirl of blackish smoke, earth and debris. Hundreds of steel balls smashed into their tightly packed ranks, puncturing flesh and bone. Metal fragments and dirt ricocheted off the steep sides of the ditch, increasing the lethal field of debris cutting through the men. The agonised cries of the wounded and the dying split the morning air.

'They won't be trying that again for a while,' shouted Webb.

'Aye, but it won't stop the rest of them,' Mallet said.

Bowman hooked the Gimpy back round to the main assault groups and fired at the next team on the move. The rebels were still pushing forward aggressively. By this point, they had covered almost three-quarters of the ground to the stronghold. In another few minutes, he knew, they would be dangerously close to the main building.

There was still no sign of D Squadron.

He fired another burst. The GPMG glowed red hot, distorting the barrel and rendering the weapon useless.

'Gimpy's fucked!' he shouted as he chucked aside the flaming machine gun. 'Switching to my rifle.'

Time became a blur. Minutes stretched into hours as the team kept on putting rounds round. Bowman's eye was suddenly drawn to a puff of smoke from the rebel ranks. He saw one of the fighters launching an RPG at the rooftop and shouted a warning at his comrades. The rocket whistled just over the parapet, missing the team by inches before it self-detonated somewhere in the distance, exploding uselessly over the forest.

'Christ, that was close,' Webb hissed.

Bowman got to the end of a clip. He fished out another from the pouch, reloaded. Then he heard Gregory's voice in his earpiece. 'I'm out. Repeat, I've got no more ammo for the Gimpy.'

'We're almost out, too,' Loader said. 'Down to our last mags. We're taking a lot of incoming.'

'Prepare to fall back,' Mallet said into his mic. 'Back to the stronghold. Josh will cover you. We'll make our stand here.'

He glanced to his right.

'Get downstairs,' he said to Bowman. 'Give the others a hand. Once you're all inside, secure the front door. Don't let anyone get through. We'll defend this place or die trying.'

Bowman pulled back from the parapet. He scrambled over to the fire exit, stooping low to avoid the bullets zinging above his head. He flew down the stairs, raced across the central atrium and shouldered through the front door. Knelt beside one of the stone bases buttressing the marble columns along the porch. Brought up his rifle, pointed it through the gap between the pillars and filled his lungs.

'Get back!' he thundered. 'This way!'

At his twelve o'clock, Gregory began sprinting back from the gun pit, AK-47 in his right hand. Bowman supported him with sustained bursts, engaging any rebels showing an interest in his old boss. The second guy in the pit, Toothbrush, lay motionless beside the abandoned GPMG. Gregory ducked and weaved his way across the front drive, bullets sparking against the ground behind him. Like a million firecrackers going off. He sprinted up the steps and shrank behind the pillar to the right.

'Thanks,' he said between ragged draws of breath.

'Thank me later,' Bowman replied. 'If we ever make it out of here.'

Further away, several of the Karatandan soldiers had hastily abandoned their gun pits, sensing that the tide of the battle had turned. Some dived into bushes, others fled towards the eastern side of the estate or threw up their hands in surrender. Still Loader and Casey fought on. They were coming under heavy, remorseless enemy fire. The rebels were roughly eighty metres from the mortar pit. They were in grave danger of getting overrun.

'Tiny! Alex! Start moving!' Bowman roared. 'Now!'

Loader emptied a final burst. Then he grabbed Casey by the arm and started dragging her towards the stronghold. She limped along, struggling to keep up the pace as they zigged and zagged across the front lawn. Almost at once a group of three rebels shot up from a small depression and unleashed a blitz of rifle fire in their direction. Bowman and Gregory replied with short bursts from their rifles. One rebel fighter fell backwards. His muckers hurled themselves into cover.

'Hurry!' Bowman thundered. 'Come on, Tiny!'

'To the right. The fountain!' Gregory called out.

Bowman whipped round. He spied two rebels kneeling beside the water fountain to the north. Seventy metres away. He fixed them in his sights and fired twice, hitting one of the enemies in the guts. Gregory nailed the other guy through the head.

A grenade detonated several metres off to Casey's right, belching smoke and fragmentation. She stumbled on, tripped, then fell. Loader stopped and reached down to help her up.

Several cracks split the air.

Loader spasmed as the bullets tore into his body. One round smashed into his face, shattering his jaw.

Bowman saw the flickering of muzzles at his ten o'clock. The two other rebels behind the depression had broken cover and aimed their weapons at Loader, riddling his body with lead.

He instantly raked the depression with gunfire, slotting both of the rebels before they could duck from view. Then he lowered his rifle and shouted at Gregory.

'Cover me!'

He shot up from behind the pillar and bouldered down the steps. Gregory continued peppering the rebel positions, keeping them busy as Bowman sprinted across the open ground. Legs chopping, lungs burning. He reached Loader, glanced down at him. There was no need to check for a pulse. His body was in rag order. Rounds had punched through his throat and right arm, his shoulder. Half of his face was missing. Bowman looked at his lifeless friend and felt something clench around his heart.

Tiny. One of the genuinely good guys of the Regiment.

Dead.

He grabbed hold of Casey and yanked her to her feet.

'Move!' he screamed at her. 'Let's go!'

They set off towards the stronghold. Casey stumbled forward, taking in ragged draws of breath. Bowman helped her along while Gregory put down covering fire from the porch. Enemy rounds slapped into the turf, missing them by inches. Somewhere to the rear a grenade detonated. Bowman gritted his teeth and urged Casey to move faster. They ran on, hit the front steps and raced up to the front door. Gregory stayed behind the pillar until they had reached the safety of the atrium. He gave the enemy a three-round burst and hurried back inside, slamming the front door behind him.

'Are you hit?' he asked Casey.

She shook her head.

'Tiny,' she croaked. 'They got Tiny.'

Bowman nodded. Rage and grief swirled inside his chest. There would be time to properly mourn his friend later. 'There's nothing we can do for him now.'

'What's the plan?' said Gregory.

'We need to barricade the door. Slow these bastards down if they try to breach the building. Stay here.'

They raced off in search of heavy furniture. Casey applied a field dressing to her wounds while Bowman and Gregory carried over a table from one of the dining rooms. They jammed it against the door frame, then reinforced it with several other sturdy items. A side cabinet, a sofa, a coffee table, several chairs.

As they worked, Mallet kept them updated on the enemy movements from his position on the rooftop. The rebels were less than a hundred metres from the mansion now. Webb's GPMG had flamed out. Both men were down to their last four clips of 5.56 ammo.

This is like the Alamo now.

Gregory closed the plantation shutters screening the downstairs windows. 'That should keep them at bay for a while,' he said.

'What now?' Casey said.

Bowman looked at her. There was blood on her shirt, her trousers. Her face and hands were caked in dirt and battle grease. Frag metal pitted her right shoulder.

'We've got to sort out the back. Do you think you can hold the front?'

'I'll be OK,' she replied steadily.

'Keep away from the door. That's where the rounds will be coming in. Stick to the window. Tilt the shutters so you've got a gap to see through. If you see anyone coming up the front steps, drop them.'

'What if D Squadron doesn't come?'

Bowman didn't get a chance to answer. Mallet's voice boomed urgently over the comms.

'Rebels approaching the rear of the stronghold. Heading for the terrace. Get over there. NOW!'

Thirty-Two

Bowman spun away from Casey. He nodded at Gregory.

'Come on!' he roared. 'Let's go!'

They broke into a run, crossed the atrium and darted down the corridor leading towards the salon at the back of the house. Bowman with his Colt rifle, Gregory gripping the AK-47 he'd taken from the gun pit. Another burst of adrenaline swept through Bowman's veins, jump-starting his shattered body. He rushed into the salon ahead of Gregory and dived across the room to the French doors. He threw the deadbolts into the locked positions while Gregory circled round to the Steinway.

'Give us a hand,' Gregory said. 'Get this thing against the doors!'

They had seconds to spare. Bowman hurried over, and the two men braced their legs and pushed hard, shoving the piano across the marbled floor. They stopped just short of the back door, then pushed up at an angle, tipping the piano onto its side. It wasn't a great barricade, and it wouldn't stop the rebels for very long. But it was the best they could do. There was no time for anything else.

'Take the left window,' Gregory said. 'I'll take the right. Don't let them get inside. As soon as they breach this room, we're fucked.'

Bowman lunged over to the casement window to the left of the central doors. He raised the C8 and peered through one of the glass panels. From his position he had a clear line of sight to the terrace. He could see the stone balustrade, the limestone steps leading down to the rear sloped garden. Bowman figured the distance between the steps at the end of the terrace and the salon was no more than twenty-five metres.

'They're coming,' Gregory said.

On the far side of the terrace, three rebels surged into view.

Gregory crouched and took aim from the fixed window to the right of the blocked door.

Bowman lined up his first target. Two of the rebels had surged ahead of their mate, running hard as they sprinted towards the stronghold.

The clicker counter in his head told him that he'd expended three clips of 5.56 × 45 mm ammo already. Two on the rooftop, one at the front of the mansion. Which meant he had one magazine left, plus the ten bullets in the clip housed in the weapon. A grand total of forty rounds. Not much. Not against a large force of rebels. Once he was out of ammo, Bowman would have to resort to his secondary weapon. The Glock 17 pistol holstered to his belt.

We'll be taking pistol shots at these bastards soon.

He centred the weapon on the rebel to the left, pulled the trigger. The muzzle flared. Two rounds blasted through the windowpane, shattering the glass into a million pieces before they thumped into the rebel. The man tumbled backwards, arms windmilling. Gregory fired simultaneously at the other guy, giving him a two-round burst to the face.

The third rebel ducked left and scampered towards a classical statue mounted on a stone pedestal. Bowman fired twice, missed, depressed the trigger again. The bullet struck the man in the ankle, shattering bone and ligament. The rebel screamed and crashed to the tiled floor, hands pawing at his fucked-up lower leg. Bowman permanently silenced him with a double-tap to the face.

Three enemies down.

Two rounds left in the clip. Thirty-two rounds in total.

'How many mags have you got, Mike?' Bowman called out.

'Down to my last two,' Gregory said.

'We're in the shit. Big time.'

'Keep fighting. Don't let the bastards win.'

Bowman threw a quick glance at his old OC. *The guy has still got it*, he thought to himself. *He might be older and worn around the edges. But he's the same tough officer I fought alongside in the Regiment. Now we're fighting shoulder-to-shoulder again. Just like the old days.*

Except this time, there's no one to bail us out.

Another four rebels ran up the stairs to the terrace.

Bowman and Gregory opened up as soon as they popped into view. They cut down two of the enemy with surgical precision. Bowman put two bullets into the lead rebel, stitching him in the groin. The man howled in agony, hands cupping his shredded balls as he sank to his knees. The other two KUF men immediately responded with a couple of bursts of their own. Bullets smashed through several of the windowpanes. Bowman felt a searing pain as a round streaked past him, grazing his cheek. He gritted his teeth and lined up the two rebels darting for cover behind the statue. Depressed the trigger. Got the dreaded click.

He dipped his head below the window, released the empty clip. Reached for another.

'Reloading!' he shouted to Gregory. 'On my last mag!'

Thirty rounds left.

He came up. Through the blown-out pane he spotted five more figures storming across the terrace. He lined up the sights with the nearest target. Double-tapped. Missed. Gregory shot a second guy through the chest. The other rebels spread out and found cover, firing at the salon from behind statues and stone ornaments. One figure bolted towards an enormous planter crowning a stout plinth. Bowman clipped him with three rounds to the guts. His body slapped dully against the floor, like dropping a bag of cement.

The six others kept up a continuous stream of gunfire, punching holes in the French doors and the Steinway. One burst struck the wooden bar on the back wall of the salon. Bowman glanced back and saw the bottles racked on the shelves exploding, spilling shards of glass and premium whisky over the counter.

As he returned fire, Bowman noticed two of the rebels were moving off to the left side of the terrace. He hooked the C8 round, but they swept out of sight before he could pull the trigger. A moment later, another three enemies sprinted up from the lower garden level to join the fight. The nearest rebels were twenty metres from the salon.

They're almost on top of us now.

'There's too many of them!' he yelled.

'Keep engaging,' Gregory shouted back. 'Don't let them get inside!'

Bowman put down another two rounds.

He didn't think about dying. He didn't think about anything beyond the next three seconds. He was operating on a purely mechanical level. Picking out targets, aiming, firing. Like a runner fixed on completing the next mile, the next lap, the next metre. His entire world had reduced to the twenty metres of ground in front of him.

He shot a scrawny soldier through the head as he scrambled across the terrace. The round uncorked his brains like champagne. Then Bowman heard the shrill crash of shattering glass. It came from somewhere to his left. His nine o'clock.

The room next to the salon.

'They're coming through the dining room windows,' Gregory said. 'Get over there, Josh!'

Bowman shrank back from the window, his heart hammering frantically. He scudded round to the open door on the left, past the abandoned teddy bear and the dried patches of blood marking the spot where the president's brother and niece had been killed hours before. Bowman stopped just inside the doorway, his rifle at shoulder-height as his eyes skated across the chandeliered room. He saw a mahogany table the size of a spaceship, pictures of bare-breasted women on the wall.

He saw a rebel in wraparound shades on the other side of the room, jumping down from a broken window. A second figure was climbing through the opening after his comrade. The rebels freeze-framed at the sight of Bowman standing in front of the door. They stared in horror at the dark mouth of the rifle barrel.

Bowman gave them four blasts from the C8. He aimed at a third figure crawling through the next window, squeezed the trigger and got the click. He tossed the weapon aside, ripped the Glock out of the holster and put two shots into the man's centre mass.

'That's it,' Gregory hollered from the salon. 'I'm out. Nothing left! Fall back!'

Bowman backed out of the dining room. At the rear window, Gregory retrieved a hand grenade from his pocket. He tore the pin out, posted it through the broken pane. Then he ran over to Bowman and the two men retreated towards the corridor. There was a loud bang from outside as the grenade exploded, momentarily scattering the rebels.

Bowman pushed the pressel switch attached to his vest. 'We're out of ammo,' he said. 'Down to our pistols. Rebels about to breach the back of the stronghold.'

'Enemies are almost at the front door,' Casey said over the team radio. 'I can't hold them off! Falling back.'

Bowman and Gregory ran on. They had only a few seconds before the building was overrun. Seconds to find a secure part of the building to hole up in. Retreating to the basement or the rooftop wasn't an option. They were too far away. The atrium would be overrun with rebel fighters by the time they got there.

Gregory stopped in front of the door to the private study.

'In here,' he said.

They darted into the room. Gregory slammed the door shut, twisted the lock. He shouted to Bowman, and they dragged over a bulky bookcase and wedged it sideways against the jamb. The sounds of splintering glass and wood came from the other side as the rebels tried to gain entry through multiple points along the terrace and the front of the building.

Bowman stepped back. He waited in front of the barricaded door. Pistol in his hand, his clothes caked in sweat and dirt and lead particles. His adrenaline levels were through the roof. Any second now, the enemy was going to storm inside.

And then it will all be over.

'Give us a couple of those,' Gregory said, pointing to the grenades Bowman was carrying.

Bowman handed them over. 'Never thought I'd die in this shithole,' he said.

'It's not over yet.' Gregory smiled grimly. 'We can still take down as many of these bastards as possible. Let's give them something to remember us by, eh?'

Bowman nodded. 'I'm ready.'

They waited.

The crashing noises suddenly cut out.

Bowman stared at the closed door.

'What the fuck's going on?' he asked after a few seconds.

'Listen,' Gregory said.

Bowman pricked his ears.

At first, he didn't hear it. Then a sound came from somewhere beyond the walls of the stronghold. A noise that was instantly familiar to any seasoned Hereford operator. The deep throated bark of a Browning .50 calibre machine gun.

'Christ, have they got more hardware coming in?' Bowman said in despair.

Gregory crinkled his brow. 'I didn't think the rebels had any Brownings.'

Bowman spoke into his throat mic. 'What's going on out there?' he asked.

Silence.

He tried again. 'John? Patrick?'

Still nothing.

Then Webb came over the radio, shouting excitedly, 'They're here! It's D Squadron! They've arrived!'

Bowman and Gregory hastily dragged the bookcase away from the door. They paused outside the study for a moment, checking for any sign of the enemy. Then they hastened down the hallway into the salon, Bowman sweeping his eyes left to right as he led the way. Gun smoke hung like a veil over the room. He hurried over to the shattered window, gazed out past the empty terrace at the rear garden.

An armoured vehicle had gone static to the east. Bowman recognised it at once. A Regiment-modified Jackal, rigged up with a fearsome amount of firepower. Twin-mounted GPMGs on the front, a belt-fed MK19 grenade launcher operated by a third man on the back. Twenty soldiers in camo kit and plate armour charged forward on foot while the bloke on the back of the Jackal pumped the grenade launcher. They were engaging the enemy using the tried-and-trusted fighting tactics of 22 SAS. The Jackal providing the heavy support fire, the men on foot sweeping forward in five-man assault groups. The soldiers blasted away with their C8s at the rebels as they bolted towards the rear fence.

Mallet had made contact with D Squadron. Bowman heard the Scot in his earpiece as he talked with the squadron over the open comms system.

'There are friendlies in the stronghold,' he was saying. 'Do not engage, repeat do not engage.'

Behind the assault groups, the guy on the MK19 chugged away at the fleeing targets. Grenades churned up the earth, shovelling clumps of loose soil into the air, atomising the few rebels left standing. Within seconds, the ground to the rear of the stronghold had been almost cleared of enemy combatants.

Bowman felt an indescribable sense of relief. 'They made it. Thank fuck.'

'They'll slice through this lot in no time,' Gregory remarked. 'It'll be over in a minute now.'

'Yes.'

He turned to Gregory. The two men shared a look. Something unspoken passed between them. A bond only those who had stared death in the face could understand.

'Check on the family,' Bowman said. 'I'll check on the rooftop.'

They jogged out of the salon. Back down the corridor, past the study, into the atrium. Casey appeared from a separate hallway to the left, a dazed look on her face.

'Is it over?' she asked in a weak voice.

'It will be shortly,' said Bowman. 'The lads in D Squadron are taking over now. Our part's done.'

'Thank God.'

She slumped to the floor, as if her tired legs simply couldn't support her any longer. Bowman left her by the stairs and climbed back up to the roof, his weary muscles making one last effort.

On the rooftop, Mallet was busy giving fire orders to D Squadron. Bowman heard him directing them onto targets from his vantage point high above the action. Webb crouched beside him, a blood-speckled field dressing wrapped around his head. There was shit everywhere. Smoke wafted up from the warped barrels on the two Gimpys. The acrid tang of gunpowder hung in the air. Bowman dropped low beside the parapet and looked down.

The battle was almost over.

Pockets of rebels were fleeing in every direction. The men of D Squadron had swept right across the field of fire, dominating the ground. One of the Jackals had taken up a support-fire position on the east side near the pagoda. The second Jackal was still mop-ping up resistance to the south. A third vehicle had sheered round the back of the estate and swung round to the west of the man-sion. Both the Jackals on the east and west side had Browning .50 calibres mounted on top instead of grenade launchers. Otherwise known as the 'relish', because that's what a human body looked like after you put a burst into it. A section of the fencing to the east had been flattened, and Bowman realised that the Jackals must have bombed in from that direction, crashing through the flimsy chain-link mesh. The guys on foot would have debussed from their transport trucks somewhere further up the main road before moving forward with the support vehicles.

As Bowman looked on, the soldiers picked off the last dregs of resistance. Half of the guys had advanced west from the pagoda. The other half had attacked from the ornamental garden. Caught between the Jackals and the assault groups, the remaining few rebels were brutally cut down, some of them ripped limb from limb. Most of them were killed before they had a chance to escape. Those further back from the struggle turned and fled up the clearing towards the main road. They ran straight into an ambush set up by one element of D Squadron. Several of the rebels tried to resist or return fire. They were swiftly dropped. The rest threw down their weapons and surrendered.

In less than a minute, the rebels had been completely routed.

To the west, through a gap in the woods, Bowman spied four tiny figures jumping into a white Toyota Land Cruiser. The wagon took off west down the main road, wheels throwing up clouds of dust.

A posh clipped voice came over the open comms network. The OC of D Squadron, Bowman realised.

'One of our fellows has just seen a vehicle speeding away,' the OC reported. 'Land Cruiser. Four passengers, he says. Pale-skinned. Any idea who that might be?'

'Aye,' said Mallet. 'It's the Russians. The guys behind the coup.'

'Roger that. We'll put a message across to SFSG. They'll set up a cordon to intercept down the road.'

'Leave them,' Mallet said. His voice was papery, hoarse. 'Let them get away.'

A short pause. 'Are you sure?'

'If you capture those guys, it'll cause a diplomatic shitstorm. Let them escape. They're not going to cause any trouble now. They'll be on the next plane back to Moscow.'

'Very well. It's your call, I suppose.'

The gunfire finally ceased, and the OC came back on the radio to report that the estate was secure. Webb threw his head back and laughed deliriously. All the pent-up stress and adrenaline and fear of the battle suddenly rushed out of him in a burst of cathartic laughter.

At his side, Bowman stepped back from the parapet, overcome with relief and exhaustion.

'It's over,' he croaked. 'Thank God, it's really over.'

Thirty-Three

They left the rooftop a short time later. As they reached the ground floor a team from D Squadron swept inside the stronghold from the rear terrace and quickly took charge. A handful of the guys searched the rooms for lurking rebels while the others brought up the family from the basement. Once the building had been cleared the guys escorted the women and children to a suite of guest rooms on the first floor, away from the chaos elsewhere. Guards were posted to watch over them around the clock.

With the family secure, Mallet and the others cleared the barricade and made their way outside.

They stepped out to a scene of total carnage. The ground was thick with the dead and the dying and the detritus of battle. Some men lay writhing in agony, clawing at their wounds or trying to shove their guts back into their stomachs. Others screamed at the soldiers, begging for help. The foul stink of death choked the air.

A platoon of Karatandan soldiers had accompanied D Squadron from the garrison at the airfield. Some of them threw up a cordon around the estate while the others assisted the Regiment as they cleared the battlefield. The lightly wounded were checked for ID, plasticuffed and then taken over to the ornamental garden to join the rest of the rebel prisoners. At least a dozen men had been taken captive. They cut a pathetic sight, with their ragged uniforms and blood-encrusted faces. Those with serious injuries were handed over to the local platoon, placed in the back of a waiting truck and driven away to the airfield to be treated by the local garrison. Or at least, that was the idea. Bowman doubted the Karatandan soldiers would show their sworn enemies any mercy. Most likely, they would be locked up somewhere and left to die.

Two guys marched briskly over to Mallet. The OC of D Squadron, Stuart Thriepland, was a buff former Guardsman, tall and ramrod straight, with a shiny blond quiff and an accent so posh it probably had a seat in the House of Lords. The man at his shoulder, Sergeant Major Craig Dundas, was a short wiry Scot, teak-tough and bulbous-nosed, with an aggressive attitude and a permanent angry stare. His voice carried a slight trace of his Aberdeen roots as he addressed the team.

'Bloody hell. How the fuck did you lot survive this?' Dundas said as he surveyed the chaos of the battlefield.

'We almost didn't,' Mallet replied. 'Another minute and we would have been overrun.'

'What took you so long?' asked Bowman.

'We ran into a rebel ambush a few miles outside the airfield,' Thriepland replied in his public schoolboy accent. 'Had to clear the area before we could get over here. Unavoidable.'

Dundas spat on the ground. 'Rebels had us pinned down for an hour. Proper ambush tactics. They knew how to fight.'

'The Russians must have sent them over,' said Mallet. 'Bastards know every trick in the book.'

Thriepland cleared his throat and said, 'I count only four of you. Where's the other fellow?'

'Loader's dead,' Mallet said.

'I see.' Thriepland nodded sombrely. 'Sorry to hear that. And the rest of you?'

'Alex took a couple of frags to the shoulder. We've got a few nicks and cuts. Nothing major.'

Dundas smiled at Casey. 'I hear you're deadly on the old mortar.'

'Something like that,' she replied tonelessly. Her expression had a faraway quality.

'Looks like you fought off half the rebellion,' said Thriepland. 'There'll be some citations coming out of this, I imagine.' He looked at Mallet, and a sarky tone crept into his stiff voice as he went on. 'Pity you guys in the Cell can't be named.'

Bowman stared wordlessly at him.

'What happens now?' asked Webb.

'We'll stick around here and guard the family,' Thriepland said. 'We've got orders to wait here until the country is fully secure. Which will take a few days, I expect.'

'It'll take us that long to clear all them bodies away,' Dundas muttered. 'This is a right bloody mess.'

Bowman said, 'Why isn't the president flying straight back? The coup will be over soon enough.'

'There's a force coming in from 2 Para,' Thriepland explained. 'A long-term training team. We're due to hand over to them in a couple of days. The president's refusing to return until the hand-over is complete.'

'Probably wants the extra boots on the ground,' Dundas added.

Webb snorted. 'Yeah, that fucker will want this place like Fort Knox before he comes in.'

'So much for caring about the welfare of his family,' Bowman said. 'If he was that concerned, he'd be flying back now.'

'Why aren't you escorting the family back to the city once the coup has been crushed?' asked Casey. 'Why wait here with them?'

'Orders from the top.' Thriepland swept a hand through his magnificent hair. 'The president doesn't want his family to return to the palace in its current state. I gather there was some heavy fighting there last night.'

'More like a massacre,' Mallet said.

Thriepland shrugged. 'Either way, the president has instructed his family to wait here until his aides and household staff have given the palace a thorough cleaning. He wants it spick and span for their return, apparently.'

Webb laughed weakly. 'Well, at least they don't want to rough it.'

Thriepland didn't look amused.

'You'll be leaving soon, I imagine?' he asked.

Mallet said, 'That depends on Six. I'll have to make some calls. We might need to be on-site for a while.'

'As you wish.' Thriepland straightened his back. 'In the meantime, help yourselves to a brew and some food. I suggest you get one of the medics to clean that shoulder up,' he added to Casey.

Dundas jammed his thick thumbs into his belt and rolled his tongue around his gums.

'What do you want to do with those prisoners?' he asked Gregory. 'They're your responsibility, not ours.'

'Colonel Lubowa and I will take care of them.' Gregory pointed out the head of the Presidential Guard. 'They'll be dealt with,' he added.

'We'll need a body bag for Tiny,' said Mallet. 'He's coming home with us.'

'Of course,' Thriepland replied. 'I'll see to it.'

He moved off, Dundas stalking him and barking orders at the men. Mallet walked away to put in a call to the Voice. Casey went in search of a medic. Gregory beat a path over to Colonel Lubowa. The latter had mustered the handful of surviving men from the Presidential Guard and Mavinda's platoon. Now they began herding the rebel prisoners towards the back of the stronghold under Gregory's watchful gaze.

'What'll happen to them, do you think?' Webb asked Bowman as they watched the last of the prisoners disappear from sight.

'They tried to overthrow the government, mate. The president's hardly going to let them off with a slap on the wrist.'

'You think he'll execute them?'

Bowman considered, then shook his head. 'Mike would never sanction it. They'll probably interrogate the ringleaders, then chuck the lot of them in prison.'

'That's as good as a death sentence over here anyway,' said Webb.

A while later, Mallet came back and gathered the team round.

He said, 'I've heard back from Vauxhall. They're arranging transportation for us now. We'll be leaving on the same Herc these lads came in on.'

'When?' asked Casey.

'Soon. A few hours. We're still waiting for clearance. Once we've got the green light, I'll let you know.'

Bowman said, 'What's going on with the coup?'

'SFSG landed about an hour ago. Along with the detachment from the SBS. They've recaptured the international airport from the rebels. Moving on to the capital as we speak.'

'It'll be over soon, then.'

'Looks that way. As soon as they've taken the broadcasting station, they'll put out a pre-recorded statement by the president, telling his people that the rebellion has been quelled. Once that message goes out, the game's up.'

'The hard core elements won't give up that easily.'

'Maybe not,' Mallet said. 'But they won't stand a chance against our guys, now that the Russians have abandoned them.'

The morning wore on. Bowman sat with the others near the steps of the stronghold, sipping boiling-hot coffee, each of them feeling physically and mentally exhausted. They looked at one another, but no one said a word. The mood was sober and quiet. There was no sense of jubilation. Just an overwhelming feeling of relief, tempered by the grief they all felt at the loss of their friend. Bowman saw a couple of men from D Squadron placing Loader in a body bag and thought about the promise he'd made in the basement.

As soon as this op is over, I'll go clean.

I'll keep it, he vowed. *This time, I won't slip. No matter how hard it gets.*

The team waited. After a while, Gregory wandered off to speak with Colonel Lubowa. Mallet was fielding a constant stream of phone calls from the Foreign Office and Six. He was answering questions about the assault and getting information about the situation elsewhere in the country. The attack on the capital was going well, Mallet said. By late morning the combined SFSG–SBS force had captured the broadcasting station, and the rebellion began to fizzle out. General Kakuba had gone silent. His loyal officers were rumoured to have fled across the border.

The sun reached its zenith, beating down on the men on burial duty. Tractors were brought in from one of the nearby farms, and then D Squadron began the grisly task of clearing away the dead. Bowman looked on as they scooped up the corpses into the loading buckets and dumped them in an agricultural trailer. Another group of soldiers from the Karatandan platoon picked their way across the battlefield, gathering up body parts and severed torsos. The dead would be buried in a mass grave by the local forces, removing the evidence of the struggle before the arrival of the foreign press corps. The Foreign Office would be keen to downplay the fighting; they didn't want some freelance photographer taking snaps of a field littered with hundreds of bodies. That would undermine the narrative they were building. The truth would remain buried for years, decades perhaps. Maybe even forever.

Ten minutes later, Gregory emerged from the mansion. He made his way over to the team, grinning broadly.

'This way, guys,' he said. 'I've got some entertainment lined up for you in the basement.'

Webb lifted his chin and frowned heavily. 'This is hardly the time for a celebratory piss-up.'

'Trust me, you'll want to see this.'

Bowman looked up at him. 'What is it?' he asked. 'Booze? Women?'

The grin stretched across Gregory's face. 'It's something better than that.'

'Like what?' Casey said.

'It's a surprise,' Gregory replied. 'But I can guarantee you'll enjoy it.'

Bowman sighed wearily. They had just lost a close friend, they were physically spent, tired beyond belief, and now Gregory was suggesting they hit the basement for a party. He couldn't think of anything worse. Or less appropriate.

'Come on, guys,' Gregory insisted. 'This won't take long, I promise.'

Bowman and Casey looked at each other. Gregory stood there, his eyes glowing with excitement. Then Webb shrugged indifferently. 'May as well go and have a look,' he said. 'Nothing else to do until we get the clearance from Six, anyway.'

'All right,' Bowman said, climbing stiffly to his feet. 'Let's see it.'

'Great.' Gregory clasped his hands together. 'You won't regret it, guys. You're in for a treat.'

Webb gave Casey a hand, helping her stand up, and then they followed Gregory towards the front door. Bowman looked round but Mallet was nowhere to be seen.

'Where's John?' he asked nobody in particular.

'Guest house,' Gregory replied. 'He's in the conference room with Thriepland. They're having a joint briefing with Six. He can join us later on.'

He led them through the entrance, past the river of splintered wood and broken glass in the atrium. As they trudged down the stairs to the basement, Bowman wondered why Gregory was so excited. He obviously had something big to show them. *Entertainment*, he had said. *I guarantee you'll enjoy it.* But not beer or women. Some sort of orgy, perhaps, Bowman reflected. He'd heard of dictators hosting private sex parties. Maybe Seguma kept a secret harem in the basement.

Gregory paced down the corridor until he reached the door on the left, several metres short of the wine cellar. The rusted hinges grated in protest as he ushered the team into a dimly lit corridor with bare concrete walls and several steel doors on either side. Bowman counted twelve of them in total. The doors were closed, with arrow-slit viewing panels and food hatches set above the locks. *Like cells in a police station*, thought Bowman. *Or a prison wing.*

'Where are you taking us?' he asked.

'You'll see,' Gregory said.

He stopped in front of one of the cell-like doors and fished out a set of keys from his pocket. A queasy feeling moved through Bowman as he watched Gregory twist open the heavy-duty lock. *Something was wrong here*, thought Bowman. *Very wrong.*

Bolts clanged. The door groaned open.

'In here, guys,' Gregory said.

They entered a damp, dingy space with bare concrete walls and strip lighting. Dried patches of blood scabbed the floor. A bucket in the far corner overflowed with faecal matter. On the left side of the room Bowman saw a bundle of bloodied cloths on a wooden bench, next to a set of DIY tools. There was a power drill, a bone saw, a blowtorch, an iron bar, several knives, a claw hammer and a selection of rusted nails. A GSh-18 semi-automatic pistol.

And a cattle prod.

In the middle of the room, a rebel had been stripped naked and chained by his wrists and ankles to a metal bedframe. A short, stocky man with a chinstrap beard. Bowman had seen his face before, two lifetimes ago. Back in London. The lobby of the Broxbury Hall Hotel. On the TV. The mountainside interview with the reporter. The man had been wearing a pair of aviator shades back then, but the face was unmistakably the same.

General Moses Kakuba.

The rebel leader's torso was covered in bruises. One of his ears had been sliced off. Chunks of flesh were missing from his arms and legs. A filthy rag had been stuffed into his mouth, stifling his screams of terror.

Colonel Lubowa stood over the prisoner, the sleeves of his army shirt rolled up to the elbows. He was beating General Kakuba senseless with his fists, delivering vicious blows to his stomach, his face. A second man dressed in the uniform of the Presidential Guard leaned against the bench, cheering Lubowa on. The dull wet slap of bone against flesh echoed through the cell as the Colonel shovelled a punch into the prisoner's ribs.

Bowman's stomach went cold. 'Jesus Christ,' he said.

'What the fuck is going on here?' Webb snapped.

'I wanted to show you the secret interrogation centre we run down here. This is where we deal with the president's enemies,' Gregory replied casually.

'This isn't an interview room,' Bowman said. 'This a fucking torture chamber.'

'More or less the same thing over here.'

Gregory flapped a hand at the terrified figure bound to the bedframe. 'We found the general hiding in the ditch with some of his men. Trying to play dead. It's a good job I recognised him, otherwise he might have been taken away with the wounded.'

Bowman felt sick. 'Why are we here?'

'The president wishes us to dispense with the general . . . once we've had our fun with him, of course. We've already enjoyed ourselves, as you can see. I thought you guys might want to take over. Think of it as a treat, for all your hard work.'

The guard roared with laughter as Lubowa struck the man again.

'Thank you, Colonel,' said Gregory. 'We'll take it from here.'

Lubowa gave the man a final punch to the face before he stepped back from the mattress. He wiped his hands with one of the dirty rags, tossed it aside and nodded at Gregory.

'He's all yours,' he said. 'Let us know when you're done. Make sure you don't get started on the next prisoner without us.'

'Wouldn't dream of it.'

The colonel barked at the guard. The latter stubbed out his cigarette and followed his boss out of the cell, closing the door behind them.

The rebel leader groaned in agony. Bowman could barely believe what he was seeing. He remembered the box of cattle prods he'd seen in the wine cellar. He remembered the look of fear in Major Mavinda's eyes when he had heard Gregory's name. Suddenly understood. *The guy isn't just Seguma's chief of security.*

He's running his own personal torture camp.

Gregory walked over to the bench, picked up the cattle prod. Held it out towards Bowman.

'This usually gets a good reaction from them. Who wants to go first? Josh?'

For a moment, Bowman was speechless.

'You're not serious,' he said finally. 'You can't fucking do this.'

'Why not?'

'It's wrong. It's against the Geneva Conventions, for Chrissakes.'

Gregory waved his hand dismissively. 'Don't pretend to be offended. You know the president's track record. How he operates. This can't come as a great surprise to you, surely.'

'I don't give a crap about Seguma. The guy's a tyrant. But I thought you would be above all of this.'

'I'm his chief of security. This is my job.'

'Torturing prisoners?'

'Sending a message to his enemies.' Gregory held up the cattle prod. 'This is the only language these scum understand. You can't sit down and negotiate with these people, Josh. They're not interested. The only tactic that works here is violence.'

Bowman shook his head furiously. 'This isn't like you, Mike. You would never have stood for this shit in the Regiment.'

'That was then. Things are different down here. Torture is a fact of life in Karatandu. I'm not just talking about the president. The KUF are as guilty of that as anyone.' He pointed the prod at

Kakuba. 'The general is personally responsible for hundreds of killings, rapes and mutilations. His men massacred the president's staff at the palace. They've razed dozens of villages. He's not one of the good guys.'

'Doesn't make it right.'

Gregory stared at him with a downturned mouth. 'I'm disappointed, Josh. I thought you'd be fine with all this. Your bosses certainly don't have a problem with it.'

Bowman frowned. 'What's that supposed to mean?'

'Vauxhall knows what we get up to down here. They're perfectly comfortable with the arrangement. As a matter of fact, they're the ones who supplied the cattle prods.'

'Bollocks. You're lying.'

Gregory chuckled. 'Do you really believe Six wouldn't sanction torture?'

'I'm not an idiot. They've done some pretty dark shit in the past, I know. But they've got their limits. They would never agree to this.'

'Why not? They've done far worse on this op.'

Something cold moved like a bayonet through his stomach. 'What the fuck are you talking about?'

Gregory cocked an eyebrow. 'Didn't you know?'

'Know what?' Bowman demanded.

'Six was behind the poisoning. In London. The attack on Freddie Lang. That was their handiwork.'

Bowman felt a cold chill on the nape of his neck. 'No,' he said. 'No fucking way. They wouldn't do that.'

'Why do you think they haven't identified the suspects yet? The middle of a royal wedding, all those people, and there's not one witness? Not even the Russians could pull off something like that.'

Bowman couldn't think straight, couldn't breathe. His mind was reeling.

'But . . . how?'

'Six contracted the job out to a couple of ex-Regiment guys. They do all the wet work for the government. They got them into the hotel disguised as bodyguards or something.'

The chill ran like ice down Bowman's back. He remembered the two men in the ballroom corridor. The face-mask strap dangling from the pocket. The absence of crucial CCTV footage.

Five has looked into it, Mallet had said. *It's a dead end. The cameras weren't working.*

'How the fuck do you know this?' Webb asked.

'My handler told me,' Gregory replied simply.

'You're working for Six?' said Bowman.

Gregory nodded. 'They approached me soon after I took the job. They wanted a second source close to the president, you see. To verify the information they were getting from David Lang. They suspected he might be feeding them bullshit. So they came to me. I've been working for them for a couple of years now.'

'But why would they tell you about the poisoning?' Casey said. 'Six would keep something like that top secret, if it was true.'

Gregory said, 'They didn't have a choice. I was the one who tipped them off about that backstabbing bastard Lang.'

'You knew about the meeting with the Russians?'

'I'm the president's chief of security, Josh. It's my business to know everything that goes on around here.' Gregory ran a hand down his beard. 'I knew Lang was sneaking around, having lots of meetings with shady Russian businessmen. More than usual, anyway. So I had him followed by my people. We ran a huge surveillance operation on him. That's when we realised Lang was double-dipping with the Kremlin. I heard about some big meeting in Monte Carlo and told my handler. Said they might want to look into it. Stop it from going ahead.'

'And?'

'And nothing. I didn't hear back from Six. Lang went about his business as normal. A couple of weeks before the meeting, I decided to lift the sneaky prick myself. Give him a taste of this.' He waved the cattle prod in the air, like a magic wand. 'Find out what he was planning.'

'You were going to torture David Lang?'

'That was the plan. Then my handler got in touch with me out of the blue. Demanded an emergency meeting. Not like him at all. He said he had big news. When I got to the meeting, the guy was very twitchy. He looked panicked.'

'What did he say?' asked Casey.

'He told me to leave Lang alone. I asked him why. My handler said Six was going to deal with him. I told him I had ways of making Lang talk, but he claimed Six had a better plan. When I asked him for details, he just smiled and said that his brother was going to have a nasty accident. His exact words.'

'That's why they used Novichok to kill Freddie Lang,' Casey interjected. 'To make it look like Moscow was behind the attack?'

'Exactly.' Gregory pointed a finger at her. 'You're a sharp one.'

'Why would Six want to poison him?' said Bowman. 'Why not just arrest David, if they knew he was up to something dodgy?'

'Isn't it obvious? They needed a way of turning the screw on Lang. Pressure him into calling off the deal with the Russians. Subjecting him to a hard interrogation wouldn't get them anywhere. So they decided to kill his brother and pin it on the Russians. Make it look like Moscow was planning a double-cross.'

Bowman shook his head in disbelief. 'But . . . that means Six carried out a chemical weapons attack. On their own soil. People were poisoned, for fuck's sake. Hospitalised.'

Gregory shrugged. 'Best way of getting David Lang to spill his guts.'

'Who else knew about this?' Webb demanded.

'Only a handful of people. The higher-ups at MI6, myself. The guys tasked with the wet work. And your boss, of course.'

'John knew?' Bowman said. The bayonet sank deeper into his guts.

'He runs the Cell. He's plugged into everything that goes on inside Vauxhall,' Gregory replied. 'He knows all their dark secrets. John would have known about it from the start.'

'He wouldn't lie to us.'

'Are you sure about that?' Gregory parted his lips into a cruel smile. 'I hear David Lang took a nasty fall from his apartment yesterday. That was John's doing, I imagine. In fact, I wouldn't be surprised if he'd planned to kill Lang all along.'

'No.'

But even as he shook his head, a voice of doubt crept up on Bowman. He remembered the briefing back at the Shed. Mallet's last-minute decision to go with the team. We need boots on the ground, he had said. But maybe he had a more sinister reason for tagging along with the team to Monte Carlo. Maybe Mallet had orders of his own from the Voice. *Make sure Lang doesn't come back alive.*

'You should be careful, Josh,' Gregory went on. 'John's a great soldier, but he's slippery. None of the guys in the Regiment ever trusted him . . . and neither should you.'

Bowman stayed quiet for a beat. He was beginning to see the dark side of the Cell. The extreme lengths they would go to in order to defend British interests at home and abroad. Poisonings, executions. Covertly funding the torture of foreign nationals. Bowman thought he had joined the Cell to fight mobsters. But he was beginning to realise that the truth was far more complicated than that.

Gregory offered him the cattle prod.

'Here,' he said. He grinned manically. 'Give it a try. A bump to the bollocks is always good fun, I find.'

Bowman looked at his old boss and shivered. He thought: *Mike actually enjoys this shit. He's getting a kick out of torturing people.*

'Hit him, man. Make him scream. Go on.'

Bowman said nothing. He just stared at Gregory. The man was unrecognisable from the charismatic officer Bowman had once fought alongside in B Squadron. The years of working for Ken Seguma, doing his bidding, had warped his mind. *He might have been a first-class officer in the past*, Bowman thought. *But he's just a deranged psychopath now.*

'You've lost your fucking mind,' he said.

'Don't give me that nonsense.' Gregory pointed to the chained rebel leader. 'The general and his men killed your mate. Christ, they almost wiped us all out. Don't you want to get your revenge?'

Bowman looked down at General Kakuba and felt a pang of nausea. The leader of the KUF whimpered hysterically through his gag and looked up at Bowman with wide pleading eyes. His face was swollen with bruising, his lips were bleeding heavily. At some point during the torture session, the man had voided his bowels. The air reeked of shit, piss and sweat.

He grabbed the electric prod.

Gregory beamed with delight. 'That's better! Now crack on with it,' he said, rubbing his hands expectantly. 'Let's get started. Don't hold back.'

Bowman held up the prod. The general gave out a muffled scream. His eyes were so wide they looked as if they might pop out of their sockets.

'Well, what are you waiting for?' Gregory said.

Then Bowman hit his old boss with the shock end.

Gregory let out a grunt as the current shot through his system. His body jerked wildly and his legs buckled before he dropped to the concrete flood with a thud. Bowman bent down before he could recover and bumped him again. Gregory groaned through his tightly clenched jaw as another wave of pain ripped through his body. The voltage wasn't powerful enough to kill or knock someone out, but it would still hurt like fuck. He hit Gregory repeatedly, delivering shocks to his legs, his stomach.

He gave Gregory a final bump to the groin. Then he tossed the prod aside and stood up.

Gregory lay in a shrivelled ball at his feet, moaning softly. Bowman watched him for several seconds with a look of cold contempt. He gave his back to Gregory. Nodded at Casey and Webb.

'Let's get out of here,' he said.

'Good idea,' Casey said. 'I don't know about you, but I've seen enough shit for one day.'

Bowman started towards the cell door.

'Look out!' Webb cried.

He spun round.

He saw Gregory gripping a pistol. The gun he'd seen on the bench. The GSh-18 semi-automatic. Colonel Lubowa's weapon. Gregory had snatched it up and swept it across his front in a flash.

The barrel pointed directly at Bowman's chest.

Bowman had no time to react. It would take him a couple of seconds to thrust a hand down to his holster and bring up the Glock. By which time Gregory could have pulled the trigger. At a distance of four metres, there was no way he could miss.

Bowman waited to die.

Two cracks echoed violently inside the cell.

In the corner of his eye, he saw Webb standing with his Glock already drawn. The barrel flamed as he fired twice at Gregory. The bullets double-tapped him in the forehead and punched out of the back of his skull, splattering the wall with blood and brain matter. The pistol clattered against the concrete. Gregory's arms and legs sagged, and then he dropped to the ground, as if someone had cut his strings.

Webb lowered his Glock.

Bowman nodded at him. 'Thanks, mate.'

'No need,' Webb said as he stuffed his weapon back into his holster. 'That animal had it coming.'

'I thought you said he was a really great guy,' Casey said.

'He was,' Bowman said. 'Once. A long time ago.'

He stared at Gregory for a long moment. The former hero of B Squadron. One of the best officers in the history of the Regiment. Now he was dead. Slumped on the floor of a torture chamber in the heart of the jungle, his brains slicking down the wall. He didn't feel a pang of sadness, or pity. He didn't feel anything at all. He just wanted to get the hell out of Karatandu. And never come back.

They left the chamber, walked back past the cells and up the spiral staircase to the atrium. They stepped outside, into the sweltering midday heat. Mallet spotted the team and beat a quick path over from the guest house. Behind him, the tractor dumped another bucketload of bodies into the agricultural trailer. The trailer was almost full, but the battlefield was still thick with enemy dead. Torn limbs and glistening entrails putrifying beneath the burning sun.

'Where the fuck have you lot been?' Mallet snapped. 'Where's Mike?'

'He's busy,' Webb said. 'Tied up in the basement.'

'Grab your kit. We've just been given clearance. We're leaving on the Herc. We're out of here now.'

He marched off in the direction of the Land Cruiser. Bowman paused and looked briefly back at the mansion, Gregory's warning about Mallet ringing in his ears. *John's a great soldier, but he's slippery.*

None of the guys in the Regiment ever trusted him.

He wondered about that. He wondered about the lies Mallet had told him. He wondered what the future held for him in the Cell. He wondered if he could keep his promise to Loader and stay clean.

Casey gently placed a hand on his shoulder.

'Come on,' she said. 'Let's go. We've got a friend to take home.'

THE END

If you enjoyed *Manhunter*,
why not join the
CHRIS RYAN READERS' CLUB?

When you sign up you'll receive an exclusive Q&A with Chris Ryan,
plus information about upcoming books and access to
exclusive material. To join, simply visit
bit.ly/ChrisRyanClub

Keep reading for a letter from the author . . .

Hello!

Thank you for picking up *Manhunter*.

I've always wanted to write a thriller set in the murky world of organised crime. Mobsters are everywhere these days: in some places, they've become more like professional corporations than traditional gangs. In Russia and elsewhere, the lines between government and the criminal underworld have become completely blurred, leading to the term 'mafia state'. It seemed to me that the SAS would be perfectly suited to tackling this emerging new threat, working hand-in-glove with the security services and the police. So when I first sat down to think about *Manhunter*, I knew straight away what kind of story I wanted to tell.

I also knew that my hero would be radically different from anything I'd done before: an elite soldier with a talent for fighting mobsters. He would need a background in law enforcement before joining the army, with an insider's knowledge of how criminals think. He would have grown up in a rough part of London, a world where violence and gangs are rife and only a lucky few escape – a world he can never quite leave behind. But that wasn't enough, I knew. The character also needed a powerful personal motivation for wanting to take revenge on the criminal elite, so I gave him a tragic family backstory. This incident would only be revealed slowly, through the prism of the hero's ongoing struggle with addiction. All that was left was to create a new covert SAS unit to combat this new threat. The Cell was born, and the idea snowballed from there.

Writing *Manhunter* has been a genuine pleasure. I've had great fun spending time with Josh Bowman, John Mallet and the other members of the Cell, and I hope you've had as much fun reading about them. Hopefully, this is the first of many adventures to come.

If you would like to hear more about my books, you can visit **bit.ly/ChrisRyanClub** where you can become part of the Chris

Ryan Readers' Club. It only takes a few moments to sign up, and there are no catches or costs.

Bonnier Books UK will keep your data private and confidential, and it will never be passed on to a third party. We won't spam you with loads of emails, just get in touch now and again with news about my books, and you can unsubscribe any time you want.

And if you would like to get involved in a wider conversation about my books, please do review *Manhunter* on Amazon, on Goodreads, on any other e-store, on your own blog and social media accounts, or talk about it with friends, family or reading groups! Sharing your thoughts helps other readers, and I always enjoy hearing about what people experience from my writing.

Thank you again for reading *Manhunter*.

All the best,

Chris Ryan